COMATOSE

By

JANE BADROCK

?

Question Mark Press

First published in 2021 by Question Mark Press

Cover art by Emmy Ellis @ Studioenp

1

Hertfordshire, England.
Thursday 13th December 2012

The driver stared ahead at the road, her face set. Determined. She'd made her decision and she was going to see it through. It was all his fault. He deserved it. He had it coming.

Her eyes flicked to the dashboard clock. Every second counted. She needed to be there. She had to do it; it was now or never. Why had she waited so long?

She put her foot on the gas and the yellow car zoomed along the deserted road. Then it wasn't deserted. Something was happening.

'What's that ahead?
No! It can't be!
What's he doing?
He's stopping. NO!
STOP!!!
MY BRAKES!!!
OH MY GOD!!!'

***

The bright yellow Porsche now damaged beyond repair, glimmered in the rapidly falling dusk. Ahead was the white Transit van, its bonnet rammed against the crash barriers and its back crushed in. It shone in the remnants of sunlight in the dank December air. Now both vehicles lay in the right-hand lane in near silence. The ear-shattering bang of the collision followed by the crunching of metal on metal, now a faint echo.

The first passing car was on the opposite side of the dual carriageway. It pulled up and stayed long enough for the driver to report the accident. The car sped off; the driver anxious not to get caught in the congestion of the rush hour that was about to begin.

Swiftly other cars arrived and parked on the left-hand-side verges. The first responders surveyed the vehicles then scattered purposefully. Traffic had to be stopped and space cleared for the emergency vehicles.

From another car, two paramedics in high-vis jackets emerged then broke ranks. The first one ran to the van. Finding the driver's door open, she only needed a swift check, her fingers on his neck, to confirm what her eyes told her.

'This one's gone!' she shouted. She moved on to help her colleague. Time was critical.

Unable to open the door of the Porsche, the other paramedic gently pushed through the web of shattered glass crystals and reached through the window frame to search for signs of life. The airbag had done its job; he felt a pulse. He saw the relief on his colleague's face then looked towards the fire engine parking up.

'Over here.' A fireman rushed towards him and made a rapid inspection of the driver's side of the car.

'We'll have to cut her out,' he said. The fireman's face, calm and determined reflected the flashing blue lights of the arriving ambulance.

He shouted 'Over here. LIGHTS.' Then he turned to speak to the woman through what was left of the window. 'Listen, love, we're going to have to cut the car open.' There was no response.

Moments later light flooded the scene, and the mangled yellow wreckage was revealed. The woman, her serene and unblemished face framed in golden hair, looked a picture of tranquillity amidst the frenzied activity.

'We're going to stabilise the car first,' the fireman said. Then we have to get the metal cutters. You'll hear a noise, it's a horrible screeching but it won't last long.' Still no response. 'You'll be fine, love. I promise. We'll get you out.'

Awake, the woman would have howled at the damage to her car and lamented the irredeemably ripped handmade blue silk suit. Unconscious, she put up no resistance to the frantic hands exploring her body for signs of injury.

'Suspected traumatic brain injury and possible spinal trauma,' the paramedic said, giving his initial assessment to the ambulance team. 'No seat belt,' he shook his head.

Painstakingly the woman's head and neck were braced before she was gently lifted from the wreckage. Immediately other hands searched the footwell of the car for the scattered contents of her Prada bag.

'I've got ID. Stella Cary,' someone said. Stella's purse was handed to the waiting police officer. 'There's a phone.' As items were retrieved, Stella was placed on a bodyboard, covered with a blanket and placed on a trolley inside the ambulance.

'Call Desk Sergeant Bill,' the Road Scene Manager said. 'We need a uniform to tell her next of kin.'

Once clear of the other vehicles, the ambulance sped off, blue lights still flashing and siren wailing.

***

Ten minutes later, a young orderly stubbed out his cigarette and watched the ambulance pull into the Accident and Emergency bay. He stood back from the doors as Stella was transferred to a waiting trolley. Mesmerised, he stared at her face.

'Get her to the ICU!' a paramedic shouted at him. Jumping to attention, the orderly took over the trolley and wheeled it as if it were made of glass down the corridor to the intensive care unit. He held it tight, seemingly not wanting to let go.

'We'll take her now.' A doctor wrestled the trolley away. As Stella was guided through the doors, the orderly watched, unable to move.

'Look after her!' he shouted.

2

Constable Macy Dodds had recently taken up her new position and had soon discovered she was the only black officer at the station. 'Yuh show dem gyal, ow good a Jamaican be,' her mother had encouraged. She'd never even been to Jamaica, but it had become her mantra. She'd smiled and done anything asked of her. She was always the first to put a hand up when volunteers were needed. Now, a few months in, her enthusiasm was waning. The station always ran at full stretch and the promotion of her first manager to Inspector elsewhere left her saddled with his newly promoted replacement. Detective *Sergeant* Karen Thorpe. And she'd gone on compassionate leave.

There was no work-life balance; it was all work. Especially today, when the Serious Collision Unit was short on numbers because of the funeral. *That's why*, she realised. It was Karen's father's funeral. Bill had called her from his private phone because he was there. Bill knew she'd do it, she always did. Naturally, she'd agreed but it helped that it was on her way home. She stood on the doorstep and unnecessarily patted her immaculately straightened bob.

Now what? Looking around she realised that apart from the porch light the house was in darkness. As she reached for her radio, she heard a vehicle approach; a red sports car zoomed up the drive, halting millimetres from the garage door. A Triumph Stag MK2. Pimento red. The driver, a middle-aged bearded man, emerged cigarette in hand. He took a long drag then exhaled and coughed when he realised Macy was standing there. His shoulders drooped as he faced her, his voice flat.

'Good evening officer. How can I help you?'

Was he expecting her? 'Are you Robert Cary?' she asked. He nodded. 'Husband of Stella Cary?'

'Yes.'

'I'm Constable Macy Dodds. I'm sorry, I have some bad news for you.' Macy paused, watching him. He frowned, confused.

'Something's happened to Stella?'

'There's been a major incident on the London road. She's been badly injured. She's in the county hospital.'

'Oh,' Rob said.

Macy was perplexed. *Am I too unsympathetic or is he in shock?* 'Is there anything I can do to help? Would you like a lift to the hospital?'

'No. And the car?' he asked. Macy frowned. 'Sorry. Not important. How is she then? Any broken bones?'

'I don't know any details, Sir. She's in intensive care.'

Rob stood still, thinking. Suddenly his eyes widened. 'Kids,' he announced. 'I can manage. I'll get there ASAP.'

As Macy turned back to her car, she was aware of him crossing over to the house next door. He rang the bell and glanced back at her over his shoulder. The door opened and outlined in the porch light Macy saw a blonde woman of a size her mother would call 'fluffy'.

The woman, her hand shielding her eyes, looked towards Macy, clearly curious to see a woman in uniform. Macy turned away, not wanting to get caught up in conversation. Safely out of view, she smiled.

Job done.

***

Rob Cary gazed at the satisfyingly rounded big-bosomed lady, as she watched Macy drive off.

'Rob! Where's Stella? Is there something wrong?'

'Hello Amanda. There's been an accident...'

'Oh no! Stella?' Rob blinked away pretend tears. 'Poor you. Poor Stella. What happened?'

'I've only just heard. I wonder, can I leave the children with you?'

'Of course,' Amanda nodded. 'Take as long as you need. They can stay overnight if you like. Do you want to see them now?'

'Best not,' he replied. 'Until I know what's what.' He turned and went back into his house.

After a large Scotch and an illicit indoor cigarette, Rob set off to the hospital. When he arrived, he was pleased to discover he wasn't welcome. He wasn't allowed near the ward and none of the staff seemed able to say anything more than 'We're doing all we can. We'll call you if anything happens.'

Done my duty, he concluded on his way out, first visiting the men's toilets. He stared at himself in the mirror, oblivious to the young orderly standing in the corner. He stroked his beard, which was dark, flecked with white, and ran his hand through his floppy dark hair, which had the beginnings of a satisfying streak of grey. *Quite the don.* He pulled in his stomach. *Not Oxford; more Don Juan.* He smiled for a second then remembered something. *That little tease and her threats... Forget her. Think of all those adoring women dying to comfort a poor widower...*

A noise. Rob turned around, startled, to see the young man standing there. *Damn!* Rob recognised him from the ICU. He gave a weak smile. The man narrowed his eyes and glared at him before going into a cubicle. Rob hurried out making his way to the main entrance. Once outside, he fumbled in his pocket for his cigarettes and lit up next to the 'No Smoking' notice, sucking hard as he watched people coming and going. Then treading out the cigarette, he walked towards his car, which he'd abandoned in the A&E Bay.

As he turned to get into the car he looked back and noticed the orderly kicking something into the road then looking straight at him. *Is he staring at me? Or my precious motor?* It was only when the man had disappeared around the corner that Rob pulled the door shut and moved off.

3

Friday 14th December

Detective Sergeant Karen Thorpe hauled herself out of bed, her nose desensitised to the dusty stale scent of her bedroom. She stepped over the small heap of yesterday's outfit, her hazel eyes scanning the floor for something. Moving the clothing with her foot, she uncovered and bent down to take the folded white card headed **Order of Service**. She stared at the photo on the front. A smiling balding man in uniform looked back at her. Her mouth attempted a smile, but the rest of her face was unmoved.

She held the card up and looked around pensively until her eyes settled on a drawer. She opened it and wriggled the card underneath the collection of pens, pencils, drawing pins and small change.

Turning to the wardrobe, Karen rummaged through what was left hanging in it. All her clothes were either blue or black, apart from the odd white shirt, and ranged from smart-casual to casual. Wondering what to wear was never an issue. Finding clean clothes, however, was. Pulling out a shirt and a pair of trousers, she went into the living room where her gaze turned towards the window under which lay the large green hospital bag containing her father's things. She could feel his presence; he was telling her off. She could hear him saying it. 'Move on. Put the stuff away and get on with it.'

'But how Dad? Who can I talk to now?'

She could see him shaking his head. 'Go get 'em, girl!'

'OK, OK!'

Going into the bathroom, Karen couldn't avoid her reflection. With short near-black hair sticking out in all directions she looked even paler and scrawnier than usual. She rarely paid attention to her appearance but did wonder what the impeccably dressed Macy might think if she saw her like this. She'd never dare say anything. Their partnership was intermittent and not

7

well established. As for the others, well they'd probably stop the zombie jokes now she had her promotion. She scowled at her reflection and began her ablutions.

Ten minutes later, Karen emerged wrapped in a big blue towel and went straight into her tiny kitchen, which still harboured the remains of last night's late snack. Retrieving her phone from under a kebab wrapper, she looked at the time. Eight-thirty. She called the office. Macy picked up straight away.

'Sergeant? I wasn't...'

'What have we got on?' She could almost see Macy's shock.

'I'm still working on the paperwork of yesterday's Road Traffic Accident.'

'Where? Casualties?'

'London Road, past the intersection. One fatality, one serious injury.'

'Anyone we know?' Silence. *That's unreasonable. She couldn't possibly know*. Karen spoke again before Macy could attempt a reply. 'Never mind. I'll see you at the station.'

'You're coming in?' Too late, Karen had hung up.

***

Five minutes later, with her smoothed-back hair still damp, Karen was on her way. She drove to the station on autopilot and parked in the general area, forgetting she had a tiny degree of priority now.

'Morning Bill,' she said, sailing past the uniformed man sitting at the front desk, avoiding the sympathetic look she knew he would be wearing.

'Morning Karen. It was a good send-off...' Karen had already gone into the main room. As soon as she entered, she knew they had been forewarned.

'Karen, how are you?' someone dared to ask.

'I'm fine.' She headed towards Macy's desk and pulling up a chair, sat down with her back to the others, sensing them getting back to their work.

'OK. RTA. Give me the lowdown. Anything suspicious? Any

witnesses?'

'Yes. I'm working on it.'

'What have you got?'

'The Serious Collision Unit needed me to speak to Robert Cary, husband of the injured woman. She's in a coma. There's something not quite right about him. His reaction.'

'Explain.'

'He wasn't surprised I was there.'

Karen raised her eyebrows. 'Excellent. Sounds like guilt. Any other family?'

'Her parents and three children.'

'And the deceased?'

'Tom Westbury. Widow, Mrs Rosalind Westbury and one son. SCU saw her, them...'

Karen was distracted by the ringing phone on her desk and went over to answer it. 'DC Thorpe. I mean, DS Thorpe.' She listened. 'Just looking at it now.' Karen turned to see Macy creeping towards the coffee machine.

'No time for that. We're going to have a look at the scene, then we're going to call in at the hospital to make ourselves known, and *then* we're going to visit Mrs Westbury.'

'Right.' Before Macy had time to get to the coat stand, Karen was already out of the door.

'I'll drive!' she yelled without looking back. Macy ran behind, struggling to put her jacket on. She jumped in the car, catching her breath.

'Do you know where?' she puffed.

'Yes.'

***

They arrived at the scene of the accident with not much to look at. Karen took photos from several angles. 'Hospital next,' she declared.

'It's a nice bright day today, isn't it?' Macy said, trying to make conversation.

'Is it?'

The silence was only broken when they arrived at the hospital. Something had been bugging Karen ever since Macy had mentioned the name Robert Cary. Now, as they were at the door of the ICU and a plump grey-haired nurse looked towards them, she realised she didn't know his wife's name. She looked at Macy, a question on her face.

'What's...?

'It's Stella Cary,' Macy interrupted efficiently.

'What?!' Karen's brain clicked into gear. She was transported back to school days, a career advice seminar with a guest speaker, but not any old has-been. This was a woman who dazzled. She'd looked like a film star, had a voice like polished steel and blue eyes that bored into you; yet you could still see the twinkle in them. She'd commanded the room and intoxicated her audience.

Rarely impressed by anyone, Stella Cary had bowled Karen over, but it wasn't only her appearance. For Karen, it was Stella's passion for her profession, her dedication to her clients and her belief in justice. *She's why I went to university to study law.*

A rush of adrenaline cleared out any remnants of self-pity; Karen stood to attention as Gwen, the nurse, approached then handed her a card. 'I'm Detective Sergeant Karen Thorpe. Stella Cary is a very special lady and I promise that I am going to do everything I can to find out what happened to her.'

***

'What else have we got on the case?' Karen barked as they got in the car.

'You know her?' Macy asked.

'Long story. Well?'

'There's a story in the local paper today...'

Before they arrived at the Westbury house, Karen was fully briefed. On the doorstep, Macy looked at Karen - who nodded vigorously - adjusted her hat a fraction then rang the doorbell. A slim, tall grey-haired woman appeared. She looked older than her file age of forty-five.

'Mrs Rosalind Westbury?' Karen asked, looking straight into her eyes as she nodded. *She's angry.* 'Detective Sergeant Thorpe and Constable Dodds.' Ros pulled back the door to let them in. They both heard, and ignored, a muttered comment in the background. 'Bloody black and white minstrel show.'

'Through here.' Turning from Karen's gaze, Ros led the policewomen into her living room. An older, wizened woman, petite with iron-grey hair and beady brown eyes sat on the sofa; *the mother*, Karen guessed, *and the originator of the comment*. She sat straight and proud, an old-fashioned matriarch.

As far away as you could sit, a small, slim balding man perched on the arm of a chair. *Those eyes... the other son*, Karen thought.

As Ros settled next to her mother-in-law Martha, Macy absorbed the room; the walls were adorned with photos of Tom Westbury, the deceased. The man stood up.

'Do you want us out?' he asked bluntly.

'Stay,' Martha ordered. Macy looked to Karen.

'This is primarily a procedural visit to let you know where we are with our investigations. Technically it is a criminal matter until we know otherwise...' Karen said.

'But that bitch was on her mobile!' Ros spat.

'Forensics haven't confirmed that, Mrs Westbury.'

'It's a fucking disgrace,' the man piled in. 'It's in the papers and all. Stupid bitch!'

'Sorry, you are?' Karen looked at him.

'Westbury. Jim Westbury.'

Karen ticked a box in her head. 'Mrs Westbury, we know the car was fitted with a hands-free device and there is no evidence of a mobile phone being used. I have no idea where the paper got that story, but we are looking into it.'

'Go do your job and don't come back till you know the truth.' Jim said.

'The senior officer in charge will be in touch as soon as the facts are established. In the meantime, may I ask where you all were on the night of the accident?'

Ros spoke first. 'I was at home, here. Waiting for him.'

'We was at mine,' Martha said, looking at Jim. 'All evening.' Jim nodded.

'Thank you, Mrs Westbury.' Karen turned to leave the room.

'We'll see ourselves out,' added Macy.

Outside, Karen turned to Macy. 'What's the intel on that mobile?' she growled.

Anonymous tip-off direct to the paper,' Macy replied. 'I've asked for a copy.'

'How far have you got with the witnesses?'

Macy bit her lip. 'I haven't...'

'Get on it then and cross-check them against the caller. See if one of them held back info to get a story in the press or something. And there's something not right about Jim Westbury. He's too quick to point the finger.'

4

Stella struggled with her thoughts. She was disoriented. *Where am I?* After several hour-long seconds had passed, she began to realise she was awake, but she couldn't see or feel anything. She was suspended in space, a gigantic flotation tank with no beginning and no end. At last, she heard something and strained to listen: a faint buzzing. *What was that?*

Now a bleep. No, a bleep, bleep, bleep. Now a soft rhythmical padding noise, getting louder, coming towards her.

'Nurse? Page Miss Shah. Tell her brain activity's increased. Stella? Can you hear me?'

'My name is Gwen. I'm taking care of you, you're in hospital, my love. You're safe now. We're looking after you.'

The voice was unbearably loud. Stella wanted to block it out. *Of course, I can hear you,* she said in her head. She couldn't open her mouth or her eyes. She tried to move her head, hands, feet. She couldn't remember how to make the connections to move anything.

Stella? Hospital? How did I get here? Where was I before?

The strain of thinking was too much, and Stella drifted off to sleep; a wonderful, sensual place.

I'm awake, she rationalised. She touched her face. *I can move, see things, touch things.* A waft of something sweet reached her nostrils. *Even smell things.*

Stella was thrown backwards. She felt herself moving, rushing forward so fast it made her head spin. She turned to look around - there was a red shape. It passed her and she followed it but as suddenly as it had appeared it was gone, melting into the distance ahead.

Stella woke up again; immobilised, helpless, unfeeling, unseeing, only hearing. She remembered remnants of the dream and it reminded her what normal sensations were like.

13

Is this a deeper sleep? Is this the dream? Or is this my life now?

She heard a faint rustle of clothing and realised that someone was close by.

'Stella, I am your doctor. My name is Reeta. I think you may be able to hear me.'

What did she say? Stella struggled to concentrate but it was too hard. Oblivious to the gentle hand prising open first her right, then left eyelid, shining her torch directly into each eye, she tried to concentrate.

'Sorry, Gwen. Just a blip. Let's hope it's a good sign. Urine needs doing.'

A tapping noise.

'Gwen? Don't take it personally.'

'I know. I've been here long enough, but comas are the worst. Mrs Reader has even come to see her.'

'That's good of her. She hardly ever leaves her office these days. Did you say Stella's parents are due soon?'

'They're coming down from Derbyshire. I'll let you know when they're here.'

'Call me if there's any change.'

Footsteps moving away.

'Try again Stella. You have to keep on trying. It's hard, but you can do it.'

Something was pulling Stella down again. She was slipping away, dreaming. Here she had no idea what she was, who she was or where she came from. All she knew was that she could feel the wind on her face and see the green fields below her. She was flying, and she swooped down, nearly touching the grass, then up again so high that she was above the mountains. She felt so alive and it was as if every one of her senses had been turned up to the maximum. She was deliriously happy.

***

Reeta Shah opened the door of the relatives' room and looked in before entering. She saw a middle-aged man, whom she guessed was the husband and an older couple, both well-rounded, the man almost bald, the woman with shoulder-length white hair. She briefly wondered if it had once been blonde.

'Relatives of Stella Cary?' she asked.

'Yes.' They said as one, all eyes on her. The woman, clearly distressed, jumped in.

'She'll be all right, won't she? Our Stella?'

'Calm down Ma, let her speak.'

Reeta braced herself. Stella wasn't dead, but sometimes this was worse, delaying death. Worse still, an unbearable existence devoid of contact or human interaction. She saw in the woman's eyes the desperate hope that her daughter would survive unscathed. Reeta stepped into the room.

'Hello. My name is Reeta Shah. I'm one of the consultants for this ward. It's Mrs Baxter isn't it?' Molly nodded. 'And you must be Mr Baxter?' Harry stared at her. *He's daring me to tell him bad news.* 'And Mr Cary?' Rob sat expressionless, acknowledging her only with a glance. *What's he hiding? Disinterest or hatred? They've all got one thing in common. Anxiety. Anxious for recovery, or anxious for death.*

'It's still too early to tell anything for sure. You know that Stella's experienced a traumatic brain injury and she's in a coma?'

'We do,' Rob answered for them all.

'OK. At the moment Stella is functioning completely through the life support system. She is unable to breathe on her own, but her heart is beating strongly. We have begun to detect brain activity, but this may or may not be an indicative sign of recovery. She is stable and that is the best thing we can tell you for now.'

'How severe is the brain damage?' Rob said, as if he were asking about the weather.

'The CT scan shows that there is damage to the cerebral cortex caused when her brain hit her skull. We have drained the haematoma - that's the blood under her skull - so there's no pressure on her brain, but it's impossible to tell how severe the injury is and what impact it will have, should Stella come round.'

'You mean when,' Harry corrected.

'She will come round, won't she?' Molly asked, tears

beginning to trickle down her world-weary face.

'It's too soon to say.'

'What normally happens in situations like this?' Rob asked. 'You've seen this before, right?'

'Yes Mr Cary, I am a brain trauma specialist, but there are no rules here. Every patient is different and if I told you anything specific about recovery,' she paused, 'or not, I would be sure to be wrong. I know it is difficult, but we must wait and see.'

'May we see her?' Harry asked. Reeta looked at Molly's pleading face, then turned to Rob.

He shrugged. 'Is that allowed?'

'Yes. Yes, of course. No more than two at a time though.'

Molly and Harry instantly stood up together. Rob remained seated. Harry turned to Molly, tipping his head back towards Rob. 'Let him go first. He is her husband. You go in with him.'

Molly looked at Reeta. 'Can she hear us?'

'Maybe. We think that it can help if people talk to coma patients. It can stimulate memories or normal communication needs. Please try. It will help you too, to know you could be doing something useful. Come this way, please.'

Reeta led them to Stella's room, nodding at Gwen to let Molly and Rob in. Harry stood outside. As she left, Reeta glanced back to see Molly flinch as she took in the sight of her daughter, head bandaged, with tubes everywhere.

Molly leaned over Stella and gently touched her shoulder before sitting down.

'It's Mum. We're here now, Stella. You're going to be fine. You've been in a terrible accident, love. How did it happen? We've been so worried about you, Dad and me, but now they say that your brain is functioning, and you can hear us. Can you, love? The children haven't come today. Rob said it wasn't right, yet. But they are missing you and want to see you.'

She navigated the drip-feed connector to place her hand on Stella's. 'Can you feel my hand, love? Can you squeeze it?'

Rob leant forward. 'Better not Ma,' he urged. 'Keep to the talking.' Molly ignored him. Rob sighed. He looked over to the nurse for confirmation, but she didn't seem worried. He looked at his watch. 'I'd better go and get some supplies in. I assume you're staying tonight?' Molly nodded, then looked at him accusingly. Rob bent over Stella as if to kiss her then kissed his fingers and touched her forehead instead.

5

Harry was waiting outside the room. 'How is she?' he asked Rob.

'You go in, Harry. I'm off to Waitrose. Tell Ma to stop going on about the accident. That can't be helping much.'

'It can't hurt her either,' Harry snapped. 'Anything that gets her mind going is good as far as I'm concerned.'

Harry walked into the room and flinched at the sight of his daughter. *Poor, poor lass. What happened love? I can't bear to see you like this.*

Molly was still going strong. 'Rob's saying how good that Amanda one is. I thought you'd had a falling out with her. Shame she doesn't have a man of her own. No, don't say she was after your Rob? It's Christmas soon. I've told Sandra but she won't come, you know what she's like and all those kiddies ...'

Harry sat back in the chair and snoozed. He smiled as he saw Stella in front of him in a dream; a young, pretty, happy girl laughing at him and dancing with her arms above her head like a ballerina.

'Can I get you two a drink?' Harry was jolted awake by the young orderly. 'We'll look after her, Sir. Don't you worry,' he said.

***

Stella woke. Someone was talking; it felt close but not loud. 'Oh, Stella, were you two having problems? Kids are sensitive to that sort of thing you know, especially the boys...'

Now another voice. Deeper, louder but further away.

'Let's concentrate on getting her well, give her something to look forward to.'

'Oh, Dad. Supposing she doesn't get better?'

'She will, love. She will.'

Stella heard many words but could not interpret them. *Am I Stella? I'm sure I'm Stella. Am I?* The chatter was relentless; she wanted it to stop. She longed to dream again and waken her senses. The voices were still going on. There were names. *Mum, Dad, James, Daniel, Laura. Mum. Dad. Mum and Dad*.'

'Come on, love, time we were going.'

'She's my baby. I need to make sure she's all right.'

'Look, love, another nurse.'

Nurse.

'This young lady's got things to do and we don't want to get in her way. I'm sure she's looked after Stella before.'

'She's not going anywhere,' the nurse agreed.

A new, sharp voice.

'I'm Janice. Is it Mr and Mrs Baxter? Have you come far?'

Janice

'Aye. From Chesterfield.'

Dad.

'You must be tired with all that driving. She'll be fine.'

Janice.

'You'll ring us if...?'

Dad.

'Of course.'

Janice.

'Bye love.'

Mum.

'Now then. What are we going to do about you? Bandages off tomorrow.'

Janice.

'Let's see what you look like then, Mrs High and Mighty lawyer lady.'

A rustling sound.

'And we're short-staffed. Meant to be one to one in here. That'll be the day.'

Footsteps moving away.

Another voice, but kind and gentle.

'I'm here now, Stella. I'm going to look after you. Just like I promised your Dad. I'm here with you in the room. Behind the screens. You're safe with me.'

***

Rob Cary arrived home to find the local paper on the mat. The headline stared out at him. **LOCAL LAWYER IN COMA AFTER CRASH**. *Jesus. That's the top story?* **WAS SHE USING HER MOBILE?** Before he could throw it away, he was accosted by Solomon, their permanently starving black and white cat summoning him to the kitchen.

Rob wrinkled his nose with disgust as, kneeling, he forked the rest of the tin's contents into Solomon's bowl. He shivered then fiddled with the boiler control panel, waiting to hear for the rush of gas followed by ignition.

Shopping unloaded and a couple of cigarettes later, Rob went outside, stepping over next door's overgrown box hedge to call on his neighbour.

'Hello Amanda,' he quickly altered his lustful gaze for one of sadness. 'Time to get the kids.'

'Come in,' Amanda smiled. 'You must be shattered. Drink? The kids are fine, and I've got some mulled wine on the go.'

Amanda's house was everything that Rob's house wasn't. Untidy, cobwebs in every corner, a blazing fire in the living room and wonderfully uncoordinated floral wallpapers and curtains.

'Perfect.' Rob sighed, seeing all hopes of a hug being extinguished by the presence of his sons playing on a games console connected to the television.

'How's Mum?' asked James the fourteen-year-old.

'Is she coming home?' Daniel, eleven, asked.

'Not yet, lads.' The boys looked at each other.

'Is she all bandaged up?' Daniel sounded worried.

'Yes, at the moment, but they'll take some off soon.'

'Has she talked yet?' James asked.

'No son, she's still sleeping. You'll see her soon enough.'

'OK,' James said for both of them. They turned back to the game.

Amanda reappeared. She nodded her head backwards and Rob followed her into the big, cluttered kitchen. On the range, a huge stainless-steel jug of wine was mulling creating a wonderful aroma. She swept a space clear on the big chunky wooden table with her arm and placed big mugs directly onto the wood.

Rob sat down in the cushioned wooden chair and took a large gulp. *Bliss*. Amanda sat next to him and touched his arm.

'Any progress?'

'Serious brain damage. Her brain is working but they don't know what it's doing. She's still on life support.' *God Amanda, I could screw you senseless.*

'That's awful. What's the prognosis?'

'No prognosis, just wait and see,' Rob replied. *Look sad!*

'Poor you. It must be awful.'

'And the in-laws are coming to stay tonight.'

Amanda smiled. 'That bad?'

'Yes. Hell! Things to do. I should never have let Sofia go.'

'Bad timing.' Amanda agreed. 'How is her mother?'

'No idea.' Rob downed his mug and stood up. 'Laura?'

'Upstairs with Joely. She can sleep over if you like?'

'Might be best. She doesn't understand.'

'The boys could stay too...'

Rob shook his head. 'In-laws,' he muttered, looking at his watch. 'They'll be here any minute.'

Amanda nodded. 'Of course.'

***

When they arrived, Molly ran straight past Rob to find the boys. He followed, leaving Harry with their bags. Harry spotted the scrunched-up paper on the floor and picked it up, grimacing at the headlines before tucking it under his arm.

Molly burst into the living room, raising an eyebrow at Solomon snoozing on the sofa.

'Where are my boys?' she said, scooping them up and planting sloppy grandma kisses on their cheeks, which were promptly wiped away when she turned to speak to Rob. 'Where's my little Laura?'

'With Amanda,' Rob replied. 'It was what she wanted.'

'Grandma's here now.' She hugged the boys again. 'Everything's going to be all right.'

'Hello, James, Daniel. Grandpa's turn, or are you too old to hug me now?' Harry teased. The boys obliged, looking relieved to have an excuse to escape Molly's clutches.

'Where is your young lady?' Harry asked.

'Sofia? Gone home for a few weeks. Her mother's not well. Now, what can I get you to drink?'

'Scotch will do me fine,' Harry replied. They both watched Molly disappear through the door with a loud 'I'll sort out some tea.' Followed by a louder 'Scat cat!'

In the living room, Harry retrieved the paper he'd managed to stuff down the side of the sofa. 'What's this, Rob? It says she was on her...'

'It's a rag,' Rob interrupted, his eyes darting towards the boys. Taking the paper, he went into his study, coming back without it. He opened the drinks cabinet. 'Ice?'

'Nay. As it comes.'

As Rob handed Harry the glass, the doorbell rang. 'I'll go.'

'It's the police!' he shouted from the hall.

'Mr Cary? I'm Detective Sergeant Karen Thorpe.' Her outstretched hand was ignored.

'I've met her already,' Rob said, looking at Macy.

'We're not stopping, Sir. I wanted to introduce ourselves so you have a point of contact.' Molly and Harry appeared behind him.

'We're her parents. Baxter's the name,' Harry said.

'Good evening Mr and Mrs Baxter. I'm Detective Sergeant Karen Thorpe. Here's my card. We'll let you know as soon as we have anything to tell you.'

'Thank you, officer.' Molly reached past Rob to take the card.

'We have to know what happened to our daughter,' Harry said.

'It's my top priority,' Karen reassured them.

'That's good to hear,' Harry nodded. 'Are you coming in?'

'We're about to eat,' Rob said, looming large at the door. 'Sorry.' He shut the door before Karen could say another word.

6

Karen sat in Detective Chief Inspector Winter's office. The kind and sensitive man who had spoken such comforting words to Karen at her father's funeral had succumbed to the boss. Karen knew the rules; if you turned up for work, you were on duty. No easy rides here.

'That RTA should've been wrapped up by now.'

Karen grimaced. 'I've got an inkling about this one, guv.'

'An inkling? Not good enough.'

'There's something fishy about the husband. And the Westbury family and the accident. The lab hasn't finished yet. Someone's trying to finger Stella Cary for causing the crash - the mobile phone story...'

'What's the prognosis?' DCI Winter took a sip of coffee.

Karen looked enviously at his cup. 'Permanent brain damage a possibility; definite brain activity but no other signs, no reflexes, responses to stimuli, nothing.'

'What about the phone?' DCI Winter swilled his coffee cup gently, almost teasing her.

'The entire contents of her bag were all over the car floor. There was a phone, it's in the lab now. But she had hands-free installed and there were no recorded calls or texts at the time of the accident. Witnesses only saw the aftermath.'

DCI Winter pushed back on his chair and put his hands behind his head, making a giant eye while looking at her condescendingly. 'You have to come up with more than that.'

'Guv, someone caused that crash. There's no evidence of bad road or weather conditions, animals on the road, no instantaneous mechanical failures. Both cars were in the overtaking lane when they collided. That's weird.'

DCI Winter took a last, long mouthful of coffee, savouring it for a few moments before swallowing. 'Firstly, Karen, you did very well to make Sergeant. But it doesn't mean that you're going to be handling murders often. It's almost always going to be traffic accidents, burglary and assaults. You can't invent something that doesn't exist.'

Karen bit her lip. 'But guv, I'm sure about this.'

After a long pause, DCI Winter responded, simultaneously looking at his watch. 'You can have one of the incident rooms while we're not busy. No extra resources and I don't care what you uncover, absolutely no pre-Christmas overtime.' Karen began to smile.

'You can have Dodds too, for now. How are you two getting on?' Karen shrugged noncommittally. 'She's a good kid. Be nice to her. She's a quick learner.' Karen nodded. 'Pick away at it if you must, but no formal procedures without my say so. That means no interviews, especially the Westbury family. And Karen...' He gave her his intense look. 'This is only until something else comes up.' His face was softening. 'Just one thing...'

'I'm fine, guv.'

Karen walked to Macy's desk. 'Incident room two. Put the RTA papers together... please,' she added as an afterthought. She approached the vending machine with a gait somewhere between stroll and strut. Her win wasn't quite enough to merit a trip outside for a latte; instead, she selected a hot chocolate, which was the only vending choice that had some resemblance to the description.

She walked down the corridor holding the plastic cup and kicked the partially open door. The room was small but well-equipped. Large whiteboards filled the walls. Tables and chairs populated the floor. She took a large black marker from the holder, took the lid off, and sniffed in the fumes as if it might give her inspiration. Her first case as a DS. With aplomb, she headed three boards: **RTA, CARY** and **WESTBURY**. As she wrote **SUSPECTS** under the two names, Macy came in and stared at Karen's cup.

'OK. Let's start with Stella Cary. Was somebody trying to kill her?'

Macy sat down in astonishment before she responded. 'But

she crashed into Westbury. Isn't he the victim?'

'Initial report says her brakes were faulty. They could have been tampered with. Who had a motive?'

'Her husband, Robert Cary?' Macy suggested. 'When I spoke to him, he seemed more concerned about the car than her. But wouldn't he simply divorce her?' Karen frowned at her. Macy sat up. 'Sorry. I know she's a divorce lawyer. I forgot for a moment.'

'Maybe he needs Stella's money, or wants the house to himself...' Karen mused. 'What does a two-bit lecturer get compared to a top lawyer? I bet there's life insurance somewhere.' She wrote **ROBERT CARY** on the board.

'There's a sister,' Macy said, leafing through the papers. 'Sandra Atkins. Lives in Dorset.'

'Bit far, but not impossible. Sisters...' She wrote it up.

'There's a nanny too, or au pair, I think. Not on the scene, not sure where she is.'

'Good.' Karen beamed. 'She'll know all the family secrets. What's her name?'

'Sofia Koba.'

'Clients' husbands. Or wives.' Karen said. 'I bet there are loads of men out there who hate her.'

'She got terrific settlements. I read up on her,' Macy said.

'She's certainly dynamic. But are there any of special interest?' Karen wrote up **CLIENT** and **SPOUSES.** 'What's the firm's name?'

'Spalls.'

Karen wrote **SPALLS**. 'I'll ring them.' She wrote **OTHERS**. 'Neighbours, friends... were there any social clubs? School associations?'

Macy made notes. 'I'll check on that.'

'OK. Tom Westbury. What have we got on him? The guv said I'm not allowed to interview the family without his permission.'

'He looked shifty enough in his photos.' Macy leafed through the file. 'Worked for a carpet place, in that industrial site near the motorway turn-off.'

'Look for dodgy deals, stuff going missing.'

Macy looked up at her. 'Murdered over some stolen carpets?'

'My nose is never wrong.' Macy bit her lip. 'And our friend Jim?' Karen asked.

Macy scratched her head. 'Second-hand car dealer. They're always dodgy.'

'The wife. Rosalind. Anything?'

'No.'

'Wasn't there a son?'

'Ryan. Eighteen.'

'That's more like it. Tearaway son.' Karen rubbed her hands together enthusiastically. 'OK, let's look at the accident, then.' She turned to the other board and drew out the road layout. 'This is the nub of it. No adverse weather conditions, but both vehicles were in the overtaking lane. Why would that be?' She turned to Macy.

'There must've been something in the left-hand lane.'

'Exactly. But what? Witness statements?'

Macy scrabbled through the file. 'Only Mr and Mrs Dixon. They were the first on the scene. Mr Dixon rang 999 but saw nothing of the crash itself. He commented that there were often deer on the road, but he didn't see any.'

'CCTV?' Karen asked.

'Only at the speed trap but that's three hundred yards before.'

'Check with SCU. They'll have got that. There's got to be a reason that they were both here,' she said, tapping the board.

'Maybe they were racing?'

Karen raised an eyebrow. 'Stella's car was a possible target. Porsche, personalised number plate. But as you said, she crashed into Westbury. Was someone hogging the inside lane?' She narrowed her eyes, thinking. 'What about that damned call to the paper?'

'I've got that now. It was a message left on the answerphone on the night of the crash. It's on my laptop.'

'Good work! Go get it.' Macy went out smiling.

Karen turned to tidy up the board while she waited. An idea was forming. *It's like a crash for cash without the cash. Could Tom Westbury have misjudged it that badly? But why would they be there?*

A moment later, Macy was back with her laptop under her arm. She set it up on the desk and fiddled with the mouse. 'Got it.'

Karen sat next to her as Macy tapped the volume key. After a crackling sound, they heard a male-sounding voice, very muffled and at an unusually high pitch.

'I saw the car crash on the London Road. It was her fault. She was holding her phone. Stupid bitch.'

'Someone else called her that recently,' Karen mused. 'It's a common enough phrase but I wonder if we've heard that voice before. Jim Westbury?'

'It could be,' Macy agreed.

'If it is, I'm right.' Karen smiled. 'He was trying to set Stella up. But why?'

7

Karen's afternoon had not gone well. Partly fearing ridicule if not from Macy, then from some of her colleagues, she'd waited until evening, when everyone else had gone home, to sort things out. Alone in the incident room and staring at the whiteboards, she was stewing over DCI Winter's words. He hadn't even bothered to tell her to her face. He'd just rung her from his office.

'There is no case. SCU are dealing with it. My decision Karen, and it's final.'

Was it because of the Westburys? She wondered, or was he simply right? Either way, she was off the case, if there was a case. *But I'm sure there is.*

She studied the boards, taking photos of them before wiping them clean. Then gathering up the loose papers, she tucked them into her posh briefcase, aka the Waitrose-bag-for-life that everyone laughed at and headed out.

Bill was on the desk. She smiled at him. *Good old Bill. Always cheerful no matter what.*

'Been clearing out the room?' he asked. Karen nodded. 'Happens all the time, Karen. Don't let it get to you.'

'You too?'

'Many a time. I've seen cases much stronger than yours get dropped. Hey, I'll give you something to cheer you up.'

Karen watched curiously as Bill went back to the desk and rummaged underneath for something. 'Here it is!' He pulled out a messenger bag. 'Someone left this here years ago. Finders' keepers?'

Karen smiled as she took the bag. 'Thanks, Bill. You've made my day. Just one thing?'

'Shoot.'

'The Westbury family. What's that all about?'

'No idea.'

'Why don't I believe you, Bill? You know everything.'

'Bill smiled. 'Not always. Night night, Karen.'

Karen returned home both invigorated and shattered, slinging her new prized possession on the sofa. She turned to see the still-languishing hospital bag on the floor. 'Sorry, Dad. Can't deal with this now.' She picked it up and took over to a cupboard already filled to bursting point. Reaching high, she pushed it onto the top shelf and shut the door quickly before the entire contents toppled out.

'But just so you know, Dad, I'm getting them. Or him, or her or it. Remember the lawyer I told you about? When I did my A-Levels? She's been hurt. I don't think it was an accident. I'm on the case. Happy now?'

She went into her bedroom, returning a minute later in a tiger-print onesie. Settling on the sofa with the file, she pulled out the paper headed **Initial Forensics Report,** then got up again to get a bottle of wine from the kitchen. But before she opened it, Karen had an overwhelming desire to talk to someone. The next best thing to her father. She picked up her phone. 'Auntie Sal? Yes, I'm fine. Honestly. Is Uncle Jack there? I'd really like to talk to him.' She waited until she heard his voice. 'Uncle Jack? What do you know about the Westbury family?'

'Why do you ask?'

'The guv. A man called Tom Westbury was killed in an RTA and he wouldn't let me talk to the family. I saw them straight afterwards and I'm suspicious of the brother. I'm sure there's something not right.'

'Karen, first you know that there's no point challenging Bob.'

'You know him well, don't you?'

'Well enough to know that.'

'Give me something, please Uncle Jack.'

She heard Jack's long deep breath before he spoke. 'All I can tell you is that they, that is the family, were petty gangsters back in the day. Old Nick was the big Daddy. He was into all sorts. Gambling, prostitution, probably drugs too.'

'Was he ever arrested?'

'Yes, as I recall we got him on a charge. Only minor though, he was a crafty so and so. But he'd started to wind things down a bit towards the end.'

'What happened to him?'

'He died. Years ago. Cancer, I think it was. His partners moved on and that was the end of the family business.'

'You don't think his sons carried on afterwards?'

'No. I know they didn't. They didn't have his balls. Which was a good thing. Nick's reign was over, and the crime rates dipped because of it. I wouldn't stoke them up if I were you, Karen. You leave them well alone, love. Don't go near them.'

'And would Dad have taken your advice?' She paused. 'Thanks anyway.' She heard a chuckle at the other end. 'See you soon.'

She spread the papers all over the table and poured herself a glass of wine.

8

Tuesday 18 December

Stella was awake, but Reeta's comments had interrupted her thoughts. She had almost pieced together a memory, something from her past that would tell her who she was. And she had nearly understood who *Mum* was but now there was a babble.

'Right, Gwen, let's get these bandages off and see how she's doing.'

'Stella, nothing to worry about. They went a bit overboard with bandages because of the drain. They had to shave your head, my love, but your beautiful hair will grow back in time.'

Stella heard the sound of breathing very close to her.

'Look, I can see it's all growing back already.'

More breathing.

'It might itch a bit. Oh, I hope it does Stella, that would be such a good sign. There now, we're going to change to a smaller dressing.'

Now a sigh.

'What a pretty lady you are. I bet you were... are... a heartbreaker. I'm going to adjust the bed a bit, help avoid those nasty bed sores.'

A creaking sound.

'Your Mum will be here again soon.'

Mum.

Footsteps. Getting faster.

'Dad? Look, the bandages are off. Can you move the chair? Over there? Hello, love, it's Mum.'

Mum, Stella thought. *I know that voice. Where does it come from? What does it mean? This is so hard.*

'Dad's here too.'

Dad. Stella held the word in her head. *Mum and Dad. They go together. Mum and Dad. Mum and Dad.* She tried to move, to talk, but still, nothing happened.

'Hello again, Mr and Mrs Baxter.'

Baxter. Mister and Missus Baxter.

'Doesn't she look better now? We're going to try to see if she can breathe on her own later, when Miss Shah does her rounds.'

'Is that a good sign?'

Dad. Dad?

'It only means her reflexes are kicking in. But sometimes it triggers other things. Let's say it's better out than in.'

'Oh.'

He's sad.

'Dad, talk to her.'

'I don't know what to say.'

'The doctors say it's good to talk to them about when they were little. Childhood memories are the strongest ones sometimes.'

'I'll try.'

Scraping noise; getting closer.

'Hello, love. It's Dad here.'

Dad. He's close.

'Do you remember when we used to go to the Peak District?'

Too many words.

'Describe it all. Detail, lots of detail.'

Where's he gone?

'It was a lovely sunny day. The sky was as blue as your party dress, with big white fluffy clouds. You wanted to touch them...'

Stella was dreaming. She was barefoot again on the grass, but now there was a little brook running through the countryside. She could see stones on the bottom. Big stones. She stood on them and looked down into the water. She was small and smiley, with long yellow hair and she was wearing a dress and it really was as blue as the sky. She reached up...

'Be careful Stella!' A voice shouted at her. 'Don't fall in the water.' She knew that voice. It was Dad's voice. Yes, she was there with Mum and Dad.

Stella woke to another voice calling her.

'Stella, this is Reeta again, your doctor.'

Reeta. Doctor.

'We're going to try something new, OK? Your parents are still here, they're right outside. I'm going to remove the mouthpiece. It might feel strange but it's all right I promise.'

Stella knew something had happened. It was different. Instead of the soft, regular background noise, there was a new one. Closer. Not regular like the other sound. Not outside. Instead, it was coming from *inside* her. It was irregular at first, but it felt good.

'Stella, you're breathing on your own now. This is very good. You're making really good progress. Gwen?'

Gwen.

'I'll get her parents.'

Gwen's the other voice.

'She looks like an angel again.'

Dad.

'A sleeping princess,'

Mum.

'I know you say it doesn't mean much but it must be a good sign, surely?'

'It may be.'

Gwen.

'I'd better ring him. Let him know.'

Dad.

'Yes, Dad. I suppose.'

Mum. Him? I have a Mum and Dad.

'Hello again, love. I forgot to tell you. That Amanda one took little Laura to school today. Were they close? Your Rob and her? There's definitely something odd about her. Dad's gone to call him. Rob, that is. And that man from your firm. Tim Strange? I always want to say "what a strange man" when I hear his name. Is that naughty of me? He's coming over to see you tonight. That'll be nice, won't it? Dad's here.'

'Hi love. I'm back. Now, where were we? D'you remember that time you hurt your foot? After jumping into the swimming pool? It were only when you put your tootsies in the brook that the pain went.'

Yes. My toes. I do remember.

I am at a place I know well. Somewhere they took me to.
Somewhere I was happy. Where am I going?

When she drifted back off to sleep, there was something different about her dreams. No longer a fantasy place, Stella now knew exactly where she was even if she couldn't yet name it. Padley Gorge in the Peak District.

***

Rob Cary sat in his car in the university staff car park. Now that he had extricated himself from the pressure of home and his in-laws, he felt much better. He'd assured them it was essential for him to go in today; the first semester had ended but he'd got important things to do and he needed to see how the land lay for his own peace of mind. *Out of the frying pan...* He gave himself a few moments' peace with a smoke.

He looked at his watch. *Showtime.* He put on his perfected miserable face and made his way to the modern glass and brick building, eager to lap up the attention of his colleagues - especially the female ones. He was rewarded with some attention, but not the sort he wanted.

'Rob, Rob!' he heard, the unmistakable voice of the Vice-Chancellor Vera Fontaine behind him. He turned to face her, unable to disguise the dread on his face.

'Rob, my dear boy. What's the latest, how is poor darling Stella?'

'No change,' he replied, as dolefully as he could. Vera had been his don in his final year at Oxford - and Stella's. Rob could convince almost everybody he met that he was the brains of the two of them. Most people were more than willing to believe that he, as a professor, was the clever one. Vera knew the truth.

'Poor girl. She's a tough cookie though. She'll pull through I'm sure. I should pop by one evening, have a chat with her. See if I can't get those brain cells working like I used to in the old days.'

'She'd like that,' Rob nodded, trying to look sincere. 'If she can hear you.'

Vera looked at her diamond-studded watch.

'Must fly.'

Rob watched as Vera flew past him to wherever she was going. *Like a bat out of hell*, he thought. *Hades*, he corrected himself. He perked up a bit. There had been no mention of that incident. Maybe it had all blown over? *She'll definitely be back for more now,* Rob told himself. *Now for the witch.*

Barbara was, as he had anticipated, hovering outside his room. She came close up to him, but he pulled away, unable to disguise the disgust he had for this rather plain woman with dyed brown hair scraped back into a bun. *Even her clothes are plain.*

'I've been so worried about you Rob,' she stammered. 'I know things weren't good between you and Stella, but it still must have been a terrible shock.'

'It was, and thank you,' Rob replied, edging closer to the door and the relative safety of his study. His eyes momentarily rested upon the photo of a young girl. Barbara followed his gaze.

'I understand you're under pressure, but you have responsibilities to me too. Us. It's nearly Christmas...'

'That's impossible,' he interrupted. 'I have the whole family to look after now. I'm only here for duty's sake. Any urgent messages?' Barbara shook her head.

Grabbing the study door handle with determination, he went inside, shutting the door behind him then letting out a relieved sigh. Slumping into his chair, he turned round to open the cabinet behind him then stiffened as the phone shrieked at him. Gingerly he picked up the receiver. 'Yes?'

'It's Mrs Baxter,' Barbara snapped. *Thank heavens.*

'Yes, Ma. I'll be there as soon as I can.' *They can't accuse me of running away now.* He poured himself a peg of Scotch. *I was here, ready for them. Clearly, she's let go, the little tart.* Knocking back the drink, he left the glass on his desk and headed out. Barbara was waiting for him.

'Where were you that day?' she asked. 'I know you weren't here.'

'Otherwise engaged!' he harrumphed as he left, muttering 'Merry Christmas to you and yours.'

9

Karen's frustration was turning into irritation. Pretending to attend to paperwork, her mind was still on the case. *Nothing's happening. Why is the guv holding back? They haven't even identified the caller yet. It's obviously Jim Westbury. Is that why? Is he protecting him?*

And why isn't there any evidence? No film in the CCTV camera, no witnesses. Something's not right. We can't leave it...

She jumped when her phone rang. It was the lab. 'DS Thorpe,' she answered.

'We've got something on the mobile. Since you kept ringing Morris, we've been working on it.'

'What?'

'It's a photo, of sorts. Well possibly.'

'And?'

'It's on Cary's phone. Mrs Stella Cary.'

'I'm coming over.'

Karen raced to her car and drove the ten-minute journey to the lab. She was still puffing when the technician handed her a printed image. She squinted at it. It was blurred with what looked like a thick red streak in the bottom half, but there was no discernible shape or recognisable feature that she could make out, even after the enhancing techniques had been employed.

'It was probably snapped by the impact of the crash.' The technician said wearily. 'It's the best we can do. I'll email it to you. Will you leave us alone now? Please?'

'Thanks!' Karen's reply hid her excitement, which was enough to lift her spirits. On the way back to the office, she sang along with the car radio, which was playing one of the few Christmas songs she didn't mind. She was still singing to the tune when she got back to her desk. 'Oh Winter, you tosser, you useless old rozzer, you think you're Gene Hunt, but you're just a ...'

'You sound happy.' Macy's surprise was evident as Karen sat down and immediately pulled up her emails to look for the promised image.

Simultaneously, Karen's phone rang and DCI Winter's head appeared round his door.

'DS Thorpe? RTA A1M. Junction five.' He paused for a second. 'Are you still here, Karen?'

'On our way, guv. Macy? You drive.'

**

In the car, Karen was silent until her rambling thoughts had been considered and shaped. 'About that photo. It could be a red car...' she began.

'Do you mean the Westbury and Cary RTA? I thought that was all settled.'

'It is. I mean, it's meant to be. But suppose we've got a serial killer driver out here?'

'A what?' Macy turned to stare at Karen then flicked her head back to look at the road. 'Do they even exist?'

Sarcastic cow. 'Well, a regular drunken driver then. There!'

Karen's foot hit the floor as Macy braked. Ahead of them they saw a mass of shattered glass, wrecked vehicles and flashing lights. 'If there is such a thing, he'll have had to have been damned clever to avoid being in the middle of that lot,' she said as she took in the scene. 'More bloody paperwork too. Here's fine to stop. Let's go see what's what.'

Outside the car, Macy stood still, watching. Her expression reflected the shock of the appalling tragedy - the twisted vehicles, the smell of petrol and the screams of an injured victim.

'What have we got?' Karen approached the Road Scene Manager while a paramedic tried to comfort and treat a woman covered in blood.

'My babies!' she was shouting after a stretcher was carried to an ambulance, the covering blanket made the shape of a small body.

'Three fatalities, two children and the driver of the BMW,' the officer told Karen. 'The driver stank of alcohol.'

Karen noted the black BMW. 'This early?' She frowned.

'There were golf clubs in the back. Might be pre-game tipples. It's a thing, apparently. There are several witnesses. He was tailgating. Didn't see the queue signs ahead, went straight into the back of the Ford.' He pointed to the silver-coloured vehicle out of which another small body was being recovered.

'Thanks,' Karen replied. 'No sign of any other drivers on the scene, then? No red cars?' He shook his head.

She turned around to see Macy in floods of tears. 'Constable Dodds! Buck up. We're on duty here!'

'It's kids, Sergeant Thorpe. Don't you care? Don't you have any feelings at all?' Karen looked blankly at Macy then watched a guilty expression appear on her face. 'I'm so sorry Sergeant. I forgot about your loss...'

'We can't get emotionally involved. We've got work to do,' Karen snapped.

* * *

On the way back to the office, Macy was the first to break the uncomfortable silence. 'That photo you mentioned, Sergeant...' Macy paused and spoke without looking at Karen. 'Robert Cary had a red car.'

Karen's head snapped round. 'Really?'

'It wasn't on the drive when we went there, or you'd have seen it yourself. It's a classic.'

'A classic what?'

'A classic car. Triumph Stag.'

'Now that is interesting. Thank you, Macy.'

'It's my job.'

'Yes, but I wouldn't know a classic car from a banger. Very well done. That's quite a skill.'

Macy's tone softened. 'I'm pleased to have helped. I've always loved cars.'

'And I know bog-all about them,' Karen laughed.

Macy, emboldened by the conversation spoke again. 'By the way, do you do midnight mass?'

'What?' Karen threw her a look as if she came from Mars. 'No.

Why are you asking?'

'I was wondering what you were going to do for Christmas now that...'

'I do my usual thing. Don't need to worry about me.'

'Do you mind me asking? What do you do?'

'I go to my aunt and uncle's every year.'

'You have family? That's good. My family love Christmas.'

'What do you do then?' Karen nearly sounded interested. *And why am I asking her this?* she wondered.

Macy responded enthusiastically. 'Well, first Mum will have decorated the entire house in black, green and gold for Jamaica and red, because... she'll cook a turkey, although she's always going on about curried goat. Ugh! And goat's head soup. I can't even think about that. Then my little brothers will be so cheeky. I'm the first one in my family to ever be a policewoman and they think I'm absolutely mad.'

'That sounds nice,' Karen replied. *You asked for that,* she thought. And as she suspected, a very animated Macy chatted the whole way back to the office.

'You get off, Macy,' Karen said when they got back. 'I'll sort it all. Enjoy your Christmas preparations. See you tomorrow.'

'I will. And you have a good evening too.' With a fleeting backward smile back to Karen and her paperwork, Macy sped off.

'Thank God for that,' Karen muttered. 'Must have a look at Robert Cary's car.'

10

Janice had begun her shift but was irritated to see that there were even more people coming to visit Stella. The curtains were drawn back and Stella, now lying in a slightly raised position was clearly visible through the glass. *Short-staffed again. We should get extra money for the evening shift,* she sulked. *It's like being hospitality, traffic warden and nursemaid rolled into one. Gwen only gets those two...* She glanced at Molly and Harry. *Such a nuisance.* Now a busy-looking little man in a smart suit was coming over. 'Only two at a time,' Janice told him. 'I'll have a word.' She went into the room and spoke to Harry.

'Another visitor. Shall I send him away?'

'No lass, don't do that.' Harry nudged Molly who was in mid-prattle. 'Mother? Someone else wants a turn.'

Molly looked around, startled at being interrupted. 'P'raps we should call it a night, Dad?'

'Mebbe.'

Janice scowled when three more people arrived. *Like flipping Piccadilly Circus in here tonight!*

She looked them over. There was a tall, broad-shouldered, rather good-looking man who looked like he'd forgotten to shave and two women; one fat mumsy one, the other was skinny. *Little and Large.* The skinny one wore a long coat and carried a large bouquet of flowers. They headed directly for Stella's room. *Popular bitch, aren't you?*

Janice fleetingly wondered how many people would come to visit her in hospital if she was in a coma. She walked over to head them off.

'I'm sorry,' she began, then they all stepped back as a painfully thin woman in fur hat and coat swished past them.

'Who was that?' Amanda said, caught between admiration and shock.

'Vera Fontaine,' the waiting man answered. 'I'm a work colleague of Stella's. Tim Strange,' he introduced himself.

'I've heard Stella talk about her. I'm Amanda. Her next-door neighbour.' They shook hands.

'We'll have quite a wait,' Tim said, wearily. 'I'm going to get a bite to eat,' he added, before wandering out of the ward.

***

'Stella darling! Stella? How are you?'

Stella stirred again. *Who's this? Not Mum. I know this voice. Slow down, slow down.* She knew the voice was especially important to her. She listened and concentrated with as much strength as she could muster.

Vera delivered an incredible resumé of Stella's early years as an applicant to, and thereafter a law student at Oxford. Not a detail was spared, from the length of Stella's hair to the colour of her shoes.

Stella felt a slow transformation taking place. She couldn't follow everything that was being said, but she knew she was changing.

I'm growing. What am I wearing? Where am I now? The landscape had changed. No reflections here but she looked down to see the blue dress had been replaced by blue jeans. She felt her yellow hair, which was now falling past her shoulders.

Ahead of her, she could see something white. As she stared, the white began to take form. Buildings. There was a city in the distance, somewhere that was important to her and she knew she needed to reach it.

I remember.

Vera.

'Stella, dear girl, I have to go now. I'll be back soon.'

Stella heard the shuffling and squeaking of furniture being moved.

'Hello, Stella. It's Tim here. Tim Strange from Spalls.'

Tim?

Stella drifted back to sleep for a while, then something roused her.

'... and that chap Brandon's been on. He seems very keen to

41

talk to you. But Stella, I couldn't find your files. He'll have to wait for now.'

Brandon?

'Other than that, we're coping. Stella, don't you worry about a thing. I've reorganised the casework. Although, we absolutely must have you back ASAP after Christmas. You know what it's like then.'

Tim.

Chair legs scraping. Footsteps walking away. A shuffling noise. Who is it?

'Hello Stella, It's me, Amanda. Penny's come to see you too, but she wasn't allowed to bring the flowers in. She'll be along in a minute. We've been chatting to your parents. Iain's been telling them about the tennis club. Fabian's coming back for New Year's Eve. Your mum was worried about who's looking after the children tonight, but the boys are with friends and Rob's got the girls. He's sorry he can't come tonight. I bumped into your work colleague, Tim. He seemed very nice and very concerned for you. Naturally, I didn't mention that you'd refused to take on my divorce.'

Divorce.

'Anyway, I want you to know that that's water under the bridge now. The woman you recommended did so well. Did I already tell you what a terrific settlement she got me? Maybe better than you could have done.'

Laughter.

'Only joking. Iain's here and Penny is on her way. Better go. Bye for now.'

Footsteps.

Shuffling.

'Stella, It's Iain. I haven't got long...'

Iain. Iain. I know this man.

'I was devastated when you didn't come that evening. There was so much I wanted to tell you. Darling, you must get better. I love you so much. I don't know what I'll do without you.'

Iain. Iain loves me.

'I'm missing you so much, it hurts. I'll come and see you

whenever I can. Oh, Stella, I wish I could get on the bed and hold you properly. I promise we'll make our baby... '

Baby.

'Can't talk anymore. She's coming.'

So faint.

Heavy footsteps.

'Hello, Stella. Penny here. I was horrified to hear about your crash. I always worried about that car of yours. Funny how things work out, isn't it? I could have checked it over for you, if you'd wanted. Well maybe I'm not up to doing a full service yet, but I will be if I finish the course. If I'm honest, I'm not really sure it's my thing. It's getting so cold outside, now. Besides, Iain won't let me near his new car. Men, eh?'

Car.

'Did you need to say all that? It's stupid...'

Iain. Faint.

'We should go.'

'I'm sure there's something you can talk to her about, Iain. Where was she going that night?'

'Leave it. For God's sake, she's in a coma. She may never recover...'

Chairs moving again.

Am I alone?

No. He's here. I can tell.

'They've all gone Stella. I'm here.'

Him. I knew it.

Stella drifted off to sleep.

11

Rob was skulking on the way to his study when Molly grabbed his arm.

'Look, see what Harry's done.'

'Very good,' Rob muttered, with barely a glance at the highly decorated and pungent Christmas tree.

'Look at the top.' Molly insisted. 'Our Stella made that fairy. How it survived all Sandra's mauling I don't know. We'll tell her about it when we see her.'

'You do that, Ma.'

'I should ring our Sandra too.'

Rob visibly flinched. 'Things to do.' He disappeared into his study.

It was there that he was the recipient of Sandra's call. *Summoned by the devil herself.*

'I'm coming to see you and the old folk,' she announced. 'I'm completely boracic. Piers is working away somewhere, and I don't know when he'll be back. He was mad with Stella; I'm only surprised he didn't do her in himself.'

'Sandra!'

'Look, Rob, I've got to get some dosh from someone soon or me and the kids will starve. And if they don't cough up, I'll have to work the streets up there; there's not much business doing in the village. That'll get your posh neighbourhood talking and what will bloody Stella think of *that* when she wakes up?'

'We've no room here Sandra. Besides, I'm sure he'll be back for Christmas. You can't leave an empty house for him to find. Anyway, Ma and Pa are in too much of a state at the moment.'

'I've got airbeds, Rob.'

'Will a couple of hundred tide you over?'

'OK. Let me get my bank details.' He sighed as he input the transfer. He knew she'd be back for more. A dislike of Sandra was

44

possibly the only thing Rob and Stella had left in common, children excepted. *How could sisters be so different?* Stella had clawed her way from nowhere to that highly esteemed place at Oxford. Sandra had stayed there grabbing everything she could, whether it was merited, earned or even legal. 'She's every bit as clever as me,' Stella would say. 'She's just a lazy bitch.'

At first, he'd first appreciated the pretty, half-clad teenager who'd deposited herself on their doorstep on the pretext of going to a local music festival. He'd noted that Sandra too, had dropped her Northern accent after meeting the vainglorious and odorous Piers. She'd turned into one of those hippy sorts. Hairy legs, armpits and scant use of washing facilities. As for Piers, disowned by wealthy parents for blowing all their funding on drugs and festivals, well, he'd have cut him off too. And he had form for disappearing. He'd probably gone off to join another hippy commune or something.

Nothing changes, he thought as he pressed the 'send' button. It had cost him before to get rid of the pair of them. He and Stella later heard about their marriage on the back of a postcard from Dorset. A miserable mix of metaphors. 'Up the duff, so we tied the knot.'

After that, they apparently lived entirely off the state. It had seriously annoyed him when he worked out that the value of their benefits was about the same as the taxes he and Stella paid. Then Stella had stuck the knife in. Hard. And twisted it.

Rob topped up his Scotch. *I bet Amanda's having a very lonely Christmas. She'll be desperate for male company. Primed and ready to be plucked, like a luscious peach.*

***

That evening, Karen drove home early via the scene of the accident noting the time. 16:31. It was approximately the same time as the actual crash had occurred and it was similarly dry and cold, but darker. *A rat-run. Packed at peak times, deserted afterwards*.

She watched the road then checked her watch. 16:36. In that

time a solitary car came from the north and only two had gone south; Stella's way. She walked across to the central reservation. The barriers were still bent in the place where Westbury's van had impacted, and a fresh bunch of flowers had been attached. *Interesting.*

Across the other side of the road, there were woodlands and what looked like a broken fence. She stepped over the barrier and walked across to the wooded area. The fence had either rotted away or been removed at one point and there was a clearly trodden unofficial path leading into the woods. *Escape route?*

She turned to go back to the car and walked straight across; there were no other cars around. *Three cars that night must have been a traffic jam, hardly scope for a crash. If it was murder or attempted murder, the murderer certainly knew their road.*

She walked back the way she had driven. *Isn't there a building around here? Yes. There it is.* In the darkness, the corrugated roof structure was almost invisible. Nothing indicated what its use was and it looked somewhat neglected. She shivered. Fog was beginning to descend, and it was getting colder.

Karen got back in the car and sat for a while still going over the same old ground. *Why would Stella go this way? Why would Tom Westbury go this way? What was the damned connection? Where does the red car fit in? Robert Cary had a red car, I've checked that. But Stella would have recognised it. Maybe she did? Better go and see.*

***

Karen entered the ICU ward, immediately recognising Stella's nurse, who was talking to someone outside her room.

'I've come to see Stella Cary,' she said, reading the name badge. 'Miss Williams.'

'Hello, again Sergeant. You know where she is. I'm sorry, I should have gone by now.'

'I want to talk to her this time.'

'Nothing stressful please,' a puzzled Gwen said as she

watched Karen enter the room.

'Hello, Stella. It's Karen here. You won't remember me, but you came to talk to us at school once. I was the one who wanted to be a copper and you said I should do law. But that's not why I'm here. I'm investigating your accident. I think that something or someone caused that crash and that a red car was involved. Your husband Robert Cary had a red car. Was he on the road when you were? Did you see it there? I'm not accusing him or anything, but if he appeared suddenly, it could be...' Karen tailed off, aware that Gwen was looking at her with an irritated expression. 'What? Is this a problem? Maybe it will help her come round.'

Neither woman knew quite what the next step should be, but they were both rescued by Karen's phone ringing. With a nod to Gwen, Karen spoke to Stella first. 'I'll be back Stella, I promise.' Then she left the ward talking into her phone as she went. 'Hi Auntie Sal. Yes, I'm fine.'

'Yes, of course I'm coming. It wouldn't be Christmas without... Anyway, what would you like? OK. That's easy. And the usual for Uncle Jack? No problem. I'm going shopping on my way home.'

***

When she got home, as Karen changed into her onesie, she remembered her father's reaction when he'd asked her what she wanted for Christmas.

'It's a what?' he'd said, bemused. 'A baby outfit for adults?'

'Something like that,' she'd laughed. 'Don't worry, I'll buy it for myself. You can get me a bottle of something.'

'Bailey's it is then,' he had declared.

Karen reached for the precious bottle that she kept on a shelf above her television and opened it. 'Cheers Dad. I need it today.' She poured herself a large measure and savoured the warm soothing feeling which began to spread over her body as she drank. She refused to call it depression or recognise the grief. She self-medicated with alcohol. Tonight's potion of choice was doing a very good job.

Briefly glancing at the paperwork she'd brought home with her, she topped up her glass until she reached the point where she couldn't read anymore. Pushing the papers to the floor, she stretched out on the sofa.

Soon dreaming, Karen sat at her desk in the middle of the road, looking at a gigantic picture suspended in the air. Half-red, half-black, she watched as it transformed into something she recognised. Then it moved, no, it *drove*. There were other shapes around. 'Of course!' she shouted out. 'That's it!'

She woke instantly and re-ran the image in her mind but before she even sat up, it had gone. Banging her head with her hand in frustration, she pulled out the photo the lab had sent her in case it brought something back. Nothing.

Sulking, she went into the kitchen for a glass of water and paracetamol, then sat back down. *Bed or Bailey's? Bailey's.* She poured herself a small glass and knocked it back, chasing it with the water and pill. In bed, she lay restless, still trying to recall the dream.

12

Tuesday 25th December

Molly and Harry had crept out of the house leaving the children with their presents. The ICU ward had a few Christmas trimmings, a nod to the occasion, but not enough to offend sensitivities.

'Where is everybody?' Molly looked around, a wrapped present in her hand.

'Holiday,' Harry grunted.

'Good morning, Mr and Mrs B. How are you today?' Janice's shrill voice as she appeared from behind a screen made them jump.

'Merry Christmas,' Harry said. Janice nodded, her eyes resting on a wrapped present in Molly's hands.

'It's for our Stella,' Molly said quickly, in case Janice got the wrong idea. 'It's a new nightie. It's the only thing I could think of getting her.'

Janice took the present and put it in the bedside cupboard. 'I'll let Gwen know, next shift.'

'Thank you,' Harry said.

Stella was wide awake and concentrating.

'Stella? It's Mum again. Do you know what day it is, love?' She began to sing softly. 'Every little girl would like to be the fairy on the Christmas tree...'

I'm inside. This is home.

Mum is singing. I know that song. She's singing it for me.

There's a tree. Why is a tree inside? But it's so pretty.

Shiny things. Boxes all pretty colours. Red and green and gold and blue.

They're for me. I'm awake and I can see things.

I'm awake.

'Do you remember that Christmas when you got your first job?'

Too fast. Wait.

49

'Oh, Stella, you were so happy. Even the building was lovely, you said.'

Yes. There are buildings.

'You told us you were working for a firm called Spalls.'

I can see a long row of buildings and greenery. Not long grass and water, these are squares of green, rows of flowers...

'You wanted to specialise in family matters. You've been there for years now. You're always talking about a man called Tim. Do you remember?'

Tim. Yes, Tim.

'Do you remember that Christmas when Rob's position at the university was confirmed?'

Rob again.

'He asked you to marry him. You remember your husband Robert, don't you?'

Robert, my husband?

'You were twenty-two.'

Rob. I'm dancing with him. I can't see him, but I know it's him.

'Do you remember the ring? Rob's got it now, for safekeeping.'

Something is sparkling on my finger. A ring? Yes, I'm sure it's a ring.

And I am happy. Very happy. With Rob.

'Dad, she's there. I can feel it!'

I remember, I remember...

'She was, Dad, I really did feel it.'

'Come on lass. Let's get back to the kiddies.'

***

Karen duly rolled up at Sal and Jack's place and was greeted with a long squeezy hug from the well-rounded Sal.

'New hair colour?' Karen asked.

'Had it for years, Karen.'

'Oh...'

'Only joshing. You're right. I thought I'd go blonde. Do you like it?'

Sal was prised away by the considerably leaner and thinner-haired Jack who planted a smacker on Karen's cheek. 'Come in, gal. What's your poison?'

After Karen had downed a couple of glasses of Prosecco and a great deal of small talk had passed, Sal began to talk seriously.

'Karen, I thought I'd let you know. I've been looking in on the house.' Karen couldn't stop her face freezing when she registered the words. 'You knew I had keys, didn't you?'

Karen took her time. It was something she was learning to do, to think before she spoke. The last person she wanted to upset was this lady whom she adored. 'I did Auntie Sal. I hadn't thought about the house at all. And thank you so much.'

'It's a pleasure, love. Do you want me to sort out his things? I only mean clothes and that. I can take them to the charity shop for you, if you like?'

'Please. That would be very kind. Although knowing Dad there'll be nothing worth keeping.'

Sal laughed. 'Tommy got his wear out of his clothes, that's true.'

'And if there's anything you'd like as a keepsake, anything at all, please feel free...'

'No love. You need to sort out his personal things when you're ready. I'll come with you if you like.'

'How about some pressies!' Jack intervened. 'And another glass...'

The topping-up of glasses took longer than the present opening.

'Brilliant, Auntie Sal. A new onesie. Exactly what I wanted.' Karen held up the furry brown outfit. 'It's got a proper head!' She planted one of her exceptionally rare kisses on Sal's cheek then did the same for Jack.

'Perfect,' Sal seemed pleased enough with her unwrapped bubble bath set, which, unlike on previous occasions, bore no sign of the price label.

'Thanks, love. My favourite.' Jack patted his bottle of single malt.

'Have you still got last year's present?' Karen asked.

'The policeman fridge guard one which shouted "ello 'ello 'ello" every time we opened the door?'

'Yes!'

'It died,' Sal said.

'Thank Christ,' Jack added, still holding the bottle.

'Now you savour that this time,' Sal warned him. 'It's not wine, you know.'

'I will. And talking of wine, let's toast Tommy.'

'To Tommy,' they said. 'To Dad,' said Karen. They all raised their glasses.

'Now.' Jack looked serious.' Did I ever tell you about the time he thought he'd solved the Ripper murders? It was when we'd first met as cadets, all those years ago...'

Not again, Karen thought. *But it's so funny.*

'You know he always denied that,' she laughed. 'And he's not here to defend himself.'

'I know, love. But it's how we keep him with us. With our memories.' Jack's face turned more serious. 'And we've got something to tell you.'

'What?'

'We're both agreed on it.' Sal nodded. 'Now, how old are you?'

'Twenty-six,' Karen said, sipping nervously at her wine.

'And what rank are you?'

Karen frowned. 'Detective Sergeant.'

'Then stop calling us Auntie and Uncle, you big daft bat!'

Karen nearly spat out her mouthful. 'I was going to say that too!' There were laughs all round.

After lunch, Sal went into the kitchen, rejecting Karen's plans to help wash up. 'Jack wants to talk to you,' she said.

'I do,' he agreed. 'Now love, that case that's been bothering you. How's it going?'

Karen's face fell. 'There is no case anymore. I'm sure that there's something up but the lab haven't come up with anything I can move on. Except, possibly, the involvement of another car.'

'Give me the whole picture.'

Karen explained every detail from the accident while Jack listened patiently.

'Then let me say from my experience and from what you've told me, there's nothing more to this than a tragic accident. It's how things go, love,' Jack said. 'You'll get your moment when something really happens, don't you worry.'

'But it might help if I knew more about the Westburys. The guv still refuses to let me talk to the family.'

'We've been there already, Karen...'

With perfect timing, Sal reappeared. 'Anything more I can get you?'

Karen patted her stomach. 'I've eaten more food today than I'd normally eat in a week.' She heaved herself up. 'I'd better get going while I can still move.'

'I'll give you a lift. I've only had a glass.'

'I can walk, Auntie... Sal. It'll do me good.'

'It's too far,' Sal replied. 'I insist.'

'I give in.' *No point stalling; she's bound to ask me sooner or later.*

In the car, Sal asked her about her father outright.

'Yes, of course, I miss him terribly. But we didn't live in each other's pockets. And I'm so busy at work, honestly, I'm fine.'

'He was so proud of you, Karen. Remember that. And we'll always be here for you.'

'Thank you.' There was a long silence. *OK. Get in first.* 'No, I haven't decided about the ashes yet.'

'Would you like me to collect them? I don't mind.'

'No. But I'll let you know as soon as I decide.'

'I didn't want to pry.'

'I know.'

It was only when Karen got back inside her flat that all the emotions of the past few months finally came out. That night, she sobbed herself to sleep.

13

Monday 31st December

Rob had spent most of the morning hanging around outside finding all sorts of things to do, including smoking. 'It's the stress,' he'd told his in-laws.

It was a mild day, so he'd pottered a bit, emptied the rubbish, all the recycling bins and got through five cigarettes. But mainly he had stared at Amanda's back door willing it to open. *She's probably too laid back to worry about recycling. Unlike... was that the door?*

Scuttling back to the black wheelie bin, he lifted the lid and turned back with a look of surprise to see Amanda coming out holding a large black bag.

'Snap,' Rob grinned. 'And hello stranger. Have you had a nice time? Is everything all right with you and yours?'

'Hello Rob. We've had a very jolly time. Only one mishap but I won't bore you with that. How are you getting on with the visitors?'

'It could be worse. We could have Stella's sister here too. She's threatened to come.'

'Oh, I remember you saying. It's Sandra, isn't it? Stella told me that she'd had a big falling-out with her.'

'She didn't come, thank God. And the old folks are going home this afternoon. So, all's well.'

'Poor you. You've had such a hard time.' She paused, her face reflecting her thoughts. 'How about you all come over for tea tonight?'

Halfway there. It's not friendship. Sympathy? Hell, I can cope with that. 'To see the new year in?'

Amanda shook her head. 'Sorry, I promised Penny a girls' night in with a rom-com. I think she's having problems with Iain again.'

It's a start. 'Tea it is then,' he replied.

***

Stella woke to hear a familiar voice talking in her ear.

'Stella? It's me again. I promised to come back and here I am. But Stella, I'm making you another promise. I will never give up on you. I will find out what happened. Whatever it takes.'

The one who asks the questions.

'Sergeant Thorpe? Has something happened?'

'No, Miss Williams. I wanted to tell her I was still on the case. What's with the nightie? Do you do that for all patients?'

'It was a present from her parents. We forgot about it until they reminded us. Pretty isn't it?'

'Good choice. It's much more *you* Stella.'

More me?

'We're moving her today, so as you know. Only over there.'

'Thanks. See you later.'

Moving me?

'Goodbye Sergeant. Hello?'

Gwen.

Who's there?

'What are you doing?'

It's him.

'We're going to move her today.'

Move me.

'There's nothing wrong is there?'

'Oh, no, nothing wrong. It's because we need the room for new patients, especially this time of year. We're not going far. To the end room, there.'

'Can I help?'

'Of course. I've noticed you're around here quite a bit. Is there any reason?'

'I saw her come in. She's very lovely. I wish I could make her better.'

Gwen smiled. 'We all do. What's your name?'

'Peter.'

Peter?

A rolling sound.

Rolling. Moving?
Now quiet.

'Can I come back? I'd like to sit with her a bit.'

'Of course you can, my love. She doesn't get so many visitors these days, it's nice for her to have company.'

***

Screaming echoed around the ward. 'STELLA! What have you done to my Stella?!'

Gwen rushed over and grabbed Molly's shoulders as if to stop her from taking off. She spoke firmly and quietly. 'Mrs Baxter, she's fine. It's Molly, isn't it? Molly, we've moved her to another room, that's all. She's fine.'

Molly couldn't stop the sobs coming, her shoulders heaved until she began to calm down. The panting stopped and slowly she recaptured her breath.

Harry took over, putting his arms around her and glaring at Gwen. He shook his head. 'Should've warned her. Us.'

Peter, hearing the commotion hurried back. 'She's over there Mr and Mrs Baxter.' He pointed to the new room. 'Gwen looks after her so well.' He could see the relief on their faces. 'She couldn't be in better hands. And I'll be back in a minute.'

'I'd hoped to catch you as you came in, but...' Gwen began.

'Why now?' Harry asked.

'Stella doesn't need to be in an emergency room any longer, so we have to free it up. Everything else is still the same; she'll still be looked after.'

'You mean out of the way, don't you?' Harry glared at her. 'For when the time comes.'

'No, not at all!' Gwen remonstrated. Harry shook his head. 'Come and see her now.' She led them to the new room. It was identical to the other one, but being in the corner of the ward there were only two walls visible. The Baxters couldn't see Stella until they got closer and saw that she lay unchanged and still breathing. Gwen withdrew back to her desk.

'See, Dad, they've put the nightie on her at last. She looks so lovely. Like Sleeping Beauty, ready to go back to the ball.'

'Aye, she does.'

They sat down and watched her for a few minutes, Molly holding Stella's hand, Harry sitting restlessly.

'Come on Mother. We've a long journey.'

'I don't want to go. We can't leave her now.'

'I'll talk to that nurse again.'

Gwen waited at the desk when she saw him approaching. 'Look, Mr Baxter, look here,' she said, showing Harry the monitoring screens. 'See? We don't take our eyes off her for a minute.'

'We want to make sure nothing happens without our say-so,' he declared. 'It's not that we don't trust our son-in-law, but we want to be told if there's any decision-making to be done.'

Gwen looked him straight in the eye. 'It's not even an option at the moment. We're in this for the long haul too. If Stella's condition deteriorates, then that's a different matter. But you will be the first to know, along with her husband of course, if that happens.'

Harry leaned forward and looked at her with piercing eyes. 'Is that a promise?'

'It most certainly is,' Gwen nodded.

Harry walked back to Stella's room. 'Come on, love. Let's grab a bite to eat, then we can talk about it.'

***

Amanda's tea was an authentic Hungarian goulash, precisely the right mixture of richness and comfort for a post-Christmas meal. When every last scraping from the pot had been consumed, the children were tempted away to the living room, with the remains of uneaten chocolate snowmen and bunches of gold and silver coins.

Nicely settled in the cosy kitchen, Rob and Amanda sat drinking the wine Rob had brought over.

'Have they've gone back home now?'

Rob sighed. 'Yes, thank goodness. They're nice enough but...'

'I know. You want your own space back. But it must be lonely now. Have you thought what you'll do if, you know...?' Amanda hesitated.

'All the time. I mean, no, not really,' Rob stumbled. 'Actually,' he continued. 'Things haven't been quite right between us for a while.'

'Oh?'

Did her breasts get even bigger? 'It's no one's fault. I wanted more children, but she wasn't keen. We haven't...' he coughed, '*loved* each other in years.'

'Oh, I see.' Amanda blushed a little. 'How awful for you.'

'Then we grew apart. We're simply not the same people we were when we met. It had to happen eventually.'

'That's so sad,' Amanda sympathised. 'And I always thought she loved children. It's terrible when any relationship breaks down.' Her eyes filled with tears.

'How stupid of me. I'd forgotten that, well, that...'

'That Edward walked out on me? I know. What a useless, unattractive woman I am that even someone like him would leave!'

'What nonsense is this?' Rob tried, clumsily to touch her but as they were both sitting, it didn't quite work. 'Here,' he gestured for her to stand. She smiled at him, that wonderful bosom heaving. *She's so up for this. Come to think of it, so am I.*

He went closer. She stood, but missed her footing a little. The heavy wooden chair fell backwards making a tremendous thud on the tiled kitchen floor. She wobbled unsteadily and Rob grabbed her with a little too much force. Her face was in his face. *Now, do it now!* He kissed her hard on the mouth at precisely the moment that James and Daniel ran into the kitchen wondering what the noise was. Amanda pushed Rob away and slapped him hard across the face. Rob took a step back and tripped over a chair leg, landing on his bottom. The boys stood in astonishment, not knowing whether to laugh or cry.

'Get out!' Amanda screamed. 'How could you even think...'

Rob, scrambling to his feet, called to the boys. 'Get your sister, we're going. Now.'

By the time Laura had been kidnapped from Joely's bedroom, Rob was already standing outside the door. 'Come on!' he shouted at the three of them. When they were all outside, Amanda slammed the door shut behind them.

14

Rob had finished a cigarette and gone back inside when the doorbell rang again. *Amanda. She's come to apologise!* 'I'm so sorry...' he said as he opened the door. 'No! Not you!'

A slim young woman with messy blonde hair stood there staring at him with venom in her eyes.

'You what?' Sandra said, stepping in, leaving a suitcase in the porch.

To compound Rob's discomfort, the doorbell rang again. He pushed the door to find Harry struggling with several overfull carrier bags and a holdall. He sighed, his hopes completely dashed. 'What happened?'

'She couldn't bear to leave our Stella. Not yet. Have you got company?' Harry looked at the suitcase with a hint of suspicion.

'Sandra,' Rob replied.

'Blimmin' 'eck.'

Sandra had settled herself in the living room where James and Daniel played on the games console. Laura was looking at her in confusion. Sandra gave her a big smile.

'Mummy?'

'No, darling, it's your Auntie Sandra. Don't you remember me? Shall we see who's come in?' The little girl nodded and happily took Sandra's hand as she went into the hall.

'How about some tea?' Sandra said as she saw Harry deposit the rest of the bags. 'Dad?' She stood there a little unsure.

'Sandra.' Harry hugged his daughter awkwardly.

'Where's Mum?' Molly appeared from the kitchen and was almost as uncomfortable.

'Hello, Sandra, love. Where are the kiddies?'

'I sold them for body parts,' she snapped. 'They're with friends. What did you think?'

Laura ran to Molly while Sandra followed Rob into the kitchen.

'I already gave you two hundred,' he said.

'Didn't even cover the rent.'

'You can't keep asking me for more.'

'Well,' Sandra gave a sarcastic smile. 'It all started when someone reported me.' Rob turned to look at her. 'I know who it was.' She glared at him.' It was Stella wasn't it?'

Rob shook his head. 'I don't think so.'

'One minute she's having a go at me, the next I get this call from the Social. Piers went mad when he found out. Said he'd kill her. Ha ha, she got her comeuppance another way though, didn't she?'

'I'm sure Stella had nothing to do with it,' Rob said, but Sandra carried on.

'Funny that she paid my fine, then. Anyway, they gave me a caution and put me on this work programme. I'm only stacking shelves at the Co-op in school time, but it's not enough, not now Piers has gone.'

'You said he was working?'

'That's what I thought. He got in that old banger and drove off. I didn't think it would even get very far but he did spend everything he earned on the bloody thing.'

'What about Piers' parents?' Rob asked. 'Can't they help? After all...'

'That's why I'm here. They live nearby.'

'How do you know? I thought Piers never told you where they were?'

'Not the details. But I knew he came from these parts, it's how I met him. Remember?'

'How could I forget?'

'I found an old letter, well the top bit of it shoved in one of his dirty mags. I think it's his mother's address. It's not far off. There's a phone number on it too.' She handed it to him.

Rob nodded and gave it back to her. 'I'll drive you there. Soon as possible.'

'Tomorrow then. How about a drink?'

'Don't you want to go to the hospital to see Stella?'

'What, that cow? Not until she's awake...' Molly and Harry appeared. 'Yes, of course I want to see her,' Sandra said, smiling

61

sweetly at her parents.

***

'Oh my god!' Sandra exclaimed when she saw her sister. 'She looks like a waxwork.'

'She can probably hear you,' said Rob, ignoring his own warning. 'The consultant says...' He turned to see Reeta about to leave the ward. 'I need a quick word.'

Rob caught up with her in the corridor. 'Miss Shah.' Reeta turned towards him, recognising him at once.

'Mr Cary,' she replied.

'I was wondering...' Rob paused. 'I've seen it so many times when the family have to make decisions...'

Reeta squared up to him. 'You mean when do we consider switching the life support off, don't you?' She frowned.

'I wouldn't put it quite like that...' Rob said, floundering.

'Mr Cary. Your wife is no longer on the ventilator. She's breathing unaided, her heart is pumping and her kidneys are functioning. There is no medical intervention to make. It will only be if her condition deteriorates considerably that we will even get close to making such a decision.'

'Oh,' Rob said. 'Good.'

'You watch too much television, Mr Cary,' Reeta said, sweeping away down the corridor.

Standing quietly in the corridor, Peter, the young orderly had watched and listened.

'Don't you dare hurt my Stella,' he muttered. 'She's mine now.'

He glanced at the unattended computer screen in the ward and smiled. 'I'm going to look after you Stella. I promise.'

***

Stella lay in confusion and torment as a voice railed at her.

'You bitch. You deserve all you get. How dare you rat on me, your only sister? What the hell did you think you were doing?'

I know that voice...

'Now my Piers has gone off. It's all your bloody fault.'

Who is it? What have I done?

'Rob says it was a fucking accident, but I reckon he tried to do you in. He'll be in hiding now, waiting for you to die. So hurry up, you stupid bitch. I want him back.'

Stella tried to retreat into sleep but was stopped by another voice. It also made her unhappy.

'Better get home.'

'Yes, Rob. I've had enough.'

Rob. Rob. Him?

***

Rob and Sandra arrived home to a quiet house, with Molly sitting on the sofa next to Harry. 'How is she?'

'Still comatose,' Sandra replied.

'I spoke to the consultant,' Rob said. 'She's in good working order, apparently.'

'She's not a car,' Molly snapped.

'Drink, Ma?' Rob poured them both a Scotch, then one for himself which he knocked straight back, swiftly refilling his glass. He remained standing, restless. The only thing he was sure of was that he didn't want to be there, in the company of his in-laws for any longer than was absolutely necessary. He stood for a moment, drank half of his glass and put it down. 'I've just remembered,' he said. 'There's somewhere I need to be.'

'But you've been drinking, lad,' Harry said, aghast.

'I don't need a car where I'm going,' Rob replied as he went into the hall to put his coat on.

'Happy bloody New Year to you!' he heard Sandra yell.

Outside, he stopped to look at Amanda's house. There was no sign of Penny's little run-around, he'd have recognised it. But there was another car parked there. *Maybe it was only an excuse, to wind me up,* he mused as he trudged down the path. *Or she got a better offer. God, I need a woman.*

***

Stella was shaken and beyond confused. So many voices, so much emotion had left her traumatised. She longed to hear the gentle voice of the man whom she thought of as her guardian angel. Instead, she woke to a very different noise.

She heard breathing. Not the soft regular breathing she'd become used to. Nor the breathing that came from inside her. It sounded erratic. Heavy.

'You asked for this...'

Who is this?

'It's what you deserve...'

She could hear the faint rustling of sheets.

Go away, leave me alone, HELP ME!

Now frantic, loud and increasingly rapid breathing.

I know that sound. It's a good sound.

No. It's not a good sound.

'I'm going to fuck you fuck you fuck you...'

Leave me alone.

Go away.

Who are you?

What are you doing to me?

She strained every sense in her body, searched for every nerve ending, willed herself to move.

I have to see! I... have... to... see!

Then it happened. Something amazing. Her eyes opened for a split-second.

Who are you?

She could see nothing, understand or interpret anything. But she heard the shock of somebody else.

'Shit! SHIT. You stupid bitch. Why didn't you die?' The voice got fainter. '... Better all round...'

Stella dropped suddenly into unconsciousness. She was catapulted into a wilderness, a nothingness. She could see nothing. No buildings, no grass, no sky. Somewhere in the distance, a voice was calling her. 'I will protect you, Stella.'

Slowly she began to move forward to where she thought the voice might be coming from.

15

Tuesday 1st January 2013

After breakfast, Molly began interrogating her daughter. 'Piers hasn't sent you any money at all then?' Sandra nodded then shook her head. 'What are you going to do? Ask his parents?'

'It's about time they showed an interest in their grandchildren,' Sandra replied.

'Do they even know they exist?' asked Molly.

'They must do. Bastards,' Sandra spat.

Rob came into the room. 'You have to contact them first. You can't turn up out of the blue.'

'He's right, love,' Molly said. 'They'll need a little time to get used to the idea.'

'Have you checked that number?' Rob asked. 'It looked like an old code.'

Sandra reached for her handbag and pulled out the piece of paper. 'But supposing they tell me not to come, or won't answer the door?'

'Then they're hardly the sort to give you money anyway and no point in wasting a journey.' Rob got up and walked towards the telephone. 'Especially if I have to drive you there.' He picked up the mobile receiver and handed it to Sandra.

'Here.' She handed him the paper.

'You have to put an 'O' first,' he said, handing it back.

Sandra dialled the number. For all her bravado, her hands were trembling.

'It's Sandra,' she said with perfect diction. There was a pause. 'Your daughter-in-law. I'm married to Piers.'

They all heard the clunk of the phone being slammed down at the other end. Sandra gasped.

'What...?' Molly stared at her. Sandra dialled again. After ten rings, the phone was answered. Molly and Rob strained to hear. This time there was a conversation of sorts.

'... He always called himself Piers. I need to see you, He's gone missing.'

Sandra's face flashed with shock. 'He was with you? Where is he now?'

Molly and Rob edged closer.

'I'm coming to see you. I've got an address... Forty-seven Balaclava Gardens. Is that right? See you later, then.' She handed the phone back to Rob.

'And?' he asked.

'He was there,' she said. 'Asking for money, but he's gone now. She says she won't say anymore over the phone.' She looked at Rob. 'Let's get going.'

***

Sandra sat uncomfortably as Rob sullenly drove her to her mother-in-law's address. 'Where did you go last night?' She asked.

'Mind your own business.'

'What's rattled your cage? I was only asking.'

Rob turned to scowl at her. 'I went for a walk if you must know.'

'Who goes out for a walk on New Year's Eve? Drinking I'd bet. Or is there another woman again?'

Rob didn't respond. He began to slow down and peer at the houses on the road. 'Well, I never. This appears to be it.'

'It can't be!' Sandra stared in dismay at the row of small, terraced houses.

'Only one way to find out,' Rob replied as he pulled up. 'I'll wait here. Good luck.' He waved his crossed fingers as she got out. Sandra went up to the door and knocked. After a few moments, it half-opened. She looked back and saw Rob craning his neck to see. She shrugged her shoulders before going in.

Inside, as outside, the house was small and not well furnished.

Jackie Atkins saw Sandra's look of disappointment. 'What were you expecting? Buck House?'

'Almost,' Sandra snapped. 'Piers told me that you were

66

stinking rich and threw him out because you didn't like his political views.'

Jackie threw back her head in mocking laughter. 'Sit down!' she ordered. She was also blunt. 'He left home when he was eighteen. I told him the truth about his father after he started university, and that was it. I wrote, every year, but he never wrote back, not a word, not a card, nothing... until he turned up out of the blue a couple of weeks ago.'

'What? I can't believe it.' Sandra shook her head. *Would he lie that much? This is Piers. Of course he would.* 'What happened to Mr Atkins?'

Jackie laughed again. 'You mean his dad? He was a scumbag,' she glowered. 'Had his fun then buggered off back to his wife. I never got a penny off him to look after his bastard child. Then after scrimping and saving for eighteen years, Paul goes and dumps me too.'

'Paul?' Sandra said, unused to hearing the name. *So much for Piers' pot of gold.* 'Where did he go after seeing you?'

'I told him to fuck off and see his real family, if I wasn't good enough for him. Off he went, and I haven't heard from him since,' Jackie replied.

Sandra took a deep breath. *Now or never.* 'Did he tell you that you have four grandchildren?' *There, that's got to her.* Jackie's face hardened. *No, it hasn't. Damn.*

'I ain't got no son so I ain't got no grandchildren. And there's no money so no point asking. I think you'd better sling your hook.'

Sandra stood up to leave but had one more question. *Worth a try.* 'Who is his father? Where does he live?'

Jackie scowled. 'His name was Nicholas Westbury. Old Nick, and called that for good reason. And the only thing I know about him now is he's dead.' She stood up and moved towards the door. 'Now bugger off back to wherever you came from.'

The name meant nothing to Sandra but her disappointment when she and Rob returned was palpable.

'Eh, lass,' Harry said, gently rubbing her arm. 'Happen we can sort something out.'

'Thanks.' Sandra was crushed but still calculating. *How much?*

'How about five hundred for now?'

'And we'll try to come and see you soon, love,' Molly added.

I'd rather have the money. 'Thanks, Dad. Thanks, Mum. No point in hanging around then.'

Harry booked Sandra a train ticket and slipped her a ten-pound note for the taxi at the other end, while Rob put her suitcase in the car.

Sitting on the train home, she wallowed. *They were glad to see me go. Where are you, Piers? I know you'll come back in the end but I'm not coping. I'll forgive you, you know that, like I always do.*

***

Rob sat in his study, composing a long grovelling email to Amanda. 'I'm so sorry for our little misunderstanding. You must forgive a poor fool who was so desirous of comforting you. And then in the light of the kitchen, you looked so beautiful! How was I, a poor wretch, to resist your charms? I beg you to forgive me.' He'd paced around his study for ages waiting for a reply. His email notification sounded.

'Edward's still here. Things to discuss. Maybe we can talk tomorrow?'

Edward? Ah, the car. Rob rubbed his hands together. *It's a sign. No rush, not with the old folks still here.* He joined Molly and Harry in the living room and handed them drinks. 'I wanted to say thanks, Ma and Pa, for all the help you've given me and the kids these last weeks.' He raised his glass to them. Harry reciprocated; Molly's eyes narrowed. 'Now, I think it's about time we thought about what we're going to do this year.'

Molly glared at him. 'Now?'

Harry was more circumspect. 'He's right, mother. New year, new plans. We can't stay here forever.'

'And Sofia's due back today. It is her room,' Rob added. *That's tactful, isn't it?*

'You've got masses of room!' Molly snapped. 'Ey, when we were growing up...'

Harry cut in. 'It's not about the space, love. It's about getting things back to normal.'

Rob nodded gratefully. 'The kids need their routine. And Stella wasn't a massive part of it. Sofia did all the school stuff.'

'And I've spoken to that nurse,' Harry said, shooting Rob a look. 'She's promised to keep us informed and you need to get home too love. What about all your bits and bobs?'

Molly's shoulders slumped in defeat. 'All right, Dad. You're right. We'll go.'

Rob gave a self-satisfied smile as if he had made a good move in a game of chess.

'But not for long,' Molly said, glaring at him. 'We'll be back in a couple of weeks. That will give you time to sort out your rooms.' Rob spluttered into his whisky.

It was Harry's turn to smile. 'We'll go tonight while the roads are still quiet.'

'After seeing our Stella again,' Molly added, looking at Rob.

Harry loaded the car, while Molly cooked a last tea for the family.

'We'll miss you both,' James said. Daniel nodded, Laura began to cry.

'Come here, pet.' Harry gave her a big hug. 'We'll be back soon.'

When tea was finished, the three children stood on the doorstep waving Molly and Harry goodbye. They went back inside. James looked at Daniel.

'I wish Dad played games.'

Daniel nodded. 'I'll miss Gran's pocket money. Dad never gives us any.' Both boys cuddled their little sister.

'We'll look after you,' James said. 'I'll teach you how to play.

They'd hardly got started when the doorbell rang.

'Look who's here!' Rob shouted from the hall.

A slender dark-haired girl appeared through the living room door.

'Sofia!' all the children yelled together.

16

Rob answered the phone with pleasurable anticipation. 'Amanda?'

'Amanda? Good gracious, Rob. It's Vera. Look, dear, I know you've had a hard time and poor Stella is still in hospital, but Barbara tells me there are lots of things you need to attend to. I trust that you'll be coming in today?'

'Yes, Vera. I'll be there.' *Damn.*

That was the end of a very unsatisfactory break for Rob. Amanda had not, despite her suggestion, been in touch. At least he didn't need to pretend he was miserable when he arrived at the university - he really was.

Luckily, Barbara was occupied on the phone, but he could hear her frantic attempts to end the conversation when she saw him coming. He felt obliged to speak to her but wanted her to be under no illusions. He was never going to go there again. Like most women in his experience, she had metamorphosed from 'just for fun' to 'when are you going to tell your wife?' What was worse, he had discerned a very manipulative streak in her. *Damn. She's stopped talking. Don't catch her eye.*

'Rob...'

'Barbara,' he said, half-turning towards her. 'It simply wasn't possible. It's unfortunate, I know but I've had my own family to deal with. It's been a very difficult time for all of us. I've told you before, if anything happens to me, you'll both be well-looked after. Now please don't disturb me, I have a great deal to catch up on.'

He charged straight into his room, shutting the door firmly behind him then poured himself a calming shot of scotch from the crystal decanter on the shelf. He didn't need to imagine Barbara's frustration on the other side of the door. He stood there, listening for movement. He heard a loud 'Bastard!'

followed by much drawer-banging. When it finally went quiet, he peeked out to see that she had gone.

Much later in the day, having drifted into a peaceful nap, he awoke to the bleeps of phone messages and the chugging of the printer. *Damn. She's back. Missed an opportunity there*. Settling himself at his desk, he took out some paperwork and pretended to be busy, waiting for the inevitable knock on the door.

'Come.' Barbara appeared, looking as cross as he'd ever seen her, carrying a notebook and some papers. 'Oh, it's you...'

'Messages for you.' She began to reel them off. 'Head of pastoral care rang again. She wants a word. It's about Tania...'

'What?' Rob's whole body stiffened, which Barbara pretended not to notice. She carried on reading.

NO! She can't have. Not after all this time! The little trollop!

By the time he tuned in back into Barbara's recitation, he realised he had missed some of the messages. *They'll get back if they need to,* he reasoned.

'... and lastly, there's a personal message,' Barbara continued.

'What is it?' Rob replied, curious. *Amanda? Please let it be her*.

'Someone rang. They asked you to be at the tennis club this evening. At around five-thirty? They said it was important.'

'Man or woman?'

'I don't remember. I deleted all the messages. The inbox was full. I think it was a woman. Which reminds me, there was another horrible letter. You need to see it...'

Still hope. It's the perfect place for an assignation. 'Put it with the others. I'll look at it tomorrow. Thank you, Barbara. That will be all. And I mean all.' Trying not to look at Barbara, gaping like a fish out of water, he turned to reach for his decanter.

'One more thing,' she announced with a severity that made him sit up. 'I'm going home early today. Things to do.'

Thank heavens for that. Rob grabbed the decanter the second she disappeared. After double-checking Barbara had indeed gone, he checked his watch. It was five past four. *I'm not talking to that bloody woman about the trollop today. No point going now, might as well go straight to the club. Maybe another scotch...*

***

That evening, as directed, Rob drove up to the club. It wasn't a normal tennis evening and the building was in darkness. *Still no bloody tennis club sign.* He walked around and tried the door. It wasn't locked, so he went inside to keep warm. He sniffed the air. *Ah yes. The new carpets. That's where some of my money's gone. Hasn't been painted yet. I bet they've blown the kitty. Ha ha!*

He looked at the shabby walls, still marked with blobs of Blu-tac from a presentation they'd done to attract new members. He'd only ever been there for the occasional committee meeting; dragged into it by Stella. He'd even tried playing a couple of times. *More her thing.* He sat down and began to speculate.

Would Amanda come here? No, she wouldn't be so secretive. Then again, she would because of the kids...

Iain? He'd made his confession already. Was he after more money? It's a lost cause, this place. No amount of dosh would make it smart enough for the really wealthy. And the courts are on their last legs too. That means serious money.

Maybe it wasn't Iain? Fabian? Could it be him? He was always sniffing around Stella. Isn't he away or did he come back for Christmas?

His ears pricked up at the sound of a car outside. *Looks like I'll find out soon enough.*

There was another noise, like a car door being slammed, *maybe two*, then nothing. *Someone's pulled in for something. Still, whoever it is will know I'm here.*

He heard the noise of a car revving up and driving off. Nobody came in.

By six pm, Rob was fed up with waiting. *Maybe something's held her up? Not Edward, surely that's all over? Bugger Iain. I'll go and see him anyway. It's about time I found out what all this nonsense is about. He'll spill the beans on Fabian too. If she's been unfaithful well... it's only fair, isn't it?*

He turned the lights off and went outside. The ground had already frozen and the cold hit him hard. He gasped a little as he fiddled with the car door. *Owwww! What the hell...?* He clutched at his chest, fighting to draw breath. Struggling with the car door he managed to drag himself inside and pull it shut. He breathed heavily and held onto the steering wheel to try to stop the nausea. After a few minutes, it passed. *That's the third time. Must see the doc soon.*

When he felt a little better, he turned on the ignition and set off. *Haven't been this way since Stella...* After a short distance, he squinted at something ahead of him. *What's that? A car? Why has it stopped there? I know that number...*

As he pulled out to overtake, a figure jumped out from behind the car, waving madly.

'That's not... Who the hell is it...?'

What's going on? Damned if I'm stopping for anybody.

What's he doing now?

Rob turned to the left, but the figure moved with him. His chest began to tighten. He swerved to the right, but the sensation of tightness had turned into pain. He tried to put his foot on the brake, but it felt like something inside him was about to explode. His hands automatically grabbed at his heart, but his foot hit the accelerator. The out-of-control car shot off. Through squinting eyes, Rob saw the central reservation barriers careering towards him.

BANG! He was thrown forward by the collision.

Barely conscious, he struggled to think.

What happened?

Where am I?

What's that smell? Petrol.

Must get out, must get OUT. He fought with the door handle. *Damn you!*

He managed to open the door as the car burst into flames and his heart erupted. As he slumped over the wheel, all he could see were the wilting flowers still tied to the barriers. 'Stella. You stupid bitch.'

17

Karen sat at her desk, diligently working through her paperwork. No one would ever have suspected her frustration about the case that never was. She glanced at the clock; nearly half six. Her in-tray was nearly empty, her out-tray was overflowing with the holiday accident reports she'd been working on. *Enough.*

She got up to go home then shivered a little. *Something's changed.* As she looked at her phone; it rang. She snatched the receiver and caught Macy's eye.

'DS Thorpe? RTA London Road, five hundred yards past the intersection. One fatality; male.'

Karen's face broke into a grin. 'Macy? RTA. Same place. Let's go!'

The two women grabbed their coats from the stand and rushed out of the office.

'My car!' Karen shouted as they ran into the car park. 'New toy!' she added, as she plonked a mobile warning device on the car roof. They sped off with the blue lights flashing.

'Look at them move out of the way!' Macy said. 'Wow!'

'I know. Christmas present from Facilities. It was meant to be for Harris, but they hate him even more than they hate me.'

It has to be connected. Karen was sure. She knew the way like the back of her hand and got to the scene in minutes, pulling up on the verge.

'It's a bit icy,' she noted as they hurried to the scene.

It was soon apparent that this was not nearby, it was the exact same spot as Stella's crash. The adrenaline began pumping through Karen's body as she saw the car. *A red car.* Behind her, a puffing Macy muttered, 'Triumph Stag. Like Robert Cary's.'

As they got closer, they could make out a body still hanging out of the driver's seat. They couldn't see the face - it was obscured by the forensic photographer taking pictures, but every cell in Karen's body screamed a name to her.

They shuffled and stamped their feet in the cold until they

were finally waved over. Karen walked quickly up to the car, taking in the sight before her. The bottom half of the body had been badly burned, but the top was almost unscathed. There was no mistaking it then.

'It's him. Robert Cary. I knew it!' Karen, unable to hide her excitement, turned to Macy.

'I did too!' Macy said. 'I recognised the car.'

'But what does that mean?' Karen frowned. 'Was he simply a bad driver? It means he's a definite candidate for Stella's crash, but how do we prove anything now?'

'Maybe he killed himself, the guilt catching up with him? If he's the one who tried to kill Stella.'

Karen looked around, then scurried to meet the Senior Investigating Officer. She immediately volunteered to visit the Cary household. 'I know the family,' she explained. 'You've got his ID?'

'Robert Cary.'

As they sat in the car, Karen's brain was going through the list of procedures.

'Macy, ring the office. They'll need a social worker to attend. And ask them to let us know when it's done. I'll ring the Baxters. Then we need to get round to the house.'

Macy frowned. 'Er, Sergeant, there's somewhere I need to be.'

'You're on duty.'

'But it's a date...'

'You what?'

Macy's mouth fell open. 'I've been clocking up unpaid overtime for months now and the first time I get a date, this happens?'

'Career first,' Karen barked. 'You'll have that for life. Not like men.' Macy turned her head away. 'Besides, it's good practice for you. This is real life; how people are confronted with terrible loss and how we can help them through it.'

'I know but...'

'More importantly, you can gain so much information about people when they're in shock. Their guard is down, and they say things they might not say otherwise.'

Macy opened her mouth to speak but thought better of it. Instead, she called the office to make the call.

Karen rang the Baxters. 'I'm so sorry to tell you this over the phone...' she began to explain. When she had finished, Macy relayed the latest information. 'A social worker is on her way to the Cary house now.'

'Good,' Karen said. 'The Baxters are on their way back. It'll be a couple of hours.' Macy bit her lip. 'OK, there's no need for both of us to be there. I'll drop you off at the office. But remember your priorities next time.'

'Thank you, Sergeant,' Macy said, barely holding back her delight.

***

Karen headed back out to the Cary house where the social worker had already arrived. She waited in the kitchen with Sofia while the children were being told what had happened to their father.

'I know I should not say this,' Sofia said. 'But he made my skin crawl. He made a pass at me once.'

'Ugh, what a creep,' Karen replied. 'Well, he can't do it again, that's for sure.'

'But I do adore the children.'

There was a knock on the door and the woman from Social Services appeared. 'They'll need lots of love and understanding,' she said. 'What arrangements are in hand?'

Sofia spoke first. 'I have been with the family for nearly a year now. They know and trust me.'

'The grandparents are on their way too,' Karen said. 'I'm waiting for them to come so I can explain to them what happened.'

'Good.' The woman handed them both a card. 'Ring this number if there are any issues or problems you need help with.'

When she had gone, Karen spoke to Sofia. 'The children won't want me hanging around. I'll wait outside in the car until the Baxters arrive.'

Sofia looked at her watch. 'It is past Laura's bedtime and the boys will be tired. I will get them sorted.'

***

Karen had fallen asleep when she was nudged awake by a tap on the car window. Harry Baxter's face loomed at her through the glass. She sprang up and got out of the car.

'Do you want to come in, Officer?'

Karen nodded and followed Harry into the house. She joined an ashen-faced Molly in the living room.

'You've told us the bones, now what happened?' Harry said.

'His car crashed into the barriers and burst into flames. We don't know the cause precisely. Our forensic team will be working on it now.'

'Where was it?'

Karen stiffened. 'It was at the intersection, where...' she began.

'Where our Stella crashed?' Molly said. 'You don't think he did it deliberately, do you?'

'Eh, mother. Not that one. Drinking and driving more like. What can you tell us, Officer? Is it definitely him?'

Karen nodded. 'Apart from having identification on him, both Constable Dodds and I were able to positively identify him.'

'It's late,' Harry said. 'Happen you should be on your way now.'

18

Thursday 3rd January

Karen stood with her hands grasping the back of the visitors' chair. 'Guv, there's got to be a connection. There *has* to be. What are the chances of a husband and wife being in accidents on almost exactly the same spot within a few weeks of each other?'

DCI Winter looked skyward. 'Yes, there could be a connection, Karen,' DCI Winter said, wearily. 'It could be suicide. Grief for the loss of his wife.'

'Did you meet that creep? I did, and that was no suicide. His father-in-law doesn't believe it either.'

'Karen, without a shred of evidence of foul play, it will be handled by the SCU. You know that. There's nothing we can do until then. And you do know that even with the remote possibility it was a deliberate act, DS Harris is in the line before you.'

Karen frowned. 'Yes guv. But the SCU will take weeks and we're losing valuable time. And I know a bit about the family now. And the Westburys. I've heard that they were a dodgy bunch. What's to stop me working on it too?'

'Resources,' DCI Winter replied. 'Are we done?'

'Tell me about the Westburys, guv.'

'We're done.'

Karen walked back to her desk. *If nothing comes back from the lab, I'm snookered anyway. Even if it's 'inconclusive' there's nothing I can technically do.*

But there's nothing stopping me looking.

On the other hand, even if I find something, I'll have to hand it all over to DS Harris. Then he'll take all the glory. If there is any.

She picked up the initial report from the first attending officer and read, 'RTA. 1977 Triumph Stag Convertible. Two petrol containers in the boot, combustion on impact probable. Road conditions: Poor; black ice in the vicinity of the crash.' She grabbed her phone and dialled. The answering voice was unfamiliar. 'Morris?'

'No, it's John here. John Steele.'

'Where's Morris?'

'He retired. Can I help you?'

'He retired? How come I didn't know?'

Damn! Karen was normally dismissive of the lab team but had cultured a relationship of sorts with its now former head. She'd have to start all over again. *Did he have a leaving party?*

'OK. It's DS Thorpe here.'

'Hello. What can I do for you?'

'Cary fatality, RTA yesterday. What's the score?'

'Too early.'

'You must have something?'

'Maybe later. But I have no authority to talk to you about it.'

'What?' She made a decision. 'I'm coming over.'

***

So that's Karen. John put the receiver down. He'd known who it was from the LED display on his phone but had been too polite to point it out. He was still basking in the glow of getting his dream job. At last, he could devote all his time examining the really important details of cases. Not for him the suspicions and theories, his enjoyment came from the interrogation of the soil samples, the study of tyres and the chemical giveaways inside human and sometimes animal bodies. His thrill came from discovering which way the bullet impacted, precisely the angle of the plunging knife and whose DNA was in the tiny bit of saliva.

He knew nothing about Karen, other than she had a reputation for being rude and unappreciative. Morris had passed the word around that he didn't mind if she didn't come to his leaving do.

Never conclude without evidence. His door was flung open without warning. Karen stood before him. He stared at her pale face devoid of makeup, efficient looking but unmatched trousers and jacket, then looked down at her sensible shoes. *What a girl!* They could almost be twins. Except, he estimated, he was a good six inches taller. He couldn't help but give her a cheesy grin. It stopped her in her tracks.

'Wh... what...?' she stammered.

'We should have something by close of play tonight,' John cut in. 'But it will be after hours. I've heard that you're a late worker. How about we discuss it over a drink?'

'Well!' Karen was visibly flabbergasted. John smiled again and nodded at her.

'Six-thirty in The Crown,' she said, then stormed off. John sighed after her then kicked himself. He'd have to bust a gut to get anything ready for her by then.

19

Molly sat at Stella's bedside, all her troubles flowing out to her unhearing, unconscious daughter. She was completely unaware of Stella's guardian Peter, concealed behind the curtain.

'Oh, love. It's been so hard. Your poor kiddies. That Sofia, she's been a blessing. It's all cramped now, of course. We're not using your room so we're in the spare. Ey, I'm not happy but we'll manage till you get home. I've been helping with organising the funeral. That Vera one, she's been good. Oh no. You don't know, do you, love? It's...' Harry sat down next to her. 'Stella, it's been awful here, bloody awful. I don't know what to tell you other than we need you to get better. Please, love. Can't you try?'

Harry touched Molly's arm. 'Don't love. Don't upset her. We need her to think positive now. She needs to know she's got something good to home back to.'

'No, Dad. We've tried that and it didn't work. Now we need to call her.' She looked back to her daughter. 'Stella? Come back to us love, we need you.'

Harry turned round to see that someone else had arrived to see Stella. 'Oh, 'eck, Mother. It's her. We'd better go.'

Molly looked up to see the formidable figure of Vera Fontaine talking to Janice. She gave a deep sigh then got up to greet her.

'How are the plans coming along?' Vera asked.

'Getting there,' Harry answered, seeing Molly getting flustered.

'I shall take charge on the day,' Vera said. 'And the funds will come from Rob's estate. Thankfully I talked him into arranging a funeral plan a while back.'

'Thanks, Madam.' Harry almost bowed before they left. 'Can you see if you can wake her up? We need her back.'

'I'll do my best,' Vera said. Her face broke into a rare smile.

***

'Oh, Stella, my darling girl. I had to come. I've been thinking so much about you recently. You were wasted on that man. You've had your children. Now you should have been having fun. He certainly was. Oh, I know you had a fling with the tennis man, I remember how you blushed when you told me, but was that for real? I hope you got something out of it before... Now, how can I tell you this? It's important.'

Stella drifted into a light consciousness.

'Stella, dear, you know I've never had much time for Rob, don't you? Well, even I didn't wish this on him. I'm afraid it's bad news. He's been killed in a car crash. Heavens, dear, it looks like that stupid extension of male inadequacy has let him down. The car was almost burnt out. But don't worry, Stella. Your parents have been wonderful, and your parents are there. As is that dear girl, Sofia.'

Rob. Killed.

'And all that business with Tania happened the day... Let me start again. This might make you so furious that you'll wake up. You remember that pretty little thing I told you about? Tania, the girl from the local comprehensive who's set for a first degree? Apparently, Rob assaulted her. He forced himself upon her. My God, he must have been getting desperate to do that. He damn near raped her.'

Raped her.

'Can you believe that? One of the students? I mean we both know about... '

Raped her.

'Anyway, she screamed the place down and eventually one of the maintenance men heard her. The poor man got such a shock when he ran into Rob's study. There he was on top of her. He pulled Rob off and she ran away. Can you believe he actually blamed her? He told the man she'd been pestering him. Wanted better grades. What nonsense. She's a natural. I'd have killed him myself if I'd known. I'm sorry, Stella that was too much, I take that back. Unfortunately, the head of pastoral care hadn't had a chance to interview him before it happened.'

Tania. Tania?

'But the most important bit is the night it happened. That's the night when you crashed, Stella. He must have been in a real tizzy. He wasn't involved in it, was he? Your crash? Did Tania call you? Were you going to report it? Was he trying to stop you? Maybe some God-almighty power has taken revenge on him for his sins at last. Or the drink. Can you hear me, Stella? I know one shouldn't speak ill of the dead, but do you know what Stella? I'm pleased he's gone.'

Pleased he's gone. Rob's gone.

'My dear sweet girl, if you could only remember that wonderful old city with her dreaming spires. You were so happy there. I'm sure you would return to us if you could remember that happiness.'

Stella watched as the wilderness began to fade in her world. She saw the ground slowly turn green and above her, dull grey began to take on a hue of blue. She looked past the meadows and saw something in the distance. The city was rising again; a sparkling city of towers and domes was forming behind the hills far away. She was happy.

I must go there.

'Goodbye, my precious girl. I'll come back soon.'

Don't go! Don't go...

The city began to crumble in the distance and a veil descended around her. Stella was back in nowhere. Back in desolation.

20

The Crown was the station's local; even John had been there for New Year's Eve drinks and, he recalled, a certain leaving party. Now the harsh January fall in trade had kicked in and the place had lost its sheen. The shabby decor was no longer disguised by sparkly Christmas trappings. John arrived early and watched the door intently.

That's her. Look away. No. Take it in.

Karen, in contrast to her surroundings, seemed to be bursting with life but not smiling. This had all the signs of a business meeting. *Fair enough. Early days. At least she won't be put off by small talk about dead bodies and bloodstains.*

She looked over, presumably noticing his pint. He half-stood, but she shook her head then ordered a glass of wine at the bar and came over with it to his table.

'What have you got?'

'Well,' John began. 'It looks like a simple accident.'

'Really?' She looked unappreciative.

You can't call her out for nothing. Give her something. He couched his findings carefully.

'The boot doesn't appear to have been locked and he had two petrol cans in the back of what was a very old car. It looks like the lid was loose on one, or at least it wasn't melted into the container like the other. With the right conditions, and there was black ice on the road, the impact could easily have caused the petrol to ignite then spread to the fuel tank. There are enough warnings about not carrying petrol in the backs of cars.'

Karen leant her chin on her hand in a way that John found most appealing. 'And how often does that happen? I've heard the warnings too, but there would be a lot more accidents if it was that dangerous.'

'You have a point,' John agreed. 'But it's not impossible. In fact, it's very likely. Old cars are far more susceptible than modern ones. That one especially so. Lots of combustible materials in there and few safety features. Anyway, there's no other evidence I've seen so far and it's plausible enough for a verdict. The only surprising thing is he didn't have much petrol in the tank, otherwise the whole thing would have been burnt out.'

'Is that why he was carrying so much?'

'It's not unusual. These classic car owners can get neurotic about their cars. Maybe he didn't like leaving it unattended at old petrol stations? Some don't have modern security features. But we'll never know about his habits unless someone can tell us.'

'What do we know for sure? Would the impact on the barriers have been big enough? They're not that strong, they're meant to take reasonable force.'

'We know the car swerved,' John said. 'It might even have spun first; it's feasible. If it gathered momentum, all that petrol swimming around on the ground, then even a small impact might do it. Imagine a petrol bomb. And it looks like he was accelerating when it happened. The car hit a post as well as the rail; they're concreted in so it could easily be enough. Whoosh!' he added for dramatic effect.

'The suicide theory,' Karen said, taking a large swig of her wine in dismay. 'But isn't that too uncertain? Why there, why not a brick wall? And it's a horrible way to go. Burning. What about the cause of death? Anything there?'

'Ah yes,' John nodded. 'But nothing that helps you if you're looking for foul play. There was a definite smell of alcohol on the body, which again, maybe helps the suicide theory. He gets tanked up and drives at the nearest obstacle to where she died.'

'There were flowers tied there,' Karen said. 'But I don't believe it. He seemed indifferent to her.'

'Maybe he had other worries? Anyway, strictly off the record, the pathologist suspects a shock-induced heart attack. It wasn't the impact or the fire that killed him, he was almost certainly dead before the explosion. But we've *got* to wait for his report.' Karen gave a slight pout. *God that's sexy,* thought John.

'What about the photo, in the Westbury crash. Could it be a red car?'

John frowned, his mind whirring. 'The Cary Westbury RTA?'

'Yes. That was his wife.'

'His wife? Strictly speaking before my time. But you think the Triumph could have been involved in the Stella Cary RTA?' Karen nodded.

'I think that's pushing it a bit. A lot actually. We couldn't make out anything. It could just be an aberration caused by the impact.'

'But it could be? Have you looked at it?' Karen pushed. John couldn't stop himself smiling.

'Yes, I did as it happens. It could. To my eye, I think there's a tiny portion of a door handle there. But that's unofficial. And the case is closed.'

'Come on, what do you really think about it all?' she asked.

'I have to agree there is something fishy about where it happened. But if I'm brutally honest, I'd say it was one of those times where lots of small things add up to a whole and it's simply another accidental death. And that's what I think the SCU will say too.' He turned to give Karen his most enticing smile. 'But for you, I'll take another look at it all. I don't believe in coincidences.'

He raised his glass to clink it with Karen's and was thrilled when she reciprocated. Thinking quickly, he pounced. 'Tell me, what you do in your spare time?' he asked and saw instantly that he had misjudged the situation.

'What spare time?' Karen stood up and downed her wine. 'Keep me posted, won't you?'

John shook his head as he watched Karen stride to the door. *Dammit!* He looked at his shandy, which somehow didn't look so appealing now. It was catch twenty-two. He loved the idea of a relationship with someone as committed to their job as he was, but that commitment was the reason they wouldn't get into a relationship in the first place.

'I'll be in touch!' he shouted after her. She turned briefly and gave him another smile.

'Even if I have to eke it out a bit,' he muttered under his breath.

21

The days had turned to weeks and not a crumb of a lead had come Karen's way. She was head down at work engaged with the paperwork in front of her when her phone rang.

'It's Gwen Williams here. From the hospital. One of our orderlies has told me something. Peter was too nervous to ring you himself.'

Her curiosity was aroused. 'Please tell me more,' Karen replied.

'Well, as far as I can tell, it was about three weeks ago. He's been off sick you see. He said the posh woman, the one in the swishy coat had come to see Stella. He's a nice boy, a bit *special*. He's taken with Stella. He looks after her - in his own world at least. And he sits with her, so he *hears* things.'

'What did he hear?'

'I'm not completely sure really but I think Peter thinks that Stella's husband was trying to rape someone. A student. And it happened the day of her crash. He thinks Stella knew about it and her husband crashed into her to stop her from reporting him to the police. I mean you. Does that make any sort of sense?'

Karen frowned. 'It may do. I'd need to speak to him.'

'Well, without wanting to doubt the poor lad, I'd suggest you talk to her, you know the woman. As I said, he's a little special.'

'But who was she? Posh and swishy isn't good enough.'

Gwen laughed. 'It does describe her perfectly though. Yes, I think she's someone very high up at the university. I heard the name Vera. Does that help?'

'Thank you, Miss Williams. I'll make a note.'

Karen slipped easily back into enquiry mode. *First Robert Cary tries to run Stella off the road to stop her reporting him to us. It doesn't make sense - unless the girl had decided not to report him, and we don't know that. But she hasn't so far.*

Would Stella care enough to come to us? Yes, of course, if she believed the girl and wanted to out him as a sex pest. That would make sense.

It indicates he was behaving erratically though, but suicidal?

Sure, it was strong reputational damage.

Maybe the girl was going to report him after all.

And he'd been drinking.

Looking around, she saw that DCI Winter was free and went into his office without waiting to be asked.

'... And supposing he tried to murder Stella, then this student called him out and he was plotting something, some way of killing her too and it all went wrong?'

DCI Winter sighed and put his hands behind his head in that irritating way.

'Is that the best you can come up with, Karen? Besides, even if he did try to kill his wife, or this girl, what are we going to do to him? He's dead.'

'There's evidence,' Karen took a huge gamble. 'There may have been another car involved in the accident that killed Westbury.' DCI Winter put his hands down and leaned forward. 'Says who?'

'The new guy. John Steele. Forensics. He's looked at the photo. He thinks it's a red car. Robert Cary had a red car.'

'The new man?' Karen nodded. 'And no Westbury connection?'

'Not that I know of yet, guv.'

DCI Winter put his elbow on the table, his head resting in one hand and made Karen wait for his answer. 'Interviews only. Talk to everybody - except the Westburys - about their whereabouts on the nights involved. Normal procedure, no more. Let me know if you come up with anything. And Karen?'

'Yes guv?'

'No treading on the toes of the SCU. Liaise with them, tell them everything you're doing.'

'Yes guv,' Karen replied with her fingers crossed under the desk. She left his office and went over to Macy.

'We're on again. Incident Room two. I'll set it up.'

By the time Macy had joined her, this time with a cup of something indeterminable but definitely hot, Karen had begun to write up headings on the boards.

'OK. We've got a possible connection of Robert Cary to Stella's crash. And a possible attempted rape of some girl by him. We need to interview everybody as soon as we can. That's friends, neighbours, acquaintances and most importantly a woman called Vera from the university.'

Her mobile rang. She picked up. 'John.'

Macy twiddled her fingers while Karen took the call.

'And? What have you got for me?'

'Sorry. I've been through everything and I can't find anything that will substantiate your theory.'

Macy stared open-mouthed as Karen exploded.

'Are you serious? Why did you get me out to the pub then? I even told the guv you'd got proof of the red car.' There was a noticeable pause. 'That's why he let me carry on investigating the case. Not that I've had any time to do anything more.'

'WHAT?'

Even Macy reacted to John's booming outrage coming from the receiver.

'What the hell did you say that for? I told you it was off the record. And it's not even my case. Don't you realise departmental liaisons are critical? I'm on probation here, my job's at risk.'

'And it should be, you idiot.' Karen went bright red. 'So much for your red car and partial door handle.' She hung up. 'Doesn't anybody know what they're doing round here?'

Macy shook her head nervously then jumped as the door opened. DCI Winter stuck his head round the door. 'Possible major incident at The Galleria. Both of you. Now. And Karen?'

'Yes, guv?'

'Clear the room. It's going to be needed.'

'Bastard,' Karen muttered. 'They all are.' She looked at Macy who turned away.

22

Karen's frustration with her paperwork was growing. By the end of the day when her phone rang, she snatched it off the cradle. 'DS Thorpe.'

John's voice sounded at the other end. 'How's things?'

'OK. What do you want?'

'Perhaps I was a bit hasty. Fancy a drink?'

Ten minutes later, Karen entered The Crown and bypassed the bar to join a miserable-looking John. *He's my only hope, but it's some hope at least.* 'What have you actually got for me this time?'

'I want to know why you're so convinced about this case. Maybe if I know where you're coming from, I can help.'

'Another half?'

He nodded. 'Shandy.'

Karen walked to the bar. *Grit your teeth. Keep him sweet.*

When she returned, she grabbed some beer mats from the adjacent table and began to place them on their table. 'This is Stella's car, this is Westbury's van, both in the overtaking lane. We now know that Robert Cary could have had a motive to kill, or at least stop his wife.' She placed another mat on the left. 'Maybe he was here. Forcing them to pull out. That would explain the photo too.'

'OK, there's something in that. But I'm not going to risk my job for it.'

Now what do I do? 'What are you doing tonight? We could talk completely off the record at mine. I'll cook dinner?'

'Well, yes. OK.' John's smile was a giveaway.

He's hooked. 'Follow my car,' Karen said as they left the pub. 'It's the blue one.'

'I know,' John replied absentmindedly.

***

Karen's idea of cooking meant getting a takeaway from the local Chinese, washed down with expensively priced cheap plonk from the corner shop, but she took John's silence for interest as he entered her flat. Here were no pretty flowers, candles or even photos and it was very untidy.

Dinner was eaten on their laps as Karen's only table was still covered with paper on which roads had been drawn and toy cars placed. The conversation was solely about the case.

'... And the speed camera here,' Karen pointed, 'was activated a short time before Stella's car hit Westbury's van. No film of course.'

'You think it could have been Robert Cary in the left-hand lane? Did you interview him about his whereabouts that day?'

'No. There was no reason to at the time. Constable Macy Dodds told him about the accident. But she reckons he was expecting someone to be coming for him and didn't seem at all bothered when he heard it was because of his wife.'

'Why now?' John looked perplexed.

'Someone at the hospital overheard someone else saying he'd attacked a student and that Stella knew about it. The woman who was overheard was called Vera, and it turns out she's the Vice-Chancellor of the university. If she's not a good source of intel, I don't know who is. It's possible that Stella was going to rat on her husband, and he tried to stop her.'

'OK. Let's look at the SCU report again.'

'You've got it with you? That's great.' *I like this man.*

'Easy peasy. On my tablet.' He pulled the reports up on the screen. Karen noticed his smile as she shuffled closer to him.

'Nope. There's nothing to suggest that there was a third car from the positioning of the other two. The witness statements added nothing of any importance. The only thing we've got is that even though the Porsche was valeted every week, the brakes hadn't been checked since the previous service. They were worn, and the fluid diminished.' He turned to look at her. 'And the photo's definitely been ruled out.'

'What set off the camera then?'

'Could have been anything. A bird even.'

'At over seventy miles an hour?'

'Yes, if it was wrongly calibrated. It was an old machine and unfortunately it's been junked now.'

'You checked that out?'

'I'm thorough.' *You certainly are. I really like you, John Steele.*

'You're telling me it's going to be "accidental death", right?' Karen pouted.

'Yes, but it's not your problem is it? The SCU won't want you poking your nose in now it's closed.' Karen coughed. 'You're not still pursuing this, are you?' John stared at her.

'The guv hasn't withdrawn his permission to do some questioning. SCU haven't bothered to speak to anybody so I might turn something up.'

'But why, Karen? Why are you bothering?'

'Because I care. Especially about Stella. And that reminds me, the guv warned me off the Westburys but there was a voicemail left at the local paper's office. It said that Stella had been on her phone. I'd like to get that checked against Jim Westbury's voice.'

John shook his head. 'We'd have to have a sample and you'd need absolute authority to obtain that. Besides SCU have ruled it out as vexatious.'

Karen snorted. 'I see you've done your homework. But I don't care what the SCU says. I think we've got at least two people in the frame. Robert Cary and Jim Westbury. Accidental death is too easy.'

'OK,' John said slowly. 'What's next?'

'I'm seeing Vera Fontaine, the university Vice-Chancellor, tomorrow to check out the student incident. And that's another thing...' She stood up in an unmistakable gesture. 'I'd better prepare for the meeting.'

'Thanks for the meal,' John replied, looking glum. 'Keep me posted, won't you?'

'Will do,' Karen muttered, but she was already leafing through her papers as he left.

23

Vera sat in her chair, fingers touching fingers like a skeletal cat's cradle until she heard the knock at the door and Barbara appeared.

'That policewoman is here.'

'Bring her in. And join us, if you will. You knew Rob as well as anybody.'

Barbara dutifully led Karen in and both women sat down opposite the Vice-Chancellor who very imposing. Karen could imagine how impressive she would have been in court.

'Sergeant Thorpe, this is Barbara Spinnard. She was Rob's PA. I thought she might have some insight.'

'Fine,' Karen agreed. 'I'm interested in anybody who might have been involved in his accident. And anyone who may have had a grudge against him.'

Vera cleared her throat. 'Did anybody dislike Rob Cary, you ask? Yes, certainly many people did. But some liked him too. My late husband Donald for one. We will find out if there were any more at his funeral tomorrow.' She looked Karen in the eye. 'Would he kill himself? Absolutely not. But I saw an accident waiting to happen ages ago with that silly car of his. Heaven knows it should have been scrapped years before.' She turned to Barbara. 'Thoughts? Anyone come to mind?'

Barbara squirmed in her chair. 'He did seem to upset a few people. Like Tania.'

'Is that the student he tried to assault? That happened on the day of Stella Cary's accident, I believe,' Karen said. 'Tell me more.'

'Tania? How on earth did you hear about that?' Vera said. She didn't wait for an answer. 'Sergeant, we have a college full of silly girls and boys experiencing that first full-blooded freedom from their parents. Tania is no different. A bright girl yes, and I'm sure perfectly aware of what she was doing. The problem being that once she'd got Rob's attention, she didn't know how to handle it.'

'Are you saying she provoked it?'

'Yes. In a way. Obviously, we have to see the appropriate procedures through and before you ask, I do not doubt that Rob would have been cleared again.'

Karen frowned. *Again?* 'Are you saying you think he would have no reason to stop his wife from finding out?'

'Gracious no. Stella knew what he was like.'

'Was she threatening to go to the police?'

'No.'

'Are you sure? The constable who went to see him after the accident said he acted like he was expecting a police visit.'

'It's possible I suppose. But she would be aware of our procedures, as would Rob, which is to investigate internally first.'

'What about Tania taking revenge on him?'

'What time was the accident?'

'Around five past six on the evening of the second of January.'

Vera thumbed through her diary. 'The head of pastoral care called me at around two fifteen and I went to meet with her at two thirty, with Tania present. I listened to what Tania had to say and told her to go home and reflect on things. You can check that with her parents.' Karen noted it. 'Then I told our pastor to arrange a meeting with Rob as soon as possible and let me know the time and date. As you know, that never happened.'

Karen frowned. 'Could she have tried to take her revenge out on him by causing Stella's accident?'

'I think that's extremely unlikely. He was the alleged perpetrator, not his wife.'

'Was there anybody else who might have had reason to want to harm Mr Cary?'

Vera looked thoughtful. 'Do I think anybody was bothered by it? Undoubtedly. Tania had enough time to tell people what had happened. Do I think any one of them was capable of organising an accident? Absolutely not. He was a heavy drinker driving a toy car. Barbara?'

'There was that boyfriend,' Barbara said.

'What boyfriend?' Vera glared at her.

'Let me think. Tania's boyfriend. Yes, he was a rough sort. He pushed his way into the office here a day or so before Christmas. He threatened to...' Barbara searched for the words '... punch his lights out. Mr Cary wasn't here.'

'Not a death threat but still menacing?' Vera said.

Barbara nodded vigorously. 'Yes. Could he have tried to kill him?'

'I have no idea. But we must let the police here do their job and not overlook anything.'

'What did he look like?' Karen asked.

Barbara squeezed her eyes closed. When she opened them there was no enlightenment. 'They all look the same after a while. Not especially tall. Dark hair. Unshaven.'

'Would you recognise him if you saw him again?'

'I might.'

Karen gave a small smile. 'Good. Are you going to Mr Cary's funeral?' Barbara nodded, her eyes beginning to tear up. 'Will you contact me if you see him there please?' She handed Barbara a card.

'I will.' Barbara took it, her chest beginning to heave.

Vera ended her embarrassment. 'Thank you, Barbara, you may leave.'

'But I wanted to talk to you about...'

'Not now, please, Barbara.'

Barbara left and both women heard 'Stupid bitch...' muttered as the door slammed shut.

Karen leant forward. 'You mentioned a previous case? You said he was cleared *before*.'

'Gracious, that was years ago. Nothing to it and all relevant parties moved on.'

'And I assume you wanted to say something about Barbara?'

'Only that I know she has some secrets of her own. I am Rob's executor. I haven't gone through everything in detail yet, but there are a couple of sealed envelopes I need to open, and I have my own theories. I know that she was very angry with him about something, and I'm not prepared to speculate here and now. But somebody could easily have sabotaged his car while it was parked here.'

Karen's eyes lit up. 'I see.'

'And I am about to make her redundant soon. I thought it was useful for you to talk to her while she was still on site.'

'Oh.'

'Are we finished, Sergeant?'

Vera stood up and Karen took her cue to leave

***

On the way back to the office Karen mused. *Vera's account was markedly different from Gwen's, or rather Peter's,* she thought. *What did she call him? Special? Probably unreliable.*

She rang Tania's parents as soon as she arrived at her desk.

'Mrs Hayes? It's Detective Sergeant Thorpe here. May I speak to Tania please?'

'The police? What's it about?'

'I wanted to ask some questions about her whereabouts on the evening of the second of January.'

'Why? Is it about that dreadful man, Robert Cary?'

'In a way. He was killed in a car accident.'

'That same day? Well, I'm not sorry to hear that. Tania was most distressed. She's in France staying with relatives.'

'I see. When will she be back?'

'Not for a few weeks.'

'Can you tell me where she was on that evening?'

'She was at home all afternoon and evening. In tears.'

'May I ask if she drives?'

'Are you suggesting...'

'I'm making enquiries. It's my job.'

'No. She hasn't passed her test yet.'

'Does she have a boyfriend?'

'No. She doesn't.'

'Thank you, Mrs Hayes.'

Karen put the phone down. *Tania couldn't have been there, at least to cause Cary's accident. But his car would have been parked all day at the university. Anybody could have planted that petrol in his car and loosened the lid. Barbara could.*

Am I flogging a dead horse here? The funeral's tomorrow, and nothing, not even the guv is stopping me going there. Even you, Dad. Especially after Vera specifically told me about it.

It was practically an invitation.

24

'You can learn a lot from who attends funerals,' Karen said as they entered the crematorium chapel.

'Really Sergeant?'

Karen failed to detect Macy's sarcasm. 'If nothing else, we're bound to get to speak to some of the others we listed. Friends and neighbours. I'm interested to see who turns up and why.'

The **Order of Service** leaflet was devoid of religious content, but the podium had been prepared ready for someone to make a speech. Karen and Macy made their way to the back. They watched as two men and two women took their places in the third row in front of them.

Macy nudged Karen. 'That's the next-door neighbour, the largish blonde woman. I saw her before.'

'Good. We can ask her who the others are.'

'I didn't actually speak to her.'

'That's OK.'

Next, some obvious student types appeared and after some discussion, sat mainly together on the left-hand side. Karen peered at them trying in vain to match them to Facebook profiles she'd looked at.

Vera, stunningly dressed in red and black sailed to the front pew on the right.

'That's the Vice-Chancellor,' Karen whispered. 'Vera.'

'Do you think that student he allegedly attacked will be here?' Macy whispered back.

'Tania? No. She's abroad. But keep your ears peeled for mentions.'

Several older men and women appeared in a group. 'Lecturers,' Karen and Macy said together. Macy giggled a little at their synchronisation then stopped when she caught Karen's frown.

A few more people of assorted ages arrived and took various places. When it looked as if no one else was coming in, the Officiant walked up the centre aisle and stood at the front. He nodded to someone at the back and the coffin was carried in to Chopin's Funeral March, which prompted sniggering, mainly from the students.

'They didn't like him much, did they?' Macy remarked.

'She did apparently,' Karen said, nodding towards the middle-aged woman sobbing her heart out in front of them at the end of the second row. 'That's Barbara, his PA. I saw her yesterday when I interviewed Vera. She reckons that Cary and Barbara were at loggerheads. Even suggested she could have sabotaged his car. Look over there.' She turned to the left, where a student was making an obscene gesture towards the oncoming coffin, not realising he could be seen by them. Her eyes followed someone else who was sneaking in. 'Shit! SCU. No, don't look at him!'

Macy turned her head, while Karen looked down as the man settled in a seat on the other side. Something was happening at the side. All eyes watched the funeral procession enter. James and Daniel, both in smart suits, walked immediately behind the coffin, with Molly and Harry following. Harry rested a hand on Daniel's shoulder. They sat together in the front pew.

The service was brief and the Officiant did a reasonable job, but it was left to Vera to add the personal touch. When the time came for her to speak, she rose steadily to her feet to take her place at the podium. Her voice was clear and calm.

'I am not going to stand here before you all and pretend that Robert Cary was a saintly man, or even a particularly good man,' she started. There were some exchanged glances across the rows; some of the students whispered to each other. Barbara's sobs got louder. 'But he was a good scholar. No, he was an excellent scholar. He understood his subject almost to perfection and there is many a good solicitor, barrister or even a future judge who has been well-taught by this man. And so it is this that we must pay tribute to today and remember him as a truly gifted individual.'

There were no funny anecdotes. Rob had not been an

amusing man and Vera was not a hypocrite. There was some muttering from a couple of students a few rows in front of Karen and Macy; they caught the whispers 'Paedo' and 'Pervert'. But Vera was not one to let any occasion at which she presided fall into disrespect. One steely glance from her shut them up. Nobody took on Vera, least of all an undergraduate.

'And today we must remember his family. His wife, Stella, as you all know still in hospital. And his three children, his daughter Laura, and his two sons, James and Daniel, of whom he was immensely proud.' Karen nudged Macy. Barbara was getting to her feet.

'What the...?' Karen began.

'Don't forget Catherine!' Barbara shouted. 'She was his daughter too. She deserves to be mentioned!'

A sea of heads bobbed to and fro and the mutterings began to get louder.

Vera resumed control, glaring at Barbara who immediately sat down. 'We must remember all of Robert's family indeed. Please, may I have your silence and your respect for the departed?' Surveying the ensemble and daring anybody else to speak, Vera nodded to the Officiant and returned to her seat.

Someone at the back pressed something. The mechanism activated and the curtains emerged to close around the coffin. Then a more modern classic began to play. The volume was a little too high and the song choice inappropriate. Robbie Williams' 'Angels' blasted out and even Vera couldn't suppress a smile. But when the line about loving angels was sung, nearly all the students started laughing out loud. Someone shouted, 'Or Tania!'

Vera stood up. 'Please turn it off,' she said, gesturing towards whoever was in the back room. The music stopped and Robert Cary made his final journey into the furnace in relative silence.

After an appropriate pause, Vera got up again, prompting others to do the same. She ushered them towards the door and while people exited, she turned to speak to the Officiant.

'What do we do now?' Macy asked.

'We hope to be invited to the do,' Karen muttered

100

sarcastically. 'Damn. Look away, the SCU guy's leaving.'

They weren't asked back. Vera did not even acknowledge them. Even the Baxters sat in stunned silence. Harry's arm was tightly around Daniel's shoulder. Karen and Macy waited and watched where everyone was going.

'He had a lovechild.' Macy whispered. 'Creep.'

'Yes. And where does that leave Barbara? Could she have wanted him dead?'

'She was crying.'

'Guilt,' Karen snapped.

25

Outside the crematorium, people were walking to a pub not too far away, where a prominent blackboard advertised the wake for Mr Robert Cary. Inside Karen saw there was a small luncheon set out in a private room. She and Macy stayed sitting at the nearby bar, close to the entrance to the toilets.

'This'll do.' Karen perched on a bar stool looking around for the SCU officer. 'They'll all come past here to go to the toilet. Keep listening.'

Almost at once, a now dry-eyed but mascara-smudged Barbara came up to them.

'Hello Sergeant. I didn't see that young man here today. I did look out for him.'

'Thank you.'

'How is the investigation going?'

'No more progress, Ms Spinnard,' Karen replied. 'Are you all right? You seemed very upset.'

Barbara burst into floods of tears again. 'He was a wonderful man. Very handsome. All the others were jealous...' She stopped in her tracks.

'Yes?' Karen urged, but the moment had gone.

'Nothing. Ignore me, I'm being silly. Do they think it was an accident then? Nothing to do with Tania?'

Karen fumbled in her coat pocket. 'Yes. That is the conclusion. But please take this, Ms Spinnard,' she said, holding out a card. 'And if you see the man who threatened Mr Cary or think of anything you would like to tell me, however small, please ring me, day or night. It's no problem.'

'Thank you, Officer,' Barbara declined the card. 'You gave me one yesterday. But I might do that. To make sure. Excuse me...' She disappeared into the ladies.

'That didn't sound like guilt,' Macy noted.

'She's had years of bottling it up,' Karen replied. 'And drink loosens people's tongues.' She looked towards a couple of students quietly getting hammered at Robert Cary's expense. 'Bladders like camels,' she sniped. 'We won't get anything from them. I was hoping to hear more about Tania.'

'What have you got on her so far?'

'She was at home when the accident happened. And very distressed. The criminal prosecution service will have dropped any potential criminal case against him, now he's dead.'

'Supposing someone took revenge on her behalf?' Macy asked.

'My thoughts precisely, Macy,' said Karen, almost fondly. 'There was an aggressive boyfriend on the scene, but unfortunately, not Tania's.'

Macy turned to see Amanda walk past them towards the toilets. She stopped for a second, as if to say something to Macy, but shook her head and carried on instead.

'That's the neighbour.'

'We'll catch her on the way out.' Karen looked at Macy knowingly.

When Amanda emerged, she immediately went towards Macy, who put on her best smile through gritted teeth.

'Excuse me,' she began. 'Are you the policewoman I saw when Stella had her accident?'

'Yes. And you are?'

'Amanda Denning. I lived next door to poor Rob.'

Karen jumped in. 'I'm DS Thorpe and this is Constable Dodds.'

'Are you investigating the crash then? I thought it was an accident.'

'It's routine, Mrs Denning. And paying our respects. It looked as though you were going to say something?'

'Not here,' Amanda whispered. 'Can I contact you…?' Karen passed her a card. 'Call me whenever you like. By the way, would you mind telling me who the other mourners were, the ones who sat with you?'

'Tennis club,' Amanda said. 'They were the regulars at her club. Stella and Rob were both members although I don't think Rob played. That's where she was coming from, that night she crashed, or at least I assume she was.'

'Yes of course,' Karen nodded, knowing nothing of the sort. 'Thank you. And don't forget to call me and we can talk in private.' *Tennis club? Why didn't I know about this?*

Macy sensed Karen's anger. 'Did you know about the tennis club?'

'It could be the missing link, Macy,' Karen replied. 'Social clubs are minefields for suburban passions.'

Macy and Karen stayed a little longer, but the gathering had dissipated quickly and only the family and a couple of hangers-on remained.

'Better get back,' Karen said. 'But I'd love to be a fly on that wall,' she nodded towards the private room where Vera was in an animated conversation with Barbara. 'Bet it's about his love-child.

'Is it relevant?' Macy asked.

'Could be. If she wants something from his estate.'

26

Karen and Macy arrived back at the office with Karen still deep in thought. She pined for the incident room. *Writing on the boards helps me think. And what's with the tennis club?*

She'd hardly managed to get herself a hot chocolate when she picked up a bad vibe around the office. The others looked at her with a sense of expectation.

DCI Winter's door opened, and he roared at her. 'My office NOW!'

Karen braced herself and walked into the office, closing the door behind her. It didn't make much difference; everyone in the vicinity heard as DCI Winter splattered her around the walls.

'... And I get a call from DCI Ed-fucking-Jenkins from SCU wondering what my DS and her constable are doing handing out cards to funeral-goers like sweeties!' Karen sat, fused to the back of her chair. 'I say, well, we've got intel on the other crash. A photo. Just seeing how the land lies in case we're looking at a connection. Possible homicide. And guess what he fucking says, Karen?'

'Guv...' Karen began.

'There is no fucking intel, is there? The lab already eliminated the photo. What the fuck is wrong with you? You don't go on someone else's patch without a good fucking reason and without fucking telling them!' Karen was beginning to cave. 'And don't you DARE even think about that!' he added, pointing his finger straight at her, searching her face for signs of tears. 'I know you think you've got something to prove, especially since... but you've got to stop imagining crimes where there aren't any.'

Karen was made of stern stuff and the oblique reference to her father stiffened her resolve. She pulled herself up and looked him in the eye. 'I had a hunch, guv. Don't tell me you've never had hunches.'

'Get out. And if you do anything like this again, you'll be a constable back in uniform before you can sit your sorry arse down on your chair. DO YOU UNDERSTAND!?'

Karen, somewhere between shock and fury, left DCI Winter's office in silence. Like the ripples from a stone thrown into a pond, heads looked away and bodies went back to their desks and sat down. Except for Macy. She stood, looking on like a rabbit caught in the headlights.

'This is all your fault!' Karen yelled at her. 'They recognised you. I'm going to make sure I never work with you again!'

Macy's face crumpled. Her eyes were watering but she looked calm. She walked over to Karen's desk and eyeballed her. 'At least we agree on that. But I don't want anyone else to have to put up with your shocking behaviour. I'm going to see HR and I'm putting in a formal complaint.' She turned round and left the office.

'Good riddance,' Karen said. She looked around for support. There was none. *Was someone applauding Macy?* She searched for the clapping hands but the noise stopped and all the heads in the office turned away from her. *I don't care.*

***

When Karen's anger subsided, she ran through the case in her head. There was no denying it. The guv was right. There was no evidence of a crime, no one really to interview, the families weren't even pressing for justice. The only thing she'd turned up was an illegitimate daughter, and that didn't fit with anything, not if she was honest with herself. *I need new ideas. And a new number two who won't stand out and who doesn't turn on the waterworks at every opportunity. I must talk to Bill. He'll know what to do.*

She was interrupted by her desk phone ringing. It was a similarly tormented John, but not for the same reasons.

'You got blasted too then?' Karen asked, assuming he was ringing to compare notes.

'No, not at all. You got all the blame for that.'

'OK, thanks a bunch. That makes me feel better. See you.

'No, wait!' She heard something strange in his voice. *Panic?*

'I've got something for you.'

'It had better be fucking brilliant, John. I'm on desk duty for weeks now. I might even get fired. I have to have something to get me out of this mess. John?'

There was a long pause. 'It's not brilliant but it is something unusual.'

'Spit it out,' Karen urged.

John didn't tell her of the hours he'd spent in the lab going over the mechanic's report, analysing every scrap of matter and finally finding something new; he came straight to the point. 'The remains of a cigarette butt. In the boot.'

Is that it? 'Cigarette butts get everywhere,' Karen retorted. 'They stick to shoes, bags. What about DNA?'

'Nothing yet,' John replied.

Karen clunked down the receiver. Then like a cigarette butt that hasn't been put out properly, Karen's mind began to smoulder again. A tiny bit. She stored it in a compartment in her brain, right next to the tennis club.

27

The weeks had not been kind to Karen. She had been relegated to traffic cases and spent almost all her time on paperwork. As far as she knew, Macy's absence was due to her being assigned elsewhere. But the perceived injustice of a claim of racist behaviour was making her miserable. The only person who'd given her any time was Bill.

'Macy's a good kid,' he'd said. 'Works hard and tries harder. If only you'd apologised...'

'She let me down.'

'No, Karen, she's the junior. You let yourself down.'

'Ouch.'

At the time, DCI Winter had not been supportive at all. 'Did you or did you not tell her she was the wrong colour?' he had said.

'No. I didn't. All I said was that she was too easy to see. Guv, the SCU guy would never have spotted me if she hadn't been with me. That's the truth.'

'Karen! Don't you realise how that sounds? It's inexcusable behaviour and if you were keeping low-key, and may I remind you that I did not give my approval, you should have gone on your own. Why take her with you? That was stupid.'

'I was trying to give her some good background experience. I never expected...'

'Enough. Constable Dodds has been an exemplary officer and you are a very recently promoted Sergeant. You should have thought of that before you shot your mouth off.'

'What's going to happen, guv? You might as well tell me now.'

'These things take their time. There are procedures to be followed and sensitivities to be observed. I'll tell you as soon as I know anything.'

That had been ages ago, but the words had reverberated in

Karen's head, making her flinch every time he stuck his head out of his office. Until finally the day came.

'My office. Now, Karen.' She looked up to see DCI Winter standing at his door. Swallowing down her nerves, she got up and strode into his office as if she was about to be given a promotion, not a dismissal.

'What's up, guv?' she said as casually as she could manage. 'Is it about the grievance? It's about time they got it sorted, it's been going on so long.'

'Shut the door.' Karen obliged before sitting down.

'We've been through this, Karen. Constable Dodds lodged her entirely justified complaint well within the time limits and these processes take a great deal of time. But yes, I have some news.'

'Is there a date?'

'No. She wants an informal meeting with you and me.'

'What for? To hammer it all home? Doesn't she realise how much damage she's done to my career already?'

'Karen, do you *ever* listen to yourself?'

'Sorry, guv. When's the meeting?'

'She asked for it to be arranged as soon as possible.' He looked at his watch. 'I'd say any time now.'

'Now? But I haven't prepared anything!'

'The only thing you have to do is listen and say "sorry" when the time comes. Can you do that?' He peered at her so sternly, even she took the message on board.

'Yes, guv.'

'Best behaviour Karen, she's coming now.'

They turned round to see Macy's outline through the partially drawn blinds. She knocked.

'And don't forget. Apologise. Now, open the door.'

Karen got up and greeted Macy with a sheepish smile. Macy was stony-faced.

Karen moved over to the far chair to allow her to sit down. 'I kept your seat warm,' she muttered.

'Sir?' Macy addressed DCI Winter. 'Thank you for agreeing to see me today. I've had a long think about things, and I've come to a decision.'

She what? Karen shuffled in her chair.

'I'm sorry to have wasted everybody's time. I've been thinking about things over Easter. Which as you know is a very spiritual time. And the Lord Jesus did preach forgiveness. And although she...' Macy turned to look at Karen. '... is a complete pain in the backside, I don't think she is racist.'

Now what? Karen sat frozen to the spot. 'No, I'm not,' she butted in. Both heads turned to look at her. She visibly shrank.

Macy picked up where she'd left off. 'I've decided that I'm willing to withdraw my complaint.'

'Thank God for that,' Karen sighed.

DCI Winter held his finger to his mouth. 'Constable Dodds. You were saying?'

Macy's expression relaxed. 'If I'm honest, I understand what she meant. I do stand out. But there's nothing I can do about that. If the force had more black officers, it wouldn't be an issue.'

'Exactly.' Karen nodded furiously. DCI Winter glared at her.

Karen looked at Macy. 'I'm very sorry. I got frustrated and took it out on you. It won't happen again, I promise.'

Macy acknowledged Karen with a slight nod and turned back to DCI Winter. 'That's all I wanted, Sir. And Sir? There's no need on my part to separate us anymore.'

Karen grinned. 'I knew it, you can't stand working with Harris!'

'Sergeant Thorpe!' DCI Winter boomed.

'No sir,' Macy held her hand up. 'She's right about that.' She looked at Karen and couldn't resist a smile.

'Well. I can assure you both that comment will not be minuted. Please, to confirm to all of us, you are formally withdrawing your complaint.

'I am, Sir.'

Thank you, Constable Dodds. I'm pleased we have come to a satisfactory conclusion.'

'Thank you, Sir.' Macy got up and left without looking back.

Karen waited before letting out a loud 'phew!'

'Karen? Don't you ever dare...'

'Never, guv. Never again.'

28

Molly had been waiting patiently for Harry to arrive. He went back up to Chesterfield every so often to check on things at their house, but this last time he'd been especially mysterious. It was Laura's seventh birthday and Molly wanted to make the day as normal as possible for the little girl.

She caught sight of him through the window. He was wrestling with an exceptionally large present wrapped with yellow paper and ribbons. It made her smile as she opened the door.

'Take this,' he said, handing her a carrier bag. He grunted as he carried the precious cargo into the living room. 'How many little beggars have we got coming?' Harry puffed.

'Only the little girl next door.'

'Where's the birthday girl?'

'In the living room.' Molly opened the door for him where Laura was playing with Joely.

'Happy birthday, Laura!' they said in unison. Laura squealed with delight when she saw Harry with the huge present. He put it down on the floor next to her. Within seconds, the paper was ripped to shreds revealing an immaculately restored and beautiful old-fashioned dolls' house.

Molly's jaw dropped. 'Is that what you've been up to in your shed?' she said. She looked inside the bag she was still holding and smiled even more.

'I love it!' Laura was genuinely thrilled.

'It was your mother's,' Molly smiled. 'Your grandpa made this for her, and he's given it a real going over for you.'

'It's the best thing ever!' Laura said, hugging both grandparents in turn. Even Joely looked impressed.

'And he's bought these too.' Molly handed her the bag, which was full of little wooden figures and pieces of furniture. 'It's a proper house, not like your modern plastic rubbish,' she added.

Sofia appeared and went to inspect the present. 'That is so special,' she said, smiling at Molly and Harry. 'Can I get you some tea?'

'Yes please, lass, I'm spitting feathers here. Where are those boys?'

'Playing football in the garden. Shall I call them in?'

'Nay lass,' Harry said. 'Let me get some tea inside me first.'

***

Stella lay in uneasy consciousness. She was scared. Unable to rationalise sounds and the passing of time, she had reached a crisis point.

This is hell.

'Hello, Stella my love. Your parents are here today. I bet you've missed them.'

Let me die.

'What's this blip here... Stella, are you stressed? Please, my lovely, everything will be all right, you'll see.'

'Something wrong?'

'Stella? We're back love.'

Mum. Mum's back.

'Hello, love.'

Dad.

'Did you remember the date? It's Laura's seventh birthday today...'

Laura.

'We gave her your old dolls' house; do you remember it? Dad cleaned it up and gave it a lick of paint and it looks like new. He gave it to you for your seventh birthday too. Ee, love, that's thirty-two years ago today. You must wake up before your next one. They say life begins at forty. Do you remember it, Stella? Dad? Talk to her...'

Mum.

'It were pale yellow outside and you insisted it had a proper red roof.'

Dad.

'You never did like pink, even as a babby. And inside it were green downstairs and blue up, with matchstick floors upstairs and downstairs. Mum crocheted little rugs and I made beds. You called it Buttercup Cottage, and the Butter family lived there. I made them all out of lollipop sticks and matches. You said it were your real home.'

Home.

Stella opened her still sleeping eyes and turned around. The wall was still there but an opening had appeared, an adjoining wall. She followed it, realising that it was turning from a reddish colour to yellow. It led her to a house. A yellow house with a red roof.

Safe.

The door was open and she gazed around in wonder, recognising but not understanding what it was. She got into her bed and pulled the covers up tight.

Safe at home.

***

'Lovely to see you both again.' Gwen greeted Molly and Harry. 'I haven't seen you for a while.'

'I had to go back home to sort things out,' Harry said. 'I'm here now for a bit.'

'I don't like to leave the children for long,' Molly explained. 'It takes ages for me to get the bus here and back again and our au pair isn't there during the day. But it's the end of term now. And...' she hesitated.

'Is there something you wanted to ask, Mrs Baxter?'

'I wasn't going to say anything,' Molly replied. 'But Stella looks a little different today. Fuller in the face. That's all.'

Gwen smiled. 'That's probably fluid retention, nothing to worry about. I'll check her medications with the consultant when she next comes. I'll ring you if it's anything important.' She glanced at the chart. 'She's fine, I'm sure she is.' *Am I? Let's have a look.*

Gwen waited for Molly and Harry to go. 'Now, Stella my love. The monitor is back to normal. Can you hear me? Your mother's worried about you. But I think you're looking very well, Stella. I would almost say blooming.'

It's very strange. It can't be that. She's had no periods but that's common after trauma.

'Let's get you moved a little. Onto your side for a while... Ow!' A searing pain ran up her spine. 'Oh no!' She was so loud one of the nurses came running over.

'Gwen? What's up?'

'I know exactly what it is. It's my back,' Gwen explained. 'It happens every couple of years or so. Nobody seems to know what causes it. Can you get Monica in physio, please? She'll sort me out.'

When Monica arrived, she tutted at Gwen as soon as she saw her struggling to sit down in her chair. 'Exercises, Gwen. You've been slacking, haven't you?' Gwen nodded weakly. Monica hurried off, returning with a wheelchair. She helped Gwen sit in it.

'Luckily for you, I've got an examination room free. Let's see what we can do with you.'

29

It was a gloomy evening. Karen's mood, substantially lifted after Macy's declaration, was beginning to darken. The air had cleared, but the day job she'd become accustomed to was the same. It was demotion by another name.

She looked around the room. Macy had been called away to help the dreaded Harris, and the rest of the office was almost deserted. *Soon I'll be back to investigating. And the sooner I shift this shit, the sooner it will be.* She carried on working doggedly until a call came through.

'Break-in, seventy-eight Crown Hill Road. Mr and Mrs French.'

'No uniforms?' Karen replied automatically.

'All on call-outs,' came the reply.

She quickly thought through her response. It was an escape route, albeit a minor one. No one would question her absence and there were some things she might be able to check out. Like whether there had been more flowers placed at the accident site. And it was considerably better than doing paperwork. 'On my way,' she replied and reaching for her coat, dashed to the door.

Outside, the light was fading fast and it was very cold. *Black ice, I bet. More bloody accidents. More bloody paperwork.*

She got into her car, all the time rehearsing in her head the formal procedures for investigating break-ins. It wasn't especially busy on the roads and she was soon on very familiar territory. Suddenly a car pulled out from nowhere to overtake her.

'Whoa! What the fuck?!' She could see the lights of an oncoming car, so she braked hard. The car cut in front of her just in time. *Bloody idiot!* she thought. *And he hasn't even got his lights on!*

At the same time as the thought entered her mind, the headlights of the car ahead came on, but all Karen saw were the red lights. She instantly assumed they were brake lights and instinctively hit her own before realising what had happened. 'Fucking tosser!' she shouted. 'I've got a good mind to pull you over!' But something jarred in her brain. *Why was that important? Brake lights... Could that be it? Did Westbury hit his brakes, thinking something in front of him had braked?*

The thought played in her mind all the way to her destination.

***

When she arrived at the address, she remembered to be polite to Mr and Mrs French, but was incapable of giving the matter the attention it deserved. After listening to what they had to say and making a fast but thorough inspection, she found her eyes focusing on a battered old tennis racquet lying amongst the general mess accumulated in the French's front hall. That object was telling her something. Reminding her. *What?*

'... Can we tidy up now, Officer?' Mrs French was asking.

'Did they break the tennis racquet too?'

'No, our son did that.'

'Is there a tennis club around here?'

'Yes. Does that matter?'

'Oh yes. It might be really important,' Karen mused out loud. Snapping to attention, she looked at the woman. 'Yes, you're OK to tidy up. I've taken some pictures and we'll try to send someone round to dust for prints.'

'You'll try?'

'I'm sorry, Mrs French. We are very stretched at the moment. We have to prioritise all our cases now. You've told me that nothing of value was taken. All we can do on a practical basis is make sure you get a crime reference number for the insurance.'

'Typical,' Mr French grunted. 'What do we pay our taxes for...' Karen had already let herself out not noticing the door banged shut behind her.

***

Karen started searching on her phone before she even got into her car. An address popped up. She knew exactly where it was and drove straight to the location. When she arrived, she was

116

taken aback. *This is a tennis club? Why the hell didn't I investigate it before? Damn.* She hit her forehead with the heel of her hand in annoyance, then got out of the car.

She stared at the little building she'd noticed before but hadn't studied. When she walked up to it, she could see a couple of tennis courts at the back of the clubhouse, all well secured with chain link fencing. But what was important now was not the building or the fact that it was a tennis club. It was the location. When she had completed a walk around as much of the building she could access, she went back to her car and got in, still thinking.

A few hundred yards from Stella's accident. And Robert Cary's. It had to be connected. It was part of the puzzle. She immediately thought of John. *I've got to ring him now,* she decided. *He understands.*

30

John had agreed to go to Karen's flat in a millisecond. Almost before she'd had taken her finger off the entrance button he'd appeared outside her door, a bottle of wine in his hand. But the smile was wiped off his face as he followed her inside.

'What the hell...?' He surveyed the scene. Almost every square inch of wall space was covered with charts, maps and post-it notes. The coffee table was now completely buried. 'Karen, you need help, seriously.'

'That's why you're here, dumbo.' She smiled at him. 'Look at this.'

'No, no, no, Karen.' John turned round to peer into her little kitchenette. The whole area was taken up with foil tins and paper bags from the local takeaway. 'You are turning into an a... a cliché. You have to sort this mess out. I'm not going to even look at anything until you do. You'll make yourself ill living in this... this shit.'

Karen was gobsmacked; this was nearly an outburst, from John of all people! *And he said shit! It must be serious.*

Blinking, for the first time she saw her life through the eyes of someone else. If she'd walked in on it, she would probably have been horrified too. But living on her own, she hardly noticed it. *What would Dad have said?* 'Mucky pup.' *That's what he'd say. Not the charts though. I remember him doing that.*

But it's my place, mine to mess up if I want to. Do I need him coming here and telling me what to do?

She watched John still staring at the walls. *Damn. Yes, I do need him. There's no one else and besides, he's seen the worst now and he hasn't run away.*

Had she been able to hear John's thoughts, she might have been appeased that he was worrying that he'd gone too far. They spoke at the same time.

'It doesn't matter...'   'OK. I'll get some black bags...' They laughed simultaneously.

Karen spoke next. 'But I can't touch the walls, the guv made me clear the incident room.'

'I'll help you by starting in the kitchen,' John replied. 'I'm an expert in this stuff.'

'Is it that bad?'

'I've seen worse, but only six years after the occupant died.'

Karen left, returning shortly afterwards with a roll of black bags. Waiting for her she found towers of stacked foil trays and piles of greasy wrappings.

John took one of the bags and held it open for her to drop the detritus in. 'Sorry planet,' he muttered. He turned to look at the sink. 'Has this ever seen bleach?' he asked, causing Karen to rush into the bathroom.

'I think there's some here... No. Better pop out again.'

'Scouring pads!' he shouted after her.

'Twice in one day,' the local shopkeeper said. 'New man?'

'Oi!' she replied, but nodded at him. She returned to a cleaner and clearer kitchen with two full black bags by the door.

'Can we start now?' Karen's patience was exhausted.

'One minute.' John looked past Karen who had, without forethought, opened her bedroom door and was now standing defensively in the doorway. 'Jesus Christ!' he spluttered.

Karen's bedroom was in a worse state than the kitchen and probably even less hygienic. The laundry basket was buried under a clothes mountain and judging by the carrier bags and clothes tags lying around, Karen was buying new things rather than washing anything. John couldn't hold it in any longer.

'Bloody hell, Karen! This is disgusting. And I know you can't afford to carry on living like this.'

Why, oh why did I let him come here?

But he's right. My bank account is in the red again.

John seized on her hesitation. 'Now we've uncovered your washing machine, how about doing some washing?'

'OK, OK. But you're not rummaging around in here. You go to the takeaway. I'll put a wash on and sort this out. But you know you have absolutely no right to look in my bathroom, don't you?' John cocked his head on one side and raised an eyebrow.

'Suppose I need to use it?'

'Hold it or go outside or something. Use a bottle.'

'Or you could clean it.'

Karen harrumphed.

'OK. On my way. Which takeaway?'

'The Thai's the furthest away. Take the rubbish too. Out the back, right-hand block,' Karen said. *Now, where's that bog brush...?*

When John returned with food and drink, the little flat was almost clear and the washing machine was spluttering into life. Karen was in the kitchenette, getting out newly washed glasses and cutlery. John came up behind her and put his chin cheekily on her shoulder. Karen laughed.

'OK, Mum. Nearly done.' She brought the glasses over to him. 'Can we start now?'

'Food first,' he ordered. 'If you're going to call me Mum, I'm going to act like one.'

Carefully, he picked all the model cars off the makeshift road on the coffee table. Karen begrudgingly joined in and the two of them lifted the paper off the table, putting them in the only space they could find on the floor. Karen put out the glasses and began to open the foil containers.

'Plates.'

'Shit. Really?' Karen sulked but retrieved two plates from the kitchen while John poured the wine.

'How long have you lived here?'

'A while. Why?'

'Just making conversation. Were you born near here, then?'

'What's this? I do the interrogating.'

'It's called small talk, Karen. Nothing sinister.'

'You talk, then. Why did you want to work in forensics...?'

31

Finally, the meal was finished and Karen restored the road and model cars to the table.

'At bloody last. Now, what if this happened? Someone's leaving the tennis club, here.' She picked up a car and put it in the left-hand lane. 'But it's only starting off, so these vehicles overtake.' She put the two other cars in the right-hand lane, one level with the first car, one still behind it. John nodded. 'Let's say Cary, or our boy racer or whoever sets off the camera, undertakes Stella but Westbury's van is still getting in the way. So he undertakes Westbury too.'

'But why wouldn't the other vehicles return to the left-hand lane?' John said. 'And where's the vehicle leaving the tennis club got to? Not only that, the lanes merge soon afterwards, why bother?'

Karen shuffled all the cars along. 'Because he's trying to cause the crash. This is the best bit.' Karen became even more animated. 'He's got past the van now, but he has no lights on. He turns them on. Stella's still recovering from being undertaken, Westbury thinks the boy racer is braking - he slams his brakes on and...'

'And Stella goes straight into the back of him?' John finished.

'Would it work?' she pressed. 'Is it feasible? Something like that nearly happened to me today.'

'How about this,' John countered. 'Pretend these are deer, for a moment.' He took the cork from the bottle and broke it into two, placing one half in the left-hand lane. 'Westbury sees a deer on the road and pulls out to avoid it. Stella does the same. Then as Westbury is congratulating himself for missing it, this one runs across to find its mate.' He put the other half of the cork in front of the other car. 'He brakes, job done. No damage to deer, they run off.'

'What about the speed camera, though? Unless they're Santa's bloody reindeer.'

John mused. 'We've already been through that. Let me think about it a bit more.' He scratched his head.

'Then let's talk about the Westburys.' Karen said. I'm hitting a wall every time I mention the name. I can't find anything in the records, so why would everyone tell me to shut up about them?'

'No idea.'

'Even Uncle Jack had heard of them.'

'You have an uncle?'

'No,' she shook her head and turned to her notes. 'Not really. Anyway, Tom Westbury's father was called Nicholas. He died on the fifteenth of October 1989.'

'How about a coffee?' John asked, hopefully.

'You go ahead. No, actually I think I'm going out. Why the hell didn't I think of that before?'

'What?'

Karen barely turned round to look at him. 'Thanks, John. You've been a great help.'

'I have?'

'Oh yes. There's somewhere I have to be. See you... whenever.'

'Karen...'

'Oh, I almost forgot.'

'Yes?'

'Let me know about that butt, won't you? Tomorrow would be good.'

'OK Karen, I get the message.'

Karen made some clattering noises in the kitchen while John put on his jacket. She waited for his 'bye then,' and the sound of the door shutting.

Jack knew about the Westburys. What about you, Dad? Did you know too? 'Only one way to find out.' She looked outside and waited until she saw John's car pull out, then grabbed her coat and set off to her father's house.

***

Karen sat in her car for ten minutes before she could bring herself to get out. Checking she had the keys for the third time, she walked up to the little terraced house with mixed emotions. The last time she had been here was when she and her father had taken part in a pub quiz. He was fond of them. He'd been telling her all about his latest cold case investigations, which he did in his spare time. She hadn't listened. Now she wished she'd paid more attention to him.

Oh, what I'd give to have you back now, Dad. Opening the door slowly, her immediate impressions were that it was very cold, but everything looked clean and tidy. *Thanks, Sal.* She dithered over whether to put the heating on or not and concluded that she should, if only to make sure everything was working properly.

She thought of all sorts of other things she needed to do, to put off what she had actually come to find - her father's notebooks. She checked her old bedroom. It hadn't changed since before her mother had died. Another surge of older, painful memories flooded her brain and she went downstairs to avoid them.

Would you mind, Dad? She looked up to the ceiling as she thought it.

'Silly girl', she heard him say. 'Copper first, last and in the middle. Do what you have to.'

'OK Dad. Now, where are they?'

Karen had pretty much moved out of the house when she went to university, only staying there briefly before settling in her tiny flat. Tommy had got used to her being away from him. Having discovered the occasional boy, she had wanted her own space. Now she regretted that.

'Move on gal, you can't undo the past.'

She went into the back room where she knew her father used to keep most of his important things. *There*.

The back wall of the room was fitted with sturdy metal shelving, upon which sat neatly labelled storage boxes. *You were efficient when you wanted to be, Dad.*

Her eyes scanned the boxes and rested on one on the top shelf bearing the label *1981 - 1990.* 'That's the one.'

Standing on a chair, she pulled the box down and put it on the floor. Sitting next to it, her heart began to race as she started to look through the notebooks. *Date order Dad, naturally.*

She skipped through quickly to get to October, not noticing at first that the dates didn't tally. Then taking each page at a time, she realised that a whole section had been neatly cut from the notebook.

'Nicholas Westbury died on the fifteenth of October 1989. Where are all the pages from the first to the fifteenth? What the hell was going on, Dad?'

32

Sergeant Julia Jones pulled up outside Sandra's ramshackle rented cottage on the edge of the Dorset village. Above-average height, she had a slim athletic build from years of gymnastics, before choosing her final career. If she had anything in common with Karen Thorpe, it was her love of flat shoes. Her brown hair, however, was long and kept in a neat French plait.

After checking her face in the car wing mirror, she studied the cottage. The garden fences were almost non-existent and she could see through to some of the back garden, where the clothesline was full of pegged-up washing. It looked like a tip. She caught some movement at the window. The door opened before she reached it. 'Mrs Atkins?'

'Yes. It's about Piers, isn't it? Have you found him?'

'May I come in?'

The inside of the house was even worse than the outside. *I'd ask her to sit. But where?* Julia gazed around the cluttered room. 'Please, Mrs Atkins, you sit down.'

Sandra cleared a pile of comics off a chair with one sweep of her still-wet arm and sat down, staring into space.

Julia stood. 'Mrs Atkins, there's no easy way to say this. We have recently found a body and we think it might be someone you know. There was an envelope in his pocket with what looks like an old postmark. It was addressed to a Mr Paul Atkins and redirected to this address here.'

Sandra, at first silent, suddenly screamed. 'Noooo! Not Piers!'

Julia checked her notebook. 'The name we have is Paul.'

'That's his birth name. I only just found out!' Sandra sobbed.

'Would you like a cup of tea, Mrs Atkins?' Julia turned towards the kitchen. She could see that the table was covered with jam jars, breakfast cereals and half-drunk cups of milk and juice.

'Tea's in the cupboard...'

Tentatively, Julia opened the most likely cupboard. A cereal box fell out, making her jump.

'For fuck's sake! Leave it!' Sandra yelled.

Julia went back and watched Sandra pull a chair over to a rickety-looking bookcase. She wobbled a little as she stood on it, reaching for a bottle of supermarket-brand vodka.

Oh God, don't fall... Phew. She's down. Julia stared as Sandra emptied a glass of water from the windowsill into a dead houseplant and poured herself a large shot of vodka.

'Ah, that's better,' Sandra said. 'Where did you find him? It.'

'The body was discovered in a shipping container in Harwich Docks. It had been there a long time.' Sandra looked at the floor. 'Mrs Atkins, is there anyone I can contact to be with you?' There was no response. Sandra sat still, hardly breathing. 'Mrs Atkins?'

'No one ever cares about me. Just my fucking perfect sister. It was always the same.'

'You have a sister? Could we ring her?'

Sandra laughed. 'Good luck with that one.'

'Mrs Atkins, do you have any family we can contact? Or friends?'

'Well, it's about time they took some notice. Ring him. It's Baxter. Mr H. Baxter.' She handed a phonebook to Julia. 'Phone's there.' She pointed to the hall. 'At least that hasn't been cut off, yet.' Julia went to the phone. Sandra was still talking. 'How am I going to tell the kids? What will I do for money now?'

Julia listened to the ringing tone. 'Mrs Atkins, there's no answer. Is there someone else we can ring?'

'Try Cary. Stella. They're always bloody there.'

Julia rang but there was still no answer. 'Is there anyone else?'

'No. Say what you have to.'

Julia took a photo on her phone of the two numbers, then stood opposite Sandra as she took another swig from her glass. 'Perhaps I can ask a few questions?' Sandra waved her glass at her in response. 'When did you last see your husband?'

'Late last year. I'm not sure. December sometime.'

'Don't you know the exact date?' *She doesn't know?*

'No. It was a Thursday because that's when I go to the post

126

office, and he's normally there with his hand out.'

Julia checked her phone calendar. 'The sixth? Thirteenth?'

Sandra's face became animated as if she'd remembered something. 'No. It was the twentieth. Yes. Definitely.'

'I'm sorry to have to ask this but as I said, the person we found has been dead for a while. It won't be appropriate to identify him visually. Do you have any personal items of Mr Atkins you can give us? We need to run a DNA test.'

'What?' Sandra screwed up her face in revulsion.

'A comb? Toothbrush?'

'No. I meant how long? How long since...'

'They're working on that. But we can't be sure it is him without doing the DNA test. If you have something...'

Sandra hauled herself up. 'His razor is still around somewhere.' She went upstairs while Julia took in the scene. *Mustn't judge.*

Sandra reappeared with Piers' toothbrush and a disposable razor. 'Will these do?'

'That's perfect.' Julia took a plastic bag out of her pocket and opened it for Sandra to drop them in. 'I'll be off then. I'll let you know as soon as we find out the results.'

Sandra nodded. 'Yes. I understand.'

Julia sat in her car wondering how she could help. She was aware of Sandra's recent conviction and assessed that she was on a downward spiral. *Better to get the family involved before she had to call Social Services.* She looked at the phone numbers she had snapped and rang the first one.

'Hello. Harry Baxter here.'

'Mr Baxter? It's Sergeant Julia Jones here. I've been to visit your daughter Sandra?' She paused for confirmation.

'Aye. What's she done now?'

Harry listened in silence as Julia explained about her investigation.

Ending with 'I think she needs her family around her.'

'Oh 'eck,' Harry replied. 'I've only just got back.'

33

Thursday 4th April

Gwen arrived early for her shift and rushed straight in to see Stella. If she had worried about her condition before, there was even more reason to be concerned now. *You don't notice gradual changes daily. But something's definitely going on here.*

When she drew back the bedding, it was clear that even the standard-issue nightdress she was wearing was tighter round the chest.

No! It can't be... But as she gently felt around Stella's abdomen, her worst fears were confirmed. With the blood draining from her face, she realised what she had to do.

As discreetly as she could, she walked to the desk and rang one of her colleagues. 'It's probably my imagination,' she whispered into the phone. 'A fluid build-up or something. But would you mind? Off the record, to put my mind at rest?'

Gwen was like a cat on hot bricks for the rest of the morning, jumping whenever the phone rang and continually looking out to see if anyone was coming. When her colleague finally arrived, Gwen grabbed her and led her towards Stella's room

'The one in the coma?' Gwen nodded. 'My goodness. Let's hope you're wrong then.'

Gwen drew the curtains across the window as they went in. Hardly daring to breathe, she watched her colleague bend over Stella and begin her examination.

'You're not wrong Gwen. She's pregnant all right.'

'That poor woman, as if she hasn't been through enough. I wonder if she knew she was pregnant before the crash. Could we have missed it?'

'Unlikely. It's a routine test. I'd say she's only around twelve, maybe thirteen weeks.'

'Oh, my word! We must get her to come round. I can't imagine the problems we'll have if she doesn't. What on earth am I going to say to the family?'

'Never mind the family, Gwen. You'd better get on to the head of nursing. Mrs Reader. This is way above your pay-scale, and you know it.'

'Will you guard me when I ring her? We can't let anybody know yet.'

'OK. But I've not got long.'

Gwen rang Helen Reader and whispered to her, 'It's Stella Cary. She's pregnant.'

'What?' Helen replied. 'Why didn't we know? We could have unwittingly damaged the foetus. I'm coming right down.'

'I'll check the obs.' Gwen went to the desk and called up Stella's records then waited in her room. Helen, a woman in her forties who oozed confidence, arrived quickly. Gwen was immediately reassured.

'Let's start at the beginning,' Helen said. 'Obs?'

'She was definitely tested for pregnancy. Maybe it was too early to show up conclusively?' Gwen replied.

'Well, that's a possibility,' Helen said. 'Let me have a look. Pushing her shoulder-length grey-streaked hair behind her ears, she slowly repeated the examination of Stella's abdomen. 'I have to be absolutely sure,' she said. 'When was she admitted?'

'The thirteenth of December,' Gwen replied.

Helen closed her eyes, counting. 'Sixteen.' She turned back to look at Stella and felt around her abdomen again. Gwen felt fear permeating her body.

'No, don't say it. It can't be...'

Helen stood and spoke firmly and clearly. 'In my opinion that foetus is around thirteen weeks. Even allowing for the patient's exceptional circumstances, the absolute maximum is fifteen weeks.'

'You mean...? Gwen stuttered.

'Let's not jump to conclusions yet. We need to get it confirmed. But if you're thinking what I am... Yes. She's been raped.'

***

Even as she made her way to the lift, Helen Reader was thinking, and not only about Stella. *OK, Tiggle you old dinosaur. I've been warning you about security here for years. Let's see how you deal with this.* She marched into his office without knocking, leaving his PA open-mouthed.

Martin Tiggle, the Deputy Director looked over his pince-nez in astonishment. 'Yes? Have we got a fire or something?'

'I have reason to believe that a patient has been raped,' Helen said.

'Gracious me!' Tiggle sat back in his chair. 'What happened?'

As Helen relayed her findings, she watched his face carefully. The expression of shock soon relaxed. 'Nothing that can't be sorted,' he said.

'I beg your pardon?'

'Let's be practical. There's no need to put this woman through anything unless it's entirely necessary. Get her scanned and look for any abnormalities. She's at the age where things start to get tricky and her state might have had an impact too. Let's see what we've got before we make any decisions.'

Helen nodded. *Can't argue with that.* 'OK. I'll organise it Mr Tiggle.'

'Get her into a private room and I want you to personally take charge of her. We need total discretion here.'

'She's in one already but there's another one free now. It's along the corridor. It will be easier to police and service discreetly.'

'Perfect. I want to know as soon as you've done the scan.'

When Helen returned, it was to relay the Sonographer's confirmation. 'Thirteen weeks, give or take a few days. The baby looks perfectly healthy, certainly no obvious abnormalities.'

'That's a shame,' Tiggle sighed. 'And when was she admitted?'

'Sixteen weeks ago.'

Tiggle tilted his head on one side. 'Can't we deal with this? Internally, so to speak?'

'Are you saying what I think you're saying?' Helen's voice was noticeably louder.

'I'm thinking of the family. They've already had too much to take on board.'

'No, we most certainly can't!' Helen exclaimed. 'Even if it was possible to keep a termination secret, the woman's in a coma, who knows what damage we could do to her if we even tried?'

'Bloody hell.'

Helen stared at his use of the profanity.

'And the father?'

'It doesn't matter who the father was,' Helen shot back. 'A woman in a coma cannot possibly consent. It's a criminal offence. It's rape.'

Tiggle slumped back in his chair. Helen could almost see his brain ticking.

'Who knows about this?'

'Only me, the ward nurse and the midwife who did the scan.'

'Go then. Tell them to keep quiet. It's in no one's interest to let this get out. This is not only my reputation at stake, it's yours and that of the whole hospital.'

***

'It's not my reputation, Sir,' Helen replied from the other side of his door. *And I'm not collaborating in a cover-up. Oh no, not her again...*

Gwen was approaching. 'I had to talk to you,' she said. 'Poor, poor woman. What have we done to her? We've let her down so badly.'

'We haven't done anything, Gwen,' Helen said, touching her arm reassuringly. 'It was some sick individual. Not us. I can see how it might have happened,' she postulated. 'That other room is so out of the way. Anybody could have sneaked in.'

'But there's the CCTV, isn't there?'

'If it was on.' Helen said. 'And there will have been thousands of people through those doors. I'll get on to the head of Critical Care. Maybe we can close it off. Anyhow, it's too late for her, though. Unless it's a situation of ongoing abuse.'

Gwen shuddered. 'You don't think...'

'I don't know. But we can't take any chances.'

131

'What does Mr Tiggle say?'

'He wants to deal with it,' Helen said with a nod of her head.

Gwen frowned. 'Deal with it?' Helen raised an eyebrow. 'He can't! You don't mean... No! Over my dead body. I'm not going to be part of any...' She searched for the words 'Forced termination.'

'But you could be implicated,' Helen said, testing her. 'Everyone on the ward could be. If nobody knew...'

Gwen stood firm. 'I've done nothing wrong and nobody's ever set a foot near her on my watch, apart from proper visitors.' Gwen hesitated for a second. 'And hospital staff. Let them investigate, I've got nothing to hide. Besides, it'll be all over the hospital by now.'

'What?' Helen exclaimed. 'I thought this was between us.'

'I got a midwife friend to check her over before we did it officially.'

'Oh, I see. You go now, Gwen,' Helen said. 'Nothing's going to happen imminently. And don't you worry. You've done your best. I'm going to make another call, which will make sure this terrible event never happens anywhere, ever again.'

34

Friday 5th April

Max Billingswood, the chair of the Hospital Trust, had received an anonymous message. It was short and to the point. It set out in brief and graphic detail what had happened, and it questioned Tiggle's ethics. Max was furious that he had not been informed immediately about what had happened in the ICU. A short conversation with Tiggle had elicited the man's immediate resignation. He'd then called an urgent meeting with the newly appointed CEO Clive Evans. Coincidentally, Helen Reader had been brought in to assist in Tiggle's place.

'When did it happen?' Clive asked.

'End of December, early January,' Helen replied.

'Damage limitation,' he said. 'Many of these scandals erupt because management didn't do the right thing at the right time. We'll manage this internally. I'll get our PR people onto a strategy ASAP. We must anticipate legal action by the family. The insurance company will want a say. I'll pass that to the Finance Director.' He looked at Max. 'And we'll have to inform the police, too.'

Max sighed. 'I'll ring the Chief Constable as soon as this meeting is over.'

'What's the Trust's perspective on this?'

'Early days. I've called the Committee Chairs and got everyone on board with it all. The Audit Committee will be reviewing procedures urgently. As you know, Tiggle's fallen on his sword, so heads have already rolled and that's reassuring for everybody.'

'Thanks, Max. I think we all know what to do. For the moment we must act as if nothing's happened. The longer we can keep this under wraps, the better our chances of managing it.'

'I'll warn the appropriate staff on the ward,' Helen said. 'Once the police come to investigate, we'll have a devil of a job to keep it quiet.'

'Discretion all the way,' Tom said. Helen nodded, trying hard not to smile.

***

On the ward, Gwen, despite acting as normally as she could manage was still in shock about the situation. Needing a breather, she sat, head in hands at the desk. Peter came by. He touched her gently on the arm then shrank back when she sat up suddenly.

'Peter? Sorry. I was miles away. I haven't seen you for ages. Have you been on nights?'

Peter nodded, but he looked worried. 'Where's Stella? Is she all right? Have you moved her again?'

'Yes dear. Sit down, Peter. I suppose you'll find out soon anyway. Something's happened. It is bad, but not in the sense that she's ill.' She hesitated.

'What's wrong with her, then?'

'I'll tell you, but you must promise not to tell anyone else. Do you understand?'

'Of course. What is it?'

'She's pregnant, Peter.'

Peter shook his head, not understanding the significance of what she was saying. 'That's not bad, is it? Maybe she wanted another baby.'

'No, it's not necessarily bad. But her husband may not be the father.'

'She was in here before he died. Wasn't she pregnant when she came in?'

'No, Peter.' Gwen thought it through. *He's not a kid; he must know about these things.* 'Someone must have done it to her. Even if it was her husband, she must have been raped.'

Peter jumped up and shouted, 'Some bastard hurt my precious Stella? I'll kill them!' His face turned red with rage; the veins in his forehead bulged. He clenched his hands into fists.

Oh my God, he looks like a maniac! 'Peter, Peter, calm down.' Gwen stroked his arm. 'Shush, you'll upset the other patients.

And Stella!'

Peter slumped back down almost as quickly as he had got up. His face creased up in anguish. 'What are they going to do?'

'They're going to get the police to find out who did it. They will find out in the end, I promise. But for now, there's nothing you can do.'

'I'm going to sit with her. I'll never leave her side again. I'll protect her.'

'Peter, you can't. And it's too late now, you'll have to wait and let the police do their job. Now Peter, think carefully...'

'What?'

'Do you remember that conversation you heard before?' He nodded. 'Have you heard other conversations in Stella's room?'

Peter blinked and nodded earnestly. 'Yes. I try not to listen. It's private. But I've heard lots of things.'

'Then you can help her, Peter, you must tell the police everything you know.'

Peter smiled. 'Yes, I can do that. There's a lot I can tell them, for sure.'

35

Monday 8th April

DCI Winter sat in his office, twiddling his thumbs. He'd put the phone down after speaking to Chief Constable Burns. 'It's the new chap at the County Hospital,' he'd said. 'Clive something or other. Evans. Clive Evans. Nice chap. Don't rain on his parade. Winter? Give the man a chance.'

'But it's rape,' he'd replied. 'It's a serious crime. There should have been systems in place; safeguards.'

'All happened before his watch. Go easy on him.'

DCI Winter stood up and paced a little. He peered through the blinds at Karen, sitting at her desk.

Who gets this one? She's exactly like her father. And me, when we were that age.

She's got a good nose. And she bounces back from a slap-down.

But Harris? He's the senior. But he's got the attempted murder.

He sat down.

But she's a woman and it's a woman's thing.

But she pisses me off, big time.

Then again, so does Harris.

But she's worked her socks off recently.

And Dodds is coming on really well.

He sat down.

But this is high profile.

I'm in charge, I'm the public face.

He flipped a coin.

Tails, it's Karen.

It was tails.

Best of three.

He flipped again, heads. Then again, tails.

Coffee time.

He glared at Karen as he left the office. He was still glaring at her as he came back in clutching his espresso. 'In my office,' he barked as he went past her.

'Yes, guv.' Karen followed him in and sat down.

'I have a new case for you.'

'What? Yes, guv!'

'It's Stella Cary.'

Karen was confused. 'What? Has she died?'

'No Karen. She's been raped.'

'Blimey.' Karen let the information sink in. 'And you're giving me the case?'

'Yes, Karen. DS Harris is on the Hatfield attempted murder.'

'Guv. I can't thank you enough. But...'

'Dodds, Karen. Final offer. You'll have to make it work.'

'OK, guv.'

'And what will your first action be?'

'Get the incident room set up,' she said.

DCI Winter glared at her again. 'This isn't a fucking TV drama. It's real human beings you're dealing with. You will make contact with Clive Evans, the CEO of the hospital. Your first task is to go and see Stella Cary's parents, Mr and Mrs Baxter and reassure them that we are on the case.'

Karen sat frozen to the spot. *Of course.*

'And this has to be completely discreet. We do NOT want the story getting out into the public realm. Plainclothes only.'

'Yes. But....'

'Don't you dare even think it. And one more thing.'

'Yes, guv?'

'This is nothing to do with the Westburys, OK?'

'But there is something about them guv. I found...'

'Do you want the case or not?'

'Yes, guv.'

'Then get going. Now!'

'Yes, Sir.'

***

Karen went straight to her desk to make a call. Noticing Macy coming in, she gave her a small nod before she picked up the phone.

'It's Detective Sergeant Karen Thorpe. I need to speak to Mr Evans.'

'Yes, Sergeant Thorpe. I'm his PA. I've been expecting somebody to call. Mr Evans isn't available at the moment, but I'll tell him you rang. I'm fully aware of the situation regarding Mrs Cary.'

'Have Mr and Mrs Baxter been informed yet?'

'No. Mr Evans is seeing them tomorrow morning to tell them in person.'

'Thank you. Could you mention that I'd like to meet with them - after they've been told?'

'I will.'

Karen put the phone down and looked over at Macy. She swallowed. 'Did you mean what you said about working with me again?'

'Of course, Sergeant.'

'Good. And you can forget all that Sergeant nonsense. We've known each other long enough now.'

'Yes, Karen.' Macy grinned.

'And incident room two will be back in action tomorrow. It's really, really shocking...' she said, but, unable to hide her smile she added, 'We've got a corker now!'

36

Helen sat to the side of Clive's desk, watching as Harry and Molly were shown into his office.

'Mr and Mrs Baxter. Thank you so much for coming.' Clive held out his hand.

This was too much for Molly. She ignored his hand. 'What is it? Budget cuts? Are you going to let her die because there's no money to keep her alive?'

'No! My goodness, no, Mrs Baxter. No, that is not why I asked you to come here at all.'

Harry also refused to shake Clive's hand. 'Get on with it then. What's this all about?'

'Let me introduce myself. I am Clive Evans, the *newly* appointed Chief Executive of the hospital. And this is Helen Reader, Head of Nursing.' He turned to Helen. There was a very pregnant pause. 'Mr and Mrs Baxter, Helen has a great deal of experience in this area.'

Helen sat up, realising that this was her cue. 'Mr and Mrs Baxter, we have examined your daughter carefully and we need to explain what is going on in her body.'

While Molly glared at her, Harry braced himself. 'Get on with it.'

Helen breathed deeply. 'I have to inform you that Stella is pregnant.' Molly and Harry stared at her, unable to respond. After a suitable pause, Helen carried on. 'She is around fourteen weeks pregnant. That's as accurate as we can get at the moment.'

Molly's mouth dropped open. Harry counted on his fingers. Helen waited for him to speak.

'Now wait a minute,' Harry said, turning red. 'How can that be, eh? How can that be?' Molly turned to look at Harry while Helen and Clive waited anxiously for her reaction.

'What Dad? What?'

'She's been raped,' Harry said, bluntly. 'In here. While these...' he spat out the word, '... *people* were meant to be looking after her. God almighty! Have you no shame? How could you let something like this happen?'

'Oh, no Dad, no...' Molly sat, shaking her head.

Clive looked at Helen helplessly.

Well thanks for that, Clive. Helen got up and walked round the desk. She crouched and spoke to Molly. 'Mrs Baxter, whatever we have done wrong we'll do our very best to sort it. But our main concern is for your daughter's health, her life, and now, that of the child she is carrying. I promise you that no stone will remain unturned in finding out how this happened. But our chief priority is Stella and looking after her.'

Neither Harry nor Molly seemed able to speak. Clive   broke the silence. 'Mr and Mrs Baxter, I realise that this is a terrible shock and that you need time to let it sink in. I should tell you that we have already contacted the police and there will be constant security outside your daughter's room...'

Harry found his voice. 'Bit bloody late for that!'

Helen spoke. 'Until we know who the perpetrator is, we have to take every precaution.'

Harry blanched. 'You mean some bugger's been doing it all this time?' He shook his head.

Clive took over. 'You have my complete assurance that we will find him, and I will take personal responsibility for your daughter's care.' Clive leaned forward. 'I must ask you to maintain complete confidentiality about what has happened...'

'Oh no you don't! I'm not having you trying to cover it up. We won't stand for that.'

'No, Mr Baxter. Of course not. We will all have to face our shortcomings in the fullness of time. But your daughter is our top priority and we do not want to have to deal with the publicity this would generate if news of this terrible and unfortunate event got out. That's in no one's interests. It may also hamper the police investigation.'

Harry sat back in his chair, contemplating this.

Clive spoke again. 'You're going to have lots of questions you want to ask when you have absorbed it all. Please take my card. It has my direct line. Feel free to call me anytime.'

Harry reached out to take it then looked at Helen. 'How does this affect things? Will the babby hurt our Stella? Does it mean you can't...' He stumbled over the words. '... do anything, now she's pregnant?'

'Generally, Mr Baxter, when a woman is pregnant, she is at her most healthy. In normal circumstances, it is safer to proceed with a pregnancy than, for example, to terminate it. It is also a good sign that her body is functioning normally. That means that despite her coma, she is healthy. It has been known for women to safely be delivered of their baby even in a coma. We have done a scan which shows that the foetus appears to be perfectly normal.'

'Suppose she doesn't want it?' Harry said.

Molly came to life. 'Dad? Our Stella loved children. She'd never...'

'Aye. I take that back.'

'Is there anything at all we can do for you now?' Clive asked. 'Do you have any more questions?' Molly shook her head.

Helen spoke. 'Detective Sergeant Thorpe has been trying to get hold of you. May I tell her that you'll see her? She can come to the ward as soon as you like.' Harry nodded.

'Stella.' Molly declared. 'Take us to see Stella.'

Helen held out an arm to help Molly to her feet, but she shied away from it and stood up unaided. They walked out of Clive's office with Harry following closely behind.

On the way down to the ward, Helen talked to them. 'They are trying their best,' she said. 'But it's all about procedures and systems to them. My job is more about how we care for people, like your daughter Stella. I don't want to speak out of turn, but I have been worried about our security in the past. It's something I intend to raise with the Police Officer. I'm about to phone her to tell her you're here. I'll be with you in a minute. Stella's room is over there,' she said, pointing.

'We know where we're going,' Harry muttered.

'Wait, Mr Baxter, she's in a new room now. That one,' she

said, pointing again. 'With the orderlies sitting outside. Here's Gwen. She'll take you in.'

Gwen walked towards them. But as soon as she saw her, Molly's face froze. They stood staring at each other for a few seconds, then Molly did something she had never done in her life before. She charged at Gwen and with great force slapped her round the face. Gwen reeled as Harry pulled Molly back, shocked at what she had done. Helen came running back.

'You should have protected her!' Molly shouted. 'You should have looked after our little girl!'

'Hey lass, that's not fair. I'm sorry Miss Williams. We've only heard this minute.'

'I understand, Mr Baxter.' Still stung from Molly's blow, Gwen walked calmly back to her desk while Harry tried to calm his wife down.

'Nay lass, we can't let Stella see us like this. Come on love. Calm down.' Molly breathed deeply and sighed. 'All right Dad. Let's go and see her now.'

37

Helen had been too late to intervene in the incident, but she got to Gwen as soon as she could. 'Are you all right, Gwen?'

'It's nothing,' said Gwen stoically.

An angry-looking Nurse walked up to them. 'It shouldn't be allowed. There are notices everywhere about assaults on staff. Are you OK, love?'

'I'm fine,' Gwen said, rubbing her cheek. 'They've had very bad news. I'll tell you later.'

'She's right, Gwen, that's assault,' said Helen.

'Mrs Baxter's upset. She's a right to be.'

'But she can't take it out on you. I'll have a word.'

'No,' Gwen said. She took Helen's arm. 'Please leave it, Mrs Reader. She has enough to deal with.'

'I will, for now, but I'll make sure it's noted. She might do it again.'

'She's upset, that's all.'

'All right, but I'm going to be talking to the police soon. I'm quite happy to tell them...'

'Leave it,' Gwen said.

***

Helen approached Karen who was waiting at the desk. 'Sergeant Thorpe?'

'Detective Sergeant Thorpe. My card.'

'Helen Reader, Acting Deputy Director. Mr and Mrs Baxter are with their daughter now. There's a separate room over there if you want to talk privately.'

Karen nodded and first went over to Stella's room. 'DS Thorpe,' she said to the orderlies and gave both of them her card. 'Ring me if you see anyone or anything suspicious.'

She tapped on the open door. As Harry looked up, she stepped in. 'Mr and Mrs Baxter? DS Thorpe. We have met. I wanted to have a word if that's all right with you?'

'Molly love, it's the policewoman. Same one.' Molly turned round.

'It might be better if we went into a relatives' room,' Karen said.

'Yes,' Harry agreed. 'No point upsetting our Stella.' They joined her outside.

Karen led them to the room Helen had pointed out. 'This will do.' She held the door open.

When they were all sitting, Karen clammed up. Her head was so full of car crashes, that she hadn't even begun to properly contemplate the rape. *Shit. What do I say now?*

'Mr and Mrs Baxter,' she began, her lack of confidence showing through. 'As I'm sure you realise, this is going to be a very difficult case to investigate...'

'Is it?' Harry's hackles were up again. 'Are you making excuses before you've even begun?'

'No, not at all. I'm trying to explain that it will be difficult. Normally we'd have a conscious victim, a time, a date, a description...'

'Are you telling me that in a hospital that's supposed to protect people you can't find out who did this?' Harry stood up. 'I'm not listening to anymore. You call us when you've got something worth telling us. Come on Mother; our daughter needs us.' Molly stood up too.

Do they know about Cary's attempted rape? 'It might even have been her husband...' Karen speculated.

'Have you no respect? Do you think he'd have raped his own wife in her hospital bed?' Harry boomed.' I've had enough of your rubbish.'

They left, leaving Karen standing in the room in complete disarray. *Bugger DCI Winter and his helpful hints. Why didn't I stick with my instincts and get it all written down first?*

Helen, still waiting in the ward, watched Molly and Harry charge out of the relatives' room.

'Problems?' she said to Karen.

'Only with bosses and their stupid ideas,' Karen replied.

'I know exactly what you mean,' Helen said. 'Excuse me, I have one of my own to sort out.'

***

Stella was sleeping soundly in her little dolls' house bed.

'Calm down mother.'

Leave me alone.

'I can't calm down. What'll we do, Dad?'

I want to sleep.

'Our girl's been hurt and now there's a new little one to worry about.'

Mum? Who's been hurt?

'There's nowt we can do.'

Dad's sad.

Harry said, 'Be quiet or you'll upset her.'

Her? Her? Me?

'You can talk. There was no need to be so rude to that police girl.'

Not me. Her.

'Happen.'

'Go and get us a coffee. I want to talk to our Stella.'

Something's changed.

'Stella, love. We've got something to tell you. I don't know how to explain it. But best not think about that. You've got so much to take on board when you wake up. But this is important.'

Important.

'Oh, Stella love. There's a new babby.'

Baby?

Stella pulled back the covers and looked around. Memories were coming back. Happy memories.

What was that? She looked down and saw a gurgling baby lying on the floor, arms and legs waving in the air.

'We're all here for you love. Stella, you must wake up, you really must.'

A baby.

She smiled and tried to touch it, but it changed. It began to cry and scream.

Don't cry, don't cry.

'Molly, lass. Let her be. We've got other problems too.'

'It's about our Sandra...'

Sandra.

'Oh no, Dad. Will it never end?'

'Has Piers turned up at last?'

Piers?

The baby had gone. Stella shivered and got back into her little bed.

'I'm afraid so, lass. We're going to have to go and see her soon. They've found a body.'

Stella pulled the covers up and over her.

Too tired.

Stella drifted back to sleep.

38

'You what?' Sean O'Malley could hardly believe his ears. He looked at his watch. *Nearly knocking off time. Should I?*

'You have to give me your private number. I'll call you from a phone box,' the woman said.

He reeled off the digits. 'This had better be good,' he replied, staring at his phone. *Hurry up, I'm wasting valuable drinking time here.*

He jumped when it rang.

'Who is this?'

'How do I know you're telling the truth?'

'OK. What's the story?'

'Shit! Is this for real? What's the name?'

'Jeez. I read about her.' He clicked the call off.

Now, what do I do? This is big, really big. Too big for a lousy local paper. This is red top time.

But no one will take it without proof.

Better get down there fast, O'Malley. And get it right or your career will be trampled out like a discarded cigarette. And get your butt home now.

Jumping into his car, he drove like he'd just heard his apartment block was on fire. He nearly fell through the front door of his studio flat to get to his wardrobe. He steadied himself. *First, let's see what we're looking for.* He called up Stella's image on his phone and took a screenshot. *Right. Let's play the part properly then.*

He changed into his only suit, brushed his hair and after checking himself in the mirror, headed out again. He stopped by a florist's to pick out a small bunch of flowers then headed to the hospital.

After looking at the main board in the hospital entrance area, he checked Stella's image on his phone. Then summoning up his courage, he followed the signs to the ICU, strutting in as if he owned the place.

'I'm sorry, Sir,' a shrill female voice sounded. Sean turned round. *Shit. What have I done?* 'We don't allow flowers on this ward,' the voice continued.

Sean breathed a big but inconspicuous sigh of relief. He hesitated as Janice came up to him and took the flowers. 'Sorry, I didn't realise.'

'Not been here before then?' asked Janice suspiciously.

'Er, no,' Sean replied, putting on his broadest brogue. 'I'm from the Irish side of the family; haven't been able to get away before.'

'And you've come to see...?' Janice asked.

'Stella. Stella Cary. She's me second cousin, so she is.'

'Over there.' Janice pointed in the general direction of Stella's room.

Sean panicked when he saw the room with two orderlies sitting outside. 'I'll be going there then,' he said.

As he walked towards Stella's room, Peter looked up and glowered at him. 'Haven't seen you before.'

Sean was a little scared. *How do I get past these two?* Through the window in the door, he saw a sleeping blonde woman lying in the bed. *That looks like her, but does she look pregnant? There's all this security. It's not here without good reason. Has to be.* He hesitated, desperate to get an opportunity to take a picture but conscious that Peter was watching him. 'Is there a coffee machine round here? I'm gasping.'

Peter stood up and pointed down the corridor. *Thank Christ for that. There's a window. If I'm really careful...*

Sean walked past the big window to the room, but the curtains were drawn. *Jesus.* He scuttled off down the corridor and bought himself a coffee, taking a few small sips. He practised holding his Smartphone behind the cup then wandered back towards the room. He hovered outside the door and managed to take a photo through the window.

Have I got her? Hell, he's looking at me. 'Aww, she's sleeping. I'll come back later.'

Peter rose like a tigress, protecting her cubs. 'She's in a coma. Are you lying? If you cared about her, you'd know that.'

'Of course I knew,' Sean stuttered. *OMG He's coming for me.* He turned round, dropped the cup and ran, leaving hot liquid flying everywhere.

'Look after her!' Peter shouted at his colleague, but he slipped on the spilt coffee.

With a quick look backwards, Sean took his chance and hid. He sighed with relief from the safety of the Disabled Toilet.

When he reached the relative safety of the outside, Sean leant against a wall, congratulating himself. He examined the photo. It was nearly perfect. *You clever young sod.* He studied the contact list on his phone.

'Not you, you're too small for this. I'm going with the really big fish. The red top.' He made the call. 'Put me through to Stacy, please. I've got a story she's gonna love.'

39

Wednesday 10th April

'Got something nice?' Stella's PA said as she walked into Tim's office.

'Look at this.' He held up the piece of paper he'd been looking at and pushed it towards her. It was an undated A4 sheet. The text had been made of carefully cut letters and words, each stuck down.

She read out, 'STELA CARY YOUR FUCKED NOW YOU STUPID BITCH. That's not very nice. Do you think it's one of our clients' exes?'

'No. It's too... too common for most of our clients and there's the misspelling and the missing apostrophe. I found it stuck to something else in a general file. Probably put there by that useless temp. More likely it's some idiot responding to the news. But there is a small chance it might be connected to us, so I am, reluctantly, going to ring the police. There may be something they can get from this. Fingerprints maybe, or the rag it was extracted from. But first, I do want to know if any recent clients threatened Stella?'

'They all did. She was so bloody good at her job.'

'Any particularly nasty ones? Any that swore at her? Used these words?'

'Gawd, now you're asking. It's been a while since Brandon. But he was pretty sore. She always kept every letter, good or bad. I'll have a look through her files.'

'No, perhaps I should do it. Can you unlock everything and leave the keys on her desk, please? I'll be in there in a minute.'

'Will do.'

Tim entered Stella's domain and stared around the room. *If anyone's going to breach your confidence Stella, it should be me.* He started with a small filing cabinet, where he guessed she kept files from her more difficult clients. It was a practice he had instilled in her from the beginning. The cabinet was locked, but like most people, Stella kept a ready key somewhere. Tim found it on top of a framed photo of the children. 'Let's have a look and see what we've got here. You'll maybe thank me for this one day.'

***

Vera Fontaine sat at her desk, reading through a pile of letters. One letter made her blink. *Not another one.* 'In nineteen ninety-three he put his hand on my knee,' she read out loud, rolling her eyes. *Can't these girls learn how to deal with men? They are meant to be intelligent!*

All the letters were about Robert Cary. It seemed to her that every other female he had taught was now complaining that they had been molested by him. There were no actual rape or even attempted rape allegations, and for that she was thankful. Most were signed and dated, but a few particularly nasty ones were not.

'Thank God he's dead, I hope he rots in hell.'

'I'm glad he can't grope anybody else, the fucking pig.'

'I'll rape your six-year-old you sick cunt, so you know how it feels. I hope you die.'

'Evil, smelly fat old bastard, got what was coming to him.'

Even these Vera could live with. The ones that concerned her the most were those ending, 'And I hold the University responsible for failing to protect me from Robert Cary, and will taking appropriate legal action, and will be seeking compensation for the abuse caused.'

One of those was from Tania Hayes. *It's ironic*, Vera mused. *It's a compliment to our institution that we've turned out students capable of initiating their own cases. Such a shame though, that they'll damage the university itself.*

With a heavy heart, she rang the insurers and forewarned them of the claims that might be forthcoming. Then she went through the letters, sorting them into two piles: signed and unsigned.

Should I tell the police? Vera weighed up the situation. She picked up the phone and rang Karen. 'DS Thorpe? I thought you should know something about Barbara Spinnard. You were at the funeral, so I imagine you've put two and two together.'

'The lovechild?'

'Precisely. I told you I was Rob's executor. After he died, I received some papers from his solicitors. I'm still going through them all. I probably should have mentioned it to you earlier, but it didn't seem relevant then. Before I made Barbara redundant, I had to inform her that there was a problem with the trust fund he was meant to have set up for the child. God only knows what he blew his salary on, but there were no savings and Stella, quite rightly, put the house in her name. I didn't know the full story until recently, but Barbara got a fair sum in redundancy. I believe she took the child and went to stay with some relatives. She doesn't yet know that there's no money for her, but I can see from Rob's correspondence that he promised her at least fifty thousand pounds if he died.'

'Are you suggesting she may have had a motive to kill him?'

Vera scoffed. 'I live in the real world of normal people. It's for you to hypothesise and investigate. I am merely giving you the facts.'

'Thank you. That is interesting.'

'And there's something else...'

'Go on.'

'Letters. Barbara was hiding letters she received about Rob. My secretary discovered them this morning. She didn't hide them very well. Maybe she had other reasons for retaining them. Either way, some are particularly nasty.'

'Thank you, Mrs Fontaine. I'll arrange to get them picked up ASAP.'

***

Clive Evans was done with shouting. No one else cared about who had broken the story. He'd been holed up in his office since early morning and after the initial rumours had been confirmed in print, he didn't dare leave.

He'd always intended to put something *out there*, but in his own time, and that meant when the police were engaged and properly on the case. He'd been too slow off the mark. He couldn't even blame anyone. Helen had told him they'd begun the internal investigation. His phone rang and that meant his PA had put through a call. She'd been fielding them all morning.

'Max.'

'It's not looking good, Clive. They're out to get you. We'll hold them back for as long as we can. I've seen your press release. I see our PR people have emphasised old Tiggle's resignation. His head should be enough. If we're lucky.'

'I need your formal approval for it to be released.'

'Do it. Get it out there. Bad day all round. I'll call by soon.'

Clive picked up the phone and gave the go ahead. Then he waited. Max didn't come.

As the day wore on, he felt the ground slipping under his feet. He rang for the umpteenth time.

'I'm sorry Mr Evans, Mr Billingswood is still unavailable.'

Now there's a surprise. Clive tuned into the news channel on his laptop and soon wished he hadn't. The story was breaking on the programme's strapline. He put his hands to his head when he saw that the Minister for Health was being interviewed.

'I've only just been alerted to this shocking story...' the Minister said, immediately clarifying, '... this *alleged* shocking story. I understand a report is being sent to me now and I will be looking into it urgently. What I can say is that we have put more resources into our NHS than any previous government...'

Clive sighed. He knew the score. *It's absolutely not my fault but I will take the blame for it anyway.* It was his PA who finally delivered the killing blow.

'Sorry, Sir. I've seen an inter-departmental email from Mr Billingswood. Apparently, Helen Reader is now the Acting Deputy Director. Why is Mr Billingswood writing to us about this? Does it mean you're leaving us?'

'Apparently so,' Clive replied. 'It's been nice knowing you. Nice and short.'

40

In the car on their way to Dorset, Harry gritted his teeth and stared ahead. 'Will you ever stop mithering?' he snapped at Molly, cutting her off mid-sentence. 'As I've said a hundred times, she's a good woman. You had no right to do that. But I think she understands how upset you were when you did it. We've got other things to worry about now.'

'I know, Dad. But all those posters about staff assaults...'

Harry shushed her. 'Listen!' He turned the radio up.

'... the woman who has been in a coma since a traffic accident in December is reported to be in a good condition and her unborn child is believed to be unaffected. We cannot confirm rumours about the identity of the woman in question, other than she is believed to be a prominent divorce lawyer...'

Molly grabbed Harry's arm. 'Do they mean our Stella? Ee, Dad! Will anything be right ever again?'

Harry saw a service station sign on the motorway. 'We're pulling in. Find out what's what.'

Over tea, Harry held Molly's hand. 'It were always going to come out, love. Just thank goodness you'll be out of the way.'

Molly frowned. 'Out of the way? What do you mean?'

'Reporters. They'll be bound to be after us, it being in the news an' all. And if that nurse tells them what you did... ee, it's not worth thinking about. I'd better ring Sofia and warn her. You drink your tea, love.'

'But they didn't name our Stella. Surely they won't know her name?'

'They'll know,' he sighed. 'They're already halfway there with a prominent lawyer. They find out everything because people like you and me, love reading the rubbish they print, only this time, it's not someone else, it's us. I'd better ring that lass.' He found a payphone and rang Sofia on her mobile.

'Hello, Mr Baxter. Yes, I have seen the news. The boys are out with their friends, but I will ring them. Laura is next door. Please don't worry. I will talk to Mrs Denning if she is there, but I am sure we will manage.'

'Good lass. I'll be on my way back as soon as we've got there.'

***

Two hours later, Harry pulled up outside Sandra's cottage. Sandra, frowning, opened the door. Pale, with dark circles under her eyes, she was still in her dressing gown and pyjamas. She gave a wry smile when she saw her parents. 'Is this what it takes for you to come and see me? I'll have to lose my husband more often.'

Molly's mouth fell open at the state of the place. 'Where are my grandchildren?'

'With friends. I can't cope with them right now.'

'Well, that's going to change,' Molly said. She looked at Harry. 'Let me make you a bite to eat before you get going.'

Sandra's eyebrows shot up. 'There's a fucking surprise.'

'Let's go in, Sandra, love.' Molly put her arm round her daughter and manoeuvred her into the living room, where she sat on the sofa. Molly cleared enough space for her to sit beside her. 'I thought they didn't know yet. Have they said something?'

Sandra shook her head. 'They said they'd ring today to confirm, but they sounded pretty sure.' Harry came in but remained standing. Sandra looked at him. 'Go on then, fuck off, as usual.'

'Now then lass, enough of that. We don't know for sure about Piers. But haven't you heard the news about our Stella? It's all out and there's nobody to be with those poor kids.'

'So bloody what? They've got that au pair. What have I got Dad? Four kids and only me.'

'I'm staying,' Molly smiled. 'I'll be here for a while. Until we know what's what. Now, what food have you got I can give your Dad?'

Sandra calmed. 'I can manage a ham sandwich … or three?'

'That'll be grand, love.'

After they had eaten, Sandra went upstairs. Molly looked

155

at her husband. 'Ee, what a state she's in, Dad.'

'It'll give you something to do love. We've not spent enough time with the lass. She needs us now. And I'd much rather you were here than there.'

'You're right. At least I can make myself useful here and get to know them kiddies a bit better.'

'Are you talking about me?' Sandra appeared, looking washed and properly dressed.

'Nay lass. I'm on my way. Now you let me know if there's owt you need. Any time.'

'Oh, I will, don't you worry,' Sandra replied.

***

James and Daniel were in the local park playing football with some other children from school. One of James' friends came running up to him. 'Is this your mum?'

James stared at the small grainy image on the boy's phone. He snatched it so he could read it properly. 'COMA WOMAN RAPED IN HOSPITAL' *No, it can't be Mum. There must be some mistake.* 'It's shit!' he shouted, throwing the phone on the ground, oblivious to the other boy's anger. He looked around for Daniel. 'Daniel!' he shouted. 'We have to go home. Now!'

Daniel looked up and shook his head. 'No. I'm staying here.'

James charged over and dragged him away, leaving his friends staring at them both. Daniel broke free at the park gates.

'Leave off, will you? What's going on? Is it Mum?'

'Can't tell you here,' James replied, frowning.

'It is Mum... She's dead, isn't she?'

James shook his head. 'Come on.'

The boys ran all the way home, but before they got to the end of their drive, they could see a melee of people hanging around their front door, many with cameras.

'The kids!' someone shouted and all faces turned towards them. Cameras flashed and snapped away as James, holding Daniel by the arm, pushed his way through. He wrestled with his blazer pocket to get out his key and put it in the front door.

'How's your mother? Did the rapist wake her up?'

'How will you feel with a rapist's child as a brother or sister?'

The door suddenly opened from the inside and James and Daniel tumbled in, nearly knocking Sofia over. A foot appeared in the doorway. James kicked it until it moved then he put all his weight behind the door and pushed it shut. He stood for a minute, back to the door, breathing heavily.

'What's happening?' Daniel looked at Sofia. 'What did they mean? What's a rapist?'

'Come in, boys. I'm so sorry this has happened. Your Grandfather will be back very soon. Can I get you some food?'

'Yes please,' Daniel said.

'Not hungry.' James ran upstairs. He watched the horde below out of his bedroom window.

Two minutes later, Sofia knocked on his bedroom door. 'James?'

'Leave me alone.'

'But are you OK, James?' she asked.

'Yes. Go away.'

An hour later, there was another knock on his door.

'James? It's Grandpa here. I'm so sorry, lad.'

After a moment, James opened the door a little and still crying, grabbed Harry in an enormous hug. 'What happened, Grandpa?' he spluttered. 'Who would hurt Mum like that?'

'Aye lad, it's a terrible thing. We don't know but we've got the best police in the world on it and I'm sure they'll find out.'

'I'm going to help them,' James said. 'I'm going to do everything I can.'

'Good lad.' Harry hugged him. 'That's the spirit. We must all do what we can. What's that game you play? The one with all the cars?'

'Mario Karts? Want a go?'

'Aye, lad. Happen you can teach me.'

'Come on then,' James said, smiling now as he tugged at Harry's sleeve. 'Let's see how good you are.'

41

In the ward, Gwen sat at her desk, still in her own personal turmoil. *What if it was my child?* She had asked herself that time and time again and always came up with the same conclusion. *I'd have hit me too.*

When Janice arrived, she found Gwen staring into space.
'You can't carry on like this, Gwen. You have to talk to someone. HR. I'm going to ring them now, if you won't.'

Gwen nodded and made the call. She was immediately summoned upstairs and ushered into an interview room. It was clear that the HR Manager had already been advised of what had happened.

'We can bring charges,' she said.

'No. I couldn't face that. Not now. That poor family, they've been through enough.'

The HR Manager nodded. 'That's entirely up to you, Gwen. It sounds to me like you're suffering from stress. Go home now and get yourself checked over as soon as you can.'

'I've already seen my GP. He said the same thing, that I shouldn't be at work. Tell me, do you think I am a risk?'

'Only you can judge Gwen, but if you have to ask, I'd say you should go home now.'

'Then I'll go. I can see now that I might put the patients in danger and that would only make matters worse for everyone. I'll be back as soon as I can.'

'Good. Yes, you take it easy, Gwen.'

'But how will you cope?'

'There's always temporary staff, from the agency. Don't you worry.'

'But...'

'We'll manage, Gwen.'

Gwen returned to the ICU ward and stood in the doorway of Stella's room, between the two recently arrived Security Guards. She noted Stella's curtains were also drawn all the way round. *No more photographs in the paper at least*. She turned around and walked out of the ward, wondering whether she could ever face coming back again. She didn't see Peter's haunted face, watching, still clutching the card Karen had given him.

***

Sergeant Julia Atkins was amazed at the outside improvement to Sandra's house where she could hear the sound of children playing in the back garden. Even more so when she stepped inside.

'We've been busy,' Molly explained, walking over to Sandra. She held her daughter's hand tight.

'Mrs Atkins, I'm afraid it is bad news. The man we found was your husband.' Julia watched Sandra's grip tighten on her mother's hand, but otherwise, she was composed.

'I knew it must be,' Sandra responded. 'Tell me the details.'

Julia was pleased to see there was a choice of places to sit. She perched on a chair. 'As you know, we found Mr Atkins' body locked in a shipping container in the Harwich Docks.'

'How long had he been there? How did he get locked in?'

'We don't know. We think that he might have been trying to get to Europe, but unfortunately picked the wrong container.'

'Yes. That makes a sort of sense. What a horrible way to die, all alone.' Sandra said.

'Can you give me any idea of where he was going and why, Mrs Atkins? Is there anybody who would try to hurt him?'

'He was always going off somewhere or another. But no. He didn't have any enemies that I knew of.'

'You said you last saw him on the twentieth of December. Do you think his leaving was anything to do with the letter he received?'

'From his mother? I don't think so. It looked old to me. He'd torn off the top, so I only found her address. He went to see her. He got there, she told me he'd been. Then said she told him to eff off, to go see his father's family. I don't know what happened after that.'

159

'May I have her details?'

'Sure. I made a note in my address book.' Sandra went out.

Molly seized the opportunity to talk to Julia. 'Who tells his mother? You or us?'

'We have an obligation to inform her. But I have no objections if Mrs Atkins wants to talk to her too,' Julia said.

'No way,' Sandra said, emerging showing the book to Julia. 'Not that cow.'

Julia noted the details. 'What about Mr Atkins' father?' Julia asked.

Sandra frowned. 'Apparently, he was called Nicholas Westbury, or something like that and he's dead. His mother told me that.' Molly blinked at the mention of the name.

'Thank you. There's one thing more I need to tell you, Mrs Atkins. Your husband's body will be released shortly. You are free to make any arrangements you feel appropriate.'

Sandra gasped as if it had finally hit home. 'He did say something about his funeral,' she said. 'Thank you.'

Julia walked to the front door with Molly close behind. She whispered, 'you don't think it's murder, do you? That would be too hard to bear. There's been enough tragedy in my family without all this.'

'If there's something suspicious about his death, we'll find it, don't you worry about that.' Julia replied.

***

Molly returned to find the room had been returned to near chaos. Sandra had emptied drawers and pulled books and papers out of the bookcase. 'I swear I saw it somewhere. His funeral...'

'Gracious. I'll put the kettle on.' Molly didn't get far into the kitchen before she heard Sandra squealing. But this was with delight. 'What is it, love?'

Sandra waved some papers in the air. 'Guess what?' Molly shook her head. 'He wanted a humanist funeral and guess what else?'

'Spit it out, lass.'

'He had life insurance! Poor, mad, disorganised, broke Piers actually did something right for once. Fifty grand. And listen to this...' She pulled out a handwritten letter from the pile on the sofa. 'Dear Squidgy, if you're reading this it means that I'm dead. I've been a rubbish husband I know, never done anything much to look after you or provide for you and the Squidglings. But if I'm not around, I want to make sure you've got enough money to buy that shit-heap we live in, so you've got a roof over your head. Love you, Poo. Kiss kiss kiss.'

Molly was flabbergasted. 'Dear God, please let him have kept the premiums up to date,' she muttered.

42

Karen's self-confidence, never far away, returned before she met with Helen Reader.

'Hello Sergeant. The Chair of the Trust has asked me to be the liaison between us to keep things simple. If you'd like to follow me to my office, I think I've got everything covered. The ward staff have all been briefed to expect you too.'

'Good,' Karen turned to Macy, now in plainclothes. 'Macy, you start interviewing all the ward nurses. Get their names, anything they know, saw or heard. I'll ask for all the staff rotas, so we know we've got everybody.' Macy nodded and moved off.

Karen followed Helen into her office and sat opposite. She got straight to the point. 'Can you do an amniocentesis test? We need to obtain a sample of DNA to help us identify the rapist.'

Helen shook her head. 'Amniocentesis has a risk of spontaneous abortion associated with it. We can't do it without the consent of the mother, and as you know she's not able to consent.'

'Don't women of Stella's age have it routinely these days?'

'When they've been fully informed of the risks and what the outcome might mean for them, yes. Some do decide to go ahead.'

'Can't her parents give consent?'

'I don't think we have a protocol for that. But in any case, for a woman in a coma, such a procedure might endanger the patient's life.'

'Can you ask her parents?'

'It's not a simple thing to ask. It's incredibly complicated and it's never happened here before. Probably anywhere, so it's uncharted territory.'

Karen frowned and looked at her notebook. 'Can I ask you something a bit more anatomical?'

'Of course.'

'How easy would it be for a man to do it. I mean, wasn't she catheterised?'

'The urethra sits above the vagina. The catheter is quite secure; you'd only have to move the tube out of the way.'

Karen paused. 'What about observations? If she was agitated at all. Would they pick it up?'

'Any increase in heart rate would have been spotted. I've looked at the notes, and there was something detected on the thirty-first of December, but it's been attributed to an incident in the ward when Mrs Cary was moved to her previous room.'

'What sort of incident?'

'Her mother was extremely distressed when Mrs Cary wasn't in her usual room. She was very loud. She's quite an emotional character. She...'

'She what?'

'Nothing. Sorry.'

'What about her bedding or clothing being disturbed?'

'Patients in comas often make involuntary movements. I expect someone would have simply straightened it.'

'OK. Can we talk about security?'

Helen nodded. 'There are entry procedures for access to every ward. And CCTV covering ninety per cent of the corridors. I've got a room organised for you to view everything.'

Karen was impressed. 'Good. I'm working on the basis that if Mrs Cary was assaulted, it's most likely to have been at night. Is that a reasonable assumption?'

'Almost certainly. There are so many more people around during the day. If there's an emergency, naturally people get diverted but there was nothing severe over the Christmas and New Year period. It was exceptionally busy, though.'

'Are you saying the wards might not have been functioning quite as well as usual?'

Helen frowned. 'ICU is strictly one-to-one care twenty-four-seven. But the staff have to do what's physically possible. Being completely honest, things can go wrong.'

'Thank you. I would have been suspicious if you'd said anything different. How do you know who is going in and out of the ICU?'

'We don't... Didn't. We've put in new measures today. Security in hospitals has always been a reactive thing.'

Karen frowned. 'Why?'

'Years ago, it was unheard of for patients and visitors to attack a member of staff. Now it happens all the time, so we've increased security staffing. It's like when we had a baby snatched the first time. And drugs were always kept reasonably securely but became targets for drug addicts and petty criminals, as did our IT equipment...'

Karen gaped. 'I see.'

'In poor Mrs Cary's case, we couldn't have anticipated such an attack. We can't put a guard outside every patient's bed - we don't have the resources. Now this has happened, we will *have* to find ways of making all our patients safe. But it's another cost in a decreasing budget. And there will be shockwaves through the whole NHS over this.'

'And there could be copycat rapes too,' Karen added, sadly. 'Can I have all the staff rotas for the evening and night shifts from the thirteenth of December till the seventh of January?'

'I have it electronically. I can email it to you now if you like.'

'Yes please.'

Helen tapped on the keyboard, frowned and tapped harder.

'Something wrong?'

'Excuse me,' she said, picking up the phone. 'Hello? IT? Can you check something for me? Screen ACUR oblique four zero one. I can't seem to find any records before the first of April.' She smiled weakly at Karen and carried on the conversation. 'What? Isn't it backed up?'

Karen held back her own smile. *It's either incompetence or it's an inside job.*

Helen leaned forward. 'Between you and me, I've been suspicious about our IT for a long time. We have so many guest logins allowed.'

'Do you mean anybody could have deleted that data?' Helen nodded. 'But it would have to be someone proficient with IT, surely?'

Helen sighed. 'No. Everybody has basic IT training these days.

There is a library of IDs of all ward and security staff you can access. Unfortunately, there are a lot of them. Especially agency staff.'

'Well then. We'd better take a look at the CCTV. I hope that is secure?'

Helen stood up. 'I double-checked this morning. This way, Sergeant.'

Macy was waiting outside the door. 'We've got a possible witness,' she whispered.

Karen's eyes widened. 'To the rape?'

'No, it's someone who may have heard something.'

'Ah. OK. In the meantime, we've got some films to watch. You'd better join us.'

Helen led them further along the corridor to a small room, set up with a projector fed by a laptop. 'I'll leave you to it,' she said.

43

'I'm Andy,' the young, casually dressed and clean-shaven technician said. 'I've got our data on here.' He tapped a few buttons on his keyboard and a frozen image appeared on the big screen. 'This is outside the ICU. It's at the end of the corridor, so it captures all movements. Helen told me to concentrate on the night shift, so these are all clips from ten pm till six am.'

'That's good,' Karen said. *Impressive even*.

Andy continued. 'Ordinarily, I'd expect to see a Security Officer walk this corridor up to here.' He pointed at the screen. 'Then turn round again. There's no need to go in. They should do this every half hour. I suggest we fast-forward and stop when we see somebody.'

'So,' Karen said. 'If somebody snuck in there before ten we wouldn't capture them then, but they'd have to have been there all night?'

'Exactly,' Andy nodded. 'I've added ten minutes either side in case someone comes in or out with the staff shift change.'

'Excellent! Let's get going. From the twenty-fourth of December please.'

Andy ran the film covering several nights, stopping it each time he saw a figure in the corridor. There were many visitors, mainly couples. A few times there were drunken-looking characters, but they were quickly escorted out. Andy could identify most of the others from personal knowledge.

Macy, who had been fascinated watching the footage, noted each one. 'Hang on,' she said, pointing at the screen at a bearded visitor. 'There's something about that one.'

'Can you take a picture?' Karen asked.

'Sure.' Andy pressed a button and after some clunking noises, an image sprang from the printer. Macy collected it, resisting the urge to study it.

'Carry on, until he comes out again.' Karen said. 'There he is. What was that? Eleven fifty to five past twelve? Fifteen minutes?

OK, carry on again.'

Andy continued with the film until they saw a partial grainy image of a bearded man in uniform, right at the edge of the screen. Whoever it was seemed to disappear into the ICU. Andy re-ran the film but couldn't get a good picture.

'Well?' Karen looked at Andy. 'Who's that?'

'Agency staff. I'm positive he's not permanent. I'd know.'

'Play the tape. Let's see how long he was in there.'

Andy ran the film at six times speed. The figure emerged eight minutes later, but looking down, away from the camera. 'He might have been having a chat with one of the nurses,' Andy speculated.

'It's enough time,' Macy commented. 'And he was trying to dodge the camera.'

'Yes.' Karen turned to Andy. 'Is this the same day as the other image?'

Andy read the date from the bottom of the footage. 'Yes. Both January the first.'

'Can you identify who he was from the rotas and get back to us? We'd better carry on looking at the rest.'

* * *

'Well, that was interesting.' Karen turned to Macy as they left the room. 'Who did you think the first one is?'

'I know the face, I'm sure I do. But the name won't come.'

'OK. What have you been up to?'

Macy grinned. 'The Ward Sister, Janice Dugdale said that Gwen Williams is the best person to speak to but she's off sick. Janice normally does the evening shift but wasn't looking after Stella that night. She said it was very busy. She's scathing about agency staff and ranted quite a bit about security. ICU should always be one-on-one care. But there have been quite a few lapses. Then she told me she'd seen people sleeping at their desks at night. She also commented on men all wearing beards these days...'

'And?'

'After she'd finished moaning about her shift over-running, she mentioned that there'd been a few visitors she recognised that evening. She's not sure if they were all coming to see Stella, but she remembered a couple of them.' Macy looked at her notebook. 'Medium height, longish thick grey hair. Sounds like Robert Cary?'

'Cary? Well, that might fit. Unless we've got him all wrong. But wouldn't she know his name?'

Macy shrugged. 'I'm sure she would have said if she knew. And we don't know if he normally came to visit in the evenings.'

'Kids to look after,' Karen agreed.

'There was another man, good-looking, bearded. He could be the man in the picture. And a thin woman.'

'Vera Fontaine? I wonder...'

'Then she mentioned this orderly chap. Peter. She said he was a bit odd.'

'Peter? Yes, Gwen Williams told me about him. He overheard some very useful things. And?'

'And I interviewed him. He's very shy. He caught Robert Cary talking to the consultant about switching Stella's machine off.'

'When was that?'

'He can't remember exactly, other than it made him very angry. But he also overhead another conversation at some point. Another bearded man. He kept talking about the tennis club. He called Stella "darling". But Peter said he had a wife too. Penny somebody.'

'The tennis club? Of course!' It's about time we looked there. Good work, Macy!'

44

The Riverside Tennis Club was poorly named, as there wasn't a river in sight. And since the mysterious disappearance of the sign a year before, nobody cared.

Penny Matthews and Amanda Denning stood head-to-head at the board table, while Iain Matthews began sorting papers.

'Have you seen all that stuff on Facebook?' Penny said. 'All those memes? Shocking.'

'Twitter's worse,' Amanda countered. 'I've seen at least two spoof Stella accounts.'

'And someone's organised a protest outside the hospital.'

'The NHS is really going downhill.' Amanda nodded.

'How is the family coping?' Penny asked. 'I'm still shocked about Rob.'

Amanda sighed deeply. 'Yes, that was too awful.'

'I've often wondered about you and him,' Penny ventured. 'Was there...?'

'Of course not!' Amanda snapped. Then she gave a little smile and softened her tone. 'But there might have been, one day.'

'He never made a pass at me,' Penny added. 'Not that I would ever dream...'

'He did have a bit of a reputation. And remember that woman at the funeral?' Amanda paused. 'What about...' she nodded her head in Iain's direction. '... and Stella? Anything in that?'

Penny stiffened. 'I'd have known if anything was going on. I always thought there was something between her and your ex, actually.'

'Edward? I doubt it but he did seem to be very interested in Stella's condition. He came round to see me a few weeks back.'

'I remember. New Year's Eve. He left a few minutes before I arrived, didn't he? You never told me that, though. And nothing would surprise me about *her*,' Penny scowled.

'I liked her,' Amanda said. 'But I was disappointed she wouldn't help with my divorce.'

'She was a class-A bitch!' Penny spat.

'Is,' Amanda corrected. 'And her poor parents... Shush. Jan's here.' Both women looked around to see the slight, short-haired woman come in. 'She reminds me of a greyhound,' Amanda sniped.

'Evening.' Jan Price came to join them.

'Ladies!' Iain clapped his hands. 'The meeting?'

Penny took her place to Iain's right at the head of the table and put on her executive reading glasses. Amanda was joined by Jan Price, while Fabian Denson, the Tennis Coach strolled in and sat opposite Iain.

'Shall we start?' Iain looked around the table.

'Are we quorate?' asked Fabian, out of habit.

Penny Matthews looked at him over her spectacles. 'Yes. We are.'

He winked at her. She blushed.

Iain opened the proceedings. 'Minutes of the last meeting... Thirtieth December 2012. Absent: Robert Cary and Fabian Denson.' The committee members turned the pages of the notes in front of them. 'Any comments?'

Amanda put her hand up. 'Well, only to say how sad it is that we've lost another member since that meeting.'

'That's in AOB,' snapped Iain. 'Minutes approved. First agenda item. Refurbishment. Jan, would you like to update us, please?'

Jan Price sat up straight. 'Good progress, as I hope you have all seen. Luckily the carpets we bought were fitted before...' she faltered. 'It wasn't so lucky for that poor man. That dreadful accident.'

Iain butted in. 'Jan, we've been through this before. The carpets were *donated* to us, remember? Tom Westbury merely gave us some informal advice about what to get and where. What's been achieved since then?'

'Um...' Jan was thinking what to say. 'The painter says he can't start on the outside until the end of this month. He's still working on the sign and we've picked the colours for the walls, now.'

'So, bugger all?' said Iain, impatiently.

'Bugger all,' Penny repeated

'That is not for minuting.'

'Sorry, dear.'

Iain sighed. 'Item two. Club membership. Fabian, over to you.'

Fabian, toned, tanned and with gleaming white teeth sprang into action and distributed the small pile of papers he had been fiddling with since he sat down. 'I got on it as soon as I was back. These are the flyers we agreed. They've gone out to all the appropriate neighbourhoods in the vicinity. And we've had agreements to put them up in The Bull, The Garden Restaurant and even a few private doctors' rooms.' The others nodded their approval. 'We've had twenty-three enquiries, five membership applications and three bookings for lessons,' he announced proudly. 'And Wimbledon is still to come.'

'It's not exactly a mad rush though, is it?' Iain sniped.

'It's a jolly good start,' Penny said, conscious of her husband's eyes burning into the back of her neck.

Iain moved on. 'Any other business? I have an item so I will start if I may?' The others nodded.

'The committee would like to reflect on the sad loss of our member Stella Cary's husband, Robert Cary. Although not a tennis player himself, we all met him on several occasions and he always paid his membership on time. And made a most generous donation recently.'

'I think you'll find it was Stella's money,' Fabian said.

'Anything else?' Iain looked around, challenging them. Everyone shook their heads. 'Meeting closed then.'

As the others gathered up their papers, Penny re-joined Amanda. 'You were telling me about the family...?'

'It must be so hard for them,' Amanda said. 'Especially with all the publicity. But their grandparents are around. He's all right. Not sure about her.'

***

Iain was in the gents. He squirmed as Fabian stood right next to him. 'How are you doing, now...?'

'I'm fine.' Iain snapped.

'I had no idea...'

'There's nothing to know.' Iain zipped up.

'Penny still doesn't know about you and...?

'I said...'

'I rather fancied her myself. After all, I have a lot to offer.' Fabian glanced downwards.

'Tan's faded, Fabian. Better top yourself up if you still want to attract the ladies.' Iain strode out to where Penny was waiting for him. They walked to the car together.

'I wish we could afford a decent car, for once,' Penny whined. 'Stella had a Porsche.'

'And look what happened. This car's a good little runner, a bargain and it looks well enough. And if it does break down, I might even let you look under the bonnet.'

'I did, dear. It's fine. I wish we could afford a holiday too,' Penny sighed. 'People who run tennis clubs normally have money.'

'Then you should've married somebody with money. If it hadn't been for that stupid torn ligament, I'd have won all the grand slams and be worth millions. OK, maybe not the millions they get these days, but enough. I might even be coaching Andy Murray. We can't live on what-ifs. Are you coming or what?'

'I'm sorry, dear.' Penny got in the car and put her hand on his thigh. He brushed it straight off. She began to muse. *Why, oh why did I fall for Iain?*

Because he was absolutely gorgeous. Still is.

Apparently, she thought so too. Bitch.

If only we'd had children.

And now she's pregnant. It should have been me.

She had it all. Looks, money; even her husband was sexy.

But you're tainted goods now, Stella. No one will be interested in you now, even if you do wake up.

'It's so sad,' Penny said. 'This is such a quiet road. How could two people be killed here? I wonder why Stella came this way at all. Surely it's easier to go through town to hers?'

'I expect she was coming to see me,' Iain replied, confidently. 'Committee business. I was hoping for corporate sponsorship.

172

You know we were working together on that.'

'Yes. I knew,' Penny replied.

A deer appeared from nowhere and ran out in front of the car. Penny screamed. Iain slammed on his brakes. The deer ran off, leaping the central reservation barrier with ease. Iain, still breathless, turned to Penny.

'That's how it happens.' He was shaking inside despite his composed voice.

'Poor man,' Penny said, hastily adding, 'Poor Stella.'

Iain steadied himself and drove a little further, before turning off the road and up the long shingle lane to their house.

45

'We've got a major witness we can't interview, the perfect evidence that we can't access and a potentially huge number of suspects,' Karen said. Macy now back in her uniform, nodded sympathetically. 'And on top of all that, I've been sent letters by Vera Fontaine and Tim Strange.'

'About?'

'Letters. Poison pen, threats, all sorts. Mainly about Robert Cary. I've sent the originals to the lab. These are copies.'

Karen sat back. 'Let's prioritise. Start with what we know already.' She looked at the muddled boards, the result of yesterday's late-night scrawl and wiped them clean.

STELLA RAPE
STELLA RTA
WESTBURY RTA
CARY RTA she wrote.

'OK. The rape. What are the reasons for rape? It's normally a power thing but if the victim's unconscious that can't work, can it?'

'Opportunistic?' Macy suggested.

Karen shook her head. 'We know it would have been practically impossible except during the night shift. And we've seen all the CCTV. It would have to have been planned. I'd guess revenge.'

'Who wanted revenge against her, though?'

'Maybe someone wanting revenge for Tania's attempted rape? Or for Tom Westbury's accident? Remember we already think Jim Westbury was trying to pin it on her.' She wrote up **JIM WESTBURY** and underlined it twice.

'Wouldn't her accident be enough of a punishment?'

Karen shrugged. 'Who else hated Stella?'

'Her clients' ex-spouses.'

'Precisely. Look at this.' She handed Macy a copy of the composite letter sent to Spalls.

'That's horrible!' Macy exclaimed. 'No apostrophe.'

'Spalls are searching Stella's files in case there's anything else. But spiteful letter-writers are usually people with nothing better to do. If it's not revenge, or opportunistic...'

'What about love?' Macy said.

'That probably rules out Robert Cary, then. Unless he was having a poke out of habit. But we know he's got form for rape. Maybe he likes it passive. Stella's parents were horrified when I mentioned it.'

'You said that?' Macy's mouth dropped open.

'Not my finest moment,' Karen grinned. 'Who else?'

'I was thinking of the man Peter talked about. The one who kept talking about the tennis club. With a wife called Penny. He seemed to love her. And it might have been him on camera.'

'Yes!' Karen was reanimated. 'Have you remembered who you thought it was yet?'

'I'm sure he was at the funeral. With a very thin woman. And Amanda Denning mentioned they were from the tennis club.'

'You're right. But we don't have all the names yet, do we?'

Macy shook her head. 'We could ask Amanda Denning.'

'There must be something somewhere about that club...' Karen tapped into her laptop.

'Look! There! Take off the beard and what do you think?'

'It's him.' Macy read out, 'Iain Matthews. And look, that's the secretary - Penny Matthews. She was there too.'

'Bingo!' Karen wrote **Iain and Penny Matthews** up on the board. *That's* who the orderly chap was talking about.'

'And Janice.' Macy said.

'Anyone else we should be looking at?'

Macy was staring at another face. 'He wasn't, the Tennis Coach, Fabian Denson. I think I'd remember him.'

'I see what you mean.' Karen nodded, appreciatively. 'Then there's the other bearded chap. What motive? Could be anything. Anyone. We need that staffing info fast.' Karen wrote up **BEARDED MAN??** 'And what about Peter himself. Motive?'

Macy shook her head. 'He seemed to adore her.'

'Love again?' Karen wrote up **PETER??**

'If Iain Matthews was in love with Stella, wouldn't that give Penny Matthews a motive to get rid of her?' Macy suggested.

'For Stella's accident? Nice one, Macy. Do we have their address?' Karen looked at the laptop again and smiled. 'There's an administration address on here. Loxley Lane, it's off the main road. She pointed to the map. 'And look at that. It's very close to the tennis club. I think we should make them our top priority, don't you?' Macy nodded. 'No time like the present, and I could do with some fresh air. Let's go. You can drive. I'm thinking Penny first. Let's hope she's on her own. We know that she can't be the rapist.'

***

'Mrs Penny Matthews?' Karen asked.

'Yes, what's the matter?'

'Detective Sergeant Thorpe and Constable Macy Dodds. Is your husband in? We'd like to ask him a few questions, if we may?'

'He's at work.'

'In which case, we'd like to ask you a few questions, please. It's only routine.'

Penny led them into the house and gestured for them to sit. Macy stared at the photographs on the wall and glanced at Karen when she saw a wedding photo. Iain had a beard.

'We are investigating the sexual assault on Mrs Stella Cary. I understand that you were acquainted with her?' Penny nodded. 'Can you tell us what you were doing on the nights of the thirteenth of December and thirty-first of December last year?'

'Of course. I'll never forget it the thirteenth. That was the night of Stella's accident. Is that relevant to the assault?'

'We are looking into all possibilities, Mrs Matthews.'

'I see. Well, I was at college that afternoon. I go with my friend.'

'College?'

'Oh, nothing important. I was getting bored with work and my friend wanted to do flower arranging.'

'What do you do work-wise?'

'I've got a little part-time job at a dairy.'

'Oh. I see. And on the thirty-first of December?'

'Strangely, I was with the same friend again that night.'

'And who was that?'

'Amanda Denning.'

'Ah. Good. Mrs Matthews, can you think of anyone who might wish to harm Mrs Cary?'

Penny shook her head. 'I didn't know her *that* well.'

'Where was your husband on those dates?'

'Iain was at home. Both times.'

'We will need to speak to him too. Where does he work?'

'At the Biscuit Barrel factory.'

'Thank you, Mrs Matthews. That will be all for now.'

46

Karen spoke as soon as they were safely out of earshot. 'We know Amanda Denning wasn't at college that day. She didn't mention that, did she? Where was Penny? Was she really at college?'

'I'm positive that's the same man as the one on the CCTV footage,' Macy added. 'I saw the wedding photo. He had a beard then.'

'Good. We'll know for sure in a mo. Of course, she'll have warned him now.' Karen paused. 'Are there any cases of love-coma-rape things going on? Is it a known psychological thing?'

'Not that I've heard. But I bet there's some professor or another who can give it a name,' Macy replied.

'Like necrophilia,' Karen joked. 'Dead boring,' she chuckled. Macy frowned, then burst out laughing. She was still giggling when she drove up to the factory entrance and showed her ID to the man in the cabin.

'Here to see Mr Iain Matthews.' The barriers lifted.

As they walked up to the factory, Karen sniffed the air 'Ahhing' like a Bisto kid.

The receptionist was ready for them. 'Mr Matthews will be right down. Can I get you a tea or coffee?'

'What's your coffee like?' Karen asked. The receptionist's face gave her the answer. There was a water dispenser in the corner. 'This'll do. Macy?' Macy nodded and both women sipped at their paper cups, until a red-faced Iain Matthews appeared.

'Detective Sergeant Thorpe and Constable Dodds. We'd like to ask you a few questions about Mrs Stella Cary. Is there somewhere private we can go?'

Iain looked over at the receptionist.

'Meeting room one is free. I'll book it out for you,' she said.

'Thanks.' Iain led the way. 'You were at Rob's funeral, weren't you?' He said to Macy as he led the way to a small meeting room at the front of the building.

'Yes,' Macy replied, with restraint.

They sat down and Karen began. 'What was your relationship with Mrs Cary?'

Iain visibly paled. 'She was... is a member of my tennis club,' he replied. 'I've known her for about six years. She joined after she had a baby and wanted to get back into shape.'

'Mr Matthews. We have reason to believe that your relationship was closer than simply colleagues at a club.' Karen gave him her intense look.

'What? Have you been speaking to that idiot, Fabian?' he blurted out.

'Not yet Mr Matthews. Why? What do you think Fabian would have said to us?'

Iain put his head in his hands. 'He thought I was having an affair with Stella... Mrs Cary,' he muttered. 'It's complete tosh.'

'Why would he think that Mr Matthews? If it wasn't true?' Iain was silent. Karen persisted. 'Mr Matthews, have you ever had a sexual relationship with Stella Cary?'

'No, I have not.'

'Mr Matthews, we have a witness who says otherwise.' Iain's eyes began to water. 'Mr Matthews. Can you answer the question, please? When did you last see Stella Cary?'

Iain was beginning to perspire. He fiddled with his shirt collar. 'In hospital. I can't remember when.'

'Could it have been on or around New Year's Eve?'

'What? I don't know. Let me think. I did have to go out that night. I had to see someone...'

'Mr Matthews, is this you?' Karen showed him the CCTV image.

'What? How did you...' Iain crumpled into his chair. 'Please don't tell my wife, will you?'

'Mr Matthews, if you have done no wrong there is nothing to tell. I do have to ask you this. Have you had sexual relations with Mrs Stella Cary at any time since the thirteenth of December?'

Iain looked up, beads of sweat on his brow. 'What? Are you asking what I think you're asking?' He stood up and pointed at Karen. 'That's disgusting. Do you really think I would take advantage of a woman in that condition?'

Karen stalled, momentarily taken aback.

Macy jumped in. 'Mr Matthews,' she asked. 'Do you know if Mrs Cary was having a relationship with anybody else?'

'Of course not. She wasn't that sort of woman.'

'But she was the sort who would have an affair with a married man?' Macy retorted.

Iain sat down again. 'It was different. She loved me. She wanted my child. She'd have left that moron, if...'

'Mr Matthews,' Karen interrupted. 'Where were you on the night of the thirteenth of December, the night of Stella's accident?'

'I was at home.'

'And where was your wife?' Karen asked.

There was a pause. 'I was on my own,' he said, sullenly. 'Stella was coming to see me that night. Club business. Penny knew she was coming. She was at college. You can ask her *that* if you must.'

Macy began to wriggle a little. 'What about the night of January the second?'

Iain frowned. 'The day Rob was killed? I was at home. With Penny.'

'But could he have been coming to see you?'

'No. He'd have rung first.'

'Was he aware of your relationship with his wife?'

'What?'

'Could he have tried to kill her?'

'No.'

'Was he trying to kill you?'

'No. That bastard couldn't give a hoot about poor Stella.'

'But you wanted him out of the way?'

Karen and Macy exchanged glances. Macy rummaged in her bag.

'What? That's insane.'

'Mr Matthews, I must ask you to give a DNA sample please, for purposes of elimination.' Iain grunted what Macy assumed was a 'yes'. She took out a kit from her bag and swabbed the inside of his cheek.

When she'd finished, Karen stood up. 'Thank you, Mr

Matthews, that will be all for now. We may need to talk to you and your wife again.'

The two women left the factory and Karen was complimentary. 'You're getting good at this.'

Macy smiled. 'I'm sure Cary was going to see him too. Why else go that way?'

'Yes. But is he the rapist? They wanted a child together. But would he go that far? He'd know we'd find out that it was rape but maybe he'd have thought she would be happy to have another child and let it go. Let's get back and assess. We'll go via the lab and drop off the sample.'

47

Back at the office, Karen was thinking out loud. 'I think we're missing a trick here with Penny Matthews,' she said to Macy. 'She doesn't come across as being particularly bright, or vindictive, but her job is really interesting.'

'The dairy?' Macy looked puzzled. 'Why?'

'Because I was reading all about the dairy industry the other day.'

'And?'

'Do I have to spell it out? How do they produce milk?'

'From cows,' Macy replied.

'From impregnated cows.' Karen corrected. 'The cows have to be pregnant and produce calves before they can produce milk.' She nodded slowly at Macy to catch up.

'You mean...'

'Yes. She could have artificially inseminated Stella.'

'With bull semen?' Macy looked aghast.

'No, you idiot. Human semen.'

'Ah. Got you. But why?'

'I don't know. Maybe she thought Iain would go off Stella if she'd been sleeping with someone else. Who knows? She probably didn't think the dates through. The point is, we're not necessarily looking for a rapist now.'

'Fuck! You mean anybody could have artificially inseminated her?' Karen's shock at her use of the f-word was obvious. 'Sorry.'

Karen laughed. 'Or not fucked,' she quipped. 'It makes a sort of sense. It could be done much more inconspicuously I imagine. A careful and knowledgeable hand under the blanket...' She wrote up **Artificial insemination by turkey baster. Penny Matthews** under **CARY RAPE**. Then it was her turn to swear as another thought struck her.

'Fuck! Is it even rape if it's with a turkey baster?' Both women laughed. 'We need to do some research to see if it's ever been done before.'

Macy grinned. 'I'm impressed you know what a turkey baster is.'

'I've heard the term,' Karen replied. 'But that's not what I meant by research.'

'And how would we even begin to look at that one without DNA?' Macy said.

Karen nodded. 'Agreed, it's a toughie. And talking of DNA, can you chase up the lab about the letters? I'm going to give Spalls a ring, right now.'

Macy moved to another desk to make her call, while Karen was put straight through to Tim.

'Yes, Sergeant. Tim Strange here. How are you getting on?'

'We're moving forwards,' Karen replied. 'But not quickly enough. I wondered if you had found anything further since our last conversation about the letter?'

'No,' Tim replied. 'But there was something odd in her filing system.'

Karen's ears pricked up. 'Odd? What do you mean?'

'Stella was meticulous in everything she did. Of course, we all occasionally need to keep things private, but the house rules insist that somebody always has knowledge of all files at all times.'

'Are you saying something was missing?'

'Yes. How can I explain it…? There was an empty space where a client's file should be.'

'Who was the client?'

Tim huffed. 'I don't know. It wasn't there, was it?'

'Sorry,' Karen said.

'I could speculate but I'll keep that to myself for now. There could also be a perfectly good reason for the file being out of place. I'll be in touch directly if I find either the file or anything about it.'

'Thanks.' As she put the phone down, Karen overheard the tail-end of Macy's call to the lab about Iain Matthews' swab. She waited for the call to finish.

'So, we've got his DNA but no match?' she asked.

Macy nodded. 'There's nothing on the database.'

Karen sighed. 'If only we could test that baby. And the hospital still hasn't sent the rotas through yet. I thought that woman, Helen Reader was more reliable than that.'

'I expect she's having a nightmare too,' Macy said.

Karen gave her a non-committal look. 'I think we should bypass them and get straight on to the agency. We've got their details. Let's check on everyone who was engaged from the thirteenth of December to the seventh of January.' Macy was looking thoughtful. 'What?'

'Not the rape, but Robert Cary's accident. Amanda Denning, remember? I'm sure she was going to tell us something at the funeral.'

'Yes. Good.' Karen wrote **Amanda Denning** on the **CARY RTA** board. 'And talking of funerals, there's the Tania incident,' she added. 'She couldn't have done it herself if she was abroad, but she might have arranged something. Barbara Spinnard said a youth made threats against Robert Cary.'

Macy nodded. 'Yes, and she was angry with him, too.'

'Vera has hinted that she was expecting a legacy when he died. But then again, she seemed to be genuinely upset at his funeral. She's also just lost her job and apparently abroad at the moment, so we'll probably have to track her down if nothing else comes up. We need to set up some interviews ASAP.'

'Agreed.' Macy nodded, enthusiastically

'Is there anyone else we should be talking to at the tennis club?'

'Let me have a look.' Macy called up the website on her laptop. 'Mmm, Fabian Denson and there's a Jan Price named as the administrator.'

The door opened unexpectedly. 'Karen?' DCI Winter's voice boomed into the room. 'I need you. Now.'

Karen looked at Macy. 'Agency. And tennis club. Quickly, before Harris sees you and sends you somewhere else.'

Karen joined an agitated DCI Winter in the corridor. 'What is it?'

'Hurry!' he shouted.

48

The National Police Chiefs' Council was formulating new policies and priorities to assuage public concerns about hospital security, but for DCI Winter it was personal. It hadn't helped that Chief Constable Burns had ordered him to go. He was already planning to take charge, but the moment was lost. 'Yes, Sir,' he'd said. Sounding and feeling like a lackey.

Now he had to face the journalists, hospital staff, journalists, news cameras and anyone else that happened to be around.

Bracing himself, he stood outside the hospital in a designated area, with Karen at his side. He coughed to clear his throat, then spoke to the awaiting crowd.

'Good afternoon, ladies and gentlemen. I would like to give you an update with regard to our investigations into the alleged sexual assault of patient, Mrs Stella Cary. Our enquiries are ongoing and we are devoting significant resources in order to find the perpetrator and bring him to justice. May I assure members of the public that no stone will remain unreturned in our pursuit of our aim. We are pleased that the national debate about how society best protects its citizens in hospitals everywhere has now begun. And we will feed in our recommendations to the debate.' He knew it wouldn't be enough and waited for the onslaught.

'How do the police intend to protect other coma patients in the country?'

'Are you charging the hospital with criminal negligence?'

'Have you got any suspects yet?'

'What are you doing about the internet trolls?'

Karen fidgeted, bursting to talk. DCI Winter glared at her. He held up his hands to quieten the gathered throng and continued.

'Patient security is a matter for individual hospitals to consider. We are always ready to advise on security issues. Consideration will be given to all issues arising from this tragic case in due course. Our sympathies are with the family and friends of Stella Cary. I have nothing further to add at this time.'

DCI Winter shouldered through the people who had gathered behind him, ignoring the particularly pushy journalists who clung to his coat-tails and flashed cameras in his face. A door opened and he went back inside the hospital to regroup after the ordeal.

Karen followed a few bodies behind muttering, 'that was shite.'

***

Catching up with DCI Winter, Karen saw that Helen Reader was waiting for them in a corridor just off the main entrance. She led them to a small room at the end.

'And how *is* the investigation going?' Helen asked.

DCI Winter looked at Karen. 'Over to you.'

Karen took his cue. 'We're making slow progress. We've identified several possible suspects, but as you know, Ms Reader, we still haven't got all the records yet.'

Helen blinked. 'I have been pushing them. It's complicated.'

'What about the amniocentesis. Any decision yet?'

'No, not yet. I'll chase both for you. Actually, I'll get on to it now. Please stay as long as you need.' Helen left the room.

DCI Winter turned to Karen. 'We can't set any hares running, Karen. We have to be careful.'

'I suppose.'

There was a knock at the door. Helen reappeared, but turned to speak to someone outside. 'You wait here a moment.'

'Who's that?' DCI Winter asked.

'It's Stella Cary's son. James Cary. He wants to talk to you.'

DCI Winter frowned. He looked at Karen. 'That's your department. I'm going back now. I'll see you later.' He left the room muttering, 'Excuse me,' to the gawky young lad now standing in the doorway.

'Come in, James. What can I do for you?'

Helen stepped back in and James sat down, looking both determined and nervous. 'Are you DS Thorpe?' Karen nodded. 'It's about all these people.' He held out his phone. 'I want you to do something about them.'

'Show me,' Karen said. James stood close to her and took out his phone. He pulled up pages and pages of obscene messages.

Karen looked at them with increasing anger. 'That's terrible, James. Awful.'

'But can you do anything?' James said. 'Can't you catch them and lock them up?'

'Unfortunately, it's not that easy, James. They hide behind false identities. Keyboard warriors, they're called.'

'Yes, I know,' James said. 'It's not that. He might be in here. The one that did it. Can't you investigate them?'

Karen paused, thinking. *He's got a point.* She looked at James. 'Yes, I can do something, but you can too. See if you recognise any of the names or faces in there. I know they're normally fake, but sometimes people mess up. Can you do that for me?'

James nodded excitedly. 'Sure.'

'And you call me if you notice anything at all. OK?' She handed him a card.

'I will.'

Helen waited for James to leave. 'Are you sure that's the right thing to do?'

'He's fourteen and he's a smart kid. My mother died when I was ten. I'd have given anything to have been able to help her. I'm sure.'

49

Friday 12th April

'Tennis club. What have you got?' Karen asked before Macy had even sat down.

'Fabian Denson was abroad for most of the winter. He goes to Florida to coach the British Juniors. He wouldn't be drawn on Iain Matthews's possible affair with Stella and said that Iain had denied it. But we know about it now, anyway.'

Karen nodded. 'Did he come home at all?'

'Yes, for a couple of days in London for a New Year's Eve function. He said he didn't leave the hotel.'

'And?'

'The hotel confirmed his stay, but they obviously don't know all his movements.'

'OK.' Karen said. 'Did you get a swab?'

'Yes, he seemed keen enough, for elimination purposes.'

'Good. But we need to double-check he didn't leave the hotel. Where was the function?'

'At the hotel. And I checked that.'

'Good. So we just need to check his other movements. Put it on your list. Anything else?'

Macy nodded. 'Jan Price didn't seem to be interested in anything much except her new carpets.'

'Carpets?' repeated Karen, her eyes lighting up. 'Didn't Tom Westbury do carpets?'

'Yes, he did. And I asked her about him. She said she'd used him personally before and asked him for advice about it. But *apparently,* someone gave them carpets as a donation. And fitted them too.'

'Who?'

'She couldn't remember.'

'I bet.' Karen wrote **Tom Westbury??? carpets** under **WESTBURY RTA**.

'What about the agency?'

Macy's face lit up. 'They were a complete shower. The whole place was in disarray. They've lost most of their contracts now. The hospital has engaged a new cooperative instead. All their files were either in archives or about to be archived.'

'Shit. Did you get anything out of them?'

'I persisted,' Macy smiled.

'And?'

'I made them go through all their photo records. Then, of course, I realised that they were looking for the wrong date. It's the start of the shift, thirty-first of December, not the first of Jan.' Karen suppressed a yawn. 'And eventually, they came up with a name. It's Dom West. There was no sign of a file or any records '

'Aren't they meant to have copies of passports?'

'Yes. I've demanded they send us a copy and details of all his references, where he worked, everything.'

'But let me guess, nothing yet?'

Macy looked down. 'I gave them a hard time,' she muttered. 'I told them that they might have let a criminal into the hospital.'

'Fair play,' Karen mused, as the phone rang. 'I'd have said the same.' She took the call. 'WHAT?! Another one?'

'Another what?' Macy was on alert.

'RTA London Road. It's past Knockers Corner. Male. It's on the way to the biscuit factory.'

'Matthews?' Macy speculated.

'Lightning's already struck twice. I doubt it. And I hope not. Or it looks like someone's taking out all our witnesses.'

***

As Karen and Macy pulled up at the scene of the accident, they saw that the fire crew had already extricated the driver from the wreck. Both of them strained to see the driver's face. Eventually, Karen strode over trying to look important. She joined the paramedics who were beginning to move the body into the ambulance. 'I might know who this is.' She peered at the man's face, inwardly sighing. 'Yes. It's Iain Matthews. Iain with two "i"s.

'You know him?'

'Yes. Keep him alive. I have to talk to him.'

'And we have to save him first,' the paramedic snapped.

'You have to let me know if he says anything,' Karen responded, angrily. 'He's an important witness.'

'Stuff her,' said the other paramedic.

'And he's a suspect!' Karen yelled.

While the first one settled Iain in the ambulance and began to check him over, Karen hovered nearby, listening.

'Iain, mate? We're here to sort you out. Hang on in there.'

Iain's eyes opened and he looked at the paramedic. He said one word: 'Stella.'

'Quick! Defibrillator!' The Paramedic shouted and the two of them went straight into the emergency procedures. 'I think we've got him.'

Karen backed away to join Macy. 'Did you hear that? Sounds like he's going to be all right.'

'That's a relief,' Macy said.

'How the hell does this all fit in?' Karen said, leading Macy back to the crash site. They watched for a second as the ambulance sped off towards the hospital. Karen walked over to the Road Scene Manager. 'What about next of kin?' Karen asked. 'I know him and his wife.'

'If you're offering, you're welcome,' came the reply. 'Saves me a job.'

Macy drove them to Penny's house, but despite the presence of an old mini in the drive, when they knocked on the door, there was no answer. A car driving up the lane stopped, and a worried-looking woman wound down the window. 'Can I help?'

'We're looking for Mrs Penny Matthews,' Karen said, holding up her police ID.

'I've just taken her to the hospital. Poor Iain, that's her husband.' Karen nodded. 'He crashed the car. He rang her and told her the ambulance was on its way and to meet him there. It doesn't sound too serious, does it?'

'No, that's good. Very good. Thank you.'

Karen turned to Macy and talked as they walked back to her

car. 'It looked very serious to me but I'm no expert. Let's get back. I'll double-check with the hospital that she's still there. Meanwhile, we might have got some more info in. And I want to get to the lab.'

50

John beamed as Karen came into his office. 'Too early for any reports,' he told her. 'How's Matthews doing?'

'I know that. I was coming about the letters. But I rang the hospital. He's hanging on, critical but stable.'

'Ah yes. The letters. I think I've got something in from my psychologist. Nothing extensive, more of an overview.'

'Tell me.' Karen sat down and smiled.

'Out of the twenty unsigned letters, she detects only six distinct hands at work.' He noted Karen's surprise. 'Apparently, it's common. People like to make out that there have been more cases than there actually are. They send in several. But they can't disguise their style so well.'

'And are these profiles aggressive ones? Like, possible suspects?'

'Probably not. There is one though, that seems a little OTT.'

'The rape threat?'

'Yes,' John said. 'It was directed at his daughter. Look, he, and I'll assume it's he, says **I'll rape your six-year-old you sick...**' he paused '... **c-word, so you know how it feels. I hope you die**. I'm pretty sure it was written by someone who knew the family, or at least that much detail. And, of course, there's the death threat too. Maybe he couldn't get near the child, so he tried to kill Cary instead.'

'Six-year-old,' Karen repeated. 'I wonder how old Catherine is?'

'Catherine?'

'Barbara's lovechild. I'd assumed it was a reference to Laura Cary, but maybe not. It'd have to be someone really close to know that one. Was there any DNA?'

'In addition to the unknown letter writer's, there was a common set of three traces on each one. Obviously, Barbara's, Vera's and her secretary. But whoever wrote that one was clever enough not to leave any trace,' John said.

'How do we find the bastard?'

'That's your department. I can tell you one thing, though.'

'What?' Karen leaned forward.

'I'd speculate it was someone aged between eighteen and twenty-four, but it's quite verbose so it might be someone trying to sound younger. Look, I have to be somewhere now, but would you like to talk later?'

Karen smiled. 'If you insist. My place.'

***

That evening, Karen tidied her flat. She'd already instructed John to pick up a bottle and a takeaway. *He's safe to talk to, already clued up on the case, he's got no motive to wreck my career and he's logical.* The bell rang and she smiled. *I also quite like him.*

'I can't see the wood for the trees,' she said. 'Everything seems to be connected. I was always sure it *was* but now I can't separate it all out. And Iain Matthews is our main rape suspect.'

'What's the latest?' John asked.

'It's fifty-fifty. His wife's there, waiting.' John nodded and topped up Karen's wine glass. 'Everything seems to revolve around that bloody tennis club.'

'At least the accident is straightforward this time.'

'Yes. Macy worked it out. Even I did. And there were witnesses. Someone overtaking, not leaving enough room. Matthews veers out the way, crashes into a tree on the verge. Car's too old for airbags. Bang!'

'Spot on.' John raised his glass in tribute. 'Why was he your chief suspect?'

'He'd been having an affair with Stella.'

'What? You think he'd have sex with her in that state?'

Karen paused; it did sound ridiculous when John said it.

'Maybe. Stranger things. We've got pretty good ID of him at the hospital around the time it happened. He also had a motive for getting rid of Cary. He was definitely in love with her, *and* he talked about her wanting his baby. OK, it doesn't sound so good saying it out loud.'

John grunted in agreement. 'What else have you got on it? Any progress on that letter?'

'Not yet. Barbara Spinnard is away and not answering the phone number we have for her. We do know that her daughter was six when Robert Cary died. As was his daughter Laura.'

'Interesting.'

'We've also got a bearded chap, probably a temporary security bod, not yet fully identified but possibly Dom West. And there's a strange orderly. It sounds like he's in love with Stella.'

'OK. They sound more plausible. Anything else?'

'Iain's wife could have done it. With something - like a turkey baster.'

John made a terrible choking noise and spat out his wine. 'That's even worse!' he spluttered.

'What?' Karen looked horrified for a moment, and then she began to laugh. John joined in. 'OK, OK, it does sound ridiculous when you say it like that. But it is another way she could have become pregnant.'

John was now in fits of laughter. It was infectious. He turned and put his hands on her shoulders. 'Oh, Karen I do love you,' he said, still laughing. Their eyes met, the laughing stopped and they kissed. Karen quickly regained her composure and drew away.

'Now, where were we?' She gave a little cough. 'Yes, there's something else I found out. Ages ago. I put it to one side as there was nothing connected to the rape...'

'What?'

'I'm sure there's some sort of cover-up going on about the Westburys.'

John's eyebrows shot up. 'Really? What makes you say that?'

'I came across some notes belonging to an ex-copper. The pages from the first to the fifteenth of October in 1988 were all cut out.'

'And?'

'Nicolas Westbury died on the fifteenth,' Karen replied.

'But was it in suspicious circumstances?'

'No, apparently not. Cancer. But the guv is always telling me to keep away from the family. I want to know why. Can you help?

I mean, you can probably access things above my pay grade.'

'I doubt it. But for you, I'll try.'

They talked and drank late into the night, until John, reluctantly, looked at his watch. 'It's late. I should be getting back.' Karen glanced towards the bedroom then back at him.

'Is it tidy?' he asked.

'Only one way to find out.' Karen smiled, opening the door to reveal a large brown bear lying on her bed.

John nearly hit the roof. 'Jesus Christ! What's that thing?'

'My onesie,' she laughed.

51

Monday 15th April

Karen sat in the incident room, drinking her first hot chocolate of the day. An overnight stay had turned into almost a whole weekend. She was still savouring the comforting feeling of being intimate with another human being. Something she hadn't done for a long time. She'd also laughed at John's reaction when he wanted a shower the next morning. He was horrified at her complete lack of guest etiquette concerning towels and, more importantly, no offering of breakfast. He made it his mission to take her shopping first to stock up her fridge and later on, to buy some more towels.

'I'm not sharing yours again.' He'd actually wagged a finger at her. 'I'll treat you to a new set.'

She couldn't remember the last time she hadn't spent a weekend working or thinking about work. And she was loving it.

Her good humour didn't last. Finishing the thick chocolaty dregs of her drink, she ventured out to see what had happened to Macy. Another colleague answered her frown as she stood at Macy's desk.

'Harris snaffled her.'

'Bugger Harris.' *It's about time I go to visit Gwen, if Macy can't.*

***

'Good morning, Detective Sergeant.'

'Good morning, Miss Williams,' Karen replied, smiling her vacant talk-to-the-people smile.

'Would you like a cup of tea?' Gwen asked.

'Do you have coffee?'

'Sorry dear, I don't drink it.'

'Then tea would be lovely. Milk, four sugars please.'

Karen gazed around the room as she waited. *Homely little flat,*

not much evidence of family, nursing certificate pride of place.
Gwen came out holding a tray with teacups, teapot, sugar bowl and milk jug. Karen gasped. *A proper tea set.*

Gwen had a lot to say. Karen let her talk uninterrupted for a while. Most of what Gwen said was political with a small 'p'. Scant resources, long hours, too many temporary staff, doctors with not enough time; all peppered with lots of 'in my day' and 'it didn't use to be like that'.

When Karen had heard enough, she looked at her watch, which, as expected, got her subject's attention. 'We need to talk to everybody who worked on the ICU for the whole period from when Mrs Cary first arrived, until the time when she was definitely pregnant. We're still waiting for a complete list of permanent and agency staff from your hospital, but I'm told you know everything about the ward.'

'Well now,' Gwen sat back in her chair. 'There's the cleaners, and the hospital-visiting society, did you know about them?' Karen shook her head and wrote it down. 'Every Tuesday morning. Nice people, a bit God Squad.'

'Not your sort then?'

Gwen smiled and shook her head. 'They mean well. Then there's the school visits...' She carried on as Karen noted all of her comments but mentally dismissed nearly all of them.

'You must have your own suspicions.'

'Only that I don't trust the night staff much. There are too many inexperienced young men and women. When Peter is about, I feel happier because he's taken a shine to poor Mrs Cary, and he likes to think he's protecting her.'

'Yes, we've spoken to Peter,' Karen said. 'What do you make of him?'

'He's a lovely boy. I'm not sure he's all there, but he wouldn't hurt a fly. I've only ever seen him lose his temper once.'

'When was that?'

'When I told him about poor Mrs Cary. He got angry.'

'What happened?'

Gwen pondered. 'It was like he was a different person altogether.'

Karen frowned. 'Was he violent?'

'No, not at all. And he calmed down very quickly.'

'Does he have a car?'

'I'm not sure. I don't think... if you understand me.'

'You mean he's not competent to drive?'

'Something like that,' Gwen agreed.

'Thank you, Miss Williams. If you think of anything else, please let me know.'

'I will,' Gwen replied. 'Do you know, I feel better already. I'm going to ring my GP and see if I can go back to work.' Her face fell.

'Are you all right?'

'There was a bit of an issue. It was Mrs Baxter, you see. She blames me, you know. Of course, she's got a right. The hospital did let her down. But I didn't let her down, I swear I didn't.'

Karen realised that Gwen might be about to cry. She tried very hard to bring out her inner mother. 'You can't possibly think of blaming yourself, Miss Williams. I've seen how hard you and everyone work around the clock. Inevitably there are mishaps. Surely things like this have happened before?'

Gwen nodded. 'Not like what happened to poor Mrs Cary. But yes, things do go wrong. All it needs is for one person to look the other way and heaven knows what could happen. But I did my best. I really did.'

'I'm sure Mrs Baxter knows that, deep down.'

'You may be right. But either way, I'm not sure I'm up to seeing her again, so soon.' Gwen clasped her hands together.

Weighing up her knowledge, Karen spoke. 'I heard she's down in Dorset at the moment.'

'Oh!' Gwen was surprised. 'Are you sure about that?'

Karen nodded. 'I heard it very recently.'

Gwen smiled. 'I do so want to see Stella again. Maybe I'll give Miss Reader a call, then.'

'You do that.' Karen got up and sidled out of the room. 'I'll let myself out.'

52

Harry was in a bad mood. He sat at Rob's desk with his list of calls in front of him. He'd phoned Molly first and she sounded unusually cheerful.

'... And our Sandra's as happy as I've ever seen her. The insurance company are paying up and she's got someone sorting out the gardens so that kiddies can play properly. Oh, and the funeral's organised,' she said. 'It's one of those humanist ones. It's what Piers wanted apparently...'

'What do you want?' Harry interrupted. 'Spit it out, woman.'

'Are you all right, love? You sound strange.'

'And you sound reet perky. I'm tired, that's all.'

'It's about the funeral. We don't know whether we should tell his mother.'

'Oh. Fair enough. Let me think. Aye. I've got her number somewhere from that time Sandra went to see her. I'll let her know. When's funeral?'

'Tomorrow. They don't hang about.'

'Good. Better sooner than late. Owt else?' Harry replied.

'That's all for now, Dad.'

'OK, lass. I'll be there tomorrow. Bye now.'

At least one of us is making progress, Harry thought. *I'm going backwards. Who's next?*

He rang the school administrator. 'It's about our Daniel this time. He said something about trolls. I've no idea what he's on about.'

The administrator sounded sympathetic. 'He's probably seen some of the things that James received,' she said. 'Unfortunately, there are a lot of horrible people out there who say terrible things on social media.'

'Oh 'eck...' Harry sighed. 'As if life weren't complicated enough. So what's happening about it?'

'We did inform the police and it seems to have subsided. I'm not aware that Daniel's been targeted at all. We take a dim view of it at school and confiscate phones and tablets with anything like that on them. But we can't control what goes on outside our gates. There have been prosecutions for things like this, so it's taken seriously.'

'That's good as far as it goes,' Harry said. 'But what about all this school he's missing? And the poor lad is in such a state about his mother.'

'We have a counselling service at the school. I'll arrange an appointment.'

'Namby-pamby mumbo jumbo,' Harry muttered. 'In our day we had to get on with it on our own.'

'Mr Baxter, there are different stresses and strains on young people today. It will help him and isn't that what we all want?'

'Can't argue with that,' Harry agreed. 'Go ahead. Let me know what we need to do. I'll be in touch as and when.'

He looked at his list. *Now for that Reader woman and that test*.

'What's the bottom line?' he asked Helen. 'Will it be good for our Stella, or could it harm her or the babby?'

'There's a tiny risk...'

She was instantly interrupted by Harry. 'That's all I want to know. Under no circumstances are you doing it.' As he put the phone down, Daniel appeared.

'What's happened, Grandpa?' asked the anxious boy.

'Nothing lad. T'hospital. Nothing for you to worry about.'

'Can we go and see Mum, now?' Daniel asked. 'I really want to talk to her.'

'Of course we can, lad. I've got to make one call then we can go. Get ready, I'll be with you soon.' He waited for Daniel to leave before dialling.

'Mrs Atkins? It's Harry Baxter here. Sandra's Dad. Sandra *Atkins'* Dad,' he emphasised.

'What do you want? I've told her that there's no money.'

'Did the police tell you about your son, Piers?'

'Paul? Yes. He's dead. What do you want?'

'I wanted to let you know about the funeral. It's tomorrow.'

'Where?'

'Dorset.'

'No bloody chance...'

'I could give you a lift,' Harry said, but she'd already hung up.

***

'Mum? Mum, it's Daniel here.'

Stella, instantly wakened by the voice, listened.

A new voice. I know this voice very well.

'Dad's gone now. We need you more than ever. Mum, come back to us please.'

Please don't cry. Please don't cry.

'James's been so upset. He doesn't talk about it, but I know it.'

I don't know. I don't know what to do. Daniel, James...

'Laura misses you so much.'

Laura. What can I do?

'So do I, Mum. I miss you too. I don't understand. No one tells me anything. What's happening, Mum?'

I have to help them. I have to find a way...

As Stella listened, she looked around her. The walls of the little house were dissolving, and she was surrounded by green countryside again. In the distance, she could almost make something out.

Over there. I need to go over there.

'We need you home again, Mum. Come home.'

Yes, home. I need to go home.

But as she made progress towards home, a shadowy figure came towards her. She stood still and held out her arms as if to catch him, but he drifted past her. She could hear him. He was crying.

'I love you, Stella. I'm trying my best. But it's hard.'

I know that voice. No, don't say you're gone too? Too much. Too much to bear.

53

Tuesday 16th April

'Ah, you're back.' Karen smiled at Macy. 'Had fun with DS Harris?' Macy's expression replied for her. 'That good?'

'No, I'm still with him. I'm Just popping in to check my emails.'

Before Karen could mutter some profanities, her phone rang. It was John.

'Easy peasy,' he said.

'What does that mean?'

'Dodgy car. The whole chassis crumbled down the middle. Classic Cut and Shut.'

Karen's mind began to whir. 'Is that where they put two halves of a car together?'

'Yes indeedy.'

'Jim Westbury. It's got to be,' Karen said. 'He's a second-hand car dealer. We can pull him in for that - if we can prove he sold the car to Matthews. What about other drivers?'

'Why do you ask?'

'I've got a possible lead. Remember that orderly chap I told you about?' Karen said.

'Peter? Wouldn't hurt a fly, you said. What's changed?'

'Yes. Peter Stubbins. It sounds like he got very angry when he heard about Stella's rape. He also heard Robert Cary talking about switching off Stella's life support system. And he knew Iain was in love with Stella — and as Gwen thinks, so was Peter himself.'

'Slow down. What are you saying? That this guy's a suspect? For what?'

'All of it, potentially.' Karen said. Except for Stella's crash. He loved her, so might have raped her. He might have caused Robert Cary's accident. And Iain Matthews' crash.'

'Does he have a history of mental health issues?'

'That's something I need to check.'

'OK. I'll see if he's got a licence. What about Westbury? There's got to be a possible trail there too. Although hopefully, Iain Matthews can tell us when he comes round.'

'Yes. First, I have to convince the guv about Jim. Talk soon.'

'Tonight?'

'Go on then.'

Karen put the phone down smiling, not only about John. *Jim Westbury, I'm closing in on you.*

The phone rang again. It was Tim Strange. 'I've found the missing file. It was in her briefcase, as if she was expecting to see him very soon. He was a difficult man.'

'Who was the client?'

'His name was Edward Brandon. She was keeping it very close to her chest, for some reason. I hope she wasn't breaching any client rules, but knowing her, I'm sure she had her reasons.'

'Good. We'll check it out.'

'I was wondering if you knew that...' Karen didn't hear the rest. She was distracted by Macy waving furiously at her. With a muttered 'thanks' she put the phone down.

'What is it?'

'Iain Matthews. He died last night.'

'Fuck fuck FUCK!' Karen exclaimed.

Wednesday 17th April

'Good afternoon, Mrs Reader. Is something wrong?' Gwen asked. 'You look very flushed.'

Helen sat at Martin Tiggle's old desk, looking less than pleased. 'They've brought in a new CEO. An interim. It looks like I'll be on my way soon, too.'

'Why? You were one of the good ones.'

'I tried, Gwen. I really did. I wasn't only interested in the patients. I made it my business to see exactly what was going on in this place. You know what an idiot Tiggle was. So many bad things happened under his watch. I couldn't sit there and do nothing.'

'Of course not. You did right. I've seen it myself how silly some of the managers are. What did you do?'

Helen gave a wry smile. 'Well between you and me...' she read from the letter on her desk '... and the Trust, whilst it has a strong whistle-blowing policy, does not agree with or condone staff talking to the press without full authorisation. You are reminded of the confidentiality agreement you signed when you took up employment.'

'That was you ringing the papers? Oh, gracious!'

'You disapprove? They were going to cover it up. Don't you remember how they wanted to deal with Stella? Tiggle was suggesting a termination.'

Gwen nodded. 'Yes, I do. And you did the right thing. But it's such a sacrifice.'

'Thanks, but I was leaving anyway.' Helen folded the letter. I'm going into medical administrative consultancy. Freelance. There are trusts around who do want my expertise and I shall do my very best to help.'

'Good for you, Mrs Reader.'

'Anyway, Gwen. You didn't come here to hear my troubles. How are you?'

'Right as rain. I want to come back on Monday.'

'You'll find things have changed a little.'

'Oh no. Now what?'

'The new CEO has sacked the agency. On my advice, I might add. They're using a new worker's cooperative now.'

'That's good isn't it?'

'Yes. I'd have done it, too.' Helen sighed. 'I could have been running this hospital. Anyway, I shall be earning a darn sight more where I'm going.'

Gwen reached out to shake her hand. 'Good luck to you, Mrs Reader. Let's hope nobody else has another incident like we did. Poor Stella. I'm going to check on her now.'

'Thanks Gwen. I'll let HR know you'll be back next week. It'll be the last thing I do here.'

Gwen was sure she heard a faint 'Fuck and bollocks!' as she closed the door.

In the ward, Gwen was greeted by one of her colleagues.

'How are you doing, Gwen?'

'I'll be back on Monday. How're things?'

'Better. No more agency staff. At least, fewer of them.'

'I heard. Now I must see Mrs Cary.'

'She's fine. But we've had another fatality. Mr Matthews. He used to come and see her, didn't he? His wife's still here. Like a little lost sheep.'

'Oh no! Not another one. Poor woman. I'll go and see her.'

Gwen went to the relatives' room to find the subdued woman sitting on a chair, looking at the floor. 'I'm so sorry for your loss, Mrs Matthews. Can I get you a cup of tea?' Penny shook her head.

'You're a friend of Mrs Cary's, aren't you?' Penny nodded. 'What a terrible thing for all of you.'

'He was my world!' She erupted into tears. 'We never had children. I was still hopeful...'

Gwen sat next to her, gently rubbing her arm. 'What do the police think?'

Penny shook her head. 'I haven't spoken to them yet. I suppose I must.'

'Why don't you go home? Talk to them there, it might help if you do. That Sergeant Thorpe is a bit sharp but she's very dedicated. Is there anyone who can be with you?'

'I'm being silly. Yes, of course, I can go home. Thank you.'

Gwen watched her leave, tears forming in her own eyes as she made her way to Stella's room. She didn't notice Peter or hear him softly calling out her name as he wheeled a patient by on a trolley.

***

'Hello, Stella, my love. I wanted to see how you're doing.'

Gwen. She's back.

'I'll be around a bit more from next week.'

'Oh. Mrs Baxter...'

Baxter...

'I'm sorry. I was wrong to... er... Thank you so much for not reporting me.'

Mum?

'Being honest, if I were you, I might have done the same.'

Mum, what have you done?

'We're looking after her properly now. I promise.'

What's happened?

'I'm sure you are.'

I'm trying Mum. I've been walking forever.

Footsteps walking away.

'Stella love. We're back from our Sandra's.'

Sandra.

'Poor Piers was buried yesterday. They put him under a tree. It were quite nice really.'

Piers. PIERS.

'Oh Stella, we need you, Stella. Your sister needs you. Please come back to us, love.'

I'm trying.

'The boys need you, love. And Sofia's not going to be around forever. Tell her, Dad.'

Dad? Dad's here.

'Stella lass, you need to come home. We can all manage, yes, all of us. Even the boys. They'll cope. We'll get through it, somehow. But there's someone else. You've another one to take care of now. A new babby. Now, think on.'

Baby?

Inside her head, Stella could hear something new. A beat. A fast heartbeat. She knew she had to protect it.

What's happening to me...?

54

'What now?'

Sergeant Julia Jones waited for Jackie Atkins to stop growling at her. 'I thought I might have seen you at your son's funeral, Mrs Atkins.'

'And? Doesn't mean I don't care at all. He was my flesh and blood. Who would do something so awful? Lock him in like that. I want to find out what happened.'

'We don't know if it was deliberate. Tell me what happened when you saw him. His wife thinks he left on Thursday the twentieth of December. Is that the day he came to see you?'

'Pension day. Yes. Sounds about right.'

'Can you tell me exactly what was said when he came?'

Julia listened patiently while Jackie relayed the conversation. 'And what do you know of Nicholas Westbury's family?' she asked. 'Do you know if your son found them?'

'No. He never got in touch again. Old Nick was a bit of a racketeer in the day, a right bastard. Martha's still around, I heard. And I read about a Westbury being killed a few weeks back, but it's a common enough name. I know one's a car dealer. He had a yard, up the way there.' She waved her arm, randomly. 'I told Paul.'

'Why did he change his name to Piers?' Julia asked.

'After some author who wrote lots of fantasy, suited him well, that did. He had all the books; I've chucked them now.' Then she added, 'What happened to his car? Did he sell it?'

'His car?' *Sandra mentioned a car.* 'Do you know the make? Registration number?'

'It was red and old. That's all I know.'

'Thank you. I'll be in touch if I find out anything.'

***

Julia sat in her car and rang Sandra. 'Mrs Atkins, do you know the registration number of your late husband's car?'

'Easy. I've paid the bills often enough. He spent a fortune on that car. Fuck knows why. It always looked like a banger to me. RJC 479R. It's a Triumph Herald.'

'Thank you.' *Now for the widow.*

'Hello? Is that Mrs Martha Westbury, widow of Nicholas Westbury?'

'Who wants to know?'

'Sergeant Jones, Ma'am. I'd like to ask you a few questions, if that's all right?' There was a slight pause before Julia heard the response.

'This about Tom again? I'm getting fed up of your lot.'

'No, it's not... It's about a missing person. Your husband's son, Piers, known as Paul, Atkins.' *She must know about him - when he came looking.* The line went dead.

Julia rang her office and spoke to a colleague. 'Hi. Can you look something up for me? I want to know if we've got anything on a Nicholas Westbury and family? Hertfordshire area. He had a criminal record, apparently.'

'Give me a minute.' Julia waited patiently for the return call. 'OK. Quite a lot of activity, no convictions that I can see. He had two sons; birth names are the short versions. Jim and Tom, but Tom was killed recently.'

'Good. That tallies with what I've been told. What do we know about his death?'

'RTA Thirteenth of December.'

Julia frowned. 'That's a week before Piers Atkins supposedly went missing. Can you check out this car reg? And text me the address for Mrs Martha Westbury.'

'Fire away.'

***

Julia pulled up outside Martha's house. She watched as the door opened and a bearded youth emerged. 'You lose that strange and weird,' a voice inside the house yelled. 'Before the inquest! Do you hear me?' Julia heard a faint cackle of laughter.

The lad jumped a little when he saw the uniformed Julia get out of the car. 'Nan,' he yelled. 'It's the ...' he hesitated. 'Someone to see you. Catch you later, Nan.' He ran off.

Julia waited for Martha to come to the door. There was no laughter now. 'You'd better come in,' she muttered.

'Sergeant Jones,' Julia showed her ID as she stepped inside.

'Who's gone missing, then?'

'I told you on the phone. Piers Atkins, also known as Paul.'

'I ain't seen that little bastard. He never come here.'

She knows something. 'But did he meet up with your son?' Martha glared at her. *Hell, her son died.* 'I'm so sorry Mrs Westbury. It's your son Jim, I mean. The car dealer?'

'I don't know nothing. You'll have to ask him.'

'And where can I find him?'

'It's off the end of the High Street. Right out, until you get to the industrial estate.'

'Do you mind if I ask you what happened to your son Tom?'

This time there was a different response. Martha's expression changed and the defiance melted away. 'It was a car crash. No cause. One of those things, your lot say. But I don't believe it. Inquest is next week.'

'Can you tell me the name of the investigating officer?' Julia asked. 'It will save me bothering you again.'

Martha walked over to her mantelpiece and picked up a small card

'All I've got is this.' She showed it to Julia.

'DS Thorpe,' Julia read. She took out her mobile to key in the phone number. Thank you, Mrs Westbury, that's all for now.'

***

After driving round the industrial estate for a few minutes, Julia's eyes alighted on a rusty old sign hanging on a chain-link fence. **Westbury's Motors Best cars Best price's**

She followed the fence around until she found the entrance. It was securely chained and locked, despite the relatively early hour. She got out of the car and walked up to the tall metal gates, giving them a shake in case they were open. She peered through them. There were about twenty cars, all polished and shining, parked outside a mobile cabin.

'Yes?' A gruff voice sounded.

'I'm looking for Mr Westbury,' Julia replied, turning round to see a very tall and dirty-looking man perfectly matching the voice. He had a large German Shepherd on a lead.

'Can't you read?' He pointed to a notice. Julia's eyes followed his arm to a white notice fixed to the fence.

'Call this number. Anytime day or night.' *Some detective you'd make.* She chided herself and looked at the number.

'Thank you,' She took out her mobile and punched in the digits.

The man loomed over her. 'You won't get a signal down here,' he sneered before strolling away.

Julia walked around the perimeter of the yard. She could see that there were more cars round the back but there was a garage blocking the view. Her eyes caught something red, with a distinctive shape, but she couldn't see the plates. She looked at the fence and thought about scaling it, but it was topped with razor wire. *And I don't have a warrant.*

The approaching security man appearing in the corner of her eye made her decision for her. She snapped a picture on her phone before he got too close, then gave a loud pretend sneeze and turned round, smiling before walking away.

After driving a short distance, she tried the number again. This time there was a ringing tone, but it went straight to voicemail. She ended the call. *I don't think I like this Westbury much.* She looked at her watch. *It's late and it's a long drive home. Time for a quick conversation?* She rang the phone number for Karen Thorpe.

'DS Thorpe's not here. Can I help, or take a message?'

'No problem. It's Sergeant Jones here, from the Dorset Police. I'll ring her in the morning.'

55

Karen walked into the incident room to find Macy drumming her fingers on the table. 'Oh. You're back.'

Macy nodded. 'How's Penny Matthews?'

'I've left a message for her,' Karen said. 'Forensics have confirmed it was a dodgy car. I've been trying to track it back to Jim Westbury but without the logbook, I'm stumped. And we might have a dangerous driver in the frame. Peter Stubbins. He had a valid licence.'

'I thought there were witnesses.'

'Yes, but no IDs or car reg numbers. He might have had a pop at Iain if he thought he'd hurt Stella. Anything for me?'

Karen's phone rang. She looked at Macy as she spoke. 'Yes, Mrs Matthews. Thank you. I'll meet you there.'

'OK Mace, I'm going to see her now. Can you try Amanda Denning?'

'Mace?'

'Is that a problem, me calling you that?'

Macy blinked. 'No.' She grabbed her coat. 'I'll call you.'

***

Karen was startled when Penny opened the door slowly. *She's stick thin and hasn't slept for days,* she surmised. 'Mrs Matthews, I am sorry for your loss.'

'Come in.' Penny replied. 'In here.' She led the way into her small sitting room where the women sat opposite each other.

'We've looked at your husband's car. Do you know where he got it from?'

'No. It was a good deal he said, that's all. Why?'

'We believe it was not fit for purpose.'

Penny became agitated. 'What? It looked fine. Iain told me so often it was a good little runner. I knew it was too good to be true.'

'We think it was put together from halves of two cars.'

'What? I... But that's illegal, isn't it?'

'Mrs Matthews, I don't want to cause you any more grief, but we must investigate all possibilities. Do you have the logbook?'

Penny hauled herself up as if the whole world was on her shoulders. 'I'll have a look. He was very well organised.'

Karen watched through the door as Penny searched the hall telephone table drawer. 'Here,' she passed it to Karen, who held open a plastic bag for her to drop it in. 'If you find the seller will he go to prison?'

Karen sighed. 'We have to find him or her first, then prove enough about it to stand up in court. But I promise you I'll do my utmost to get them locked up.'

'Good.'

'Mrs Matthews, may I ask you about the other case while I'm here?'

Penny frowned. 'Do you mean poor Stella again?'

Karen nodded. 'You told us before that you didn't know Mrs Cary very well.'

'Only at the tennis club. I thought she was a bit stuck-up, to be honest.'

'Do you know of anyone who might have wished her harm?'

'I already told you, no.'

'And you were at college on the evening of Thursday the thirteenth of December, last year?'

'Yes. Amanda was meant to be there. She couldn't come. She had to look after the children. It was a dreadful day.'

'What about New Year's Eve?'

Penny frowned again. 'Iain and I don't *do* New Year's Eve. We're more Christmas people. We were...' Her eyes filled with tears.

'You were both in, that evening?'

'No. I was keeping Amanda company. Iain was out for a drink with someone, I think. I don't keep him on a lead.' She bit her lip. 'Didn't.'

'Did you know he was at the hospital that night?'

Penny shook her head. 'No. Why would he go there?'

'We think he went to visit Mrs Cary.'

'He wouldn't do that.'

'Mrs Matthews, your late husband admitted that he was in a relationship with Mrs Cary.'

'No, he wasn't. He wouldn't. Please go away now, I've had enough of your questions.'

Karen stayed firm. 'There's one more question if I may? About your work at the dairy?'

Penny blinked. 'What's that got to do with anything?'

'I'm interested. What's a typical day?'

'Sterilising containers, checking temperatures, testing for bacteria, that sort of thing.'

'Breeding?'

'No. Never. What's this about?'

'I've read a bit on dairy practices and it would be nice to know that the cows are looked after well,' Karen said.

'I'm sure they are but it's nothing to do with me.'

'Thank you, Mrs Matthews. Please don't be surprised if someone else from another department calls. We have several specialisms at the station. If you want to speak to me at any time, here's my card.'

Penny took it. 'Tell me if you find anything out about the car, please.'

'I will.'

***

Macy sat in Amanda's comfortable, cosy home. She had got off on the wrong foot by referring to Amanda as Mrs instead of Ms and was now trying to redeem herself. 'It must have been hard for you the day Mrs Cary crashed. It was very kind of you to look after her children.'

Amanda nodded. 'It was the least I could do. The au pair was away for a couple of weeks, so I had them most evenings. No trouble at all. And Stella came home early on Thursdays, that's my college night. Except she couldn't that day. She had an important meeting or something.'

'How well did you know Stella Cary and her husband? What were they like?'

Amanda started with relish. 'We didn't see that much of each other normally. We were good but not close neighbours. Stella was... is one of those people who had everything. Clever, beautiful and quite fearsome. If she didn't like someone, they knew it.'

'Do you know of anyone who might wish to harm her in any way? Or damage her car?'

'What, that yellow monstrosity? I expect there were a few who wanted to damage that. She treated it like another baby, you know.'

'Anyone who maybe had a grudge against her?'

'She was good at her job. I expect lawyers make enemies, sometimes.'

'We understand she had a relationship with Mr Iain Matthews.'

'Poor Penny. I've asked her and she denies it. But I think she knows.'

'And what did you think about Robert Cary?'

Amanda went quiet for a moment. 'It was quite useful having a man around sometimes, after my husband left. But he got the wrong idea about me.'

Macy pounced. 'When we spoke to you at his funeral, I thought you were going to say something to us.' Amanda looked blank. *What's she hiding?*

'Ah, he made a very clumsy pass at me on New Year's Eve,' she said. 'Immediately after, he told me he hadn't had sex with Stella in years. Then I heard the rumours about him at his funeral. But I'm sure no one would have killed him for that.'

'Do you think someone may have killed him?'

'Goodness no! I didn't mean that at all.'

'Can you confirm where you were on the evening of second January?'

'I was here then too. It was a terrible day. I waited with the au pair until Stella's parents arrived.'

'You're clearly a very good and kind neighbour, Ms Denning.'

214

But you're not telling me something.

'There is one thing that's been bothering me...'

At last. 'Yes, Ms Denning?'

'Rob told me that Stella and her sister had a falling-out. And Piers, that's Sandra's husband, went missing. I think that's what Rob said.'

'Thank you, Ms Denning.' Amanda gave a little nod. 'I'll be in touch if I need to talk to you again.'

Macy went back to her car and switched her phone on. **KAREN. FIVE MISSED CALLS.** She rang her.

'And?' Karen said.

'Robert Cary's accident. Amanda says he tried it on with her on New Year's Eve.'

'Interesting,' Karen said. 'So he was feeling randy.' Anything else?'

'Yes. She also knew something was going on between Iain Matthews and Stella. But she said Penny knew it too, she thinks. And apparently, Robert Cary told her something about Stella and her sister Sandra falling out. And that Sandra's husband Piers had gone missing.'

'OK. That could be interesting. Penny Matthews is definitely keeping something back, but I've got the logbook now. I'll drop in into the lab on my way home.'

56

Thursday 18th April.

Karen arrived at the office to find a multitude of messages waiting for her, but the one that caught her eye was from Julia Jones. *Dorset Police? Doesn't Stella's sister live there*? Karen tilted her head at Macy to join her as she rang the number.

'Sergeant Julia Jones speaking.'

'DS Karen Thorpe.'

'I'm investigating the death of Mr Piers, aka Paul, Atkins. Husband of Sandra Atkins.'

Sandra and Piers. He's dead? Now that is interesting.

'Are you the officer who was investigating Tom Westbury's accident?'

'Yes. What about it?'

'It's possible, I mean I'm not sure, but there could be a connection.'

'What?'

'Piers Atkins was the illegitimate son of Nicholas Westbury.'

'Bloody hell!'

'Is that important?' Julia asked.

'It could be. I've only just heard that he's gone missing. When was that?'

'He was last seen at his mother's house on or around December twentieth. His body was found two weeks ago.'

Karen checked the file. *That's a week after the accident. Connection? Westburys. Has to be.* 'Did Mrs Atkins mention anything about her sister, Stella?'

'Stella? Yes, no love lost there. Why?'

'Because the crash that killed Tom Westbury is the one that put Stella Cary in a coma.'

'Oh. I see. Yes, of course. Sandra mentioned Stella's coma but nothing about an accident. Heck. Did I read about that one in the newspapers?'

216

'Probably.'

'OK.' Julia paused. 'Then I need to tell you this. I think Pier's car may be in Jim Westbury's dealership place. Although it may be that he sold it to Jim. It seems he was trying to raise some money.'

'What colour was it?'

'Colour? It was red and quite small'.

'Red?!'

'Yes. I couldn't make out much more, the place was all locked up. I could only look through the bars.'

'We should meet up and compare notes,' Karen said. 'The inquest into Tom Westbury's death is next week.'

'Yes. I think I should be there. Have you interviewed Jim Westbury? I'd like to know what happened with Piers. If he did see him, he may have been the last man to see him alive.'

Karen grimaced. 'No, I've not yet had enough evidence to see him. But I'm going to the inquest. It starts at ten, could you get here for eight? Two heads and all that. I've got my suspicions about him too.'

'What?'

'I'll tell you when you're here. Make sure you set up an interview with Westbury, for after the inquest. All indications are the verdict will be accidental death, so it should be over by midday.'

'I will.'

'And can you give me that car reg? I'll check it out.'

'I couldn't see the plates in the yard, but I can tell you what Piers Atkins' car's registration was. I've also managed to take half a picture. I've got your email. I'll send it all now.'

'Great.' Karen put the phone down and turned to Macy. 'Well, well, well. We've got a new name to check up on now, and a possibly missing car.' She paused to wait for the details to come through. PING. 'Here. I'll forward it to you.'

Macy went to her desk and called up the image. 'Triumph Herald. That's all I can see from this.'

Karen nodded. *Impressive*. 'You get over to Westbury's, the car place. Say you're looking for a classic car. In red. See what he does.'

'Won't he recognise me? Everyone else does.'

'Men rarely remember faces out of context,' Karen replied. 'No uniform, change your hair. Wear a low top. Short skirt, something colourful.'

Macy nodded. 'What makes you think I've got a short skirt?'

Shit. Not this again. 'Er, I'm sorry. I didn't mean...'

'Don't worry. It's not a problem.' Macy said.

'Thanks.'

***

Macy smiled as she turned her back on Karen. She was still grinning when she got home. *This is going to be fun.* Karen was right, she had a large and colourful wardrobe which included several short skirts and low tops. She put together the most noticeable outfit she could and fluffed up her hair. To complete the effect, she added loads of bling and some oversized sunglasses. Stepping into high-heeled shoes, she set off to the yard. She parked a hundred yards or so from the back of the industrial estate, where the dealership was.

When she arrived at the entrance, the gates were open. She wandered in and had a good look round. Macy could pick out a Triumph Herald on a cold night in the fog, but she saw nothing remotely resembling one. She checked the picture on her phone and tried to work out exactly where it had been taken. She could make out the edge of the cabin office from the picture and quickly took another photo from the same angle for comparison.

That's it. No need to hang around now. As she turned to walk back to her car, she heard the sound of an engine revving. *What's that? That's not a car.*

She double-backed, following the direction of the sound and watched as a lorry with a large trailer came out of a side road. She could make out a car-shaped canvas cover in the back. Snapping the lorry as discreetly as she could, she called Karen as she hurried along.

'I think there's a car being moved in a lorry,' she said.

218

'Can you follow it?'

'Not in these heels,' she puffed.

'Do what you can,' Karen said.

By the time Macy got to her car, she realised it was too late. She drove around the area in case the lorry was still around but had to admit defeat. She looked at the photo she had taken. *Damn. Missed the number plate.* She rang Karen. 'Sorry. I lost it.'

'Reg?' Karen asked.

'No. But I've got a new picture of the yard to compare with.'

'Good work.'

'So, he's on our list now then?'

'Definitely.' Karen said. 'Get back here ASAP. We need to do some thinking.'

***

Karen mused as she updated the boards. *Another Westbury connection and the sister. The sisters fell out. Robert Cary had a red car. Could he be the missing link? And he disappeared. Maybe Jim bumped him off as revenge for Tom's death? Talking of possible revenge, what course was Penny on?* She picked up her phone.

'Hello, Admin office, please...'

Karen was beaming when Macy arrived.

'Guess what Penny Matthews was doing at college?'

'I thought it was flower arranging.'

'Car maintenance for beginners.'

'Wow! If Penny knew about Stella's affair with her husband...' Macy started.

Karen continued. '... And Amanda fancied a pop at Cary...'

'They could be in it together.' Macy finished.

'Where did she park her car? Who could have got to it? Macy, check out the station car park. And talking of cars there's another Westbury connection I should tell you about.'

57

Gwen got into a conversation with Janice as soon as she arrived to take over the shift.

'... And that funny bloke's been looking for you. He asked if you were on today.'

'Peter?' Gwen looked at the clock. 'He knows my shifts.'

'If you hurry, you can get away before he comes back.' Janice smirked.

'He's a nice lad. I shall wait for him. It's nearly time, anyway.'

On the dot of four, Peter arrived. 'Can we go outside? I want a ciggie.'

'Yes, my love.' Gwen could hardly keep up with him as he charged out, looking back to make sure she was still behind him. She followed him to a bench near the A&E entrance. He sat down and lit the last cigarette from the pack, without talking.

'Peter...' Gwen began.

'Not yet. I'm thinking.'

They sat for a few more minutes, Peter drawing hard on his cigarette. He dropped the butt and trod it out, throwing the empty pack on the floor. Gwen held her tongue and waited. Peter took out his phone and stared at it.

'If you thought that someone was going to hurt someone else, would it be wrong to stop them?'

Gwen didn't let her face react. 'No, it's the right thing to do but it must be done in the right way.'

'And what if you loved someone but you did something bad, something that might hurt them...' He tailed off then looked Gwen in the eye. 'I've done a terrible thing, Gwen. A terrible, *terrible* thing.'

'Not Stella, Peter, don't tell me you...'

Peter turned on her furiously. 'I love Stella! Do you think I would hurt her on purpose?' he shouted, then calming down he added: 'But I've hurt her anyway. I've hurt her family, her children. I had to do it. She told me I had to do it.'

'Who told you to do it? What did she tell you to do?' Gwen looked away for a second, distracted by the stopping of a siren as an ambulance approached. When she looked back, Peter was on his feet. 'Sit down Peter and tell me what you've done. It will make you feel better, it really will.'

Peter muttered something about a car. She didn't hear him. 'What did you say?' She grabbed his wrist. He struggled to get away. He pulled himself free and in a moment that would stay in Gwen's memory for the rest of her life, he backed away from her. The next thing she saw was him falling into the path of the ambulance. She screamed like a madwoman... 'PETER!' It was too late; the ambulance hit him square on.

Gwen watched in horror as the ambulance reversed away from his body. Peter lay in a horribly contorted shape on the tarmac, a pool of blood slowly spreading from his head.

She ran up to him as fast as she could. The ambulance stopped and the paramedics rushed out to look, frozen for a moment, torn between the emergency patient inside and Peter, lying on the ground.

'Oh Peter,' Gwen moaned, holding his hand. There was still a pulse, a faint one. 'We'll save you and sort this out I promise.' She called one of the paramedics over.

'Do you recognise this chap?'

'Yes, he's one of our orderlies. Please hurry.' She watched as they tended to him. *What was that on the ground? His phone. Better put it somewhere safe.*

The man called another paramedic from the hospital entrance. Peter was checked over and strapped into a stretcher. No need for the ambulance, they carried him between them into the hospital where he was put on a trolley and taken straight to the ICU ward. Gwen followed them all the way in. Peter was slowly drifting but as the harsh strip lights of the hospital corridor flashed over his head, he felt strangely comforted. He spoke, but she couldn't make out the words.

'This is how I first met Stella,' he said.

***

'Hello Stella, it's me.'

Another familiar voice woke Stella from her slumber. She left the greenness of the countryside for the blackness of wakefulness.

The one who asks the questions.

'Stella we're getting closer, but it would really help if you woke up. You see, you're carrying a baby now and we need to find out who the father is, or was. I don't want to put you under pressure but whoever he is, he needs to be locked up.'

Father.

'Stella, did you have an argument with your sister Sandra? Or her husband, Piers?'

Sister. Sandra. Piers. Too much.

Stella slipped back into sleep and began to walk again in the direction she knew would take her home. Then after many years, she saw another figure coming towards her, a young man. He was smiling at her.

'I love you, Stella,' he said, as he drifted past. Stella knew that voice and became a little sad.

'I love you too,' she replied. She turned to see him, but he was gone. 'I love you!' she shouted. 'Thank you.'

The sound of her own voice woke her up again briefly but there was nothing else to hear, so she drifted back to continue her journey.

58

Friday 19th April

Gwen woke early, her back already regretting her decision to sleep in a chair on the ward. *What did he mean? What had he done?* She couldn't believe he had ever done anything bad, but then she remembered she'd seen his temper. Her guilt had spread, she somehow blamed herself for Peter. *I should have listened,* she said to herself over and over. At last, one of the doctors emerged from the operating theatre.

'Gwen? What are you doing here?'

'I don't think he has anyone else. How is he?'

'Not good. But he's holding on.'

Gwen fumbled in her handbag and pulled out Karen's card. 'Hang on, Peter,' she whispered, as she left the ward and went outside again to make the call.

***

Karen answered her phone straight away, jumping out of bed and heading towards the bathroom. *Six-thirty? Must be serious.*

'It's Gwen Williams. Peter Stubbins, the orderly we talked about? He's had an accident. He's very badly injured.'

Karen gaped. *Another one?* 'What happened? How serious is it?' Karen sat on the toilet.

'I think...' Gwen could hardly bring herself to say it. 'I think he may have tried to kill himself. I don't know. It happened so fast. He stepped out in front of an ambulance...' She paused.

'Hello? Gwen? Are you still there?'

Gwen breathed in deeply. 'He said something. He said he'd done something terrible.'

'I'll be right there.'

***

Karen arrived to find Gwen wandering aimlessly round the ICU ward. 'Miss Williams?'

Gwen looked at her as if she were a stranger at first. 'Ah yes. Let's go to the relatives' room. It's empty. The poor lad has no one.'

'How is he?'

'Not good. I don't think he'll make it.'

'What happened? Tell me from the beginning.'

Gwen relayed the story slowly and carefully, rubbing her eyes a little as she spoke. Karen listened intently, keen to hurry her up, get to the important bit. She was disappointed.

'He didn't say what he'd done?'

Gwen shook her head. 'He talked about hurting Stella but not hurting *her*, hurting her family, her kids. He said he'd done a terrible thing and that she had told him to do it.'

That doesn't make sense. Karen thought. *Could he have killed Iain Matthews? That would certainly upset Stella, but not her kids. Anyway, Matthews' accident seemed straightforward, with witnesses. Could he mean Cary? That was months ago and technically it was a heart attack. But then again, would he know that? Who was "she"? Stella? Did he think she was talking to him? Telling him what to do?*

'Ring me, Miss Williams. Ring me if there's any change.'

***

Macy had woken up that day with her head full of questions. *It must be catching*, she decided, as she got out of bed. *Where would Stella park an iconic car like that? Karen was right. Again. It had to be at the station and probably within range of a security camera.*

She drove to the train station car park. *This is busy. Is there someone about? Yes.*

'Excuse me.' She flashed her badge at the parking attendant. 'Do you remember a yellow Porsche? Registration 5T33LL4?'

'How could I forget? Haven't seen it in a while though. Lovely car, shame about the colour.'

'The owner was in an accident in December last year. Can you remember where it was parked?'

'Yes. She had a season ticket. See, there.' He pointed. 'No one's taken the space, her ticket's still valid.' Macy followed the direction of his arm then looked left and right. Sure enough, there was a camera pointing, if not exactly at the spot, certainly covering the area.

'Do you keep all the CCTV records?'

'We do but you'll have to speak to the manager for that. I'll tell him we're on our way.'

Macy was shown into a small cabin-style office where the manager was waiting.

'It's about the Porsche,' Macy began. 'December, last year.'

'So I hear.' He handed her a stack of disks and nodded towards the laptop. 'You're looking for camera two. I'm in the back, catching up with paperwork if you need me.' He paused. 'Better get you started.' He loaded the disk for December, showed her a few buttons and left her to it.

Macy was in a state of near bliss. She enjoyed working with computers, had a very good eye for detail and had developed a love for watching CCTV. It was even better than paperwork.

Camera two captured an area covering about fifty cars, including all those in the season ticket area, with varying degrees of clarity. She looked up Monday the third of December first. There she saw the Porsche in the far row to the left-hand side of the picture. *Would it necessarily be a college night? Let's start there anyway.*

She forwarded the disk to college nights looking at the sixth of December first. *She came home early to look after the kids on Amanda's college nights. There she is. Fifteen hundred precisely. What about the thirteenth? Amanda Denning mentioned a meeting. Ah, there she is. Sixteen ten. Exactly what I'd expect. But the damage could have been done at any time. Brake fluid, if the tank is damaged, drips out slowly.* She flipped back to the third of December and began to look at every single day from the time that Stella parked it to the time she took it home each evening, which most days was seven am to seven pm.

'Yes! There!' She shouted so loudly the manager came out to see what had happened. He peered over her shoulder as she rewound the footage and looked at the details on the screen. At 18:00 on 11/12/2012, she saw a figure approaching the car. It dipped down as if it had dropped something. Whoever it was, wore a long coat and a trilby style hat, but it was impossible to tell whether it was male or female.

'Is that who you're looking for?' The manager said.

'Maybe,' she replied. 'Do any camera's cover the entrance and exits?'

'Indeed they do.' Now intrigued, he sorted through the pile of disks and loaded one. 'There!' he said, as they watched the footage of the figure walking towards the camera, wearing long boots.

Macy peered at the screen. *That's a woman for sure. And it's too thin for Amanda Denning. Penny Matthews?*

'Do I get a reward for this?' The manager asked, hopefully.

'May I have the images?'

'I'll get them.' He went out and returned with a disk.

'Thanks,' Macy said.

'What about my reward?'

'No chance.'

59

Karen paced around the ward, waiting to talk to Gwen. She went over to Stella's old room. There was a new patient in there, so she didn't go in. Instead, she walked around the side and along the back, until she reached a few large mobile partition screens in front of the wall. Being nosey, she looked behind them.

What the hell?! She'd exposed a fire escape door. *How did I not see this?* There was no green arrow or any signage above it. *Must be disused.* A big sign across the bars read **ALARMED DO NOT OPEN.** *I wonder...*

Bracing herself for the chaos she was expecting to initiate, Karen pushed at the door. It opened. There was no sound. Nothing, as far as she could see, had been set off. She looked around, half-hoping for some security people to materialise. But still, nothing happened. *Bloody hell! Anybody could have got in here.* Pulling the door shut again, she went to find Gwen.

'Miss Williams, this is important. The fire escape door behind the screens. Next to the room where Stella was attacked. It's open. Who had access to turn the alarm off?'

Gwen shook her head. 'It can't be.' She got up and with Karen following went to the door and opened it. 'Is this what he meant?'

'What? Peter? Could he have turned off the alarm?'

She nodded. 'It's possible. But I doubt it. I expect it was missed when they did the last building reorganisation. Yes, Peter knew his way around the place. As you know he used to sit with her. He told me he was protecting her. Maybe he came in that way, sometimes?'

'Can you get in from outside?' Karen asked. Gwen frowned. 'I don't think so.'

'I'm going out. Shut the door.'

Gwen did as she was told and waited as Karen struggled to open the door from the outside. She banged on it for Gwen to let her back in. 'OK. He may have let someone else in, or he may have wedged it so he could get in at any time. That opens up the whole case to almost anyone. How well do you know him?'

'I was beginning to get to know the poor lad. He had no family at all, as far as I knew. He was in care all his life. One of those who slipped through the system. But he was a gentle soul.'

'No family then, but do you know where he lives? Have we got an address? A key to his place?'

Gwen frowned. 'Yes. They gave me his things to look after. They're locked up in my desk. HR will have an address for him. What are you going to do?'

'We need to check his place. We have to find out what he was talking about. He may have left some crucial evidence.'

'But you need permission or a warrant, don't you?' Gwen followed Karen's gaze, to see a grim-faced surgeon walking towards them.

'Oh no, don't tell me...'

'I'm sorry Gwen. We did all we could.'

Karen seized the moment. 'I need those keys, Gwen. Now.' Gwen, tears pouring down her face, searched her pockets and shook her head.

'Have you no respect?' the surgeon said. 'Can't it wait a little while?'

Karen sighed and looked at Gwen. 'Ring me when you find them. Please. I'm sorry for your loss. But you know we have to help Stella Cary too.' The surgeon took her arm and manoeuvred her away.

'Tomorrow,' he said. 'Come back then. I'll make sure you get what you need.'

Saturday 20th April

Karen wasted no time that morning. Armed with Peter's address and keys, she ran out of the hospital building and called John.

'I've got the keys. Ninety-four B Peabody Terrace. Get a team together; I want that man's place searched from top to bottom.

We have to find out what he was confessing to. I'll meet you with the address and the keys. I want to see this myself.'

'What man?' John asked.

'The orderly. Peter Stubbins. He confessed to doing something terrible before he died.'

'He died? Shit. On our way.'

Karen was the first to arrive at Peter's flat. John wasn't far behind, with three of his team in tow. She ran up the steps of the concrete block, looking for the numbers as she sped along the walkway.

'Here.' She stopped outside number 94B, and for the first time, realised that there was a car key in the bunch she had been given. Her fingers picked out the smaller Yale key and she opened the door, hesitating before stepping inside. *It's not a crime scene*, she reminded herself.

The flat was small and a little untidy, but not dirty. *A lot cleaner than mine,* she noted.

John was right behind her. 'What are we looking for?'

'We'll know when we see it.'

'Gloves!' John ordered, passing Karen a latex pair. She looked around as she put them on. She scanned the living room, sparsely furnished with two chairs and a small table. The tiny kitchen was next. She was immediately struck by the sight of a fridge magnet holding up a scrap of paper, with a number scribbled on it. *That's local*. She took out her mobile and rang it.

'You have reached the voice mail of Barbara Spinnard, PA to the late Robert Cary,' it said, before giving redialling instructions.

'Why the fuck did you have that Peter? Were you the man who threatened Barbara?' Karen clicked the call off, her mind racing. She went back into the living room, where colleagues were going through and checking every item. She watched for a moment before going outside to the balcony for some air. Her heart was pumping. *This is what it's all about. And I love it.*

John joined her, a piece of paper in his gloved hand. 'He had Barbara Spinnard's phone number,' Karen said. 'Have we got his phone yet?'

'No, but we've got this. A receipt for five litres of petrol.

Unleaded petrol. Cary's car took leaded.'

'Would that matter if it was deliberate, to cause the accident?'

'Good point.'

'OK. But Peter did have a car too. I've got the keys to it,' she held up the bunch. 'Weren't you going to check if he had a licence? Can we find it from these?'

'No idea.' John was unusually flummoxed as he wrestled the car keys off the link. 'But there are other ways.'

'Is it worth me waiting?'

He shook his head. 'Not really. There's still a load of things to go through, but I suspect we've already got the good stuff. I'll ring you if I find anything exciting.'

Karen nodded. 'OK, talk later. I'm going back to the station to catch up with Macy.'

60

Karen and Macy arrived in the incident room within a minute of each other. 'Stubbins is dead,' Karen said.

'Peter? The orderly? How?'

'Fell in front of an ambulance.'

'How awful.' Macy sat down shaking her head. 'What happened?'

'Immediately before he did it, he said he'd done something terrible. John's there now, ransacking his flat. He had Barbara Spinnard's number on his fridge. And we found a receipt for unleaded petrol.'

'Wow! That's of no use for Cary's car. But he might have bought it for other petrol-driven things. A lawnmower?'

'In January?'

'Sorry.' Macy smiled. Do you think he could have been involved with Cary's accident? He seemed so passive.'

'He had a car. It's a compelling idea, especially combined with the phone number. But what would he be talking to Barbara Spinnard about? Cary's whereabouts? And if his car is red... We have to find it. What about you?'

Macy put her hand to her head, thinking. 'The CCTV at the train station car park has a woman in a long coat and hat, bending down right by Stella's car.' She paused. 'My first thought was Penny Matthews. But the image is so dark it could even be my grandmother.'

Karen chuckled. 'That's good, but half the women in the country wear long dark coats and hats in winter; including Vera Fontaine. Besides, could you damage brakes that quickly?'

'Sure, if you knew where to look. The fluid tank in a Porsche is quite low down. With the right implement, you could pierce it if you knew what you were doing.'

'Cool,' Karen replied. 'I know nothing about how cars work.'

'But there's another thing. I had a little wander around.'

'And?'

'There's a footpath from the station. If you follow it far enough it leads to the college. Anybody could easily have got between the two.'

'To interfere with brakes, you mean?'

Macy nodded. 'Or to put an open petrol can in a boot. The college is linked to the university. It's not that much further.'

'Hang on.' Karen held up her hand. 'And we've got Penny Matthews doing a car maintenance course at the college. What date was the image?'

'Eleventh December at six pm.'

'Does that make sense? If she damaged the car then...'

'Absolutely,' Macy grinned. 'It seeps out slowly so by the...'

Macy was interrupted by Karen's phone ringing. It was John from Peter's flat.

'You won't believe this one.'

'Try me.'

'We've found something in Stubbins' wardrobe. A security guard's uniform exactly like the ones they wear at the hospital. And wait for it...'

'Get on with it!' Karen spat.

'Full wig, false beard and moustache.'

'What the actual fuck?' *You're loving this as much as me, John.*

'Gwen said he was trying to protect her. I wonder if he was doing extra rounds, incognito? It puts him back in the frame for the rape too. Thanks John.' Karen put the phone down. 'It seems as though Peter had a false beard and moustache. What's that about? Some sort of identity crisis or a disguise?'

Macy piped up. 'And talking of rape suspects...'

'Go on.'

'We've possibly got Ryan at the hospital. On the first of January.'

Karen stopped in her tracks. 'What? Why didn't you say before?'

'Because I was being a bit thick,' Macy confessed. 'I told you about Dom West and the dodgy-looking ID. But there's no such person, at least not on our files. The Passport Number isn't real either, apparently. And when you look at the photo...'

'Show me,' Karen said. She peered at the image. 'It does look familiar. Those eyes. Tom West... You mean it could be Ryan Westbury using his father's passport?'

'It would need a tiny alteration before copying it,' Macy said.

'You're right; if we could get hold of a copy of Tom Westbury's passport, we could compare the two. How did the agency pay their wages?'

Macy shook her head. 'No idea. Maybe it was a one-off.'

'There's no beard either. How long does it take to grow one?' Macy shuddered in response. 'Barbara Spinnard mentioned a possibly unshaven young man.'

'It fits,' Macy said.

Karen nodded. 'If Ryan was at the hospital, he could easily have opened the fire door, like Peter could have done. Let's see where we are.' Karen turned to the boards and started a new one.

1. **CHECK STUBBINS CAR KT/JS**
2. **RING PASSPORT OFFICE MD**
3. **CHECK FABIAN DENSON' MOVEMENTS MD**

'OK. There's the Westburys. Tom Westbury. He's connected to the tennis club with the new carpets. He could have been leaving there the night of his accident. Damn, I should have gone to his funeral. Bloody DCI Winter and his red lines. We need to lean on Jan Price.' She wrote 4*.* **JAN PRICE MD** on the board. 'What else is around that building? We know that Stella was going to see Iain. That's why they were both in the vicinity.'

'Exactly,' Macy agreed.

'Now, back to the rape. As well as checking the passport, we can see if Barbara recognises Ryan as the attempted attacker. I'll try Vera and see if she's got Barbara's number. If we've got Ryan Westbury somewhere in the frame, the guv will have to give in and let me investigate properly.' Macy nodded. 'Then there's the rape threat letter.'

'Yes, that was a very clear threat.'

'Definitely. And if it was a response to Tania, it's a pretty personal one. We know now that she, or her solicitor, has made a formal complaint; but maybe someone else took it personally too.'

Karen wrote up **5. TANIA Rape letter** 'That reminds me. The other letter...'

Macy could no longer stifle her yawn. She let out a loud one and seconds later, Karen followed suit. 'OK,' she said.' Enough for tonight. Meet back here on Monday. I've got to be in court on Tuesday. We've got to prepare.'

Macy left in a flash. Karen still had things on her mind. She wrote on the board:

6. THE COMPOSITE LETTER. EMAIL SPALLS. KT
7. LOGBOOK. MD.

61

Monday 22nd April

It was late in the afternoon and Karen was already in the incident room when Macy appeared. She looked at the board where a line had been drawn through item 1.

'Stubbins.' Karen said. 'Had a car, it was scrapped two years ago. Another orderly at the hospital confirmed it and said he walked everywhere.'

'Still nothing from the Passport Office,' Macy said. 'And I tried Jan Price. I think she's avoiding me. I've left messages. Tania's not due back but I had a look on Facebook over the weekend. And guess what? She's friends with Ryan Westbury. They went to school together. She posted something the day his father was killed and told him about Cary's attack. He told her that Stella was responsible for his Dad's death. He got really angry about it and said he would sort it.'

'Excellent work, Macy.'

Bill's head appeared round the door. 'Got a young lad for you, Karen.' He looked at the boards. 'Better if you come to the desk.'

'Ryan?' Karen speculated. She was wrong. It was James.

'Hello James. Nice to see you again. What can I do for you?' She led him into an interview room.

'I've found something.' He got out his phone and held it out so she could see it. 'This one. I think I know something about this man.'

Karen looked at the post. 'She's going to fucking hell stupid bitch.' There was no face attached to the words.

'Who do you think it is?'

'That background. That's taken in my school. I think he's someone who used to go there. It's changed a bit now. That tree's been chopped down. Last year. It was diseased or something.'

'That is brilliant, James. We'll get someone working on it now. Thank you so much.' He was smiling when she showed him out.

Karen returned to the incident room and explained it to Macy. 'I reckon that post, together with what you've found on Facebook definitely puts Ryan in the frame. I'm going to see the guv. He's got to let us talk to the Westburys now. Was he at his desk when you came in?' Macy shook her head. 'Bollocks. What about the logbook?'

Macy stared at the board. 'I don't remember that...' Karen guiltily put her fingers to her mouth. 'But I'm going into town now to check with the hotel about Fabian Denson.'

Karen nodded. 'Good. And we've got a suspect for the composite. It could have been from an Edward Brandon.'

'Who's he?'

'Stella handled his divorce, but she insisted on complete secrecy. Including from him. But it looks like she stitched him up. She conceded far too much to his wife.'

'And?' Macy waited for the punch line.

Karen glanced at the board. 'He's sent a reply.'

'And?' Macy repeated.

'He was Amanda Denning's ex-husband.'

'Wow! So Amanda never knew what a favour Stella did her. That's magic. If I ever get divorced...' Macy caught Karen's eye and stopped talking.

'OK. You get off into town and check on Fabian. I bet the lab is closed, but I'll check if there's anything on that logbook or the composite letter. And I'm seeing Sergeant Jones tomorrow so I can find out more about Sandra Atkins and her dead husband.'

'For the inquest?'

Karen nodded. 'And John Steele gave me an idea about that rape-threat letter. I'll try Vera again. She gave me her home number. We need to find out what's happened to Barbara Spinnard.' Karen's hand hovered over the phone. 'Ring me if you find anything,' she said, as Macy left. 'Mrs Fontaine? DS Thorpe here. Have you heard from Miss Spinnard yet?'

'A mobile number? Yes please.' Karen scribbled it down. *Now I've got you. Ah, she's answering.*

Karen waited for the woman to speak. 'Miss Spinnard? It's DS Thorpe here. I wanted to ask you a couple of quick questions.'

'Is it essential? I'm in America at the moment, with relatives.'

'Yes, it is, Miss Spinnard. First, I need to ask you about a poison pen letter you received, a particularly nasty one. It mentioned the rape of a six-year-old child.'

'I don't remember that one,' Barbara replied.

'Who else knew about your daughter - Robert Cary's child?'

'That was about Laura, not Catherine.'

Interesting reaction.' And how can you be sure?'

'No one else knew. Only Rob.'

'Isn't there anyone you might have mentioned it to?'

'It could have been that young man.'

'What young man?'

'The one who threatened to attack poor Rob. He saw the picture. He asked me if she was Rob's and I said yes, on instinct.'

'Have you ever heard of a man called Peter Stubbins?'

'No,' Barbara replied, without hesitation.

'He never rang you or spoke to you?'

'No. But there was a call to Mr Cary, the day he died.'

'Why didn't you tell us before?'

'I've only just remembered. Whoever it was didn't leave a name. And I can't be sure if it was a man or a woman.'

'We do have a possible suspect for the attempted assault. Can you make yourself available so we can show you an image?'

'I'm sorry. I can't hear you. Reception...' The line went dead.

There is something very suspicious about that woman. Karen rang John. 'Ah, you're there? Any technicians around?'

'One or two sad souls.'

'Good. How are you on tracing Twitter and Facebook posts?'

'Karen, for you, I'll have a go.'

'And Stubbins' phone?'

'Sorry. It wasn't at his flat.'

'What are the chances that the university switchboard monitored calls coming in?'

'You mean Stubbins calling Spinnard? It's possible...'

62

Tuesday 23rd April

Karen got to the office early only to be disappointed. There was a message from Julia: 'Stuck in traffic. See you at the court.' She did, however, have a glimmer of success with DCI Winter. He was in his office. She marched in and after a short preamble, got to the point.

'But we've got to talk to them all now. Ryan at the very least. It's totally legit.'

He stared at her for what seemed to her like ages. 'You're going to the inquest?'

'Yes, of course.'

'Don't you dare talk to anyone at all. See me afterwards. I want to know the verdict before I do anything else.' His hand hovered over his phone. 'Shut the door please, Karen.' He picked it up as she closed the door.

***

Karen made her way to the courtroom and hung around inside, trying hard not to look like a police officer. But a uniformed Julia walked straight up to her.

'Sergeant Jones.' She held out her hand. 'Julia,' she added.

'DS Thorpe. But you already know that,' remarked Karen shaking Julia's hand. Both had firm handshakes, both liked that they did but none the less, they were sizing each other up, Julia clearly miffed at the mild snub.

Karen led the way into the courtroom where they sat at the back. The family were already seated. Karen identified them to Julia in a whisper.

'Mrs Westbury Senior, who you've already met is sitting next to Rosalind Westbury, Tom's widow, then Jim, the car dealer is at the end.'

'He's the one you think made the call to the press about the phone?' Julia whispered back.

'Can't prove anything. I've got him in mind for something else too. Nasty piece of work I reckon.'

'I've arranged that meeting. Can't you join me?'

Karen shook her head. 'Protocols. Try and get him into a conversation about the accident. It's fair enough, you're here.'

'OK.'

'No sign of the son, Ryan. I'm really keen to see him, never mind interview him.'

There was a slight movement in the public gallery. Both of them turned to see a young dark-haired man joining the family.

'I see he shaved,' Julia noted.

'Shaved? Is that Ryan?'

'I'm guessing it is. I saw him leave Martha's house. He had a beard and moustache then. She told him off about it.'

Karen threw Julia a strange look, then smiled. 'Perfect. Tell you later,' she whispered, nodding her head to the front of the courtroom. They joined everyone standing as the Coroner came in.

The stern-faced, plain-suited man sat down, and the formalities began. Evidence of the deceased's identity was presented and accepted, the pathologist's report was read out in full, concluding that death was through multiple organ failure following massive trauma to the torso. No witnesses were called but some statements were read out.

Throughout the hearing, there was almost total silence, the exception being some stifled sobbing from Ros Westbury.

When the policeman from the SCU was called, a few people sat up and took notice. This was more interesting. There were pictures of the aftermath of the crash to see, and everybody wanted to look at them apart, perhaps, from the family.

'In conclusion, we found no evidence of any particular reason for the driver to apply his brakes other than the possibility that an animal, such as a deer, ran out in front of him, which is a frequent occurrence at that location. It is also likely that the lack of airbag and the impairment of the brakes of the car that

239

crashed into him added significantly to the impact of the collision. However, we are unable to detect any conclusive evidence of tampering with the brakes. Unfortunately, it has not been possible to interview the driver of that car, but we do not think it likely that any further information that might come to light will alter our conclusions.'

Someone in the room shouted 'Shame!'

The Coroner asked only one question: 'There was an article in the local paper about the possibility of the second driver being distracted by a mobile phone. Could you clarify that, Officer?'

'Yes sir,' the policeman replied. 'The accusation came from an anonymous call to the local paper. We have asked for the caller to come forward. He has not, and we have been unable to trace the call since it was made from a pay-as-you-go mobile device. Nobody witnessed the collision. A phone was recovered after the removal of the driver of the other car. There was a working hands-free system already set up. We have examined the phone, and although there was a photo taken at the time of the crash, we believe that this was caused by the impact. In the absence of sworn evidence, we have concluded that this phone call was vexatious.'

Karen and Julia both watched Jim Westbury as the policeman spoke. He looked as shifty as ever but gave nothing away.

The Coroner looked up. 'Thank you, Officer.' He then addressed the attendees. 'Ladies and gentlemen. Having read the witness statements and heard the Officer's report I have reached a verdict on the death of Tom Westbury of Cedar Lodge, Yewlands on the thirteenth of December 2012. I hereby record a verdict of accidental death.'

Everybody stood as the Coroner left the courtroom. After a moment of reflection, the family trooped out in silence. Karen and Julia stayed behind, watching them leave.

'When are you seeing him?' Karen asked, looking at her watch.

'Two. Anywhere round here we can get a quick meal?'

'Yep. Walk this way,' Karen replied. Five minutes later, Karen and Julia were sitting in The Crown, waiting for their Ploughman's

Lunch to arrive.

'What was it with the beard?' Julia asked.

'We have a bearded suspect at the hospital. We're pretty sure we have a name, but nobody to identify him and our only image is poor.'

'And still nothing on the car?'

Karen shook her head. 'It was definitely a Triumph Herald though. My Constable ID'd it from your photo. We're pretty sure it was carted away under a cover to be disposed of. Buried or something; crushed wouldn't do it.'

'Or re-sprayed, new plates?' Julia suggested.

'In my experience, they don't take chances like that these days.'

'What about Jim Westbury, then?'

Karen shook her head. 'I need him at the scene of the accident on the thirteenth.'

'And I need him in Harwich on the twentieth,' Julia grunted. 'Why can't you interview him yourself?'

'It's complicated. If he mentions his father, ask him about it.'

'OK.'

63

Julia found her way to Jim Westbury's house where grimacing, he opened the door. Without speaking he nodded her inside. He was clearly in a bad mood following the inquest. When Julia explained she wanted to ask him a few questions about his half-brother Piers, his story sounded well-prepared and he was tight-lipped.

'I only saw him the once. It was the thirteenth of December.'

'The thirteenth? Are you sure?'

'Do you think I'd forget my own brother's death?'

'I'm sorry. I didn't know it was the same day. What happened when you saw him?'

'He was sniffing around looking for money. I gave him a monkey and told him to bugger off.'

'Fifty pounds?'

'It's five hundred. And he was bloody lucky to have that.'

'That's a lot of money for somebody you've only met once, Mr Westbury. How did you know he was who he said he was?'

'Family resemblance.' Jim pointed to his eyes. 'No mistaking Dad's peepers. I take after Mum meself. Besides, the old man told me before he died that there was a Paul or someone out there.'

'He died? Was it recent?'

Jim puffed himself up and glowered at her. 'None of your business. It was years ago.'

'I didn't mean to pry. He must have been young then, like your brother?' Jim folded his arms. *What was that all about.* 'Please tell me again, where did you meet and where did you last see him?'

'He came to the yard.'

'Could he have had anything to do with the accident?'

'No.'

'How can you be sure? Where were you the night your brother was killed?'

'Because that cow caused the accident. I don't care what that ponce said, she was on her phone. And it's none of your business, but I was with my mum.'

'How did he come to the yard? By car?' Jim hesitated. *I'm on to something here*

'He was on foot when I saw him.'

'But he drove up from Dorset in a car. In a very distinctive car. A red Triumph Herald. You're a car dealer Mr Westbury, think again. Are you sure he came on foot?'

'Then he must've sold it to someone else.' Jim snarled 'There was no car.'

'What's this then?' She showed him the photo.

'Customer parking.'

'A Triumph Herald?'

'We get all sorts.'

'OK. What happened when you saw him?'

'We had a bit of a chat, then I gave him the money and told him to do one.'

'Do you have any interest in finding your half-brother?' *Why isn't he curious? He's thinking what to say.*

'No. And when you find the little bastard tell him to keep away.'

'Mr Westbury, Piers Atkins is dead,'

There was no reaction from Jim, no surprise, no concern. 'I don't give a stuff.'

***

'Anyone seen the guv?' Karen shouted across the room. It was answered with a wave of shrugs. 'Aha,' Karen said optimistically, as her phone rang. 'Julia.' She walked back to the incident room as they talked.

'Westbury's definitely hiding something,' Julia said. 'And he says Piers came on the thirteenth...'

'What? Was he definite?'

'Oh yes, he even mentioned his brother's death later that day. I'll have to have words with Sandra Atkins about that. He also said there was no car.'

'But the photo?'

'He said it was a customer's. If you believe that. He said he gave Piers five hundred pounds to go away. I bet that was for the car, but there was no money on the body. I suppose someone could have mugged him or...'

'... Jim never gave him anything, bundled him in and threw away the key,' Karen finished.

'He also said he was with his mother all night.'

'How can we put him at either scene if his mother's lying?' Karen asked.

'Our forensics team have told me they've found another print on the container. It looks like someone cut their finger and tried to wipe it somewhere else. It may not be connected, of course. Your lab is probably better equipped than ours...'

'Absolutely. Get them to send it over here.' Karen gave a small fist-pump.

'Thanks. Do you have Westbury's prints on file?'

'I don't know, but our forensics guy John is pretty good. He's sitting on a logbook, which we hope has Jim's dabs on it. Maybe if they match, I can persuade my guv to let us get prints from him.'

'OK. I'm heading back now. Anything else?'

'Yes. Sandra Atkins. We heard she'd had a spat with her sister. Do you know anything?'

'Only that they didn't get on. Why?'

'Just a thought, but if Piers was up this way and gunning for Stella...'

'She might have lied about the date to protect him. I'll talk to her,' Julia said.

'Thanks.'

'Oh, I nearly forgot,' Julia added. 'Westbury was very touchy when I asked about his father.'

'What did he say?'

'Nothing much, told me to mind my own business.'

'OK. Talk soon.' Karen ended the call and looked at the recently arrived Macy. 'Now what?'

Macy slumped in a chair. 'Prints. There are prints on the logbook but no match. And Westbury's aren't on file.'

'Let me ring John.' Karen picked up the phone. 'Hi. Sergeant Julia Jones, Dorset Police is sending through some prints. Can you cross-check them against the ones on the logbook? We think they could be Westbury's. Macy says you don't have them on file?'

'I'm working on it.'

'And any progress with the Twitter and Facebook accounts?'

'I'm doing my best, your majesty.'

'Piss off, John.' Karen clicked off the phone and turned back to Macy. 'Anything else?'

'We know the original owner of the half with the chassis number on it, but he sold it for scrap.'

'Where?'

'Through a number in the local paper.' Macy said. 'I've rung it; discontinued, untraceable. Probably an old phone.'

'Do we have a description of the man who took it?'

'Middle-aged male, average height, no distinguishing features.'

'Even if Westbury was behind it, he might not have collected in person. We need an ID. Do we even have a picture of Westbury? Who else works for him? Do we know?' Macy shook her head. 'I'll add it to the list. Fabian Denson?'

'I got hijacked by DS Harris yesterday...'

'Bastard,' Karen muttered.

'I'll go tomorrow.'

Karen looked at the map. 'That car... If it *was* Piers' car in Westbury's yard it means that it never left the area. Supposing Westbury used it to take him to Harwich? And would he have needed leaded petrol?'

'He'd have needed some petrol somewhere. But probably unleaded. Piers and Peter weren't in Cary's league. If they had old bangers, they'd have been converted years ago, that's my guess. Shall I look at routes? CCTV?'

Karen nodded. 'What about Jim? He's meant to have been at home with his mother that evening. Could he have been at both places? How does the timing work? Why so keen to blame Stella?

If it *was* him made that call. We need a motive for him. Insurance?'

'I'll look at it.'

Karen looked at the board. 'Jan Price?'

'No. Sorry,' Macy said.

Karen's phone rang. She spoke before she answered it. 'John already. Speedy or what? John? You sound chirpy. Good news?'

'Yes. We've got matches on both the logbook and the fingerprints Sergeant Jones had from the container. Same prints. Jim Westbury; we're 99.9% certain.'

'You found Westbury's prints? How?'

'Because I'm a genius. No, very old case, twenty-five years ago. Should've been wiped. We can't use them; we'll need fresh ones.'

'Great! We've got him at Harwich that night *and* selling Iain's car. You're bloody amazing, John. Have you told Sergeant Jones?'

'Had to tell you first.' Karen could hear him smiling down the phone.

'Hang on, you said twenty-five years ago. What was the case?'

'I searched everywhere, Karen. Whatever it was, everything else has been removed from all the records.'

'Was there a date?'

'First October, 1989'

'And that didn't ring any bells?'

'Shit!' John said. 'I'll have another look.'

64

'Thank you for meeting with me here so early, Mrs Price.' Macy was as stern as she could manage, as she stood in the Club boardroom. 'But we believe that it was, in fact, Mr Tom Westbury who supplied and fitted these lovely blue carpets on the thirteenth of December last year.'

Jan wriggled a little in her chair. 'I don't want to get anyone into any trouble.'

'He's dead, Mrs Price. There's nothing anyone can do to him now. Tell me what you know.'

Jan let out a curious stifled giggle, then her face fell. 'It wasn't like you think. He explained it to me. Stock tolerances he said, and off-cuts that can't be sold. He did us a real favour. The Club doesn't get that much dosh these days. We can't splash out. It's not like he nicked it. Not really.'

'Thank you. We're getting there at last.'

'What about me?' Jan frowned. 'Am I in trouble?'

'Mrs Price, if you've told me the truth this time, we may be investigating a murder. No one's got time to come after you for a slight memory loss.'

Jan took a moment to absorb this. 'He did it. I'm sorry I forgot. Did you say a murder?'

'We're still looking at the whole scenario, including Iain Matthews' accident.'

'Poor man. I don't know what's going to happen to the Club now. Fabian's probably taking over.'

'How well do you know Fabian Denson?'

'Not well. I'm not a fan.'

'How did he get on with Stella Cary?'

'I think he tried it on with her once. Does it with everyone. Except me.'

'Do you happen to know anything about Mr Matthews' car?'

'Funny you should say that. Iain was talking about buying a car from Jim Westbury. I mentioned it to Tom, Jim being his brother. I know he got very angry, but I left him to it.' She paused. 'Oh no! Do you think that's what happened? Iain bought it anyway?'

'It's certainly something we'll look into, Mrs Price.'

***

'That's brilliant, Macy!' Karen had caught Macy in the office as she took off her coat. 'We know that the brothers weren't seeing eye-to-eye and that Tom didn't approve of Jim. That maybe gives him a motive.'

'Especially if he was going to lose a good sale to Iain.'

'The guv's absolutely got to let us interview the Westburys now. What about fingerprints? We need to check the ones on the poison pen letters. Can you run through the files? We need them for every name on those boards, please.'

'OK.'

'And don't forget petrol and timings,' Karen added. 'We, and by that I mean you, need to check the CCTV on all petrol stations for all possible routes for the thirteenth of December. Let's try and pin the bastard down.'

As soon as Karen finished speaking, DCI Winter appeared. 'Guv!' she almost shouted. 'I've been trying to speak to you.'

'In thirty, Karen. In thirty,' he replied.

***

DCI Winter sat in his office, thinking about things. He'd been getting it in the neck from Chief Constable Burns for days now. And this morning's call had been very fraught. 'Look, sir,' he'd reasoned. 'Most rape victims at least have DNA evidence. Even if they were drugged. I can't deliver the impossible and I won't try. When the baby is born, we'll be able to test it safely. There is absolutely no point in trying to arrest somebody now and make ourselves look like fools, a few months down the line.'

'Put someone who knows what they're doing on it.'

'Thorpe's one of my best officers.'

'Just fucking well get someone else,' he'd been told. 'Get Harris on the case or get off your own arse if you have to.'

Did I do the right thing? Has she got a hope in hell of sorting this?

He finished his coffee and braced himself to speak to Karen, then opening his door he yelled, 'DS Thorpe!' Karen came running in. 'Where are we? Chief Constable Burns is baying for my blood.'

'We're closing in, guv. On Jim Westbury.'

DCI Winter sat back in surprise. 'As a rape suspect?'

'Possibly, but we've got a lot more.'

'Tell me...' *Please don't say I've been holding her back...*

DCI Winter leaned forward and gave Karen his complete attention. This was no time to cover his back. It was more exposed if he didn't let her have her way. Possibly. He had a tough call to make.

When she had finished her briefing, he sat back in his chair, letting it all sink in. Then he leaned forward.

'What you've got on Jim Westbury isn't good enough. And there's protocol, Karen. We have to formally liaise with the Dorset Police. I have to. You can't simply ring up your counterpart there and get on with it. I need to smooth the way, OK?' Karen nodded. 'Even the Dorset Police won't be able to convict Westbury because his prints were found on that container, and you haven't even got him in the frame for anything much; only maybe selling a dodgy car. Keep off their turf until you've got something concrete. And let me know first.'

'He's definitely up to his neck in his half-brother's death. I'm positive.'

'It's not our case, Karen. Steer clear. I mean it.'

'What about Ryan though? Guv, we've got him at the hospital. Nearly.'

DCI Winter frowned.

'Another rape suspect? Very unlikely. Personally, I still think it's an inside job, but we must make some progress, I agree.' He paused. 'Talk to Martha Westbury. Only about the rape though, absolutely nothing else. She's a rum old bird but she has her limits and I don't think she'd approve of rape. If Ryan's involved, she'll let us know one way or the other.'

'Will do!' Karen ran out of the office.

After she left, DCI Winter picked up the phone. 'We need to talk...'

65

Karen was tingling with excitement as she waited at the door.

'Mrs Westbury? I'm here to run over a few things again. It won't take a moment.'

Martha, scowling let Karen in. 'You lot. Always have to hear everything ten times. If you got it right first time...' She walked into her living room and sat down.

Karen perched on the edge of a chair. 'I am sorry that the inquest didn't turn up anything. I know you were looking to put the blame somewhere.'

Martha looked up at her. 'Bloody disgrace. It's all down to that bitch and her phone...'

Karen nodded dismissively. 'There's no evidence to prove that Mrs Westbury. But there is evidence to suggest that somebody made that call *intending* to make it look like that. Funnily enough...' She gave a half-laugh. 'It sounded a bit like your son, Jim.'

Martha straightened her back at the mention. Karen continued, watching the old lady carefully. 'But telephone voices always sound a bit weird, don't they Mrs Westbury?' She waited for a reaction. 'Anyway, according to our notes, Jim was with you all evening on the night of the accident.'

'He was,' she replied, defiantly.

'Are you absolutely certain of that, Mrs Westbury?' Karen asked.

'Yes, I bloody am.'

Then I'd like to know, if he saw Mrs Cary use her phone at the scene of the accident, how could he also have been with you all evening?'

Martha sat back in her chair, her anger changing into something else. *Doubt?* Karen wondered. 'And Jim's name has also come up in connection with a death near Harwich.'

'Who?'

'A man called Piers, also known as Paul Atkins.' *She didn't even blink.* 'The son of your late husband Nicholas Westbury.'

'I've already had one of you lot talking about this shit.' The anger was returning.

'What about your grandson, Ryan? Could he have been at the scene of the accident?'

'Ryan's a good boy.'

'Where was he that night?'

'No idea. You'll have to ask him.'

'We will. When we can find him. We also believe he may have been at the hospital the night that Mrs Cary was raped.'

'Then you're mistaken!' Martha, now red-faced, rose to her feet.

'Rape is a serious, terrible offence. Especially committed against a defenceless woman in a coma. She didn't deserve that now, did she? Even if she possibly was on her phone?'

'Piss off before I throw you out.'

'Thank you, Mrs Westbury. That's all for now.' Karen left, shutting the door firmly behind her, but she lingered long enough to hear Martha shouting down the phone.

'What the hell have you been up to, Jim?'

Karen jumped into her car and rang Julia. 'You'd better hurry up; I think Jim's mother is on the warpath.'

***

Karen had just arrived back at the office when Julia rang her.

'I think you might have waited,' she said. 'It looks like he's done a runner.'

'Bastard,' Karen replied. 'We'll check his house.' She looked at Macy. 'I'll drive, you navigate,' she barked, as they rushed outside to get into Karen's car.

Karen, following Macy's directions, eventually turned into a small road full of run-down terraced houses. 'Is this it? The second-hand dodgy car market can't be bringing in much if he's living here,' she said.

Macy leaned forward suddenly. 'Look, up ahead. There. Red car pulling out.'

'Got it.' Karen put the car in gear.

'It's the Triumph Herald! Macy said. 'And Jim's driving.'

'I'll follow. Take your cap off and keep low.'

Macy gave her a look. 'Are you seriously suggesting that you're not as easy to recognise as me now?'

Karen frowned. 'Fair point. Still, lose the hat. It could be a fast ride.' She followed the car as it turned right at the end of the road.

'Fake plates,' Macy noted.

Karen expertly followed at a distance. 'Shit, he's turning towards the London Road.'

'And?'

'And that stretch is quiet now and we'll stick out like a sore thumb. And the guv will kill me. He's warned me off him often enough.'

'Shall I call Julia? Will she give us the green light?'

'Good thinking.' Karen took out her phone. The number's on here.'

Macy rang Julia as the car began to move off. She explained the situation.

Julia was on board. 'Follow him for as long as you can. Give me the coordinates and I'll try to get air support.'

Karen carried on matching the red car's pace as best she could. 'He's on to me,' Karen muttered. 'Now he's pulling in,' she yelled. 'I'll have to overtake.'

The red car slowed down then as Karen drew level, she stared past Macy to see Jim's face. He sneered at her through the window.

Karen looked back to the road. Jim's car began to pick up speed.

Karen slowed; Jim slowed.

She sped up, he sped up.

It's like that is it? This time Karen kept going. But Jim went faster. Karen put her foot down. Macy held on.

By the time they were both doing seventy, Jim suddenly cut in front of her. Karen slammed on the brakes, but with a glancing hit, Jim pushed them off course, sending Karen's car careering towards the central reservation. She turned the wheel, avoiding a head-on impact then scooted alongside the barriers until the car hit a bend in the barriers and came to a stop with a bang. While their airbags inflated, she watched Jim disappear into the distance.

When she'd caught her breath, Karen was furious. 'I knew it! That's how he did it. I'm positive now. But how could he go fast so quickly? In that old banger?'

'Because it's been souped-up,' Macy said, still puffing from the excitement. 'I wish I could to that to mine. Till then, I'd better look at yours.'

Both women got out to have a look. Karen inspected the dents and scratches while Macy pulled up the bonnet.

'You're lucky,' she said. 'It doesn't look too bad, considering. You'll need a new radiator, minimum. But a bit faster and we'd have been really hurt.'

'Paintwork and a few bumps,' Karen said, rubbing her arm. 'I'd better get back to Jones. She'll need to get a search on for the car.'

66

The incident room was beginning to feel crowded as Karen, Julia, John and Macy met.

'Are you sure you're OK?' John asked.

'I'm fine. I've got a courtesy car coming.'

'That's not what I meant. And have you filed a proper report?'

Karen grunted. 'We're not here to talk about me.' She looked at the others and stood up. 'Welcome, Julia. I'm sorry we lost him. But I think I need to make sure we're all up to speed with this, no pun intended. I'll start with the rape.' Julia settled in her chair and looked interested.

'Stella Cary, sister of Sandra Atkins was raped on or around first January,' Karen began. 'Husband, Robert Cary, he hadn't had sex for weeks and had form for sexual aggression. He was at the hospital at some point on New Year's Eve not long after being rejected by neighbour Amanda Denning after he made a pass at her.' She tapped the board. 'Iain Matthews. Stella's lover. Now deceased. We've got him at the hospital on New Year's Eve too. But he denied having sex with her. Peter Stubbins, an orderly and obsessed with Stella had been posing, we think, as a hospital security staff member.

We have an agency worker, Dom West, possibly Jim Westbury's nephew, Ryan, using his father's altered passport to get the job.' Karen paused to sigh. 'But it's all blown wide open because of a compromised fire escape I found in the ward. However, we know that most rapists are known to the victim. My money's on Ryan opening up the fire escape for his uncle. With me, so far?'

'Yep.' John answered for them all.

Karen looked at Macy. 'What about Fabian Denson?'

Macy sat up. 'He arrived at the hotel at eleven am December thirty-first, left two pm on January first. There's no sign of him leaving at the front or the back. I've got a copy of the reception CCTV and I'm going to run through it to double-check.'

'Good. Hopefully, that's one less.' Karen drew a dotted line through his name. 'Now the poison pen letters. Of particular interest is the composite, for which we have a possible suspect, Edward Brandon. He has a motive. He was pissed off at the settlement his ex-wife got. Stella Cary acted for him. We also think she tricked him into giving more away than he needed to.'

'Why would she do that?' Julia asked.

'She was friends with Amanda Denning, his ex-wife.'

'Clever,' Julia nodded.

'Then there's the other letter containing a threat to rape a six-year-old child, as a revenge attack for Robert Cary's sexual assault on his student Tania. Once again Ryan could be in the picture. Cary had a six-year-old lovechild with his PA Barbara Spinnard and a six-year-old daughter with Stella. We know that a youth tried to threaten him. And Ryan is a friend of Tania's. He also told her that Stella is blamed for his father's death. What's more, Ryan went to the same school as James Cary.' She looked at John. 'Any results on that troll?' John shook his head. 'Ryan could be one of the trolls. One of them posted a photo, which we know was taken in a year when he was still at school.'

'Sounds good to me,' Julia said. 'Anything conclusive?'

Karen looked at John. 'Fingerprint checks, John?'

'We're still missing Amanda Denning, Penny Matthews, Ryan Westbury and Edward Brandon.' Karen looked at Macy with accusation. 'And?'

'I've been really busy,' Macy responded. Karen stayed staring at her. 'You mean now?'

'Take the mobile unit.' Macy hesitated. Karen looked at her. 'Now.'

'But...'

'Now!' Karen repeated. Macy walked out, unable to disguise her indignation.

'OK. Where was I?' Julia gave Karen a look somewhere between horror and admiration. John smiled with adoration. 'For Julia's benefit, technically I'm not meant to be investigating Stella's RTA but to me, it seems very connected.'

'I agree,' John said.

Karen beamed at him. Julia looked from one to the other in mild suspicion.

'Here we have possible interference on Stella's car and a potential suspect, Penny Matthews. We think she knew her husband Iain was having an affair with Stella. And she was doing a car maintenance course, so she knew her way around brakes.

There's a potential red car at the scene - possibly linked to Piers Atkins and we know there was bad blood between Stella and his wife Sandra.'

'What about Robert Cary?' Julia asked. 'Did he want her out of the way?'

'Yes. He might have thought Stella was going to shop him for the sexual assault on Tania.'

'And the Westbury RTA?' Julia asked.

'It's Stella's accident only from the other angle — that someone might have been trying to kill Tom. But we've got no traction with that line so far.'

'Got it,' Julia nodded.

'But we do suspect Jim Westbury was involved in the collision somehow. And after today, I know how he could have done it. As you know, he was driving a Triumph Herald, probably Piers' car, but with fake plates. Macy reckons it had been jazzed up.'

Julia looked at the board. 'Could it have been the unidentified speeding car?'

Karen shook her head. 'It's possible but I don't think so.' She turned to the map board. 'This is what I think. Tom's here at the tennis club finishing off the carpets. Jim's coming past in Piers' car, sees Tom's van and stops. Tom was angry about Jim selling Iain a dodgy car. They had a row. Jim waits in the road here. Tom drives off.

Now, Stella comes along speeding. She's got a date with Iain and Penny's at college. She sets off the speed trap but probably knows there's no film in it, or doesn't care about a fine. She catches Tom up. Both pull out when they see Jim's car in the left-hand lane. Jim speeds up again on the inside, cuts Tom up, turns on his headlights. Tom thinks he's braking, slams his brakes on and Stella, she's only going at Tom's speed now, but her brakes are faulty, or Penny's messed with them and BANG!'

John spoke first. 'It's good. It works.'

'Where was Piers then?' Julia asked.

'Damn. No, hang on, he could've been in the boot already,' Karen said.

'A Triumph Herald?' John said. 'He'd have to have been willing to get in such a small space. Were there signs of injury on the body?' He looked at Julia. She shook her head. 'Then he could have been a passenger. Jim supposedly taking him to Harwich after he bought the car, or pretended to buy it. When was he shut in? Any idea?'

Julia looked at her phone. 'Got it. A report back from the container company. Let's have a look. OK. It's here in black and white.' She read out: 'The container was unloaded early on the thirteenth of December and was locked by the security guard on or around seven pm.'

'Perfect.' Karen looked at John. 'Timing?'

'I'd say a two-hour drive?'

'That's plenty of time, then. We have to break Martha Westbury's alibi.'

'She's a tough cookie,' Julia said. 'OK, 'I think I'm following it all. But what happened to Robert Cary?'

Karen smiled. 'Let's have a coffee. We've earned it. I'll tell you all about it. John?'

John shook his head. 'I have to get back. I'm still doing my homework on those notes.'

67

Martha sat staring at a photo of Tom and Ryan together. *Peas in a pod.* She knew that Jim was beyond redemption, but Ryan? That was a different matter. He was young. He still had his future in front of him. She picked up the phone and rang him. 'Where are you, lad? I've had the rozzers asking about you.'

'Shit. I mean, sorry Nan. I'm trying to find Uncle Jim.'

'I spoke to him, what, half an hour or so ago. What do you want with him? What have you been up to, Ryan? Why were you at the hospital when that woman was raped?'

'I wasn't,' Ryan said, unconvincingly.

'Have you been working with your uncle?' He didn't answer. 'I don't like saying this about my own son,' she said. 'But I think he's a wrong'un. Now my Nick was no saint, that's true, but he never did nothing like this.'

'Like what Nan? Nan?'

'Never you mind. You're a good lad. You keep well out of it. Now you come over here. I want to hear all about it.'

Martha sat in silence until at last, she heard Ryan at the door. 'Come in. When did you last have a wash or a bed for the night?'

'I don't know where to start, Nan.' He heaved an enormous sigh and Martha leaned forward to listen. 'The night Dad was killed Uncle Jim wasn't here, was he?'

His grandmother shook her head. 'I don't know where he was.'

'But you told the police that...'

'I know. Because sometimes that's right, sometimes it isn't.'

Ryan was almost panting as he continued. 'He came round the next day. Swore me to secrecy...' Ryan paused.

'Best out, lad.'

'He told me he'd seen that Stella one at the accident. Said she was on her phone, but he was being chased by a blackmailer so he couldn't tell the police.' His breathing slowed a little. Martha's face was frozen in concentration.

'He said she'd killed Dad.'

'Spit it out.'

'Well, I wanted to get my own back. Especially when Tania told me what Stella's husband had done.'

'And what was that?'

'That he'd tried to rape her.' Martha flinched. 'So I thought he was a bad lot and I told Uncle Jim about it. And then he told me to get a job at the hospital. They wanted night staff, no responsibilities, only a presence they told me. And to help when people got lairy.'

'What did he want you to do?'

'Watch her, he said, he wanted to know when she came round - if she did. And that he wanted to talk to her without anybody knowing. I didn't know he was going to do anything; I swear.'

'Just finish it.'

'I signed on at the agency. They told me the hospital were desperate because it was New Year's Eve and not many want to work that shift. It was lucky they put me round her ward 'cos then I was already where he wanted me.'

'Well, lad. If you're telling me the whole story, you've done nothing wrong. No harm in taking on a job. It's good to see a young man try to find his way.'

'I didn't use my real name though Nan. Uncle Jim gave me Dad's passport. He'd fiddled with it a bit.'

The old lady breathed in so deep she looked like she might pass out. *You've gone way over the line, Jim.*

She looked at Ryan. 'If the police ask you, tell them all of it. Tell them everything. You're a young man, your whole life is ahead of you. There's no need to protect your Uncle Jim. You look out for yourself and I'll look out for you too. I have to ask you one thing.' Ryan took a deep breath. 'You don't have to say, just nod. Did he *do* anything to that woman?'

Ryan blinked hard, then gave a tiny nod of his head.

'You're a good lad, Ryan. Give your old Nan a kiss.'

As he bent down to kiss her, she tucked something into his pocket. It was only after he'd gone that she picked up the phone and made a call.

'Have you been at it all this time?' Macy asked as she returned to the room. Karen barely acknowledged her and carried on talking. But Julia smiled at her, so Macy sat down and listened.

'...so Robert Cary's death might be almost entirely unconnected. We think Peter Stubbins probably put a petrol can in his boot. He didn't have a car and he confessed to doing something terrible. But that might have meant that he'd committed the rape.' She turned to Macy. 'How did you get on?'

'Still no sign of Ryan but I got the others and I managed to get hold of Brandon. He's agreed to come by tomorrow. Any news on Jim Westbury?'

'Not yet.' Julia answered. She looked at Karen. 'What else have you got on Jim Westbury?'

'He sold, or had something to do, with the sale of the cut-and-shut car that probably killed Iain Matthews. But to be honest, our best hope in getting him is for the murder of Piers Atkins, and that's your case,' Karen conceded.

'And even with the fingerprints, it's still circumstantial.' Julia nodded.

'I'll catch him if it kills me.' Karen looked menacing. 'It's personal now and I reckon he's more likely to be the rapist than an eighteen-year-old kid. We only need the right lead.'

Their joint silence was interrupted by Karen's phone ringing. She picked it up and saw 'Number unrecognised'. She frowned then listened while a voice said.

'If you're looking for Jim Westbury, try the chalet. Leysdown.'

It was an old voice, female, and Karen could sense the tears running down the old lady's face.

'Thank you...' but the caller had already clicked off. Karen punched the air.

'And we're getting closer.' Karen turned to Julia.' Sergeant Jones, we have a tip-off.'

68

Thursday 25th April

Sergeant Julia Jones was relishing the chase. She'd gone straight to the office at the crack of dawn and secured the cooperation of the Kent police. Her counterpart, DS Mays was very helpful. He seemed to enjoy a hunt as much as anybody she'd met.

'Oh, yes, Jim Westbury. We've had him on our radar often. Usually in connection with hooky motors and imports from Harwich. But we've never managed to pin anything on him. It sometimes feels like he's being protected. We know the family have a chalet or maybe two, and there are a couple of his pals who trade around here, but it's not going to be easy to catch him. We can try all the known addresses first, if you like?'

'Definitely. I'm going to scout around the chalets, try to spot the car. How many sites are there again?'

'Nine caravan parks, eleven chalet sites. It'll be busy, but not heaving this time of year.'

'Can I drive round?' she asked.

'Might mow down a few kids if you did,' the DS winked at her. He spread out a local map on the table and continued. 'These are all the sites and other places where we know he's got contacts. I'll get my teams to do a house to house on these but if he's serious about hiding, he might be on one of these two...' He pointed at the map. 'They're a little more isolated with footpaths out of the area, and I mean footpaths. We've lost a few suspects for not being able to follow in a motor. Try this one here, first. And don't forget, ring for back-up if you find anything.'

'Thanks.' Julia took the map. Her phone rang. 'Karen. I'll call you when I get something. Yes, full-scale search. We're crawling all over Leysdown. Not a stone unturned, I promise.'

'He'll have dodgy friends and other people in the car trade. Look out for breakers' yards, and welders,' Karen said.

Julia relayed this to the DS. 'She's right. I'll mark all the ones we're covering so you don't do them too.' He took out a pen and put crosses against the sites. 'My gut feeling is he'll be in one of them. But it's possible there are more we don't know about. If you find something not marked, have a look but be careful. Don't go in, all guns blazing.'

Julia nodded. 'I'll call you if I find anything. I'd better get going.'

***

Julia got into her car and her phone rang. It was Karen. Again. 'Don't forget to look for the car,' she urged. 'The red Triumph Herald.'

'I know,' Julia growled, then she set off to the first caravan site. She parked behind a blue van in a big car park at the top of the site and wriggled into her t-shirt and running shorts on the back seat. There were rows and rows of almost identical chalets, only distinguishable by their immediate surroundings. Some had little gardens, some had kids' playthings like swings and slides, and a few had cars parked alongside. She was very excited. *My very first chief suspect in a murder investigation! About time.*

Viewing the site systematically, she tried to look casual then broke into a loping run, looking either side as casually as she could. *Nothing here... nothing there.*

When she saw the end of the last line approaching, she became a little despondent. She went back to her car, a little puffed, and called DS Mays. 'Nothing here. You?'

'No one's seen him - or if they have, they're good liars,' he said.

'I'm off to the second one. I'll ring again when I'm done. We may need to spread the net further.'

At the next site, Julia's spirits lifted again. *This is much bigger, more cars.* It was more complex, not in simple rows; there were crescents and avenues on one side and all of those had small front gardens.

This map wasn't easy to follow but remembering the advice she was given about mazes when she was a little girl, she took the left-hand side and followed it wherever it went. These smarter chalets were more secluded than those at the previous site, but she could see into the back gardens. Still, she found nothing.

Disappointed, Julia did some stretches then began on the other, more regimented side. She ran down then up, sequentially. She saw kids playing, people sitting down to barbeques, hardy sunbathers and the odd car parked alongside next to a chalet, but no red Triumph Herald.

She arrived at the next site and saw a silver Astra parking up. She didn't recognise the car, but she did recognise the occupant. 'Karen? What are you doing here?'

'I finally got new wheels and I thought you might need a hand.'

'But this is against all protocol.'

'I know this place. Dad took me here for our holidays. I can help. I want to help. Where are we?'

Inwardly fuming, Julia showed her the map. 'I'm about to go here.' She pointed. 'But...' She stared open-mouthed as Karen had already raced off. Julia loped after her, shaking her head. When Julia saw Karen go down one lane, she took the next.

They saw each other when they passed gaps in the chalets. It was clear that the race was on. Julia missed Karen at the next gap and double-backed to find her. She saw Karen closing in on a vehicle covered by a tarpaulin, then watched. Karen grabbed her back as if she had pulled a muscle. But as she bent down to stretch, she lifted the corner of the tarpaulin and revealed the very thing they had been searching for, the red Triumph Herald. *Damn her! No time to argue.*

Julia caught Karen's eye as she made the call. She watched as Karen nodded, then dropped the corner of the tarpaulin. She walked around the chalet, limping a little then leant up against the wall. The only window was closed, and the blinds were down but Karen put her ear to it. Julia stared at her.

'What's the number?' DS Mays was asking Julia. Julia kicked herself to attention.

'Three-four-three,' she whispered.

'Hang on, we're a minute away.'

Julia waited and watched from behind another chalet as DS Mays and his three officers charged up to the villa. They split, two going behind, two in front.

The first two saw Karen loitering outside. As she tried to explain who she was, they heard a commotion at the front. DS Mays had banged on the door and in the absence of a reply, had shouldered the door down. His colleague went inside.

Jim Westbury came hurtling out of the back door, taking the two at the back and Karen completely by surprise.

'Get him!' Karen screamed, but the men held her tight.

Julia careered round the corner. She launched herself at Jim Westbury's legs in a rugby tackle that would have made anybody proud. DS Mays, who was still rubbing his shoulder, helped to cuff him as the other man came out of the chalet.

Karen tried to wriggle free from the two officers, but they were having none of it. She felt humiliated as she watched Julia say her piece.

'Jim Westbury, I am arresting you in connection with the murder of Piers, also known as Paul Atkins. You do not have to say anything, but anything you do say may be taken down as evidence...' She shook her head at Karen, then went to speak to DS Mays as he and his colleague marched Jim to the car. When he was secured, DS Mays came to address his team.

'Let her go,' he ordered. 'She's one of us. But a bloody strange one.' He looked at Karen. 'What the hell did you think you were doing? You were not part of this operation. You had no right to be here.'

'He's my suspect, too. I was making sure we got him.' Sulking, Karen got into her car and headed back home, not completely despondent. She rang Macy to make herself feel a little important again.

'We've got him. I'll be back soon.'

69

'What the fuck is wrong with you, Karen?' DCI Winter yelled. 'I specifically told you not to trespass on their territory. How many times did I tell you not to go after Jim Westbury, without asking me? Now you've jeopardised an arrest operation. There's been a fucking complaint. Give me one good reason why I shouldn't suspend you?'

Karen's mouth went from open to wide open. 'I could have him for dangerous driving. He nearly ran Constable Dodds and me off the road.'

'And you reported it?' Karen's face fell. 'Christ, you are such a pain in the arse.'

DCI Winter's phone rang. Karen sat down and squirmed in the chair. There was a long silence from DCI Winter. She tried but couldn't hear what the person at the other end was saying. And they had a lot to say.

'Much appreciated,' DCI Winter said into the receiver. He turned to look at Karen. 'You are so bloody lucky, Karen. Apparently, your opposite number has spoken up for you. Sergeant Jones says that it was a misunderstanding on her part. And that you were being helpful. I hope you're fucking grateful. But this is going on your record.'

Karen took in a big breath before answering. 'Thank you, Sir.'

DCI Winter began to sink back a little in his chair. 'Now where are we with the rape?'

Karen reanimated in an instant. 'Number one suspect: lover, Iain Matthews. Bearded. Spent time alone with her, after hours.' DCI Winter nodded. 'He's dead, guv.' DCI Winter rolled his eyes. Karen swallowed. 'Then there's number two. Peter Stubbins. Ex-orderly at the hospital. Obsessed with Stella. Had a false beard. Same as Matthews. Motive, opportunity...'

'And...'

'He's dead too,' Karen muttered.

'Is there anybody left alive in this investigation, Karen?'

'Plenty,' Karen answered, immediately regretting saying it.

'You have plenty of suspects?' DCI Winter asked, at his sarcastic best.

'We've got CCTV of a bearded man on the right date. It might be Ryan Westbury. We've got a name, Dom West. It could be from an altered or faked passport, probably his father's. There's a resemblance. Either way, he had a beard too. Well, he did at the time of the rape. And the alarm was switched off on a disused fire escape right next to Mrs Cary's room. This man could have let anyone else in, including Jim. However, I have to admit that it could be someone else altogether. Someone with a beard. And there's a poison pen letter, a composite that looks a possibility too. There's also...'

'Don't tell me. There are seven of them. All with beards. Dwarves too, were they?'

'What?' Karen was floored by his ridicule.

'Have you interviewed Ryan Westbury yet?'

'You said...'

'Karen, sometimes you're meant to show initiative.'

'That's what I did yesterday!' Karen exclaimed. 'And...'

'Well, you'd better bloody get him before he dies too. What about this fire alarm door? How long was it open?'

'No idea, guv. Possibly since the last refurb. But there was only a window of a few days for the rape. Unless it was ongoing abuse, but the ward staff have said that's impossible. With the exception of Stubbins.'

'Are you saying it could have been any man who had access to the hospital at the right time, then?'

'Well, there is another theory, guv.'

'Go on.'

'It could be an act of revenge. Artificial insemination.'

'WHAT?!' DCI Winter roared.

Karen held firm. 'Mrs Cary was having an affair. Someone else may have been trying to scupper it.'

DCI Winter shook his head as he rested it in his hand. 'The whole thing is a crock of shit and you know it.'

Karen stood up, her temper rising. 'The chief witness

is in a fucking coma, the hospital security was shite, we can't test the foetus so there is no DNA whatsoever to go on, and I've been busting my balls working twenty-four-seven trying to suss it all. And I want to know why someone's been covering things up. Things about the Westburys twenty-five years ago. Is that why you've been stopping me get on with my job? Because I'd be much further on if you weren't holding me back all the time!'

DCI Winter stood up, also furious. 'You'd better watch yourself, Karen. If you dare to accuse me of anything underhand...'

'No worries on that score, guv. I'll save you the trouble of adding anything to my record, I'll fucking well quit.'

They eyeballed each other for what seemed like ages, neither backing down. Karen stormed out of the office to silent admiration from her colleagues, all of whom had been listening, eager-eared, outside since the opportunity had presented itself so nicely.

DCI Winter emerged a minute afterwards and everybody turned back to their work.

'Where is she?' he yelled.

Macy piped up. 'She's gone.'

'I know that, but where?' Macy shrugged.

'Anyone?' he yelled.

'Sorry, Sir,' someone said.

DCI Winter went back to his room, where he sat staring at the wall. He picked up the phone.

'Martha? Looks like he's gone too far this time. The deal's off.'

'Understood,' came the reply.

DCI Winter put the phone down.

What now? Go crawling back to her? No way.

But I need her on this case.

Do I? Do I, really? Can't I pick up the reins?

Macy's good, but she's still raw. Harris is flat out.

She'll be back. Tail between her legs. For sure.

He picked up the phone and made another call.

70

'Hello, Karen. Lovely to see you. Come in,' Jack smiled.

'Tea?' Sal appeared.

'Yes please.'

'This isn't about your dad, is it?'

'No. I've quit my job.'

'Have you really? Better tell me all about it.'

'Well, you know I was given the rape case?' Jack nodded. Karen relayed the fundamentals of the case while he listened. The only interruption was Sal bringing in their teas.

'... And the guv's been holding me back the whole time. Jack, what happened back in 1989? I found Dad's notebook. All the pages from the first to the fifteenth of October - the day Nicholas Westbury died, were cut out.'

Jack sighed. 'I don't know what to do for the best, love. Your dad swore me to secrecy, but he also told me to look out for you and truth will out, so they say.'

'Tell me, then.'

'It's a long and murky story. Drink your tea and I'll tell it to you. Although what happened was wrong, it was for a very good reason.'

Karen took a gulp of her tea while Jack began his tale.

'There was a bent copper. DCI Gary Reeves. He was on the take from Westbury's nasty little empire. He had all sorts back then, brothels, gambling, strip joints, drugs. We could never nail him for anything, because of Gary. But we didn't know that, then.'

'How did you find out?'

'It was Bob and your dad. They got a call from Nick Westbury himself. There'd been an accident, he said. Turned out that Gary had been drinking heavily, and he'd tried to rape one of his madams. But not any old one, it was one Nick used to be with. I still remember her; she was a bitter woman called Jackie Atkins.' Karen frowned at the mention but didn't speak.

'Anyway, old Nick threatened Gary with his own pistol but then Jim turned up. Now he was only a youngster himself, but he always wanted to be a bigshot. He grabbed his dad's hand to get the gun, but the trigger got pulled and Gary was shot. They had to think fast. Nick had proof that Gary had been taking backhanders, and he didn't want his lad going down for killing a cop, especially a bad'un. He was dying, too. Cancer. They didn't know that though, not then.

On Gary's side, he had a family who adored him. Six kids. If it came out what he'd done, there'd be no chance of a pension or anything. Basically, they struck a deal.'

'No!' Karen shook her head.

'Don't judge, love. Sometimes these things have to be done. You'll learn in time. Your dad carried that guilt to his grave but at least he knew the family were being looked after, and Gary died with an unblemished record.'

'How come? How did they explain his death?'

'Easy. He was drunk and fell over on his own gun, setting it off. They left him in a position that made it feasible and the pathologist confirmed it. Even he could see there was no merit in investigating further.'

'What about his widow?'

'I think she knew him well enough. She was happy with what she was told.'

Karen went into silent thinking mode. Jack was patient.

'You told me Dad stepped back because Mum died. Is that true, or was it because of this?'

'It may have been at the back of his mind; I can't deny it. But no, he didn't do that until your mum started to get ill. It wasn't long afterwards, it's true.'

'Why are you telling me this now?'

'Because Bob wants you back on the case, love. He trusts you that much.'

Karen was shocked. 'The guv? Did he ring you? When? Do you know what he said to me?'

Jack laughed. 'I've a bloody good idea, love. Don't make him crawl. He says he'll see you at six. Don't be late.'

270

'I need time to think.'

'You know that's not true,' Jack said. 'You've a rape to solve.'

Karen sat there not speaking again. He's right. *I promised Stella. And of all the people I ever trusted, Jack and my father were right up there.*

'You're a rogue, Jack. I'll think about it.'

Sal came in. 'Everything all right?'

'I suppose so. It's a lot to take in.'

'I didn't want to mention it but while you're here. Have you thought any more about...?' she began.

'His ashes? Yes. I was in Leysdown today. I shouldn't have been, but I wanted to go. It brought back some happy memories. Only now they're all ruined.'

'Don't be silly, Karen. You're hurting a bit, that's all.' Jack said, stroking her arm. 'Leysdown you say. Well I never. Your mum was from round there. I'd completely forgotten. That's where her ashes went. Remember, Sal?'

'I remember it well.'

'Have a think about it, Karen love. We could all go there together, to the sea where we used to go paddling. When you're ready. If that's what you want.'

Karen looked at them both. 'I know what you're saying. But I want a little longer. It's too much to take in. That Dad could let something like that happen. I'd better go.'

***

Karen hadn't doubted that she would go and see him, but she wasn't sure what would happen. By six pm she was sitting in DCI Winter's office. When he spoke, his tone had softened somewhat but there was no apology, no explanation, it was all work. And at that moment, that was exactly what she needed.

'Karen, the Chief Constable is on my case. We have to get a result. I don't want you to quit. Let's go through what you've got and maybe I can throw some new light on it all.'

'OK.'

DCI Winter sat with Karen in the incident room listening

while she went through everything that she had. Every single report was examined, every interview note read, every theory interrogated. DCI Winter began to draw his conclusions.

'So. I have to admit, you have a point. At this moment in time, I can't see any obvious gaps. You've been thorough, you've been insistent. Yes, find Ryan Westbury and pull him in but other than that, I agree with you. Until someone confesses or we can do a DNA test on the foetus, there's not much more you can do.' He paused. Karen was beginning to feel better. 'There's only one comment I have to make.' He looked up at the board.

'What now?'

'Drop the fucking turkey baster theory, for God's sake.'

And with that, DCI Winter strode out of the room.

71

'Hi. You're back?' Macy asked, tentatively. 'Are you OK?'

Karen shrugged as if nothing had happened. 'Sure. Fine. Whatya got?'

'More prints. And a bit more.'

'Fire away.'

'CCTV. We've got two males at a service station on the M11. Red Triumph Herald registration is the same as Piers' and there's someone sitting on the passenger side.'

'Two men? If it was Piers, he was definitely visible and with someone. Who was driving? Let me see.'

Macy showed Karen the image. 'I reckon it's Jim,' she said.

Karen beamed. 'Me too. Have you told Julia?'

'Yes, and I sent her the images.'

'Nearly there.' Karen clenched her fist. 'It's all fitting into place, at last.'

'And we've got a match of prints on the composite poison pen letter. Edward Brandon, but...'

'Fantastic. But?'

'It's only a partial match. John doesn't think it'll stand up without a confession.'

'OK, we must get him in again. Beard?'

Macy shook her head. 'Not when I saw him.'

'What about the Passport Office?'

'They're inundated. We could try the widow, Rosalind Westbury.'

Karen shook her head. 'If it was used, Ryan will have got rid of it by now.'

'Yes. You're right.' Macy agreed. She looked Karen in the eye. 'And how is DCI Winter?'

'What? That pussycat? He's been really helpful, actually. Reckons we're on the right track.'

'That's great.' Macy smiled.

As Macy left the room, Karen rang Tim Strange. 'Hi. DS Thorpe here. Do you remember that composite letter?'

'I can't forget it.'

'We may have a partial match of fingerprints to Edward Brandon. I was wondering if there's anything else I should know about him?'

'Actually, yes. He's a slippery customer. Stella had quite a bit of information accumulated about him. He was one of those serial company director types. I would surmise that she might have been about to report him to HMRC too. She was very moral about people paying their taxes. And she made him sign something to keep his appointment of her secret. I can only imagine he assumed it was in his interests to do so.'

'Now that *is* interesting. Could it give him a motive to harm her?'

'If he had any inkling of what she was doing, I'd say yes.'

***

Later that morning, with still no sign or information about the missing Ryan, Karen arranged interviews for Penny Matthews and Edward Brandon. Penny Matthews was the first to be interviewed. When she sat in front of Macy and Karen, she still looked miserable. But this time it was about her treatment, not her late husband.

'Again? We've already gone over this,' she said, looking at Karen. 'There's nothing more I can tell you. I've been through a terrible time, you know that. I have things to do, I don't need all this hassle.'

Macy smiled at her, kindly. 'I know and we're sorry, Mrs Matthews. But there are a couple of things we need to let you know, and a couple of things we need to ask you.'

'All right,' Penny sniffed.

Karen gave a little cough. 'Have you heard of a man called Jim Westbury?'

Penny stiffened immediately. 'Don't tell me Iain bought the car from him?'

'You know him?'

'Not at all. But I'd heard he sold disreputable cars. Someone mentioned it at the Club. Oh Iain. I didn't think you could be so stupid.' Her eyes filled with tears.

'There's another thing, Mrs Matthews. Where were you on the night of eleventh December last year at around six pm?'

'I have absolutely no idea.' She was beginning to cry.

'Were you at the station car park, in the vicinity of Mrs Cary's car?'

'What?' She sat upright, eyes still brimming.

Macy pushed forward a printed photo of the CCTV image. 'Is this you, Mrs Matthews?'

Penny looked at Karen in horror. 'How... where...?' She was now in floods of tears. Macy touched Karen's arm.

Karen was unmoved. 'Would you like a tissue, Mrs Matthews?'

Penny shook her head and reached into her bag for one. 'The inquest said there was no interference with her brakes,' she spluttered into her tissue.

'And why would you mention brakes, Mrs Matthews?'

'I don't know.'

'But we know that you were doing a car maintenance course at college.'

Penny promptly looked up. The cry-baby was gone. She was glowering. Karen sat back in surprise. Penny's voice was full of steel. 'Yes. That could be me. And yes, I did think about doing something to Stella's car. It's one of the reasons I went on the course. But I didn't. Like the inquest said. There was no interference. I chickened out. OK? Are you going to charge me with anything, or can I go now?'

Karen and Macy exchanged frustrated glances. Karen spoke first. 'Thank you, Mrs Matthews. That will be all.'

'I'll show you out,' said Macy.

When Macy returned, Karen was pacing the room.

'Pathetic cow,' she snarled.

'Why? Because she chickened out?'

'OK, I take back the cow bit.' Karen realised her unintended pun.

Macy laughed. 'But not the turkey...' she began. Karen's glare stopped her.

'I'm sure she did it, Mace. And she's much smarter than she pretends. And angry. But we can't prove a damned thing without a confession.'

72

The telephone rang. Karen picked the receiver up. 'Brandon's here,' she said, and looked at Macy. 'Doesn't hurt to leave him sweating a bit.'

'Yep,' Macy agreed. 'What do we know about him?'

'He's a crafty businessman. We already know that his divorce cleaned him out.'

'Very unprofessional of Stella. But pretty cool, too. He must have been furious with her.'

Karen nodded. 'And she might have threatened to dob him in to the taxman.'

'That definitely gives him a motive. And an anonymous threat might be more his thing. An office worker. Er, have we got time for a pee?'

'Yes, but only because I want to go too,' Karen grunted.

When they returned from the Ladies, they peered into reception, where a couple of men sat waiting. Neither looked happy.

'He's the one on the left,' Macy whispered. Edward Brandon sat with his legs wide apart. He chewed on the edge of a paper cup and spat out the bits.

***

In the interview room, Karen counted to sixty before telling Macy to collect Brandon. He came in, looking miserable and sat opposite, still holding the remains of the paper cup.

'Mr Brandon, as you know, we are investigating a serious sexual assault on Mrs Stella Cary. I believe you know her?' Brandon nodded. Karen took the plastic-encased letter from her file and pushed it towards him. 'Mr Brandon. Have you seen this letter before?'

Brandon sneered, as he looked at the A4 sheet of paper with the cut-out words on it. 'Never,' he said. 'I know how to use punctuation.' But his neck went bright red.

Karen pounced. 'Then can you tell us how your fingerprints were found all over it?'

'They can't be! I...' For a second Karen and Macy braced themselves; Brandon was shaking but they couldn't read him properly at first. Was it anger or fear? They didn't have to wait long. He was a paper tiger. He broke down almost immediately.

'I've never done anything like that before. I'm so sorry. She was such a stupid bitch... No, I don't mean that. I've never hurt anyone. I...'

'Mr Brandon,' Macy interrupted. 'We'll need to take a sample of your DNA, please.'

Karen nodded firmly.

Brandon's face hardened. He stood up, dropping the cup and backed away. 'What? Why? You don't think I'd... That's disgusting. I'm not doing it.'

Karen also stood up. 'Mr Brandon,' she said in her most authoritative voice. 'You are at liberty to refuse that request. But if you have nothing to hide, you have no reason to object.'

'I refuse,' Brandon said with all the force he could muster. 'I'm not doing anything without speaking to a solicitor.'

Karen tried hard not to show her surprise. 'As you wish Mr Brandon. You have forty-eight hours from now to consider this request. Then we may contact you again.'

Brandon muttered something incomprehensible as Macy took him back to reception. When she returned, Karen was standing holding a clear plastic bag. 'Oh, I do love this job sometimes,' she said. 'It won't stand up in court but at least it'll help the investigation.'

Macy grinned as she put on a plastic glove, picked up the cup and dropped it into the bag. 'I'll take it to the lab myself.'

It's a small win, Karen thought. *But it's all too bitty. If this was Midsomer, it would all be nicely wrapped up by now, like a Christmas present under a perfectly decorated tree. What I've got is what was put into recycling; bits missing, lots of horrible straggly pieces of string and used balls of sticky tape everywhere. Then again, we've got DNA from nearly all the suspects, for when we can finally test the baby. All but Ryan Westbury.* 'Damn!' *I need to see Stella again.*

***

Karen arrived at the ICU and saw Gwen waiting outside Stella's room.

'How are you?' she asked.

'I'm very well, thank you. It was a terrible shock, but I know Peter had mental health issues. Did you ever find his car?'

Karen shook her head. 'No. Your instincts were right. He had one, but it was a while ago.' She remembered something else she needed to ask, but Gwen got in first.

'How are your investigations going? There's nothing on the news these days.'

'We have a suspect in custody. We think he may have been involved in Stella's accident, but there's no proven connection to the rape yet. Phone! Do you know if Peter had a phone?'

Gwen blinked. 'Oh heavens. Yes. I picked it up the day... It's in my locker. Let me find someone to cover for me and I'll get it for you.'

'Thanks. That could be very helpful.' Karen looked at Stella. 'I assume there's no change?'

'No. Was there anything you wanted specifically?'

'I wanted to talk to her. It sounds silly but I made her a promise.' Gwen touched her arm and smiled.

'It's not silly at all, my love. It's a very good thing.'

Karen peeped into the room. Stella's bump was very noticeable. Then she realised something as she looked at her. 'What happened to the Christmas nightie?'

'It became too tight,' Gwen said.

'But it was hers. What happened to it? Did it go in the hospital wash?'

'Gracious me, no.' Gwen shook her head. 'It wouldn't have lasted five minutes here. I took it home myself to wash it if you must know. On a very low cycle.'

'Blimey.' Karen exclaimed. *That's what John taught me, too. I*

279

wonder... 'Where is it now?'

Gwen was startled. 'Why? I haven't stolen it you know.'

'DNA. There might be DNA on it. God, I've been so stupid.'

'Don't fret, my love.' Gwen went to the bedside cabinet and opened it. 'I kept it for her. For when she can wear it again.' She handed Karen the nightie and watched open-mouthed as Karen sped away. 'What about the phone?!'

73

Sergeant Julia Jones' adrenaline rush had long since subsided, as had her anger with Karen. She'd received plaudits and her Chief Inspector had even hinted about her doing her Inspector's exams.

As she pulled up outside Sandra's house, she couldn't help but notice the transformation; the walls had been painted, the fence and gate had been mended and the grass was freshly mown. The door was opened by a woman Julia could only describe as radiant. Sandra looked younger, healthier and considerably happier than when Julia had last seen her.

'Hello, Sergeant. Have you got some news at last?'

'I need to ask you a couple of questions.'

'Fire away.'

'You told me you'd last seen your husband on the twentieth of December. Was that correct?' Sandra hesitated. 'Mrs Atkins, we have evidence to the contrary.'

Sandra took in a deep breath. 'No. It wasn't. I didn't want to get him into any trouble.'

'What was the correct date?'

'He left on the thirteenth.'

'And what trouble did you think he was in?'

'He was fiddling our benefits. Claiming for kids we didn't have and Stella, that's my sister, sussed us. I thought Piers was out to get her and had run away.'

'I see.'

'Is that it?'

Julia shook her head. 'We've arrested somebody in connection with Piers' murder.'

'At last. Who is it? Anyone we know?' Sandra asked.

'Do you remember his mother telling you Piers' father was Nicholas Westbury?'

'Yes. I remember that name.'

'The man killed in your sister's accident was his son, Tom

Westbury,' Julia said. 'And we've arrested Tom's brother, Jim.'

'Why?'

'I believe Piers saw him to ask him for money, or help, or both. I don't know precisely why, but apparently, money changed hands although nothing was found on his body.'

'Poor Piers. So he was killed by someone he thought could help him?'

'It would seem that way, Mrs Atkins. But we've still got a long way to go on this case. We have to put everything in front of the Criminal Prosecution Service for their decision, but we're reasonably confident that we will be taking him to trial.'

As Julia walked away from the house, she remembered Karen and got out her phone. 'Karen? Sandra Atkins has confirmed Piers left here on the thirteenth, not the twentieth. And guess what? He did have a motive. You were right about the sisters falling out.'

***

Safely locked up in Dorset, Jim Westbury sat contemplating his lot. He had precious little else to do. *What did that solicitor say? The fingerprint on the container was circumstantial. They'd probably have to find something more on him than that. And I'd have an answer ready.* 'What Officer? You found his car? I'd forgotten I bought it off him. Gave him a monkey? Nah, that was the price. I remember now. Had a busy day, then. And when he begged me to take him to Harwich to get a ferry, well it'd have been unkind not to. He was knackered. Wanted to kip down somewhere for the night. Early start, he reckoned, to sneak into a ferry. I helped him open the door. Even nicked my bloody finger doing it. He definitely had the money when I left him. Someone must've found him and done him over. But I never had no key, Officer.'

They can't prove nothing. Even if I did go down, what's worse? Prison or Mum finding out? No one would give a bugger about that money-grabbing little bastard, Paul. But Mum? She always loved Tom best of all.

'Bloody Tom,' Jim shouted out. 'It was always your fault. That bloody car, it was none of your fucking business. And you wasn't that honest either. Those carpets? It was all right for you to work something but not me? Bloody typical.'

'SHUT THE FUCK UP!' a voice from another cell yelled.

'It wasn't my fault Mum. Honestly.'

That stupid bitch on her phone came from nowhere. She saw me for sure, but she wouldn't know me. No, she saw him. And he saw her. He was laughing when he saw what happened. Said she deserved it, and she did. There's not a sniff of me being at that accident. Or the hospital. Yes, Ryan knows it all but he's only a kid and I've got stuff on him.

'It's all her fault, Mum. I had to do it. You don't know what happened.'

It's all down to time now, he concluded. Doing time, or time passing. Only time will tell.

***

'Mother?' I've spoken to our Sandra,' Harry said, laughing, as he saw Molly knitting. 'Ha-ha, that didn't take you long.'

'What now?'

'They've arrested someone for Piers' murder at last.'

'Oh, what a relief. But Dad...'

Harry looked at her, anticipating the question.

'What about the babby? It'll be here soon. Sofia won't be around forever.'

'I've been on to the folks from Social Services. I got a contact name from the people counselling our Daniel.'

'No, Dad, we can't do that! They'll have the children taken into care!'

'Ey, lass, no they won't. We've got to let them know. We can't manage on our own forever, not on our pensions.'

'What did they say?'

'They'll be in touch. We'll stay with the kids as long as we can. Especially now our Sandra's on her feet again, we'll manage. But if there's money we're entitled to, best we get it.'

'And that cat can be put on rations. He costs more than

kiddies.' Solomon had come straight to Molly, rubbing against her legs. 'Gerroff. Bloody cat!' Solomon purred loudly and tried to coax her into the kitchen.

'I'll put kettle on,' said Harry. 'I'm spitting feathers, here.'

In an instant, Solomon's affections were transferred and he trotted behind Harry into the kitchen, tail as erect as a ship's mast.

'Tuna,' he mewed. 'There's a tin in there, I'm sure.'

Whether or not Harry had understood Solomon's miaowing, he did indeed open a tin of tuna.

74

John was sitting in Karen's local Thai restaurant, waiting for her. He'd hardly seen her socially since that memorable weekend. Finally, he'd managed to get a proper date with her. 'I'll get on it as soon as I can,' he'd told her when she gave him Stella's nightie. 'If you promise to have dinner with me, tomorrow night.'

'How long will it take?' she'd asked.

'Don't raise your hopes. My guess is we won't find anything at all. The rapist would have had to have left traces of semen on the nightie and even then, the chances of any of it resisting weeks of washing. Well?'

She'd taken her time before answering. 'OK. You're on.' But he'd also forbidden her to talk about the case and she'd been less clear about accepting that.

John looked at his watch as Karen strolled in, looking as unhappy as he'd ever seen her. He poured her a glass of red wine and after she'd half-heartedly chinked his raised glass, he began his own interrogation.

'What's wrong?'

'You said I can't talk about it, remember?'

John smiled. 'Then let's talk about you. I don't know anything about you, Karen.'

'What? You know everything there is to know,' she snapped.

'I know that your personal habits leave a lot to be desired.'

'What is it, John? Kick-Karen-while-she's-down time?'

'You're too sensitive. Let's start with something simple. What sort of music do you like?'

'I don't even like music that much. What about the tests John? Anything?'

John sighed inwardly. *Should he tell her about the specialist tests? No. Better not to raise her hopes than dash them again.* 'No Karen. We haven't found a thing and you did agree not to talk about the case.'

'It's important John. To me. What about the trolls?'

'That's highly specialised. I'm on to the internet service provider. Enough now.'

'OK.'

'All right then, Karen. When did you decide you wanted to become a police officer?' He smiled as he spoke. 'What made you do it?'

Karen frowned. 'I didn't. I wanted to go into law; be a solicitor or something. Stella Cary came to our school. She was amazing. I think we all fell in love with her that day.'

Hooray! She's talking to me! 'What happened?'

'Ah.' Karen sat back in her chair. 'That was all Dad's fault. All the stories he used to tell me. Three years of sitting in a room writing is what made up my mind for me. I wanted to be doing things, not sitting in an office...'

'Tell me more,' he said, but she seemed to have drifted away from him. 'What's the matter? Have I said something wrong? Karen?'

Karen stood up. 'This is no good. I have to go. There's someone I have to see.' She hurtled out of the restaurant, leaving John in a mixture of all sorts of feelings, but mainly hurt.

***

Karen jumped into her car and sped off. Before she knocked on the door, she checked her watch. Eight o'clock. *Not too late.* She rang the bell and saw the light come on in the hall. Sal opened the door.

'Karen! How lovely to see you again. We were just talking about you.'

'Thanks, Sal,' Karen replied, going in. 'I'm sorry to...'

'Come inside.'

Jack was already on his feet and looking to see who was at the door. Without speaking, he gave Karen a big hug and kissed her on the cheek. 'Come in love, come in.'

'I'll put the kettle on.' Sal went into the kitchen while Jack turned the TV off and patted a chair for Karen to sit on.

'It's a lot to take on I know, love. But terrible things happen.

All we can do is make the most of a bad lot.'

'I loved Dad so much. I can't believe he'd be mixed up in something so terrible. It's not right, Jack. That man should have been exposed. And if Jim had been locked up back then, none of this might have happened.'

'But that's what life's like, love. We can't predict the future. None of us can. And your dad was one of the best. Honestly. The most straight and moral man I've ever known.'

'Really?'

'Yes, love. He agonised over it for ages. We all did, but it was different for him. He had you and he couldn't bear to think of that family left with no father, no money and hearing about what he'd got up to. None of it was their fault.'

'I suppose,' Karen blinked. When Jack patted her on the back, the tears came.

'Get it out, love. Is this the first time...?'

'... I've cried?' finished Karen. 'No. It's the second time. What a wimp I am. I never saw Dad cry, ever.'

'Shall I tell you something else?' Jack asked. Karen nodded. 'When your mum died, your dad, for all his bravery and stiff-upper-lip around you, as soon as you were in bed, he told me he cried every night.'

Karen looked up, surprised. 'Did he? I never knew.'

'He didn't want to upset you,' Jack replied. 'Your mum had been ill on and off for years; I bet you hardly remember her, do you?'

Karen shook her head. 'Not really. Mainly the emptiness when she'd gone. Dad never talked about her much.'

'He didn't want to keep reminding you of her,' Jack continued. 'That's why he brought you here so often. To give you people around you who could help a bit with, you know, women's things and that.'

Sal had been listening as she stood at the door. 'That's why he took the desk job,' she said. 'To have more time with you. He wasn't going to be running around the country all hours; not with you at home.'

'That hardly makes me feel better. You mean I held him back?'

287

'No, no.' Jack shook his head. 'It's how things were. He took to eating and drinking more after your mum died, and he wasn't getting the exercise anymore. But he still kept his hand in.'

Karen looked up. 'The cold cases?'

'Exactly. If he couldn't get out there, he could still exercise his mind. And nothing infuriated him more than unsolved cases. He couldn't bear that families were left not knowing what happened to their kin.'

'Yes. I remember the files. Always files around the house. And charts.'

'And he was damned good too. There's many a case got opened, even some solved, thanks to him.'

'What about all the frustrating cases he dealt with? What would he have done if he'd been stuck with car crashes? Unsolvable rapes?'

'First of all, he'd have realised what he could and couldn't do. For every case you solve, there are hundreds that you can't. It's how it is, and you have to get used to it.'

'Are you saying I simply have to accept it?'

'Yes, love. You know you'll get DNA evidence eventually and you have to accept that even when you get it, if the bugger's not on the database, there's nothing more you can do. He'll turn up one day, no doubt when you're retired and looking at cold cases of your own.' Karen smiled.

'That's better love. And remember there's nobody in this world that can criticise anybody for doing their best. Even Bob, I daresay.' Karen nodded.

'And if all else failed,' he said, winking at her. 'Your dad was partial to a bit of table-kicking.'

Karen laughed. 'I can see him doing that.'

Sal sat down next to Karen and patted her hand. 'And most importantly of all, Karen, he was so very proud of you.'

'Was he?' Sal had said that before, but Karen genuinely wondered.

'He was bursting with pride when you passed your sergeant's exams. He had high hopes for you, and he reckoned you had the makings of a better copper than he ever was.'

Jack agreed. 'And you're your father's daughter all right. Karen, the time will come when you have to make decisions. And sometimes it really is the lesser of two evils.'

'Thanks, Jack. Thanks, Sal. I don't know what I'd do without you two.'

***

Later, sitting in her car before heading home, Karen looked at her phone. *Macy? What have you sent me?* She saw a video labelled, 'Hotel CCTV 31/12/12'. She pressed play and watched the film closely. It was a camera's view of the main entrance to the hotel. It was mesmerising watching the constant flow of people in and out. Suddenly, a figure appeared; someone she'd seen before. It was a woman in a long flowing coat and a Trilby-style hat. But this time the camera caught the figure's face.

'Penny Matthews. What the hell were you doing at Fabian Denson's hotel?' She fast-forwarded it to the end then looked at the time. 'Four pm to five-thirty. What were you up to, Penny? Were you having an affair with Fabian? Revenge for Iain and Stella, or did it help your own deceit?'

75

Monday 29th April

Harry had begun on the paperwork when Molly shouted to him. 'Dad? There's someone here!' He looked at his watch. *Can't be Social Services they're not due till this after.* He got up to see. A woman was standing in the hall. She looked familiar. Molly whispered, 'It's Barbara Spinnard. *That* woman.'

'Bugger,' he said. 'I'd forgotten about her.' He went into the hall. 'Better come through into the kitchen. I'll put th'kettle on.'

Barbara spoke sharply as she followed him. 'I'm sorry to trouble you, but I need money. Rob promised me that he'd take care of us if anything happened to him. He assured me that there was a legacy of, well never mind, but a large sum, that I would receive if he died.'

'Oh 'eck,' Harry replied. 'I'm not sure we can help. We're broke too.'

Barbara looked him in the eye. 'I want proper support for my daughter. Your grandchildren's half-sister. I have *friends* you know.'

Harry was having none of it. 'Miss Spinnard. We invited you into our house in good faith. We are well aware of your circumstances now, and I promise you we'll see you right. If we can. But you have to leave now and let us get on with it.'

'I'm not going until I receive some solid assurances.' Barbara stood firm.

'And I suggest you leave us in peace.' He took her arm and manoeuvred her back out into the hall where Molly opened the door.

'You'll be hearing from my solicitor!' Barbara yelled as Harry shoved her out.

Molly shut the door. 'Ey, Dad. Will it ever end?'

Harry hugged her. 'Come on, Mother. Let's go to Rob's study. We've got paperwork to sort and we might find something about this bairn. I should have done it ages ago.'

Together, Molly and Harry pulled out all the papers they could find in Rob's desk and drawers, but there was nothing to suggest a will had ever been made.

'What about that Vera woman?' Molly suggested. 'She'd know, wouldn't she?'

'Aye. I've got her number somewhere.'

Vera answered the phone almost immediately. 'Mr Baxter, good to hear from you. How are the children doing?'

'Aye, well enough. But it's t'other lass I'm ringing about. That Barbara woman's been round, demanding money.'

'Oh, my dear man. I should have anticipated that. I spoke to her this morning, but I had no idea she was back in the country. You should ring the police. Don't worry, I'll be in touch as soon as.' She hung up.

'Bloody hell, Mother. She's wanted by the police!'

***

John had sat at his desk musing over the events the night before for too long. *Coffee.*

As he approached the drinks machine, he spotted a familiar face. 'Hi Macy, coming to see me?'

'Yes and no. It's for DS Harris. Why? Are you missing Karen already?' John blushed. 'I *knew* it. You're an item, aren't you?'

'Not here!' He looked around. 'Got a moment?'

'Sure.'

Moments later, Karen's ears should have been burning.

'She left you?' Macy said. 'Without a word? Wow, that's bad.'

'How do you get on with her?'

Macy sighed. 'We've had our moments, as you've seen.'

'But is she always like that?'

'No,' Macy smiled. 'We're beginning to understand each other a bit better now. But she's still a pain at times. Can I ask something personal?' John shrugged. 'Have you seen her flat?'

John sat up, animated. 'Oh yes.'

'I had to go there once. What a pigsty.'

'Except that's an insult to pigs.' They laughed in empathy. Then John looked serious. 'Maybe I should keep away?'

'No, John. I think she's really fond of you. But you know the only way you'll get her attention, don't you?'

He nodded. 'Test results.'

Macy giggled. 'Absolutely. Which reminds me. Bill gave me this, but I have an inkling you're expecting it.'

'What is it?'

Macy handed him a phone. 'It's dead and it's pretty ancient but someone from the hospital brought it in for Karen. I'd guess it's Peter Stubbins' phone.'

'Ace. More brownie points... hopefully.' John smiled.

'I'd better get back.'

'Thanks.' John waited for a moment then picked up his own phone. 'I'm after some specialist DNA services. Yes, the latest techniques. We're looking for microscopic traces.'

***

In another place not a million miles away, Karen was on her way to meet Fabian Denson. He opened the door as she arrived at the tennis club. 'Strange isn't it?' he greeted her. 'It's all my little empire now. What can I do for you?'

Karen followed him inside, talking as they went. 'Can I ask you about your relationship with Penny Matthews?'

Karen remained standing while Fabian sat down at the board table.

'There is no relationship. We know each other, clearly, but that's it.'

'Did you or did you not meet her on the thirty-first of December last year?'

Fabian scratched his head. 'Sit down, you're making me uncomfortable.'

Karen sat. 'Well?'

'It's complicated...' He paused. 'Personal. Not for me, but for her.'

'Nothing I haven't heard before,' Karen assured him.

'I think not.'

'Try me,' Karen replied.

'OK. I'll come out with it. She wanted a baby.'

'With you?'

'No, with Iain. But he was infertile. Or at least nothing was happening.'

Karen's mouth fell open. 'What? Why on earth didn't he tell us?'

Fabian shrugged. 'I'm not sure he knew, actually.'

'Why do you say that?'

'Erm, well, Penny said that they'd been trying for years. But they'd stopped sleeping together ages ago from what I assumed.'

'OK. But why did she come to you?' Karen asked.

'Look, there was nothing to it really. We'd been chatting about it at the Club one evening. She said I was someone she could talk to about it, especially because we didn't know each other too well. We couldn't talk then, because, well, Iain was around. But I told her where I was going to be on New Year's Eve, and she rang me. So yes, she came to meet me, and we discussed things. Nothing came of it though.'

'Nothing?'

'She wanted a little comforting, that's all.'

76

When Karen returned, she sat on her own in the incident room, sulking and weighing up the case. Her first thought was of Julia and Westbury's arrest. She refused to believe that she had done anything wrong.

Lucky cow. Gets all the plaudits. Probably gets the promotion too and all she's done is follow a trail an idiot could manage. And I was the one who told her how to do it.

Do I get a mention? Do I get any thanks? Do I bollocks!

She looked up at her whiteboards, which had once again become messy and cross-referenced everywhere.

The rape. But was Iain firing blanks? Peter? Maybe. Edward Brandon? No.

Jim Westbury. Rape? Not enough, there. We need Ryan at the hospital letting him in and we haven't even got Ryan yet.

I must file that dangerous driving report. The dodgy car - that's much stronger.

Old Mrs Westbury's on side now. Will she withdraw her alibi?

Robert Cary. Did he have a motive to tamper with Stella's brakes? As her husband, he'd have inherited everything unless she'd made a will saying otherwise. That would have sorted out his PA Barbara and his daughter. Maybe she encouraged him to do it? Damn! Never thought of that. She stood up and wrote it on the board.

Cary's accident. Did Barbara have a motive to kill him? Maybe for his estate? She thought she was coming into money when he was still alive.

Penny Matthews. There's much more going on in that head than meets the eye. What was it with Fabian Denson? Something doesn't stack up.

Who put the flowers on the barriers? Who has access to lots of flowers? Anyone working in the ICU. Anyone with an obsession with Stella. Peter Stubbins. Damn, even without a car he could have done it. He could have run out in front then double-backed through that path in the woods. He could have run out in front of Robert Cary too. But would it even be murder? Cary had a heart attack. All fodder for the inquest. Hell, that's coming up soon.

Stella, the enigma; the only untainted witness at the scene. Or was she? An illicit affair? Was that enough for someone to want to murder her? Jealousy yes, anger yes. Brake tampering, possibly. Was Piers involved? He certainly had the motive to kill her. Was that image on her phone his red car?

Then there's the physical evidence. That nightie. I had such high hopes and John dashed them. Any number of men could have interfered with Stella. But we'll get that DNA when the baby's born, dead or alive and I'll bloody well kill anybody who tries to stop me then.

I'll get the bastard and bring him to court.

IF he's still alive. IF his DNA is on the fucking database.

What was it that Jack said?

Karen lifted her right foot slowly, then aimed it at the table. CRASH! Papers, pens, stapler, paperclips and the contents of her hot chocolate all went flying over the floor.

Damn, that felt good.

Macy poked her head round the door. 'Bloody hell Karen, what happened?'

Karen grinned. 'I've been doing some filing. What's up?'

'Ryan Westbury's in reception.'

Karen's mouth fell open. 'Macy, you've made my day. Let's go get him.'

***

If Ryan Westbury looked like he'd been sleeping rough for days, it was an accurate picture.

Karen addressed him first. 'Mr Westbury. Are you all right? You look soaked through.'

'I am. I haven't eaten for a day at least. Can I have a coffee or something? Or a bag of crisps? I'm starving.'

'All in good time,' Karen said. 'We need to ask you some questions first. About your uncle, Jim Westbury. We have reason to believe he was at the scene and or involved in the crash that killed your father, Tom Westbury. Do you know anything about this?'

Ryan turned his head away to speak - as if like that, it didn't quite count as informing. 'Yes. He told me he was there and saw her on her phone. Said he was being blackmailed, which is why he couldn't admit it.'

'Was he with anybody else? Did he mention a Paul or Piers?'

Ryan looked puzzled. 'No. Can I have something to eat now?'

'Not yet, Ryan. Did you discuss Robert Cary's alleged assault on Tania Hayes with your uncle?'

'Yes, I did.'

'And what is your relationship with Tania Hayes?'

'We're mates. We were at school together.'

From the corner of her eye, Karen saw Macy nod. 'Did you send a threatening letter?' Karen asked. 'We've got fingerprints.'

'No. Who does letters these days?' *Fair point, he's too young*, Karen thought.

'We have a witness who says you were aware that Robert Cary had a daughter.'

'You what?'

'We have a letter which makes a terrible threat about a six-year-old child. And we know that you went into Robert Cary's office and threatened him.'

'It wasn't like that. Anyway, he wasn't there. And I didn't know anything about his family until I read the news.'

Something's not right here. And there are no other fingerprints. Unless...

Macy jumped in. 'What about the trolling? You can't deny that, can you? We've got pictures from your school...'

'Food!' He pointed into his mouth.

'Answer the question.'

Macy poured him a glass of water, which he knocked back in one.

'Yes, OK. It didn't mean I did anything. I was angry.'

'We need to take your fingerprints and a DNA sample. Do you agree to that?'

Karen remained silent. *Could Barbara have made that bit up? Could she have written that letter?*

Ryan shrugged. 'I've got nothing to hide.' Karen watched as Macy swabbed his cheek.

I believe him. I think Martha's got to him.

'Is this you?' Macy passed him the passport image. 'Using your father's passport?' Ryan blinked. Karen pressed. 'Did you know it's an offence to use someone else's identity? Not to say your dead father's?' Ryan blinked again and turned his head away.

'Is *this* you?' Macy pushed forward the hospital CCTV image.

Karen's turn. 'Ryan, we've got you at the hospital the night Stella Cary was raped. And I bet we've got your fingerprints all over the fire escape door...' Karen waited.

'No. I was wearing gloves.' Ryan swallowed. 'Fuck...'

'Now we're getting somewhere,' Karen said.

'Where was your uncle on New Year's Eve?' Macy asked.

'I don't know.'

'I think you do,' Macy said.

Karen leant forward. 'Tell us what happened, Ryan. Get it over with. You realise that you're an accessory now, don't you? The more you tell us now the easier it will be for you in the long run.'

Ryan took a deep breath. 'OK. He'd been having a good look round outside. That's when he spotted the door. He said something about it being turned off. There were no lights on it. He asked me to let him in. Said he wanted to pay her back. I didn't see anything. But I heard him.'

'For the tape, Ryan, who did you let in?'

'My uncle, Jim Westbury. Can I have some food now?' Karen nodded at Macy.

'Take him to the snack machine.' She waited until they left before fist-pumping the air.

'Thank fuck for that!' She looked at the tape machine still recording and laughed as she turned it off.

77

Karen almost skipped back to the incident room then stopped when she saw the mess she had created. Begrudgingly, she started to pick up the scattered papers, looking at them as she put them in order. *I'm getting somewhere but it's still not enough.*

'What would you do now, Dad? Wait for the DNA or call the family now? I've made a bit of progress, just not very much.' *I'm being stupid. He'd say, talk to the family every time.*

She sat down and picked up the phone. 'Mr Harry Baxter? It's DS Thorpe.'

'Good. I were about to ring you. It's about that woman. Miss Spinnard. She's been round threatening us, demanding money. That Vera lady said she's up to no good and I should call you. Or she'd call you.'

'What? Thanks. Where is she now?'

'No idea. That's your job. Now how's that case going?'

'That's why I rang you. I wanted to give you an update. When would be a good time to see you?'

'We're coming to t'hospital tomorrow morning. Around ten. Happen that's as good a time as any.'

'Thank you, Mr Baxter. I look forward to seeing you then.'

Macy reappeared in time to hear the end of the call. 'What about that poison pen letter? I thought you let Ryan off quite lightly.'

Karen frowned. 'I believe him. It's too wordy and kids *don't* write on paper these days.'

'Who do you think *did* write it then?'

'There were only three sets of prints on it. Work it out, Macy.' Karen went to the door. 'I need to speak to the guv. Can you help tidy up a bit?'

'I suppose,' Macy said as Karen left. 'Wow! It wasn't Barbara, was it?'

'Well done, Mace,' Karen shouted behind her. 'See you later.'

DCI Winter was in his office. He looked up as Karen walked in.

'I hope you've got some progress at last, Karen. I saw that young Ryan Westbury came in.'

'Yes, guv. He's been very useful.' She took in a deep breath. 'We've now got Jim Westbury at the hospital on the night we think Stella Cary was raped. Ryan said he heard Jim making *noises* too. Not only that, Ryan says Jim told him that he was at the scene of Stella's crash. So his mother's alibi for that and the murder of Piers Atkins is blown. I assume Martha will retract it now?' DCI Winter rolled his eyes. 'Was she the one who made Ryan talk?'

'Yes, Karen. What happened was a long time ago, but even Martha has her limits. We won't mention it again. Understood?'

'Yes, guv.'

'And? What are we waiting for?'

Karen sighed. 'We still can't test the baby yet.'

'It won't be long now. Have you informed Sergeant Jones about your interview with Ryan?'

'No guv. Your orders...'

'Go ahead.'

'But it won't help her much,' Karen said. 'Ryan didn't know anything about a Piers or a Paul. And she's got our CCTV images of the pair of them on the motorway...'

'Still, good practice to keep her informed.'

'Sorry Sir, will you call her? I've got things to do. Family things. I need a day or two.'

DCI Winter frowned. 'All right, Karen. Just this once. Then we're back to normal. OK?'

'Yes, guv.'

***

Macy was still tidying the incident room when John appeared. He stared at the mess.

'Karen's work?'

'Who else?'

'Where is she?'

'You've missed her.'

'Damn.' John straightened a table and moved a chair underneath it. 'Where's she going, do you know?'

'Are things no better between you?'

John shook his head. 'I need to speak to her. She's not answering her phone.'

Macy sighed. 'The only thing I know for sure is that she's going to the hospital tomorrow. We've finally placed Jim Westbury at the hospital on the night of the rape. I think she's seeing the family.'

'Thanks, Macy. Any other progress?'

'Iain Matthews has been temporarily eliminated, possibly infertile, apparently. Oh, guess who wrote the poison pen letter?'

'Barbara Spinnard, I expect.'

Macy gaped. 'How did you know?'

John winked. 'It seemed a bit too, how shall I say, practised? Which reminds me, I resurrected that phone. Peter Stubbins' one. There's a half-hour long call to Miss Spinnard on the day of Cary's accident. Now that doesn't sound to me like a quick message.'

'Nor me. I'd better have a word with the guv. It sounds like we should bring her in.'

'Good idea. Anything else?'

'There was an odd story about Fabian Denson, nothing sinister.'

'Tell me more,' John said. 'I want to be completely up to speed when I see her.'

'Well, good luck with that John. She's in a very strange mood.'

DCI Winter stuck his head round the door. 'Leave that, Dodds. We've got a lead on one of our suspects.'

'Yes, Sir. Absolutely.' Macy grinned and followed him out of the room. 'Sorry, John.'

John gave her a little wave and looked around the room. 'Catch you later.' He carried on tidying the room.

78

Karen had got up especially early that morning. She wanted her flat to be spotless before her visitor arrived. The washing machine was already whirring, she'd cleared every surface and was now dusting and wiping.

'Now for the hoover.' She paused. 'Where the hell is it?'

Retrieving it from under the bed, she got to work and half an hour later, even John would have been impressed. She changed into her matching jacket and trousers and checked herself in the mirror.

Next, she said to herself. *Can't put it off any longer.*

As she drove up to the Funeral Directors' office, the enormity of what she was doing began to sink in. She held back the tears as she opened the door, setting off the little doorbell. A suited man with a kindly face appeared.

'May I help you, Madam?'

'I've come to pick up some ashes.'

'Certainly, Madam. What is the name, please?'

'Thomas Thorpe. The cremation was on the thirteenth of December.'

'Yes, Madam. Please take a seat.'

Karen fidgeted on the padded velour sofa, trying to stop herself imagining what it would look like. She gasped when the man reappeared, holding a large purple plastic vase-like container. *I don't know what I expected but it wasn't that. It's almost trendy.*

'It's a rather heavy one Madam. Can you manage or would you like some help?'

Karen stared at it. *That's my father. THAT'S MY FATHER.* Shuddering a little, she reached forward and took the precious container and, surprised as she was by the weight, she'd carried much heavier things.

'It's fine,' she replied. 'I can do it.'

The man held the door open for her as she carried it to the car. 'You won't recognise the place, Dad. But you're not staying for long. We're going somewhere much more exciting. I haven't told you all about it yet, have I? Well, it all started with a car crash...'

* * *

Karen arrived at the hospital, parked the car and waited until she had collected her thoughts. She turned her phone on and looked at it: 'JOHN - FIVE MISSED CALLS'. 'GUV -ONE MISSED CALL'. 'VERA - ONE MISSED CALL'.

'John, you can wait. Things to do. But I better ring you, guv.'

She punched in the number.

'Where are you, Karen? I've had Dodds on to me.'

'I'm laying my father's ashes, guv.'

'Oh.' His tone changed in a flash. 'It can wait.'

'No, guv, tell me.'

'There's been a development with Barbara Spinnard. Dodds tracked her down and brought her in. We interviewed her last night. Seems like she didn't know that Stubbins' chap had died. Dodds mentioned the phone call and she caved. She's confessed to colluding with Stubbins to cause Robert Cary's RTA.'

'Well done Macy! So she's been charged? Has she admitted writing the letter?'

'Yes to both. Don't worry, you can pick it all up when you're back. A normal day tomorrow, right?'

'Yes, guv.'

Karen looked at the urn safely wedged in the footwell of the front seat. She was getting used to seeing it. 'I'm leaving you here for a moment, Dad. I won't be long.'

* * *

Karen arrived at the ward and immediately saw Gwen, looking her up and down. 'It's a special day,' she explained. 'I need to look smart. Is the family here?'

'Yes. And Mr Baxter's waiting over there.' Gwen pointed to a relatives' room. 'I'll tell him.'

'Yes please.'

Karen settled herself and Harry appeared soon afterwards. 'Have you sorted out that Barbara woman yet?'

'It's all under control, Mr Baxter.'

'Good. She were a right menace. Now, what's new?'

'We do have a prime suspect,' Karen began. 'Unfortunately, and it's not a problem, honestly, but we can't be absolutely sure until we've tested the baby for DNA.'

'Who is it? Who would do such a thing and why?'

'I can't give you a name, but the reasons are complicated.'

'How so?'

'We think the suspect blames your daughter for the death of the man killed in the crash.'

'Eh? Why rape her, then? I don't want to sound blunt, but why not kill her?'

'I'm possibly putting two and two together but there were allegations of attempted rape made against your son-in-law.'

Harry's face paled. 'By 'eck. I knew Rob were a rum'un but not that bad. Still, it excuses nowt. So, when you said what you did about him, you had your reasons then?'

Karen nodded. 'But we think this man is more likely to have been responsible. If, and when we can prove it, he'll go down for a long time. He's also being held in connection with the death of your other son-in-law.'

Harry's mouth fell open. 'Piers? How come?'

'Piers was our suspect's half-brother. It's possible his death was an accident, though.'

'Ee, this is right complicated. Keep me posted. I've got to go back to see my daughter now.'

'I will, Sir. I'll wait for you. I want to see her again myself.'

'Eh?'

'Oh, I talk to her often. Just in case.'

79

Stella was awake. *Something feels different. It's like before. I can hear, but I haven't moved, I'm still here.* She looked around at the greenery of her dream world.

'Stella love, it's Mum. I've got so much to tell you. Our Sandra's doing well now...'

Mum. Sandra.

Stella began walking through the fields but at last, she was able to make herself walk a little faster.

'Mum, it's James. I've been helping the police. I've decided I want to study law. I need you to help me. Please, Mum. You've got to wake up. No one else can help me like you.'

James. James. My son, James. Stella's pace increased.

'Mum, please wake up. It's Daniel. I hate school so much. The other boys at school were saying such horrible things...'

Daniel. My son, Daniel. Faster still.

'Mummy, Mummy. Wake up. Solomon is missing you and so am I.'

Laura! My little girl. Laura, I'm coming!

Stella could see where she was heading. She felt warmer, lighter. The words she heard were like invisible arms pulling her, urging her forwards. She was running. *Where am I going?*

'Stella. It's Dad here. We love you so much. Please come home.'

I'm trying Dad, I'm trying...

'You can do it, love. Dad, she's reacting, I'm sure she is.'

Mum? Yes, I'm coming, I can feel it. It's so strange...

Stella was flying through the clouds in her mind towards consciousness. Everything was becoming clearer to her. She saw before her a wall of light.

What's that? I'm scared. It's getting closer... I'm going through...

In a burning painful instant, Stella suddenly understood everything. She knew precisely who she was, where she was and what had happened to her. She remembered conversations and noises. Her brain rewound to the minutes before the crash. She watched in her head like an IMAX screen, her last few seconds before it all happened.

I'm driving.
Where?
To Iain's.
Hurry. I'm passing the tennis club.
What's that ahead?
I know that car.
Why has it stopped?
The van's overtaking it.
I'm sticking with the van.
The car's level with me.
Who's that man?
There's another man there.
He's looking at me.
'No, it can't be!'
Shit! Is that Piers?
It is!
Where's my phone?
Must get a picture.
Damn that seat belt!
That's better.
What's he doing?
Now he's alongside the van and the driver is shouting out the window.
He's speeding up.
He's cutting up the van.
He's braking.
'He's stopping. No!'
'STOP!!!'
I'm braking but nothing is happening.
'MY BRAKES!!!'
Lights.
Red lights everywhere.
'OH MY GOD!!!'

In the second before Stella emerged from the wall of light, she was omnipotent. She felt like she knew everything, all the secrets of the universe, the very meaning of life. She knew who had fathered the child whom she could finally feel kicking inside her.

Then she understood that, like a meteorite hitting the earth's atmosphere, all that knowledge, that last moment would be obliterated forever.

She opened her eyes. 'Where the hell am I?'

'Stella?' Molly could hardly believe her eyes and ears. She pulled her chair closer and held her daughter's hand.

'Mum?'

'Call the nurse!' Harry shouted at the security men. Gwen heard the commotion and ran over.

'She's awake? At last! How wonderful! I'll call the consultant.'

Within minutes, Reeta Shah was on the scene checking Stella over. She talked as she examined her. 'Stella, welcome back. You've had a very traumatic accident. There is a great deal I need to tell you.'

Stella didn't listen. She was blinking her eyes and trying to focus on her children's faces. All of them were crying with the emotion of it all.

'James, Daniel, Laura. Please don't cry.'

'She's made exceptional progress,' Reeta said to Harry. 'As I told you, comas are such strange things.'

Stella rubbed her belly as if she already knew about the baby. 'Everything's going to be all right,' she said. 'I know it.'

'Stella love, we've got some bad news about Rob.'

Molly glared at him. 'Not now, Dad.'

'It's all right Mum. I knew already. I can't explain it, but I heard so many things in here. Iain's dead too, isn't he?'

'Iain Matthews? Yes, love...'

'And Peter. Poor Peter.'

'Peter? You knew Peter?' Gwen was gobsmacked.

'Where's Sergeant Thorpe? She'll want to know this.'

'Aye,' Harry smiled. 'She said you'd want to talk to her. I'll bring her in.'

***

Karen's dour expression transformed into a broad smile when she saw Stella wide awake. She was also stunned to see her laughing and talking to her family. Harry gently shooed the family out. 'Give her a few minutes,' he said. 'We can come right back.'

Karen sat at the bedside. 'You're looking great, Mrs Cary.'

'I remember you,' Stella said immediately. 'The high school, a few years back. You kept asking questions.'

Karen laughed. 'I did a law degree, thanks to you. I'm a Policewoman now. How on earth did you remember me?'

'I heard you talking to me. You asked me questions in here, too. I recognised your voice. I knew you were looking out for me. Thank you.'

'Do you know what happened to you?'

'Yes. I sort of knew that, too. It was so strange. I could hear lots of things. You want to test the baby, don't you? I don't mind. I'm curious to know who the father is, too.'

Karen hesitated. 'It's not that simple, Mrs Cary. Apparently, the test may not be safe yet. And even if we obtain the DNA, it may be from someone who's not on our database. We do have a suspect, but we can't be sure. He's locked up in a cell for now, so we can wait. You need time. You've only just woken up.'

'But you're desperate to find out. I know you are.' Stella gave her a near-dazzling smile.

Karen laughed. 'I see you were definitely listening to me. Yes, of course I do, but what matters is when *you* want to do it. And I'm really sorry, but there is somewhere I absolutely have to be. I promise I'll come and see you tomorrow.'

'Then I accept it must be important. Bye-bye for now.'

Karen left a minute before a puffed-out John arrived.

80

'Come in, love.' Jack opened the door. 'Cup of tea before we go?'

'Yes, please. He's in the car, should I...?'

'He's not going anywhere, love. He'll be fine.'

'He's already been on the case with me.' Karen laughed.

'He'd have loved that.' Jack joined in with the laughter.

'What made you decide?' Sal asked. 'Have you solved it?'

Karen shook her head. 'Not quite. But we're nearly there. Even the guv had to get involved in the end. No, it was what Jack said, really. About things never really being finished. He wouldn't have held anything up to end a case, would he? He'd soldier on. Anyway, don't you remember the date?'

'We knew,' Sal smiled.

'He'd be fifty-six today.'

'And far too young,' Sal added.

'His story can be ended today. And I thought it was time to let him be with Mum again.'

'It's perfect.' Sal wiped away a tear. Even Jack was snivelling a little.

'Are we ready?'

Karen drove them to Leysdown, accompanied by lively conversation and more stories about her father. She parked the car near the caravan park she remembered so well.

'Down there,' she pointed. 'There's a little cove where we used to look for crabs. I hope there's no one around, I'm not sure this is legal.'

'This is where we scattered your mum's ashes. I didn't think you were with us.'

'I wasn't. Dad told me about it when I was older.'

The three of them trod carefully down the little coastal path. The cove was exactly how Karen remembered it. The tide was going out as she carefully tipped the contents of the urn into the water's edge.

'Bye, Dad. Thanks for everything. I'm sorry I doubted you...'

'Don't be sorry, love,' Jack put his hand on her shoulder. 'Tommy was the first to accept not everything's cut and dried. And he'd have expected and *wanted* you to challenge him. It's a difficult call and you can't change the past. Now let's watch him go and join your mum.'

The three of them stood close together. Jack, in the middle, put his arms around the waists of Karen and Sal. They watched as the sea snatched the grey mass into the water a wave at a time, until it had all gone.

'Now then, how about a quick drink at ours to toast his birthday,' Jack said.

'Definitely,' said Sal.

'Yes please,' Karen agreed.

As they walked back to the car, Karen's phone pinged. 'I've got some reception at last,' she said, as she read the message from John. 'MEET ME IN THE THAI RESTAURANT AT SEVEN. PLEASE!!!'

'If it's work, ignore it,' Sal said. 'It's been a very hard day for you, love. Sometimes you have to look after yourself.'

'I'm fine, thanks anyway. But it's not work, well, not *work* work. It's John. He wants to take me for dinner tonight.'

'Oh, is it now? I want to hear more about John, then.' Sal winked.

'OK' Karen texted back. She looked at Sal. 'There's nothing much to say, really.'

'Dinner's not nothing,' Jack said, grinning. 'Come on, let's make tracks.'

***

Karen walked to the restaurant in a much better frame of mind. She hadn't appreciated how much she had worried about her father. But now, having said goodbye, she felt more at peace. Even the investigation was no longer raging in her mind.

She arrived on time and saw John already there. She didn't notice him wriggling with excitement; she was working out what to say to him.

'Hi. Sorry, there was something important I had to do.'

John didn't ask what. 'And there was something *I* had to do.'

Karen frowned. She saw from his expression that he was bursting to tell her something. 'What?'

'Well, first, remember that butt?'

'Yes. I'd forgotten about that. What?'

'We found microscopic traces of DNA in it.'

'And?'

'Peter Stubbins.'

'That's good. But Barbara confessed.'

'How did you know that? Oh, you spoke to DCI Winter, but not me?'

Karen grinned. 'He's my boss. Is that it?'

'No,' John shook his head. 'I wanted to meet Stella.'

'You spoke to her?' What did she say?'

'She asked me if I could do the test.'

'She *asked* you?'

'Karen, what's wrong with you?'

'I didn't think it was fair to push her. She'd only just woken up.'

'Is this really you, Karen?'

'I've grown up a bit, John. That's all. What did you say then?'

'I said yes.'

'OK, when do we get the result?'

'I rushed it through, Karen. I've got it already.'

Karen's eyes nearly popped out of her head. 'What?'

'Karen you're back! That's more like it.'

'John...'

'But there's one more thing. The nightie? I didn't want to raise your hopes, but I managed to get some specialist tests done on it.'

'And? John, I'm going to throttle you in a minute.'

'I wanted you to see them first. But obviously, I couldn't not see them.' He handed her a sheet of paper. 'You were nearly right. Well, you were righter than you could imagine.'

'What?' Karen took the paper, her eyes devouring it.

'And you were also wrong,' John continued. He watched her face as she read on.